The Good Neighbour

Beth MILLER

1 3 5 7 9 10 8 6 4 2

Ebury Press, an imprint of Ebury Publishing
20 Vauxhall Bridge Road,
London SW1V 2SA

Ebury Press is part of the Penguin Random House group of companies whose addresses can be found at global.penguinrandomhouse.com

First published in 2015 by Ebury Press

www.eburypublishing.co.uk

A CIP catalogue record for this book is available from the British Library

ISBN 9780091956332

Printed in Great Britain by Clays Ltd, St Ives plc

For John, Molly and Saul

Chapter 1

Davey

Davey was glad to be leaving Gina's. Her house smelled of not nice bubble bath. His room there had a scary wardrobe, the door kept swinging open for no reason. The only thing he liked at Gina's were the two fat white sofas. They looked so soft. But Gina wouldn't let him sit on them.

'Soon be there,' Davey's mum said in her cheerful voice. Davey stared out of the window. If he scrunched his eyes the houses looked like the houses in their old town. But it kept getting spoiled by the blue bits at the end of the roads. The sea. His old town didn't have blue bits.

Lola was next to him in the back, playing with Panda. Davey had left a lot of things behind in their old house. Cars, annuals, all his posters except his American flag, which wasn't really a poster because it was made of material. And most of his teddies, except Waffles, who lay on Davey's lap now. His granny had given Waffles to him when he was born. We can get more stuff, his mum said. Stuff doesn't matter.

They had moved before, but this was bigger. They'd never left so many people and things behind. He had even left Adam Purcell. He'd started talking to Adam Purcell in his head. Today Davey told Adam his top five flags:

1. American, obviously.
2. Portugal because the last present his dad had given him was from there, a T-shirt with the Portuguese flag on. Half red, half green, with a yellow-and-red shield in the middle. Davey's dad knew he liked flags.
3. Malaysia because it was like the American one, except with a moon.
4. Uruguay because the sun on it was a proper sun with lots of yellow rays.
5. Vietnam because he could draw it easily. It was a big gold star on a red background.

Davey's mum said the new house was going to be fantastic, but Adam Purcell pointed out that Davey's mum said lots of things were fantastic. Gina letting them stay at hers was apparently 'fantastic'. Their new house in Hove was going to be 'fantastic'. Their new school was, you guessed it, 'fantastic'. Adam Purcell was a good person to talk to.

There was more and more sea now, bigger bits of blue in between the streets. Davey leaned back in his seat and closed his eyes.

Chapter 2

Minette

The Miltons' horrible Big Ben doorbell chimed out when Minette pressed it, and her mouth went instantly dry. On the few occasions she'd rung that bell before it had been to offer a timid apology, and receive a stone-cold bollocking in return.

A blonde woman opened the door, and said, 'I've got to get rid of that damn bell.'

Minette laughed, relieved, and introduced herself. 'I live next door,' she said. 'I heard you moving in this morning. I've made some biscuits.'

'How lovely of you! Come in for a cuppa?'

'You sure? You must be very busy.'

'I could use a break.' The woman called out, 'Look, kids, our first visitors!'

A little girl ran into the hall, and said a shy, 'Hello.' She was followed by a disabled boy in a wheelchair, who stared intently at Minette, but didn't say anything.

The woman told the children they could play in the living room, and she led Minette into the kitchen, which was looking remarkably sorted, only a couple of unpacked boxes on the floor. She put on the kettle. 'Have a seat, Minette. I'm Cath. So, who's this little one?'

'This is Tilly.' Minette sat down, and took Tilly carefully out of the sling. 'She's nine months.'

'That's a nice name. Wish I'd thought of it for Lola.' Cath rummaged in a drawer and put a pile of spoons and a plastic bowl on the table. 'Would you like to play with these, lovie?' Tilly immediately started clattering them together.

'Lola's a pretty name, too,' Minette said.

'My hubby wanted to call her Esmie, after his mother, but I won that one.'

Minette realised she could smell paint. 'Surely you haven't started decorating yet?'

'Oh, I'm just getting shot of the magnolia. This place hasn't been touched in years.'

'I can't believe you've done so much already!'

'Davey and Lola are good little helpers.' Cath brought over two mugs, and Minette's homemade biscuits. 'They organised most of the kitchen cupboards by themselves. They still think chores are fun. I'm dreading when they start to realise.'

'So where have you moved from, Cath?'

'We was up north. How about you, how long you been here?'

'Oh, almost a year. Whereabouts . . .'

'So you moved in just before this little lassie came along?'

'That's right. We were renting nearby before then.'

'You must like it round here, then?' Cath said.

'Love it. We went to university in Brighton and liked it so much, we stayed on.' To her surprise, Minette felt tearful. 'Though actually, it's not been that great lately.' For god's sake, she told herself, you can't start blubbing because someone's being vaguely nice. She sipped her tea, though it was too hot.

'I know what it's like,' Cath said, sympathetically. 'Babies are lovely, but exhausting.'

'Oh, it's not Tilly's fault, it's been, well – it's complicated.' Minette looked around her. 'It's so odd being in the House of Horror. I mean,' she said hastily, 'that's what we called it when the Miltons lived here. I had it in my mind as a haunted house, all cobwebs and skeletons.'

'Well, it was clean enough. But everything's so out of date.

I could run the National Grid off the static electricity in the carpets. There are decent floorboards underneath.'

'Yes, ours has the boards. Well, you got a bargain, I reckon. When we heard how much you got it for we were all a bit worried, and Kirsten over the road got a valuation. We were very relieved when they said hers was worth 30K more.'

'Oh, really?' Cath said, and Minette at once felt like a mortgage-whinging, middle-class stereotype. 'So talking of neighbours, maybe you can tell me who's who?' Cath bit into a biscuit. 'These are fantastic.'

'I don't know very many people yet. We're next to you, obviously, that's me and Abe, and Tilly. Priya's next to us, she's really nice, Indian family with kids, her mother lives with them. Then opposite, number 36, is Kirsten, who I know because she's a cranial osteopath and she's doing a few sessions with Tilly.'

'Wow, she has her own osteopath already, impressive.'

God's sake, Minette, first mortgages and now baby therapies. Cath would think she was a total airhead. She said quickly, 'Oh, Tilly's just been having a bit of trouble sleeping so, you know, it's supposed to help. Worth a try. Anyway, next to Kirsten is a student house. Then on your other side from us is, well, er, Liam.'

Cath grinned. 'Er Liam, blush blush?'

Minette hid her face behind Tilly's head. 'I don't know why I'm blushing! He's just quite cute, I suppose.'

'I spoke to someone very tasty this morning, tall guy, looks slightly like a young fair-haired Frank Sinatra. Could that be him?'

'I only know what Frank Sinatra looked like when he was old and fat. But yes, that's probably him. Longest legs in Hove, official award.'

Cath's little girl came in. 'Baby!' she said, seeing Tilly. And then, even more enthusiastically, 'Biscuits!'

'Hi Lola. Of course you can have a biscuit,' Minette said.

'Wait a minute, Lola, remember?' Cath said, as the girl's hand snaked towards the plate. To Minette she said briskly, 'Are there any milk or nuts in them?'

'No. Well, there's milk in chocolate, isn't there?'

'She's all right with chocolate, thank the lord. OK Lolly, go ahead. Take one for Davey.'

Lola took the biscuits, beamed at Minette, and skipped out of the room.

'Adorable,' Minette said. 'How old is she?'

'Four. I'm trying to train her to ask about ingredients, she's got some serious allergies, but she always forgets when she sees something yummy. Talking of yummy, you were telling me about the young Sinatra?'

Minette wished she had more to tell about Liam. She'd only ever said one word to him, a couple of months ago. Tilly had woken, sobbing, at five in the morning, and Minette, terrified of another Milton complaint, had bundled her into the buggy and pushed her up and down the dark street. On her fourth circuit Liam, wearing a dark suit, came out of his house at a jog, heading to the station. Minette looked a complete state, was wearing her pyjamas under her puffy Michelin Man coat, hair in a messy pineapple on top of her head, so she hoped he wouldn't notice her. But he said, 'You're up early,' and gave her a gorgeous smile as he passed. She giggled and said, 'Yes,' kicking herself for her pathetic lack of repartee.

She said now, 'I've just seen him around a few times. Actually, a lot more in the last couple of weeks. I was wondering if he'd lost his job. He's married,' Minette added, hastily, in case she seemed too interested. 'I don't know her name, though I say hello to her in the street. And I've no idea who lives on their other side. It's bad, isn't it? We've been here nearly a year and I hardly know anyone.'

'Well, hopefully you'll get to meet some of them at my house-warming party. I was thinking of having one in a couple of weeks' time.'

'My god, you're a breath of fresh air,' said Minette.

'Sounds like you didn't get on too great with the last people here?'

'Slight understatement. They were horrible to us. They couldn't stand the noise. Tilly, you know. They banged on the walls at night.'

'How horrible. They were pretty stiff when I spoke to them

on the phone. Babies are supposed to cry. I bet you're not even that noisy, are you, beautiful?' Cath clucked at Tilly.

'Not according to the Miltons. They were unfriendly from day one. They never got over the fact that I was pregnant but not married.'

'Old-school types, huh?'

'Totally. They behaved as if Abe was some kind of anti-social yob, just because he's got long hair. I'm sure they used to spy on us out of your funny round window, when we were in the front garden. We drank champagne, well Prosecco, when we heard they were moving out.'

'I hope you won't feel the same way about us.'

'Definitely not. I'm so glad you're here.' Minette raised her mug and chinked it against Cath's.

'Our first day in our wonderful new house.' Cath stretched her arms out wide. 'We're really glad to be here, too.'

Minette sang as she cut up carrots for a chicken cassoulet. Thank you, thank you, she prayed; to who, she didn't know. To the God of Good Things, perhaps. Everything was going to be all right.

'Minette is a glass-half-full type,' one of her school reports had said, and she liked that view of herself. She did try to look on the bright side of things, though someone narky, Minette thought, might point out that it should be easy for her, given she'd led a fairly charmed life, had experienced few sorrows in her twenty-eight years. But then again, she said to the narky voice, things hadn't been so smooth since having a baby. Not that there was anything wrong with Tilly, god no! She was perfect. Minette knew how lucky she was. She gave Tilly a big kiss as she put a bowl of raw vegetables in front of her. 'Crudités, Tilly. Can you say "crudités"?'

Yes, completely lucky. Think about all the things that could go wrong, that did go wrong every day. You didn't have to look any further than the new kid next door, in a wheelchair. Poor him, and poor his mum. But it was – fingers crossed – such a good lucky thing for her that someone like that had moved in.

By the time Abe got back from work, Minette had the radio on and was luxuriating in the noise.

'Hi honey, I'm home,' Abe called as usual. He kissed Tilly, but didn't, Minette noticed, attempt to kiss her. 'Isn't that a bit loud?' Then he remembered. 'They're gone!'

'Yes! They've bloody well gone, and the new woman is lovely. She's a bit older than us, late thirties, maybe forty? Two kids. Really friendly.'

'That's brilliant. Bon fucking voyage, Miltons. Hey, I brought you a no-more-House-of-Horror present to celebrate, look.' He held up a stack of wooden picture frames, cobwebbed and dirty, doubtless from a skip. 'Can you believe the stuff people chuck out, Dougie? They'll scrub up nicely, be perfect for those black-and-white photos Dad took of Tilly.'

His enthusiasm was contagious, so that even though Minette knew who'd be doing the scrubbing up, she smiled and took them from him carefully. Since having Tilly her life was made up of such compromises: dirty frames as a gift, curry in front of the telly instead of going out, smiles instead of kisses. Hand-holding rather than sex. Minette hadn't noticed the lack of sex at first, because it had been the last thing on her mind. Like every new mum before her, she'd laughed mirthlessly when the solemn young midwife at the hospital questioned her about contraception, the day after Tilly was born. 'If you think I'm doing that again . . .' Minette had deadpanned, and the midwife smiled wearily, having heard it many times before.

But Tilly was nearly nine months old now, and they still hadn't done it, or even mentioned it. Minette suspected it was the noise factor: Abe, always quite shy in the bedroom, had not wanted to give the Miltons something else, something more embarrassing, to bang on the wall about. So, Minette thought, ding-dong the witches are dead, lovely Cath is next door instead, and things will soon get better. She felt an anticipation that hadn't been there for months. She turned up Radio 1 even louder, and clapped as Abe danced Tilly round the kitchen.

Chapter 3

Cath

No matter how careful you were with the measuring tape, Cath told the kids, there was always something that didn't fit. The removal men yesterday had tried, god love 'em, had took the living-room door off the hinges, but in the end they had to admit defeat. They'd took the sofa to the dump for her; there was no way as she could eBay it, because it didn't have that fire label thing. It just meant sitting on deckchairs for a bit, till she got her act together.

This was a great house though. Hall plenty wide enough

for the wheelchair – see, Davey, she could measure some things properly! And of course the Miltons had put in a disabled loo downstairs for his old mum. That was one of the attractions of the house: that and the two reception rooms. There was soon going to come a point, sad to say, when Davey would be too heavy a lump for her to carry upstairs. Then she could convert one of the downstairs rooms for him. At eight, he was still just about light enough, but the last couple of months she'd noticed a twinge in her back when she took him up to bed in the old house. But anyway, another massive advantage of the new house was that there were five less stairs. So chin up, Cathykins! Just because the sofa wouldn't go in was small taters compared to the big pluses:

1. New house, new town, new start.
2. Gina just up the road.
3. Good school for Davey.
4. Away from all the bad stuff.

She didn't even want to think of the name of their last town, so associated with bad feelings was it. Troubletown, that's what she'd call it now. Where you come from? Troubletown, up north. Oh can't say as how I've ever heard of Troubletown. No lovie, you don't want to, believe me!

Like that pretty girl next door. Minette. French-sounding name, and French-looking too, with her dark hair and chic clothes, but English as you like. Not stuck-up, but nicely spoken. She was all, oh where you from, why've you moved here, but Cath was a life-long expert at asking questions rather than giving answers. 'We was up north but what about you, how long you been here, what's going on for kids, how old's your baby, isn't she sweet?' The person you were talking to soon forgot you hadn't answered them. Like when people asked – and a few of them had, the nosy whatsits, while they were staying at Gina's – about the children's father. Cath had rapped back, 'He's working abroad. So what about you, what does your husband do?' Cath laughed her throaty laugh, thinking of the embarrassment this had produced ('Oh god something in computing, I suppose I should know, shouldn't I?' or 'Um he, well, we're separated'). She went into the living room, where Davey was setting up the telly. Lola was kneeling on the floor, passing him leads, following his instructions.

'What's funny, Mum?' Davey asked.

'I'm just happy to be here. Aren't you? I slept so well last night.' Cath sat down on a deckchair and sang, 'Oh I do like to be beside the seaside, while the brass band plays tiddly-om-pom-pom!'

Lola sat on Cath's lap, but Davey just gave her one of his funny looks.

'What's up with you? We *are* beside the seaside now.'

'We haven't seen it yet,' Davey pointed out, 'except in the car.'

'Well, it's there, all right. We'll go look at it later, shall we?'

Both children nodded. Lola rubbed her head against Cath's neck.

'Fantastic. Hop off, Lolly. I just got to do something. I'll come and help you with the telly in a sec.'

Cath went upstairs, marvelling all over again at the wide staircase, the three good-sized bedrooms leading off the hall. She paused at the little round window at the top of the stairs, which looked out onto Minette's front garden. These funny old houses. They were semi-detatched, but the big bay windows, upstairs and down, meant that the right-hand side of the house – the left-hand side in Minette's case – stuck out further than the centre. The round window was on the side of the bit which stuck out, but only on her house: Minette's didn't have one, so maybe a previous owner had bricked it over. A window like this would never get planning permission now. They'd say, rightly, that it was overlooking next door. From what Minette had said about the previous owners, they were quite keen on overlooking, and complaining too. Well, Minette would find her quite a different kind of neighbour.

Cath went into her bedroom, and smiled at herself in the mirror. A room of her own. No dirty work clothes chucked on the floor, no smells other than her own, nothing moved unless she moved it. There was a bolt on the inside, but she'd have to get a proper lock on the outside too, pretty sharpish. The kids were going to go mad, especially Davey, but she'd realised, soon as they got to Gina's, that she couldn't risk them going on the computer. Gina had put hers away while they were there and told Davey it was at the repair shop. She needed the computer herself, of course, for fundraising, so she'd have to keep it in here. As Davey got older this was going to be a massive headache. Computers were everywhere, smart phones, everything. School was going to be a big problem. Well, she'd have to explain some of their situation to the head teacher, was all.

The bed looked very inviting. Five minutes, all right, Cathykins? Just till she felt a little calmer. She lay on her back and sank into the pillows, focused on soothing the tension in her arms. Lying in bed in the day always made her think of being off school, her mum coming up with soup, or to put a cool flannel on her forehead. It was such a safe feeling. Cath snuggled under the covers, and tried to hold onto the safeness, to stop worrying about everything. She consciously stopped herself thinking about Davey and computers. She'd go mad if she thought about everything she had to sort out, all at once. There was so much of it, and she was so tired. Lousy night last night, no point telling the kids that, though. She'd hoped it would be better now they were here in their own place, far away from Troubletown, but it was obviously going to take a bit of time. It had only been one night, after all.

She'd always fall asleep fine, but an hour later she'd be awake, heart racing, convinced something had happened to the children. She'd hurtle out of bed, go into each of their rooms, shine a torch on their faces, check they were breathing. Only when she'd done that could she get back into bed. Then she'd be asleep, awake, asleep, for the rest of the night. Sometimes she'd have to check them again; other times she'd manage to get into a deeper sleep, but then she might have one of her stressy, argumentative dreams.

Her dream this morning had woken her at five-thirty, shaken her so much she'd got up and gone downstairs to paint a couple of walls before the children stirred. Her dreams were frantic, her racing round, trying to do some unspecified thing. There was usually a chase in which she had to cross a road that became sticky trapping mud. Other times there was an old-fashioned phone where she kept dialling the wrong number.

Andy had been sympathetic about her nightmares. He was lucky, he always knew he was dreaming, and when things got frightening his conscious self could tell his unconscious 'it's just a silly dream'. How she wished she could do that. But her dreams always seemed totally real and terrifying.

She remembered she hadn't yet noted down the names she'd learned off Minette, and from Josie, the woman on her other side, who she'd met this morning. She sat up and grabbed a notepad and pen from the bedside table. Gina's mum had taught her, years ago, that one way to feel more in control was to focus on one small, manageable task. On a separate page for each address, so there was space to add things when she got to know people better, she wrote:

29: Priya, Rashid, Amina, Nisha and Raka. Three generations. Priya's sister = estate agent. Brother owns and lives over shop at end of the street.
30: Don't know.
31: Minette, Abe and Tilly. Her = a bit strung out. Him = don't know yet. Sweet baby.
32: Old woman, living alone.
34: Sixty-something couple. Smart red car.
35: Liam and Josie. Him = gorgeous and knows it. Her = slightly less so and knows it.
36: Kirsten. On her own. Husband left her last year. Skip outside. Post-divorce renovating. Cranial osteopath.
37: Greg and Steven. Gay?
38: Student house.
39: Don't know.
40: House-share. All girls in their twenties, Josie thinks.
41: Martin, Sarah and Callum. She walks with a stick. Accident? Kid a teenager, Josie says a menace with his skateboard.

The other houses she could just put an invite through with the house number on the envelope. No need to get everyone's names yet.

Cath surveyed her notes, frowning at her babyish handwriting. At school, boys and girls had been separated for writing lessons. Cath and all her mates had left primary with the same rounded writing, lots of loops. The boys all had nice spiky writing, straight lines, no messing. Only Gina had rebelled, had got Barry Etherington to teach her the boys' version and practised over and over till she got it right. The teacher had whinged about it, called Gina a silly tomboy, but there was nothing the school could do. It was a good lesson, Cath thought, and she didn't mean the one from school. If you really set your mind to something, what could anyone else do to stop you?

Cath locked the notepad in her bureau. She definitely felt calmer. She turned on her laptop and sent a quick email.

Dearest V

We are here! Safe. Gina was a star, did so much, helped me with all the paperwork. Couldn't have done it without her. But must admit it is so nice to have our own space. Hoping for long-ish breathing space before we see you. Has Wade gone yet? Keep me posted.

R xx

She took a last look at the neat, silent room, and went back down. The television was working and the kids were watching a cartoon.

'Well done, Davey. You're a right little electrician. I've got a good feeling about this place, don't you?'

'Mmm.'

'I'm going to sort out a party for the neighbours, really soon. Would you like that?'

'Mmm.'

'Yes Mum. Blimey, I'm talking to myself here.' Cath laughed and ruffled his hair. 'It'll be a great chance to tell people about our fundraising and that.'

'Can we have a biscuit?' Lola asked.

'What, them ones from her next door? They've all gone, Lolly. I'll do some sandwiches. I'm just going to sit for a minute, I'm cream-crackered.'

'Will Daddy be here soon?' Lola asked.

Cath caught Davey's expression, saw him shake his head at Lola. Cath frowned, not really meaning to, just thinking about what to say, and Lola's face crumpled. Cath put her arm round Lola and held her close. She put her other arm round Davey but he leaned away so that she had to stretch awkwardly to reach him. 'Ooh, you big lump,' Cath said, 'so stubborn. What'll you be like when you're a teenager? I tremble to think. I knew a kid like you, Davey, a little girl, in the hospital, very poorly she was, but stubborn? Jumping snakes! She was.'

'What was her name?' Lola asked. She loved Cath's stories.

'Libby. Cute little thing. Blonde bunches. Roll up your sleeve, Libby, I'd tell her, gotta take a teeny bit of blood for the doctor. Would she? Nah.'

'Did she die?'

Cath tried again to cuddle Davey, but he sat up straight and stiff, his arms folded in front of him. Cath gave up and pulled Lola closer. 'Yes,' she whispered, into Lola's hair. 'Yes, she died, poor little thing.'

'Daddy,' Lola whispered.

Cath wasn't sure if she'd meant to be heard. 'He's busy, like I told you. Driving his big lorry.' She let her go, and both kids turned their attention back to the television. 'I'll do them sandwiches. Jam all right?'

Neither of them replied, and she walked over to the door. When she turned to look back, Davey had put his arm round Lola's shoulder.

Chapter 4

Davey

The carpet in Davey's old room had thick red and orange stripes, with a thinner blue stripe in between. Red, blue, orange, blue. Davey liked to sit on the floor and run his finger along a blue stripe, because when you pushed it one way it went a slightly different blue.

The new carpet was green. It was old and flat. The green stayed the same when he pushed it. Lola said pretend it's grass, but Davey wasn't feeling particularly pretendy.

Davey told Adam Purcell his five favourite numbers.

1. Eight, because he was eight.
2. Seven, because he had liked being seven and it was famous as a lucky number anyway.
3. A zillion, even though according to his dad it wasn't a real number.
4. Googol, which was one with a hundred noughts after it, bigger even than a zillion which was probably a billion times a trillion or something. He knew Google had been named after googol, but it had been spelled wrong.
5. Sixty-eight, the number of their old house.

Davey wished his mum would hurry up and unpack the laptop. She kept saying it was in a box underneath another box and she would 'get round to it'. Grown-ups said they would get round to it if it was something they didn't want to do.

Davey wasn't even going to have his new room for long. His mum said she would make him a better room downstairs, in the dining room, soon as she got a minute. Getting a minute was a lot quicker than getting round to it. She'll say it's going to be fantastic, Adam Purcell said. Davey told his mum he wanted to stay upstairs but she basically did her look. 'I can't carry you anymore.'

When Davey was little, he could walk whenever he wanted. He remembered that well. Just walking around, nothing stopping him.

The best thing about the new house was the window at the top of the stairs. No, the best thing was that his mum was all happy. The window was the second best thing. It was a special window, because it was round. Davey had never seen a round window before, except in pictures of ships. You could look at next door's front garden out of it.

Davey thought about the last joke his dad had told him. Whenever his dad put him to bed, he would tell him a bad joke. 'Lola,' he said, 'want to hear Dad's joke?'

She nodded.

'Why did the birdie go to the hospital?'

'I don't know.'

'To get a tweetment.'

Lola laughed, she always did, though she never really got them. She laughed, then said, 'I don't get it.' Her doing that always made their dad laugh even more.

Now she asked him when their dad would be coming. Davey just said, 'I don't know, don't ask Mum any more,' and ran his hands over the new carpet, hoping to see the green change.

Chapter 5

Minette

As Minette walked up Cath's path, she wondered idly – she told herself it was idly – whether Liam would be there. She'd made a big effort: black trousers that made her waist look smaller, a little green top with sparkly straps. Now she'd stopped breastfeeding she could wear what she liked. She still winced whenever she thought back to Ros's wedding, when Tilly was just five weeks old. How impressed everyone in their old crowd had been to see Minette out and about so soon after giving birth, looking 'super-hot', Ros said. Tilly slept through the ceremony like an angel, and Minette was just starting to properly relax when Tilly woke with a scream at the reception. Minette automatically moved the sobbing baby to her breast, then realised that the only way to get her boob out of her new tight-bodiced dress was to unzip the whole thing, and push it down to her waist. An usher found her a quiet room that was invaded ten minutes later by a group of drunk men looking for the cloakroom. It was the most humiliating moment of her life, easily taking over from the school sports day when her period started in the middle of the egg and spoon. She'd almost cried when she got back to Abe and told him, but Abe, pissed and enjoying the party, had just laughed. And although he was horrified for her later, when he realised how upset she was, a small part of her felt she had never completely forgiven him.

Cath greeted her effusively at the door. 'Love your top, Minette! Hey, where's my Tilly?'

'Abe's just changing her, they'll be along in a minute.' Minette admired the newly sanded wooden floors in the hall as Cath led her to the kitchen.

'So many people have come,' Cath enthused. 'This really is a fantastic neighbourhood.'

'I suppose it is,' Minette said, distracted by the word 'neighbourhood', which she thought was American. Though of course there was the Neighbourhood Watch, which was very British, very Abe's parents, so maybe not. Two Indian men

Minette hadn't seen before were sitting at the table, drinking tea.

'Too early for wine?' Cath asked, holding up a bottle. 'Don't be put off by these two,' and she giggled at the men, 'they're lightweights.'

Minette accepted a glass of wine, not looking at the tea-drinking men in case they disapproved.

'Good lass. Keep me company.' Cath started pouring the wine, then her little girl toddled over and tugged her sleeve. 'Careful Lola, you'll make me spill it.'

'He wants toilet.'

'OK, tell him I'm coming.'

Cath handed Minette the glass and said, 'Davey hasn't got the hang of getting his chair up that high step yet. Come out with me, there's someone I want you to meet.'

There were quite a few people already in the garden, most of whom Minette didn't recognise. She waved at Priya, and saw Kirsten talking to a man with receding hair, who was blatantly looking down her top. This made Minette grin, and she was still smiling when Cath said, 'Minette, let me introduce you to my other next-door neighbour.'

Minette looked up into Liam's film-star face. 'Oh! Hi!' she stammered.

His eyes crinkled as he smiled, and said, 'Lovely to meet you properly.' He took her hand and held onto it a little longer than she might have expected.

'Excuse me, won't you,' Cath said. 'I just have to sort Davey out.'

Christ! Minette was alone with the handsomest man she had ever seen. She didn't know whether to give thanks to the God of Good Things, or call out to Cath, don't leave me by myself! Liam had her idea of perfect looks: tall and broad-shouldered, fair-haired, expressive brown eyes, a secretly amused expression. He reminded her dangerously of her ex-boyfriend Paul, her gold standard of maleness, who had inevitably broken her heart.

'Is, er, your wife here?' Minette asked, mentally slapping herself around the head the instant it was out of her mouth. See? She should simply not be left alone with men like this.

'No, Josie's had to go to work. Mind you, meet the neighbours isn't really her thing.'

'Oh, really?' Minette now felt naff in comparison to the cool unneighbourly Josie.

'Not me, though. I like it.' There was a pause. 'Well, I like meeting some of them.'

Was he flirting or just talking? She looked into her glass, and mumbled, 'What work does she do?' Now she'd started on the wife she might as well keep going.

'Something time-consuming but well-paid, in human resources for Hilton Hotels.'

'Ah, so do you get to stay in luxury hotels then?'

'Everyone asks that.'

'I'm super-original,' Minette said, attempting to style out her pitiful small talk.

'We do get the occasional freebie. So, where's your husband?'

'Oh, I'm not married. We're just. Um. There's no right word for this, is there? Partners, I suppose.'

Liam grinned. 'So where's your *partner*?'

'He's still at home, changing the baby.'

'What's wrong with the one you've got?'

'Very good.' Minette tried to up her banter. 'Well, we thought we'd maybe swap her for a quieter one.'

'Yes, I understand from Cath that the previous neighbours complained.'

'Oh! I was only joking.'

'So was I.'

But Cath had told him that? When? She'd only been in the street five minutes. What else had she said?

'Shall we sit down?' Liam said, indicating some deckchairs. 'I'd love to have a bitch about Mr Milton. He told me off once for mowing the lawn at the wrong time.'

It seemed extraordinary that someone who looked like Liam should be sitting next to her, his brown eyes staring into hers. It gave her a reckless, drunk feeling, and she started talking unguardedly, telling how her heart beat faster, even now, every time Tilly cried, how she'd sometimes walked her up and down half the night, and put the cot in the bathroom, as far as possible from the Miltons' side. How she'd spent hours looking at estate agents' websites, fantasising about isolated country cottages surrounded by fields.

'Were you trying to get away from them, that time I saw you early one morning?'

So he remembered that! She nodded.

'I'm glad you didn't move. Much better they did. In my considered opinion they were complete wankers.'

She laughed, and changed the subject. She didn't want him to think she was a moaner. 'So, do you work for hotels too?'

'No, I used to do flash money stuff in the city, but I was made redundant last year.'

'I'm sorry about that.'

'Sorry I was a trader, or sorry I got made redundant? No need to answer, and definitely no need to be sorry. I'm enjoying being a kept man, for now. Means I have a lot of time at home. Which is nice.' He all but fluttered his eyelashes at her. He bloody well *was* flirting. 'Plus I had an excuse to change career. I'm starting teacher training in September.'

Minette gulped down her wine. Oh my god, he was going to be a teacher, which was really cool, and he was at home a lot in the day, and he was flirting, and . . .

Abe materialised silently at Minette's side. 'All right, Dougie?'

'Abe!' Minette almost shouted. 'This is Liam, he lives next door to Cath, his wife Josie is at work, she works for Hilton Hotels. He's going to be a teacher.'

'That's a perfect summary of our conversation,' Liam said, smoothly. 'Good to meet you, Abe.'

'I've seen you around,' Abe said. 'Haven't you got one of those folding bikes?'

'Yes, I sometimes ride it to the station.' He nodded at Tilly. 'And I presume this is the changed baby?'

Abe sat down next to Minette, cradling his arms round Tilly, who was nodding off in the sling. 'She's worn out. It was an epic shite.'

'Abe!'

'He doesn't mind. You don't mind, do you? You look like a man of the world.'

'I am, I suppose,' Liam said, 'but I'm not very familiar with the ins and outs of the infant digestive system.'

Minette smiled. 'You don't want to be, believe me.'

But Abe was on a roll. 'I've got a system for categorising Tilly's craps by the number of baby wipes required.'

'Abe, pack it in.'

'You got kids?' Abe asked, and Liam shook his head. 'Not yet, but I'd very much like to.'

'With your genes it'd be criminal not to. So he might as well hear it how it is, Dougie. Yeah, a three-wipe job you've got off lightly. A bad one could need maybe eight wipes?

And on one memorable occasion I single-handedly took care of a twenty-four-wipe special.'

Minette was familiar with this little routine. 'You'll put him off kids for life.'

'Not at all, I love children,' Liam said, with a heart-melting smile at Minette. He said to her, 'Why are you called Dougie?'

'Her surname's Fairbanks,' Abe butted in. 'Like Douglas Fairbanks. Hence Dougie. It's got to be done.'

'No one else calls me that, only Abe.'

Lola toddled over and offered up a tray of tiny, professional-looking cakes.

'What ones do you like?' Minette asked her.

'I'm allergic,' the girl replied.

'Oh yes. I hope there's something else you can have?' Minette took a tiny scone and the girl moved away. 'So cute.'

'What made you decide to go into teaching?' Abe asked. 'My brother's a deputy head in Bristol. Tough old game.'

'Not as tough as unemployment.'

'I hear you. It's grim out there,' Abe said. 'See it all the time with my clients. Doing five applications a day, some of them, not even getting an acknowledgement.'

'Abe works at Citizens Advice,' Minette told Liam.

'Meant to do IT advice, but you end up helping people with CVs, forms, everything,' Abe said.

'For a while I was one of those five applications a day people,' Liam said. 'Couldn't stand it. I've always been good with children, so teaching made sense. I'm going to specialise in maths.'

'I'd have loved maths if . . .' Minette began, then realised that she was going to say, if the teacher had looked like you, and hastily amended it to, 'the teacher had liked children as much as you.' Both men looked at her, one oddly, the other with an amused upturn at the corner of his mouth. She was rescued by Cath, who was standing on a chair and tapping on a wineglass.

When the conversations petered out, Cath smiled round at everyone – the garden was now full of people – and thanked everyone for coming. 'Davey, Lola and I are truly grateful for the warm welcome and kindness you've shown us in our first couple of weeks here in wonderful Sisley Street.'

Everyone was quiet, watching Cath. She talked about Davey, about his condition, some form of muscular dystrophy, Minette didn't catch the name, and about her fundraising for groups who supported kids like him. Cath was very compelling, Minette realised. There was something charismatic about her that caught the attention.

Minette shifted in her seat so she could sneak a glance at Liam. She knew she ought to look away, but she didn't seem to be in charge of her eyes; they roamed down Liam's long legs, and slowly back up his body, stopping at several interesting points en route. When she arrived at his face, she found with a start that he was looking straight at her, with that amused expression. She looked away so hurriedly she felt like her eyes twanged, Bugs Bunny style. Abe was looking down at Tilly and hadn't noticed.

When she dared to look back again, Liam was gazing attentively at Cath. Minette wondered if he found Cath attractive. He might, easily, though she was older than him. She was very slim, with lovely shoulder-length blonde hair that Minette envied, coiled into a clip.

Cath finished talking, and people clapped. Someone handed Minette a clipboard, which she'd dimly registered being passed round while Cath spoke. She held it up to Abe with a quizzical look, and he said, 'It's for the triathlon Cath was just talking about.'

'Now we know why we were invited,' Liam said.

'It's for charity, mate,' Abe said, filling in the form.

'There'll soon be a time when everyone in the world will be begging for cash for their bungee jump or marathon or sponsored toothbrushing. It'll be like Andy Warhol's fifteen minutes, except with sponsor pledges.'

Minette knew she should find Liam's attitude repugnant – Abe clearly did – but it made him even more attractive. Perhaps because of her default optimism, her glass-half-full mentality, Minette was drawn to cynical people. Paul had been very cynical.

Abe just shook his head. 'I'll not bother passing this on to you, then?' he said.

'Of course I'll sponsor her,' Liam said, laughing, 'I'm not a complete bastard.' After he'd signed it, Minette handed the form to Kirsten, and noticed that Liam had pledged twenty pounds more than Abe.

'She's incredible, isn't she?' Kirsten said. 'Husband away, two kids, one poorly, just moved house, and she still does all this stuff for charity.'

'She's very cool,' agreed the receding man, still loitering near Kirsten's top.

Cath came over with a woman Minette didn't know. Another one! It seemed to Minette that she had been going round with her eyes closed since moving in. The new woman was very tanned and wearing a leopard-skin dress.

'Oh, you lovely folk!' Cath cried, looking at the clipboard. 'It will make training so much easier, knowing I've got such supportive sponsors.'

'Still think you're mad,' the leopard-skin woman said. 'Least this one isn't quite as barking as your parachute jump.'

'Not a bungee, then?' Liam said quietly to Minette.

'Gina, this is Minette and Abe, their darling daughter Tilly, and Liam,' Cath said, putting her arm round the woman. 'My neighbours on either side.'

Minette overcompensated for her judgmental feelings about Gina's dress by giving her warmest smile.

'Gina's my rock,' Cath said to Minette. 'She's seen me through a lot of crazy stuff.'

The two women moved away, taking the sponsor form round to other groups of people. Liam exchanged a raised eyebrow with Minette and Abe.

'Lesbian?' Liam mouthed.

Abe nodded. 'Definite gaydar there.'

Tilly stirred, opened her eyes and began to wail. 'Ah, the kraken wakes,' Abe said, and stood up. 'I'll take her home for lunch,' he told Minette. He nodded at Liam, clearly still riled by his charity comments, and headed into the house. Minette said, 'I'd better go too.' She made no move to get up.

'It was great to get a chance to talk to you. Listen.' He touched her arm gently, setting off shockwaves in Minette. 'Yes?' she said faintly. She was sure that the hairs on her arm were standing on end, hoped they weren't, didn't dare look. How long had it been, since she had felt that rush?

'Yes, what?' he whispered.

'You said, "Listen."'

'Ah yes. Listen. When I said I liked meeting the neighbours, there was only one I was hoping to meet.'

'Oh, Jesus.'

'No, not him. He lives in Brighton.'

'I'm just . . . it's just . . . well.' Stop it, Minette, she told herself. Stop being so uncool. 'I like meeting the *neighbour* too.' She emphasised the singular.

'That's good to know. I was wondering, is there ever time when you're at home during the day, bored?'

'I have a small baby, so yes, all the time.'

'Me too. Except without the baby. I'm sitting there, on my own, waiting till my course starts. I've already watched everything on Netflix and I'm just about ready to take up macramé, so if you ever fancied coffee or something . . .'

'Oh! But I'll have Tilly.'

'Sure. She can hang out too, watch telly or something?'

Minette looked at Liam. Was she really going to cross this line? 'I don't know.'

Kirsten, who'd finally shaken off her receding-haired admirer, joined them. 'We still on for Tilly's cranio this afternoon, Min?'

'Yes, please. Liam, do you know Kirsten? She lives more or less opposite you.'

Liam said, 'Hello,' but carried on looking at Minette. There was an awkward silence. 'Well, I'll head off,' Kirsten said, eventually. 'Bye, then.'

When she'd gone, Liam smiled at Minette. 'So, what do you think?'

The look on Kirsten's face had brought Minette back to her senses. Was she seriously contemplating, well, whatever she was contemplating? Flirting was lovely, but that had to be it. 'I can't, I'm sorry. I'll see you some time.' She followed Kirsten into the house.

Cath was saying goodbye to people at the door, thanking them for coming.

'Lovely party,' Minette told her. 'Amazing turn out.'

'Lots of fantastic neighbours,' Cath said. 'Hope you met some nice ones.'

Davey was sitting in his wheelchair behind her, staring at Minette. When she caught his eye he looked away.

'Bye Davey.'

He waved his hand, and Minette went home, head spinning. She knew it was a mistake, drinking wine so early in the day.

Chapter 6

Cath

Cath sat next to another mother in the school foyer, and they got chatting. The woman was the mother of a girl in the reception class, but she clearly knew who Davey was. Cath guessed that all the kids were talking about the new boy in the wheelchair. The woman asked Cath the round-the-houses questions Cath was familiar with. Have you got any other children? (Translation: how the hell do you cope?) Does he always use the chair? (Has he just broken his leg or is he a permanent crip?) How does he manage at school? (What does he do when he needs the toilet?)

Cath gave her well-practised explanations: Yes, I've got a younger daughter as well who – how bad is my luck? – has multiple allergies. What to? Oh god, easier to say what not to! Um: peanuts, tree nuts, milk, fish . . . yes, it does make catering a bit on the awkward side, thank god for pasta, ha ha. Davey on the other hand, he'll eat anything. But he has Duchenne muscular dystrophy, only boys get it, one in every 3,500, yeah, bad bloody luck, but you got to make the best of it, don't you? We only got a diagnosis when he was four but I knew something was wrong, you just do, don't you? At his last school an assistant took him to the disabled loo, but he's big enough to sort himself out now. I'm doing a triathlon to raise money for research, maybe there will be a cure one day. Yes, you spotted my Lycra, off for a run after I've had a chat with Davey's teacher, oh well thanks, I've got the sponsorship form here, that's very kind of you.

Davey's teacher, Miss Hobbs, took Cath into the library. 'Davey is such a lovely boy,' she said. 'We're so glad he's joined us. We can talk properly here.'

Cath couldn't imagine talking 'properly' to this doll-faced young woman, who looked fresh out of college, but she smiled and sat down. Miss Hobbs had with her the letter Cath sent when Davey started at the school. 'So, Ms Brooke. Could you just tell us a bit more about this; you've asked that Davey be prevented from using the internet.'

'Yes.'

'Is that for, er, religious reasons?'

'No.'

Miss Hobbs shifted in her seat. 'Ms Brooke, it would really help us if you could explain a little more. It's extremely awkward to remove Davey from all classes which use the internet, and it's going to be detrimental to his learning.'

'I didn't have the internet at school, but I somehow managed to become a qualified nurse.'

'Well, yes.' Miss Hobbs laughed nervously. 'I take your point. But these days . . .'

'Did you become a teacher recently, Miss Hobbs?'

'Yes, two years ago.'

'Where was your course?'

'At Bath.'

'Oh, isn't that a lovely city! Did you want to stay there?'

'Yes, I loved it, but I couldn't find anything suitable, and my boyfriend, anyway, where were we? Yes, the internet.' She said more gently than before, 'Are there health reasons perhaps?'

'There are, partly. When you're using a computer or tablet you're sitting very still and only moving the lower parts of your arms. That's certainly not good for Davey's muscular development. But that's not the main reason.' Cath's eyes filled with tears.

The teacher reached across to pat Cath's arm. 'I'm so sorry,

I don't want to pry, it's just I've been told that I must put down a reason.'

'No, of course, I understand,' Cath said, wiping her eyes. 'I'm just not used to talking about my problems. We've been through a hell of a time. We left our last place in a massive hurry, there was violence and threats. I'm so worried about Davey's safety, about him being traceable if he uses the internet. I want to keep him safe.'

'Of course you do,' Miss Hobbs said emphatically, her eyes two pools of concern. 'And so do we.' She lowered her voice. 'Is there something criminal we need to know about? Can we help in any way?'

'That's so sweet of you. The police are aware,' Cath said. 'Will that be enough of a reason?'

'Yes, certainly.' The teacher made some notes. 'The head has also asked me to do some data gathering about Davey's learning difficulties.'

'He doesn't have any. Bright as a button, that one.'

'He means any difficulties associated with Davey's condition. Was he statemented at his last school?'

Cath shook her head. 'He can keep up with everything, he's fine. He don't need extra help; you already have the ramps, and a disabled toilet.' She smiled, and put her hand on the table to say, that's all.

'Great. Well, I will certainly make the staff aware that Davey mustn't be given internet access. However, in light of that, and his muscular dystrophy, we will recommend bringing the educational psychologist on board.'

Cath said, 'But surely there are other children more in need of that kind of support?'

The teacher closed her folder. 'I'm really sorry, Ms Brooke, I know the Head would just tell you the same thing. If there's a request like the internet thing, and a deteriorating condition, we're now obliged to bring in psychological services.'

'So not just "recommended" but "obliged"?'

'Er, yes. I'm sorry.' The teacher stood up, and moved quickly to the door. 'I had better relieve the teaching assistant! Thanks so much for stopping by, Ms Brooke.'

Cath saw that there was no point pushing it any further. Jobsworth woman had to do her thing.

She left the school and headed towards the seafront at a fast walk, then broke into a run once at the promenade. Grey though the sea was today, it still gave her a lift. She'd grown up in Eastbourne, only twenty-five miles along the coast, did her nurse training there, and took the sea for granted till she'd moved north and left it behind. They'd gone to the beach, course, when they lived in Liverpool and the kids were tiny. Those lovely empty beaches in North Wales, at Colwyn Bay. But it was a different thing to live near the sea, just three streets along, to be able to come down whenever you liked and breathe great salty lungs full of fresh, clean air.

It had felt very odd, being back in Eastbourne recently.

Since moving away at twenty, she'd visited occasionally, to see Gina and Fay, always driving or walking the long way round to avoid the street where she grew up. She had no wish to see that house ever again. And since Davey was born, Gina had always come to see her. Being back in Eastbourne made it clear that, despite Gina being there, it was not the place for a fresh start.

Jogging along the flat path, passed by skateboarders and leggy girls on rollerblades, Cath felt bucked up, raised a hand to two women running towards her, who waved back. Hove was such a nice town, such a good move. The right move.

She wasn't mad keen for an ed psych to get involved, she knew they were generally pretty nosy, but she supposed they might have an interesting viewpoint. Though she didn't hold psychologists in as high esteem as proper medical people, like nurses. Anyway, knowing how these things worked, a referral would take months. Who knew where things would be then?

When the derelict west pier came into view Cath slowed to a halt and looked at her phone. Three kilometres. Not bad. Bit out of breath, but the legs were holding up. She reckoned she'd soon be able to do five, which was all she had to do for the triathlon. Running and swimming were OK. Cycling would be the hard bit. But she knew from other fundraisers she'd seen back in Troubletown that nothing brought in the donations like a triathlon. There was no point just doing a run anymore.

She turned away from the pier and started to walk home, making lists in her head. Cool down, quick shower, then get working, make some calls. Got to get back into the networks, Cathykins. Already been here three weeks. She'd been given some useful numbers from the local Duchenne support group. And Lola's nursery had been great, had put up notices encouraging people to sponsor her, but it was harder to get schools on board. She needed to raise her profile. Maybe put on a fundraising event there? Quizzes were always popular.

Cath was back at Sisley Street, trying to fish her door key out of the sweaty zip pocket at the back of her running trousers, when she saw the girl next door, Minette. She was sitting in her front garden, on a bench Cath hadn't noticed before.

'You've got a good view of the street from there,' she called, then realised Minette was crying. 'Oh, lovie, what's up?' She pushed open Minette's gate and sat next to her.

Minette wailed, 'Nothing!'

'Yeah, I can tell.' Cath put her arm round Minette.

'I'm so sorry, really embarrassing.'

'Don't be daft. Let it all out, lass.'

Cath didn't point out that to avoid embarrassment all Minette had to do was sob inside her house, rather than right out in front of it. Cath preferred to cry in private, but she had flamboyant friends such as Gina who liked an audience when she was upset, and she understood that. Her own need for an audience came out in a different way, that was all.

Minette's sobs slowly gave way to sniffs, and at last she sat up and fumbled for a tissue, blew her nose with a honk.

'I thought me sitting so close would do the trick,' Cath said. 'I'm well rank.'

Minette smiled. 'You are a bit sweaty, now you mention it.'

Cath raised her face to the sun. 'This is a good idea. Maybe I'll get a bench for my front yard too.'

'Oh, god.' Minette sounded like she might start crying again.

'Hey, I'm sorry. I won't get one if you don't want me to.'

Minette gave a spluttering laugh. 'No, it's just me and Abe had such a stupid row about the bench.'

'Bit of an odd thing to argue about?'

'It's been sitting in the back garden under a tarp for months, since his parents gave it to us. They thought I could sit out on it when it was sunny, and feed Tilly.'

'Abe's parents sound nice.'

'They are, they're lovely.' Minette paused, then said, all in a rush, 'Anyway, I decided it would be better in the front garden, then Tilly and I could sit here and watch the world go by, maybe see a few more people than our average day of seeing no one.

So I asked Abe to help me move it, but he just got in a mood for absolutely no reason, and went off to work in a strop. I was so fed up I dragged the sodding thing right through the house myself, and it's made a mess of the walls.'

Cath expected Minette to start crying again, but she surprised her by laughing. 'So, it's worked anyway. By sitting here whinging at you, I'm having more conversation today than in the previous three days put together.'

'It's boring at home with little ones, isn't it?' Cath said sympathetically. 'Is Tilly asleep?'

'Yes, though not for much longer. Come and have a quick cuppa before she wakes up?'

Cath looked at Minette's earnest face. She was very pretty after crying, her dark blue eyes shining. 'I really need a shower. The pong's just killed some of your plants.'

'Those are weeds. Oh, go on, you can tell me about your triathlon and everything.'

Much as Cath wanted to go home, this was an excellent opportunity for some girl-bonding with her next-door neighbour. So she followed her into the house, noting the scuff marks on the walls above the skirting where Minette had dragged the bench.

They went into the kitchen where Cath admired Minette's oak tops and gleaming tiles. 'Wish I had the money for a new kitchen,' Cath said. She'd inherited the Miltons' outdated faux-wood units and grubby Formica tops.

'We were lucky, Abe's parents helped us out,' Minette said, filling a fancy cream-coloured retro kettle with water. 'So how's the training going?'

'Not bad. Thanks for your sponsor pledge, by the way.'

'You're welcome. Really impressed you're doing it. When is it?'

'End of June.'

'That's less than two months!'

'It'll be fine. That's ages.'

'Will your husband be there, cheering you on?'

Oh, clever Minette. Valid question. Cath batted it away. 'He might. I suppose Tilly's too young to come and watch?'

'We'll definitely be there. Always good to have something different to do. Someone said he was working abroad, is that right?'

Persistent. She'd have to give her something. There was a sharp intelligence in Minette's face and Cath knew she would be harder to fob off than some others.

'Yes, he's in Poland. We Skyped last night.'

'Good heavens, what's he doing there?'

'He's in long-distance haulage.' Intelligent or not, Cath knew she could rely on Minette not to ask any questions about what that meant. No one ever did.

'Oh. Is he away for much longer?'

'Probably – he usually goes from one job to the next. Last time he was away for six months.'

'God, that's tough. He hasn't seen the house, then?'

'Not actually been here. But I sent photos. He said to go for it.'

'Is it hard, him away so much?'

'Not as hard as having no money,' Cath said truthfully, and Minette looked embarrassed.

'Oh god, sorry.'

'It's a lot better paid than local haulage. That's what he was doing before Davey came along. But when I stopped working, we couldn't manage.'

'What did you used to do?'

'Nursing.'

'Oh, that's very cool. I wanted to be a nurse when I was little.'

'Me too, and I never changed my mind. I loved going to hospital when I was tiny. It was always the nurses who knew what was what. Doctors can be so daft,' Cath grinned. 'I liked the way nurses would say "yes doctor" then do what they wanted anyway.'

'Could you go back to nursing when Lola's at school?'

'Yes, I'm hoping to. What about you, what was your work?'

'Nothing as useful as you,' Minette said. 'I worked for the council's tourism department, as a guide at Brighton Pavilion. It's such a fun job.'

'Are you going back after maternity leave? I didn't go back to work when Davey was a baby. I loved being at home with him. Happiest time of my life.'

'I was thinking I probably will. I'll have to let work know soon, actually.'

'Do think carefully about it,' Cath said. 'Babies need their mummies. You don't get that time again. Unfortunately I had to go back when Lola was small, we couldn't manage without my wages. But I regret leaving her.'

'Well, I haven't finally decided . . .'

The monitor on the counter crackled into life, relaying Tilly's crying loud and clear.

'There she is, god love her,' Cath said. 'I'd better go,'

Minette got up. 'You don't have to rush off, do you?'

'I'll just say a quick hello to Tilly, if she don't mind the smell.' Cath pulled her running top away from her body and sniffed down it. 'God, disgusting.'

While Minette was upstairs, Cath looked round the kitchen, getting ideas for hers. Everything was stylish. That kettle, and one of those Dualit toasters that Cath reckoned were one big con. Gina had a pink one that Ryan had given her, you either got your toast white or charred. The stove had a dozen buttons and knobs, like the flight deck of a plane. Abe's job couldn't keep them in single-stave oak worktops and Neff cookers. It must all be from their parents.

She examined the large noticeboard on the wall but there was nothing very interesting: a baby group poster, out-of-date Tesco's vouchers and a brochure about viniculture, whatever that was. The board was mainly covered with photos of Tilly: on her own, with Minette or Abe, or with older people, presumably one or other set of grandparents. Then a different photo caught Cath's eye. It was half obscured under the timetable of the local swimming pool, but as it was the only picture of Abe and Minette on their own, it clearly had some significance. It was taken several years ago, going by their fresh faces. Cath unpinned the photo to see it better. They were standing on a balcony in front of an ancient cream-coloured building, smiling, arms round each other, squinting into the sun, which gave off that bright yellow light Cath always associated with abroad. Abe was wearing a white T-shirt and jeans. He was thinner, his hair shorter. Minette was wearing a green dress and her hair was loose, down almost to her waist. Cath could see why it was on display: they both looked beautiful in it.

Cath heard Minette coming downstairs, talking to Tilly. There wasn't time to re-pin the picture, so she folded it, put it in the pocket of her running top, and quickly sat back down.

'Here she is,' Minette cooed.

'Aw, she's so gorgeous. Hello lovie!'

Tilly looked blankly at Cath. 'She's still a bit sleepy,' Minette said.

'Seems only a minute since Lola was that tiny.' Cath stood up. 'I'd better run. See you both soon.'

'I hope so,' Minette said.

'You'll be sitting on your bench won't you, now the weather's better? I'll keep an eye out for you.'

'Yeah, if Abe doesn't move it,' Minette said ruefully.

Minette was torn, Cath could see that. She knew Minette wanted to talk about Abe's unreasonableness, but she didn't want to be disloyal. And she wanted Cath to stay because it was boring being alone with a baby, but she didn't want to beg. Cath would like to know Minette better, but she wasn't going to rush. It took time to build up trust, even with someone as open and eager to be friends as Minette. There were already plenty of things she knew, anyway. She'd noted Minette's intense conversation with Liam at her party. She reckoned she knew why Abe had been difficult that morning.

She waved to Tilly as she went outside, past the contentious bench, and into her own house for a long hot shower.

Chapter 7

Minette

Minette kept her smile in place till Abe shut the door, then she stuck two fingers up and muttered something rude under her breath. She'd seen the meaningful look he gave to the pile of dirty picture frames still stacked by the front door.

She took Tilly up for her nap, zipping her into her soft quilted sleeping bag, pulling down the blind, and winding up the mobile Minette's mother had sent that played 'Für Elise'. Tilly was a child of routine, and her thumb went automatically into her mouth, her eyes already closing.

Minette crept downstairs and put the kettle on. The pleasure of drinking a cup of tea from start to finish, while it was hot – something she had previously taken for granted – was now right up there with sex.

Working only a fifteen minute walk away, Abe often came home for lunch. Like today. Which was sweet, but also a bit irritating, as if he imagined himself as a 1920s factory worker, with a wifey handing him a freshly made Cornish pasty before the whistle blew for his afternoon shift. Not that he at all expected Minette to get his lunch, but he invariably managed to wind her up in some way during his short trip home. In the early days of their life with Tilly it might have been a raised eyebrow that Minette wasn't yet dressed; more recently it was arch comments about the repetitiveness of their outings. 'Toys R Us *again*?' Minette had grown tired of explaining that the toy shop was like a museum to Tilly, who was too little to realise that the items were for sale. It was a great place to use up an hour, and you could be as noisy as you liked, unlike at home. But Abe thought Tilly should be learning stuff, going to proper museums and art galleries.

'Bit young, isn't she?' Abe's mum Julie murmured to Minette one time, as Abe talked about taking Tilly to see the Brighton Philharmonic, and Minette smiled at the older woman gratefully.

Today when Abe had asked what her plans were for the

afternoon, and she'd mentioned the park on the corner, he said, 'You went there yesterday.'

'Well, here's news: you can go there as often as you like,' she replied, tetchily.

She was on her second cup of tea, and reading an article in last Sunday's paper in which a divorced couple explained where their relationship went wrong, when she heard Tilly on the monitor. She bounded upstairs, calling, 'I'm coming,' in a sing-song voice. She was still programmed to rush at the first hint of noise. Tilly had only napped for fifteen minutes, but Minette had managed to drink one-and-a-half cups of tea, and read one-and-a-half articles in the papers; amazing what you could do in such a short time.

Minette gently extricated Tilly from her sleeping bag and stroked her soft leg. So plump and smooth! Minette longed to give it a gentle bite, but kissed it instead. She carried Tilly downstairs, chatting to her. 'Do you fancy the park, then, Tills?' Minette sometimes felt tired by the sound of her own voice droning on during these one-sided conversations. But then she had an idea which perked her up. 'I know! Let's clean those grotty frames and put your photos inside. We could even put them up. It would impress Daddy and maybe stop him nagging me for five minutes. What do you say?'

Tilly, as ever, didn't say anything. Minette took her out to the front garden and sat her on the little patch of grass with some toys. She filled a bucket with water and chatted as she started to clean the cobwebs and grime off the frames. 'Look Tilly, your pictures are going to go in here.' One-sided conversation or not, it was still such an enjoyable novelty not to feel that she had to whisper.

Minette finished the first frame, then realised she didn't have anywhere clean to put it now it was wet. She checked the garden gate was shut, not that Tilly was likely to crawl over there, and ran upstairs. She dug out a ratty towel, then went for a pee. It was a massively long one, as usual. Before she had Tilly – B.T. – she could wee whenever she wanted. Now – A.T. – making time for the most basic tasks required careful planning. It was easier to save everything up, including peeing, for one long burst. She was still sitting on the loo when she heard a man's voice outside, very close to the house. The gate clicked open. Jesus, he must be coming into the garden! What a stupid careless idiot she was, to leave Tilly unattended. She jumped up without wiping herself, drips spreading into her pants, and raced out to the garden, holding up her jeans. A man was crouched next to Tilly, talking to her in a low voice. Oh my god, what was he doing, what had he done, what did he want?

'Hey!' she yelled, and he looked up and smiled. For a moment she didn't recognise him, but her first thought was familiar: wow, he's handsome.

'Hey, yourself!'

Of course, it was Liam. Clearly, it was a fundamental rule of the universe that every time Minette saw him she was a mess. Apart from at Cath's party, where he had possibly propositioned her. Now here she was with her fly undone, grey granny knickers visible, his face level with that exact part of her anatomy. Was she doomed never to be cool in front of him?

Liam straightened up, reminding her how tall he was. 'I was just having a chat with your lovely daughter.'

'She's not much of a conversationalist,' Minette said, doing up her trousers.

'You look like you were caught in flagrante with the milkman.' He sat on the bench, and smiled at her.

'I was in the bathroom and I heard someone talking to Tilly . . .'

'Oh balls, and you imagined she was being abducted. I'm so sorry, that was thoughtless of me.'

'No, no, not at all.' She sat down too, to show she wasn't rattled, pushing the frames along the bench so that they were between her and Liam. 'Wha's 'appening, anyway?' For no reason whatsoever she lapsed into cockney. Oh yes, superbly suave.

'Nothin' much, blud,' Liam shot back, gamely. 'God, these frames are filthy.'

'Abe found them in a skip.' Her breathing was still uneven

from thinking Tilly was in trouble, and she tried to hide it, not wanting Liam to think that he made her breathless. Even if he did.

'What's wrong with new ones? I hear Ikea are quite good.'

'He likes reclaimed things,' Minette said, defending Abe's foraging in a way she didn't when he was around.

'Oh yes, upcycling or pre-loved or whatever is the latest terrible neologism for second-hand. But, be honest, I won't tell: wouldn't you rather have nice new frames? He's basically given you a chore, not a gift.' Liam smiled, to show he was teasing.

Minette didn't answer, because she would of course prefer new ones. And because she was distracted by the effect on her of a sexy man using an intelligent word like 'neologism'. Thank god Abe was safely back at work. Yes, he'd say, I *thought* that's why you wanted the bench out front. Handy for flirting with neighbours who've got time on their hands. No, he wouldn't say that. He'd just think it, and she'd know he was thinking it.

'How's the macramé going?' she floundered.

'Lousy. Why don't you make us some tea and I'll tell you about the blanket I had to unpick this morning.' He stretched his long legs out in front of him. 'You'll entertain me, won't you, Tilly?'

Tilly looked up at the sound of her name, and gave Liam one of her heart-stopping film-star smiles.

'Ah, she likes me,' Liam said.

Minette went reluctantly into the house. It felt weird leaving Tilly alone with a man she barely knew, even if he was going to be a teacher and was clearly not a psycho. She washed her hands, put the kettle on, then ran upstairs to change her wet pants. Look, she said to the imaginary raised eyebrow from Abe, I'm putting on another granny pair. She was safe in the knowledge that Abe was clueless about her knicker gradings – they all seemed small and frilly to him. Without making any further excuses, she pulled on a pretty white pair, and her nicest skinny jeans.

Downstairs, she made tea hastily, the wrong way (according to her dad), putting the milk in after the water, so the tea got up to colour quicker. Then she hurtled to the door, slowing down to look casual as she stepped outside. 'Ah, here's your mum now,' Liam said to Tilly. 'We'll have to carry on our chat another time.'

As Minette sat down and handed him his cup, she noticed that the frames had been moved onto the ground, so there was no longer a barrier between them. Liam was close enough that she could see exactly how twinkly his brown eyes were.

'So . . . macramé?' she asked, concentrating on her tea.

'I'm not really doing macramé, you know.'

'I know. I was just flogging the joke to death.'

'Do you want to know what I've really been doing all day?'

'I'm not sure. Does it involve porn?' Minette mentally high-fived herself at the edginess of her repartee.

'Yes, obviously. But that needn't take the whole day. No, I've been helping my mum move my gran into a care home.'

'Oh, well, that's very good of you, and sad too, of course.' Minette withdrew her high-five and cursed the crass mention of porn. It was no good her trying to be sassy and cool, she always screwed it up.

'Sorry, I don't mean to sound all noble and po-faced. I just wanted to explain why I haven't been round for a cuppa sooner. I've been up and down to Cardiff, where my gran lives.'

'Oh, no, I didn't think, er . . .' Minette wasn't sure what it was she didn't think.

'Macramé is my gran's thing. She's always making plant pot holders, though she doesn't have any plants. She's starting to lose her memory. That's why we had to move her, she forgot she put a pan of water on to boil and started a fire.'

'That's awful.'

'Yeah. God, I've really managed to put a dampener on our conversation, I'm sorry.'

Tilly started to grizzle. Minette put down her cup and scooped the child onto her lap. Tilly instantly stopped crying and reached across to Liam so she could play with the buttons on his shirt.

'See? Kids love me,' he said as he took Tilly back onto his knee.

'It's just the novelty. Wait till she gets used to you.' Minette realised the implication of what she'd just said and, to hide her red face, reached down to retrieve the cloth she'd been using to clean the frames.

'Minette, can I be honest with you?'

Minette gazed at the cloth. One of those blue-and-white ones. Nothing special. 'Yes.'

'You're very easy to talk to. The thing is, well, things aren't that great at home. I mean between Josie and me.'

'Oh god, that is extremely honest.' Clearly it *had* been a real proposition at Cath's.

'I don't want to make you uncomfortable.'

'You kind of are?'

Liam gently placed Tilly back on her blanket, and before she could protest he gave her his phone, which she started pressing with enthusiasm.

'Liam, she'll break it.'

'I don't care,' he said. Without hesitating, he reached across, pulled Minette into his arms, and kissed her.

Whenever Minette looked back at this kiss – and she looked back at it a lot – she always edited out the J-cloth in her hand. Even when the kiss became associated with guilt and regret, rather than excitement, the J-cloth was missing. But once the affair was properly, finally finished, the cloth at last reappeared in her mental image, in its proper place, held damply in her hand. Failing in its primary duty to wipe everything clean.

Minette, when reflecting, ranked this as the most significant kiss of her life. She'd not, until that moment, ever been unfaithful. Not to Abe, not to anyone. She had never so much as held another boy's hand when she was in a relationship.

But despite this unblemished track record it didn't occur to her, for even a moment, not to kiss Liam back. It was such a glorious, filmic thing to happen, such an impossibly hot gorgeous kiss, that she just closed her eyes and melted into it.

A montage of kisses from her life flickered in her mind like a show-reel, in black and white like the ending of *Cinema Paradiso*, her favourite film. The most recent, the hasty rushing-out-of-the-house peck from Abe this morning – 'Ta-ta, Dougie' – compared poorly to their first kiss, nine years earlier, at a student gig, after weeks of pretending they were just friends. Before that, the double-crossing kisses of Paul, who she didn't think about anymore, except when she did. Ah, Paul. The taste of cigarettes, and mint to cover up the cigarettes, the astonishing softness of his lips. Shit, stop thinking about Paul.

The show-reel moved onto a merry-go-round of kisses at university; before Paul and Abe there was a dark boy, before him, a bearded boy called Benjy who was shorter than her and made her sit down. A wet lunging kiss from poor Derek, who she only dated out of pity, and a thin fair-haired girl who'd demanded a snog at a party. Minette could hear the boys cheering them on, chanting 'Madonna and Britney', and Minette had drunkenly complied, and liked it, though not enough to do it again.

Going back in time, a sea of lips at sixth form college, unremembered apart from the unpleasant tongue thrusting of Nicholas Something in the student bar, and Steven from Singapore, the flicky-haired heart-throb of the college, who'd made it his mission to kiss every girl before the end of the year. Back, back, to school, to being fifteen, to Jamie, who was impossibly glamorous at seventeen with his acne scars and Ford Capri. She didn't care that her parents didn't approve, she was just grateful to have a boyfriend despite her glasses. So grateful, in fact, that she lost her virginity to him, but that wasn't as memorable as their first kiss, at a party, which Jamie turned up to with another girl and left with Minette. In between those bookends he kissed her in the kitchen, one hand holding her glasses, the other hand holding her breast.

All the way back to her sepia-tinted first kiss, aged twelve, with Ros's cousin who was staying for the summer holidays. She couldn't remember his name, only his freckles, and the cucumber green of his shirt, the sunlight on her skin, the feeling of plunging into a new, more interesting world.

That was how she felt now, too.

She dropped the cloth she'd been clutching, so she could

snake both arms round Liam's neck. His lips were warm, his breath clean, the smell of him lemony and unknown. How good it felt to be touched, to be desired, by someone so beautiful. To be touched at all was such a novelty. Thinking of how long it had been made Minette think of Abe and their non-existent sex life, and she abruptly pulled away. She couldn't look at Liam, turned instead to Tilly, who was putting Liam's phone into the cardboard box, then taking it out again, and clearly hadn't noticed anything amiss.

'So, it's true,' Liam said, his voice coming from far away. 'You *do* like meeting the neighbour.'

Neighbours. Shit! Minette scanned the pavement, half expecting to see the entire street out there, pointing and tutting. But no one was there. She glanced up at the round window at the side of Cath's house which overlooked them, the window she was sure Mr Milton used to watch the house from, and just like in those bad days thought she saw a dark shape move away. Doubtless just her guilty conscience.

Finally, she raised her eyes to Liam. She was aware that he'd been watching her while she silently panicked.

'Are you all right?' he said.

'I can't sleep with you, I'm sorry.'

He laughed. 'Wow, who's coming out with the honesty now?'

'I'd better go, got to get Tilly's supper.'

Liam looked at his watch. 'It's only quarter past three.'

God, fifteen minutes later and the kids from the local primary would be swarming up the street on their way home. Imagine them all seeing her and Liam, stopping to point and laugh at them k-i-s-s-i-n-g. How stupid, how reckless she'd been. She picked Tilly up as a kind of shield, and handed Liam back his phone.

'It's a bit smudged.'

'So am I.' He grinned. 'You sure you don't want me to come inside?'

Was this an intentional double entendre? She had no idea, which showed how little she knew Liam, so what the hell was she doing? 'I'd better go,' she said again, meaning, *you'd* better go.

'Listen, Minette,' he said quietly, 'I don't want you to think I go round randomly kissing women, because I don't. I think you're lovely.'

'Thank you.' Formal. 'I'll see you soon.'

'I hope so,' he said, and touched her arm. 'Bye ladies, have a good afternoon.' He strolled off towards his house without looking back.

Minette sat Tilly in front of the TV with a rice cake for each hand, then poured herself a glass of wine and collapsed into a chair. What just happened, what just happened? She ran her finger over her lips, trying to feel them the way Liam had done. They felt unfamiliar, almost swollen. Oh, god. She leaped up to look in the hall mirror, but there wasn't any damage, anything to see. She looked dreamy and alarmed at the same time.

God, what was she playing at? She had a partner and a baby. Liam was married. Anyone passing by could have seen them. Perhaps there *had* been a dark shape at the window. Perhaps Cath had seen them. Minette didn't know her well enough to guess whether or not she would disapprove.

She roused herself to get the tea together. It was far too early, as even a non-parent like Liam had noted, but it was helpful to have something to do. Cooking usually helped Minette think more clearly, and as she chopped sweet potato into tiny cubes she began to calm down. She ought to visit Cath. It would be neighbourly to go round, see how she was getting on. It was overdue anyway; Minette hadn't seen her since the crying-on-the-bench incident last week. That bench was fast becoming the place where it all happened. Minette let out an involuntary giggle. What are you like, Miss Minette?

She gave Tilly some of her tea early, as a treat. Tilly didn't seem to object to this unusual breach in her routine, and as soon as she'd finished eating, or smearing it across her face, which seemed to be the same thing, Minette carried her round next door.

The new doorbell gave a normal one-note ring. Cath answered the door holding a paint roller. 'Minette! How lovely.'

'You're busy, I won't stop.'

'Not at all, come keep me company while I paint. There's only one more wall to go. The kids are back from school but they're just flopping in front of the telly.'

Minette followed Cath upstairs into Lola's room. Three of the walls were already clean and white. Minette sat on the dust sheet-covered bed with Tilly while Cath climbed up a stepladder and sloshed paint about.

'Couldn't stand that damn magnolia for one more second.'

'You make it look so easy.'

'There's nothing to it,' Cath said. 'I never understand why people would pay someone.'

'Kirsten just had her entire house repainted after her husband left, cost her three grand.'

'She seems a nice lass, but what a waste of money.'

'I think she didn't care, she wanted a fresh start. Her husband had all the walls painted a different crazy colour, like lime, and purple. She went over the whole lot in Farrow & Ball Old White.'

'I use your bog-standard bottom of the range Dulux. It all looks the same once it's dry. So have Kirsten's special powers helped Tilly's sleeping?'

'Well, it doesn't seem to have done much yet. We've only had two sessions. Abe's sceptical. But I think it might help relax Tilly.'

'Is she stressed, then?' Cath grinned.

'Yeah, her high-powered job of Baby is pretty demanding.'

Cath stepped off the ladder and said, 'That'll do. Lola won't mind if it's a bit streaky. Coffee? Or I've got some wine on the go. Are you still breastfeeding?'

'No. Oh, go on then, just a small one.'

'I like your style, lady.'

They went downstairs, and Minette said, 'Talking of neighbours, er, because we were talking about Kirsten, I mean, I had a visit earlier today, from, uh, Liam?'

'Oh yes, the long-legged star of the Rat Pack.' Cath began washing her hands at the kitchen sink. Raising her voice over the sound of the running water, she said, 'So, did he pop round for anything in particular?'

'Just for a chat. I think he's fed up at home, waiting for his course to start.'

Cath dried her hands, got a bottle of white wine out of the fridge, and opened it expertly with an old-fashioned corkscrew.

'Oh, don't open that specially for me.' Tilly wriggled to get down, so Minette put her on the floor. 'I thought you already had a bottle on the go?'

'Yeah, must have finished it. Opened it now.' Cath smiled mischievously. 'So, just a chat, huh?'

'Um, yes. Sort of. I don't know.' Minette trailed off. But there was something about Cath, handing her a large glass of wine, patiently waiting for her to speak, that made her blurt out, 'He's just, it's just . . . looks-wise, he's my perfect man. Not that Abe's not lovely, he's wonderful. But Liam, he looks like someone I might dream about.' Oh god, Minette thought, why am I going on like this?

'He's your animus, I reckon.' Cath sat down opposite Minette, and took a sip of her wine.

'My what?'

'I did a year of psychology when I was nursing. The animus is like, your ideal man. Physically, I mean. You know we all have a type? So your animus is your perfect type.'

'Liam is probably a lot of women's type.'

'The animus and anima are why people fall in love at first sight. You see someone who looks like the perfect person in your head, and wham.' Cath banged the table for emphasis.

Minette regarded Cath with interest. For some reason she'd assumed Cath wasn't very bright. 'That's fascinating.'

'So how long did your animus stay for?'

'Oh, only ten minutes or so.' To change the subject, Minette said, 'So, it was nice to meet Gina. Does she live with you?'

'Gina? She's at home in Eastbourne.' Cath looked surprised. 'Why did you think she might live here?'

'Oh, I thought, um, I thought maybe you . . .' Minette ground to a halt.

Cath laughed, a loud whooping sound. 'You thought she was my girlfriend.'

'God, way off base, clearly. Sorry.' Jesus, Minette. She

berated herself: first you think she's dim because of her cockney-mixed-with-oop-north accent. Then you assume she's gay. You're like the worst kind of bigot.

'Haha, that's really funny, Gina'll love that. No, we go way back and she's my rock, but she's straight. She's not my anima.' Cath let out another blast of noisy laughter and Lola came running in.

'What's the matter Mummy?' On seeing Minette, she gave her a big smile and said hopefully, 'Biscuits?'

'I'm sorry Lola, I didn't make any more yet. I'll bring you some more soon, I promise.'

Lola nodded, then said, 'Oh, look at Tilly.'

Minette had forgotten about Tilly. She and Cath whirled round to find her sitting by the cupboard under the sink, quietly playing with bottles of cleaning fluid.

'Oh Jesus,' Minette cried, plucking Tilly off the floor. 'Have you opened any of these Tilly, have you drunk anything?' Tilly looked blankly at her.

Cath checked the bottles. 'They're all closed. She's fine.' She calmly ran water into the sink to wash Tilly's hands. 'Nothing to worry about.'

Minette was angry at herself for being so negligent, and slightly aggrieved that Cath didn't have child locks. She scrubbed Tilly's hands and arms more vigorously than she meant to, and Tilly started to wail. 'I'm finding this phase pretty difficult,' she said. 'Having to watch them all the time.

It was much more restful when she couldn't move. Please tell me it gets easier when they're older.'

'Easier in some ways,' Cath said, as Lola wandered back to the living room. 'My Lola is, anyway. But Davey, he has his own ideas, wants to do things his own way.'

'Well, I'm looking forward to that,' Minette said. 'Not having to be in charge all the time.'

'Oh, you'll still be in charge.' Cath bent over Tilly. 'You all right now, lovie?'

Tilly grinned at Cath. She smiles at everyone but me, thought Minette. All at once, she felt bone weary. 'I'd better go home. Time to start the evening sequence.'

'Honestly lovie, I know it's hard, but they're not tiny for long. I'm here if you need a break. I promise I won't let her near the cupboards again. Lola would love it, a little one to play with.'

Minette could usually only count on getting time to herself when Tilly napped, and not reliably then. This was worth more than diamonds. She felt that she might cry. 'Really? That would be amazing. But god, you've got so much on your plate already. Two kids, and Davey's, you know, and the decorating, and the triathlon, and everything.'

'If you want something doing, ask a busy person. Honestly, I mean it. I specialised in paediatrics when I was a nurse, you know. Even if it's just so you can nip to the shops. Or have a cuppa with your animus.'

She knows it was more than a chat, thought Minette. Had Cath seen them kissing, after all? But she was smiling and Minette didn't feel judged. Cath didn't seem the judging type.

'And if you decide not to go back to work, you'll need to build in some time for yourself,' Cath continued. She stroked Tilly's cheek.

'Abe says I shouldn't rush into a decision, but I'm going to have to let my boss know soon.'

Outside her front garden Minette stopped. She saw how exposed the bench was, how clearly you could see it from the street. What a damn idiot. The frames lay on the ground: one clean, the rest still filthy. 'We'll do them tomorrow, shall we Tilly?' she said, and they went inside.

Chapter 8

Davey

Davey had been waiting ages for ICT. It was called Computer Science at his last school, but Olivia told him it was called ICT here. Olivia was his buddy. He was given her on his first day. She smelled a bit of sick but she was all right. The teacher told Olivia to help Davey because he was new. Once she tried to push his wheelchair but it went straight into a wall. 'Woman driver,' he said, like his dad used to, and she laughed. She had a very big laugh. He showed her how he could do the chair by himself, and she said it was awesome.

The people in his class were all right, but in Year 5 there were two boys who called him names. Whenever they saw him in the playground or the dinner queue they basically said stuff about his wheelchair, about his trainers and his clothes. He hadn't got the right school uniform yet. Olivia told them to go away and they pushed her but then they did go away.

ICT was meant to be on Wednesdays. But his first Wednesday they didn't do it because it was their turn in the library instead. The second Wednesday they didn't do it because of a special assembly. Davey didn't know what was so special about it, it was a man in a yellow tie who talked about crossing the road. But now it was Wednesday again and at last the teacher said they were going to the ICT suite. Davey wheeled himself fast out of the classroom, Olivia running to catch up, then the teacher told him to wait. She had a frown on. 'I'm sorry Davey,' she said, 'unfortunately you can't do ICT.'

'Why not?' Davey pretended to be itching his face, and secretly pinched the top of his nose to stop himself crying.

'You'll have to talk to your mother about that,' Miss Hobbs said.

'I really want to.'

'I'm sorry. You've to watch a film instead.' She took him back into the classroom and showed him a shelf of DVDs. He chose *Toy Story 2*. The teacher put it in the machine and pressed start but nothing happened. 'What's wrong with this thing?' She kept pressing the same button. Davey found it strange when adults did that. If it didn't work the first time, there wasn't any point pressing it again. He didn't want to tell her what to do, she was the teacher, but then she said, 'What am I doing wrong?'

'It's not the right remote,' he told her. 'The DVD is Sony and the remote is Phillips.'

She laughed. There was flesh-coloured powdery stuff in the creases next to her eyes.

'Children are geniuses at this stuff,' she said, and rummaged under the TV till she found the Sony remote. While he waited for the DVD to start, Davey told Adam Purcell his top five films.

1. *The Incredibles* – this was his dad's favourite film too. They'd watched it together at least four times.
2. *Toy Story 2* – Lola loved the song about Jessie, and she learned all the words. It made Davey laugh when she sang along to it.
3. *Meet the Robinsons* – no one at his last school had seen it. One time when Sammy, his best friend in Harrogate, came round they watched it on DVD and Sammy said it was really cool.
4. *Toy Story 3* – his mum cried at the end when Andy gave Woody away. He liked the scary teddy.
5. *Toy Story 1* – not the best but still pretty good.

The teacher said again that she was sorry, and she went out to teach the others ICT.

Chapter 9

Cath

'I've still got it,' Cath joked to Minette, because Tilly was clearly comfortable in her house. She had crawled straight into the living room without a backwards glance. 'Looking after babies – it's like riding a bike.'

But Minette still hovered in the hall. 'My friend Ros got on a bike after ten years and fell off, broke her wrist,' she said, smiling anxiously.

'Go on, go. Have a relaxing time. I won't let her near the kitchen cupboards, promise.'

'I haven't left her with anyone before. But I really need a cut.' Minette ran her hand through her hair, justifying it to herself all over again. 'I haven't been to the hairdressers since before she was born.'

'Well, surely your split ends have split ends by now. We'll be fine.'

Minette looked at her watch. 'OK, I really had better go.' She swooped into the living room and kissed Tilly. 'Thanks so much, Cath. I won't be long.'

'Take as long as you want.' Cath waited till Minette was out of sight before she shut the door, and only then did she permit herself a brief eye-roll. What a fuss. She tidied the breakfast things, then settled down to watch telly with Tilly and Lola. The warmth from Tilly's small body, cuddled sleepily on her lap, made Cath feel nostalgic. How sweet and tiny babies were. But what a short-lived phase it was; in almost no time they were great lumps, like Lola, sprawled on the floor, gawping at the telly. At least Lola still never missed a chance for a cuddle. Davey, forget about it.

After ten minutes, Tilly was fast asleep. 'A proper Gina Ford baby,' Minette had said, boasting about the regularity of Tilly's naps. Cath loved that feeling of heaviness that sleeping babies gave off, and didn't want to move, but when her phone rang – she'd left it in the kitchen – she laid Tilly gently on the rug and went to answer it.

'Hey, Gee. All right? Was just thinking about your namesake, Gina Ford.'

'Yeah? Getting broody again? Listen, I wanted to let you know that he emailed to say his cheque's going to be a few days late this month.'

'Hell.'

'I can tide you over, Rubes.'

'You're a rock. You shouldn't have to, though. He should be sorting this, regular as clockwork.'

'He sounded in a right old state in his email. Listen, Ruby . . .'

'I know what you're going to say, Gee, you say it every time. It's not happening, OK?' God, maybe Gina was too soft for this after all.

'So sue me. I think it would help. Just talk to him. What can he do over the phone?'

'He could trace me.'

'You can use my spare phone. It's got no GPS or location stuff, it can't be tracked.'

It was lucky Davey was at school; this was the sort of conversation he somehow heard every word of, even from behind closed doors.

'Rubes? You still there?'

'Mmm.'

'He misses the kids so bad. Says he's been crying every night.'

'Amazed you're feeling sorry for him, Gee, after everything.'

'I know. The email caught me at a vulnerable moment.'

'Why, what's up?'

'Oh, nothing really. Bit of a row with Ryan.'

'Sorry to hear that.' Though what did she expect, shacking up with someone fifteen years younger? An even keel? Cath didn't think so.

'Anyway,' Gina said, exhaling loudly. 'I'll transfer your money as usual and sub myself when the cheque arrives. OK?'

'That's really good of you, lovie. What would I do without you?'

There was an uncharacteristic pause before Gina replied, 'No worries. Well, I'd better go.'

'Gee, you pissed off with me?'

'No. Should I be?'

Oh, don't be like that. 'Do you really think I should talk to him, then?'

'It's up to you. I can't tell you what to do.'

'I'll think about it, OK?' But Cath knew there was nothing to think about.

'OK. Speak soon. Love you.'

'Love you. Thanks.'

Cath clicked off her phone and her smile at the same time. Heaven's sake, Gina. The whole point was for her to protect Cath, not try to open the lines of communication.

She checked on the children – Tilly still asleep on the rug, Lola still staring at the telly – then brought down the laptop, sat in the kitchen and updated her sponsorship page, 'Doing it for Davey'. Cath wrote a blogpost about her twelve-mile cycle ride, and sent the link to Duchenne Together, the local support group. Julia, their communications officer, had promised to send it out in their members' newsletter. Then she opened her email, and wrote:

Dearest V
I know! We've landed on our feet. Everyone lovely. Good to be stopped for a while. To be on the safe side I've made an appointment at the Passport Office next week, it costs to do the fast track but then I've got them and don't need to worry.

You're right I must stop thinking about Darren, easier said than done, tho. Can't get his face out of my head, that cheeky smile, dream about him even, god love him. Doctors are 'always right' of course.

Wade's new place sounds peachy (see I am practising my American!), when you going to visit him?
R xx

Cath lost track of time, and when the doorbell rang she couldn't believe it was nearly midday. Shit! She was only supposed to let Tilly sleep for forty minutes. She hurtled into the living room, swept Tilly up into her arms with big shaking movements to wake her, and told Lola to turn off the telly.

'I'm hungry, Mummy,' Lola wailed.

'You'll just have to wait.'

Holding Tilly close, Cath opened the door to a revived-looking Minette, whose dark hair was cut in a glossy bob. 'Oh, you look lovely. Look, Tilly, isn't Mummy pretty?'

'Do you like it? I was worried it was a bit short. But loads had to come off. There was a bit at the back that was so matted she couldn't get the comb through, really embarrassing.'

'Like a spot of lunch? Just a sarnie, nothing fancy?'

'You sure?' Minette stepped over the threshold swiftly, as if afraid Cath would change her mind. She looked at Tilly properly, who was bleary-eyed in Cath's arms. 'Wow, she looks sleepy. When did she wake up?'

'Oh, ages ago. Maybe she's already feeling tired again.'

'Did she have most of her milk?'

Bollocks. 'Yes, she had it all. Didn't you? What a good girl!' Cath handed Tilly back to her mother and led them into the living room. 'Have a seat. I'll just pop the kettle on,' Cath said. As soon as she was in the kitchen, she tipped the milk Minette had given her down the sink, and hastily rinsed the baby bottle out, cursing herself under her breath. She returned to the living room to find Minette walking up and down, a sobbing Tilly on her shoulder.

'Sorry about the noise, Cath. Did she do this with you?'

'No, she was good as gold.'

'I don't know what the matter is. She can't be hungry yet.' But Tilly's piteous cries were obviously hunger.

What sort of monster are you?

She shook her head to get rid of Andy's voice. 'She's probably just ready for her lunch.'

'She's not due more food till one o'clock though.'

Oh, for heaven's sake, these middle-class mummies and their routines. 'Sometimes they need a bit extra. Growth spurts, you know. I'll do her some bread and butter.'

Cath escaped back to the kitchen and threw the food together. God, she really dropped the ball there. Got to be more careful, Cathykins.

Soon they were all sitting at the table, with a much happier Tilly. Minette marvelled at how much she ate, even slices of Cheddar which she'd never liked before.

'She can see Lola eating cheese,' Cath said. 'They love copying the older ones.'

'It's so nice, having lunch with other people,' Minette said.

'Haven't you met many women at mother-and-baby groups? Or NCT classes, that's where I made friends.'

'I tried a baby group, but it was awful, everyone sat round like zombies. And I didn't click with anyone at the NCT. Most of them were pretty old.'

'What, like me?'

'Oh, god, I didn't mean it like that. I don't think of you as old.'

Cath laughed. 'I don't think of myself that way either.'

'Shit, sorry Cath. You've got older children anyway. There were loads of forty-two-year-olds having their first baby.'

'I guess you're quite young to have kids these days. Mad though, isn't it?' Cath said. 'My mum was seventeen when she had me.'

'Wow, that must have been hard for her.'

'She did her best. So, have many of your friends had babies?'

'No, I'm the first one. I was hoping my mum, or even better, Abe's mum, would help more, but they're both so busy.'

So Minette didn't just have the normal baby-at-home-boring-blues, but was isolated from her friends as well. That's why she'd been willing to leave her baby with Cath, who she'd only known a few weeks. Because there was no one else.

'Can I watch telly?' Lola asked, snuggling against Cath's back.

'Again? You watched loads already. All right, ten minutes, but then we've got to fetch Davey.'

Minette said, looking disappointed, 'Wow, Davey's school finishes early.'

'No, we're taking him out for a hospital appointment.'

Cath decided to wait before asking her along. 'So how come you and Abe went for a baby, then? Was it planned?'

'Yes, though we didn't know it would happen so quickly. But we were both up for it. We've been together nine years.'

'Jeez, Louise. You must have been kids when you met.'

'Pretty much. Not quite as young as your mum. We got together the second year at university.'

'Love at first sight?'

'No, it was more of a slow-burn thing. There was this older guy, Paul, a postgraduate. We had a thing, very intense, and I guess I took it too seriously. He was unbelievably sexy. Everyone thought so. Including my friend Bella, or should I say, my ex-friend Bella.'

'One of those boyfriend-nicking Bellas, huh?'

'Someone nicked him off her pretty quickly, too. Anyway, I'd been friends with Abe for ages, and I cried on his shoulder and . . .'

'One thing led to another.'

'Yes. He was so kind, and trustworthy. He said what he meant.'

'Will you get married, do you think?'

'Lots of our friends are, but we've got a mortgage and a baby instead.'

'Those are big commitments.'

'We've done the two hard bits and not had the fun party and holiday that goes with the wedding.'

'Was Abe at Tilly's birth?'

'Yes, he was a star. It was awful, she got stuck, it was all incredibly messy. It's no wonder . . .'

'No wonder what?' Cath said, though she knew.

'Um. Nothing. Usual slow sex life with a small baby, that's all.'

'Oh god yes, we've all been there.' Cath started piling up dirty plates. 'For a while, me and Andy had such a long gap, I gave up hope of ever having a second baby.'

'Really? Oh, that makes me feel a bit better. It's been a proper drought, almost a year. Is that normal? The last time was two months before Tilly was born. And that wasn't any good really, I was so huge.'

'Sounds pretty normal to me,' Cath said.

Minette looked as if she thought she'd said enough, and busied herself turning the pages of the local paper, which Cath had left on the table.

'Have a look at page fourteen,' Cath said, sweeping underneath Lola's seat, which was a sea of crumbs, as usual.

'Oh! Is this you?' Minette read out, '"Local triathlon mum delighted by new sponsor." Hey, that's brilliant, I didn't know Hilton were sponsoring you.'

'Not that much, to be honest, only five hundred. But other companies will see it and think they should get on board. Josie next door arranged it.'

Minette looked surprised. 'I didn't realise you knew her that well.'

'I don't, we just chat sometimes.'

Minette pointed at the paper. 'This picture isn't of Davey! It's just some random blond kid in a wheelchair.'

'Yeah, I know. Local papers are not exactly the last word in accuracy.'

'You ought to complain.'

'Ah, no point, it's out now,' Cath said. 'Hey, don't suppose you and Tilly want to come to the hospital with us? It won't be an exciting afternoon out. But it'd be nice for me to have someone to talk to.'

'That'd be great.' Minette was delighted. 'Something different, isn't it?'

Cath smiled to herself. 'What about people round here, isn't there anyone in the street you're friendly with?'

'Only you, really. Priya's nice but she's out at work all day. Everyone's at work all day.'

Cath began loading the dishwasher. 'Except Liam.'

A blush spread across Minette's face. 'Oh!'

'I was only saying, because he came round the other week?'

There was a pause, long enough to make Cath wonder if she'd pushed too far. Then Minette said, 'And yesterday.'

'Did he, now?'

'Oh, god.' Minette covered her face in her hands.

'Sounds promising.'

'I'm bursting to tell someone.'

Cath slammed the dishwasher shut and sat down, propping her elbows on the table. 'If I was any more all ears, I'd be one great big elephant ear.'

'You mustn't say anything to Josie.'

'Course I won't! You're my mate, not her. Go on, lips are sealed, honestly.'

Minette glanced down guiltily at Tilly, on her lap, who was playing with a plastic beaker.

'I don't think she can understand you yet,' Cath said.

'I know, but . . .' Minette paused, then said quietly, 'Nothing much happened. Well, we kissed.'

'Holy moly! I like your definition of "nothing much happened". Just one kiss?'

'The first time he came round it was just once, outside on the bench . . .'

'Oh, it's all coming out now! And this time?'

Her hand over her mouth, Minette said, 'We were snogging like teenagers, on the sofa.'

'Bit muffled, but I got it. Fantastic! Well, I don't blame you. I'd certainly not kick him out of bed. Or off the sofa. Or bench.'

'We haven't done anything more than kissing,' Minette said fervently. 'That's bad enough, right?'

'Yeah, well.' Cath stood up again and started packing a bag for the hospital. 'You know what I always say?'

'What?'

'We'll all be dead in a hundred years.'

Minette laughed, shocked. 'But I feel really awful about it. About Abe.'

'Yes, I'm sure.' Cath guessed that Minette had expected a more censorious reaction from her. 'But still. Hundred years, know what I mean? Don't want to have them old deathbed regrets.'

Minette went home for Tilly's car seat, then they piled into Cath's Citroen and collected Davey from school. He was full of chatter on the way to the hospital, about the Aztecs or something. Cath noted how easily Minette talked to him, asking all the right questions. Minette, she decided, wasn't that great with babies, but was good with older children. Cath knew that she was the opposite. She'd never been happier than when the children were tiny. Though Lola was only four, and usually very amenable, Cath couldn't always be certain of getting her to do what she wanted. As for Davey, he was becoming difficult.

Cath parked right in front of the hospital, in a disabled bay.

'The multistorey's round the corner,' Minette said.

'Don't need it,' Cath said. 'Got the blue badge, don't we?'

'Oh, of course. Handy!'

They went up to the physiology department. 'This is our second appointment,' Cath told Minette. 'I wish they'd hurry up and refer him on.'

'Don't they have his records from your last hospital?'

'Well, they have to follow their own procedures,' Cath said.

Minette waited in the corridor with the girls, while Cath took Davey into the medical room. It was a different doctor from last time. This one, Dr Ogueh, chatted briefly to Davey about school, and getting around in his wheelchair. Then he started explaining muscular dystrophy to them both, as if they'd never heard of it before. Cath knew how much doctors liked to show off their knowledge before they got to the point. So she put a listening expression on her face, waiting till he was ready to discuss the referral.

Finally, Dr Ogueh opened Davey's file. 'I don't understand why we don't have any of Davey's notes from your previous home town,' he said.

'I explained this in the previous consultation with Dr Persaud,' Cath said, trying not to sound exasperated.

'Yes, there is a note here from Dr Persaud, but I confess I don't entirely understand. Please would you be so good as to explain it again?'

Cath turned to Davey. 'Lovie, would you mind going back outside?'

Davey silently wheeled himself out, closing the door behind him.

'He is a great boy,' the doctor said.

'He is, doctor. And that's why I'm trying to protect him.

Cath stared at her lap. 'Dr Ogueh, as I explained at our last appointment, we left our last town in a massive hurry. My kids and I are in hiding, we've all changed our names, we live in fear every day . . .'

'I am so sorry,' the doctor said, pushing a box of tissues towards her.

'I don't want to have any connection at all to that place, or our former names. I'm so frightened that we could be traced.'

'But you know, of course, that hospital records are kept confidential?'

'They're meant to be,' Cath nodded. 'But having been a nurse myself, I know that there are occasionally slips. I just can't risk it.'

'I understand. So, what this means for Davey is that, without the notes, we will have to do his diagnostic tests again. Did he previously have a muscle biopsy?'

Cath nodded. 'And I had the letter which gave the results, but I had to leave all my hospital notes behind. I had to leave everything behind.'

'I'm afraid we will have to do another biopsy before we go ahead with the referral to the neurology clinic.'

'I was wanting to ask if we could get the referral first, doctor.' Cath took a tissue and dabbed her eyes. 'The fact is, my Davey is absolutely terrified to go through the biopsy again, because of the general anaesthetic. He has nightmares about it.'

'It is a very standard procedure.'

'You try telling that to an eight-year-old boy, doctor. One who's already been through so much.' Cath knew they could postpone the biopsy if they had a good enough reason. 'We're happy to do all the blood tests again, of course, at the clinic.'

'But as I'm sure you're aware, Ms Brooke, given your nursing background, the blood test simply gives a provisional diagnosis. Only the biopsy can confirm the condition.'

'I know. But even a provisional diagnosis, from a specialist clinic, will give us certain services we can't access otherwise: benefits, physiotherapy, the latest treatments, well, you know better than anyone.'

Dr Ogueh made a note on his computer. 'It might be possible to refer you directly to the clinic before assessment. It's unusual, but so are your circumstances. I'll need to discuss it with my colleague.'

Cath knew she'd have to be satisfied with that for now. She got up, and Dr Ogueh accompanied her to the door, so he could say goodbye to Davey. He'd clearly done the bedside-manner module on his training, Cath thought, and lucky for her, because when he stepped into the corridor he immediately clocked Minette, sitting with Tilly on her lap, her arm round Davey as she read to him and Lola from a picture book.

It couldn't have worked out better if she'd planned it. Dr Ogueh looked at Cath.

'My new relationship,' Cath said quietly, 'is just another thing Davey is coping with right now.'

'I understand,' the doctor said, keen to show off his egalitarian attitude. 'Difficult times for you all.' He glanced over again at Minette, and back at Cath; was he looking at her with respect for her pulling power? 'Thinking about it,' he said, 'it would probably be best for Davey if we go ahead quickly with the referral. Get him into the system.'

'Thank you so much, doctor,' Cath said. Yes! You beauty. 'Say goodbye, Davey.'

Davey grunted. Cath turned to Minette. 'Ready to help me round up the children, lovie?' She touched Minette's arm and smiled to herself as Dr Ogueh backed hurriedly into his office.

Chapter 10

Minette

No one, including Minette herself, realised she couldn't see properly until she got into trouble at school, aged six, for copying from the girl next to her. 'I didn't copy her answers,' Minette protested, 'only the questions, because I couldn't see the board.'

Minette's mother often described how guilty she felt at Minette's first eye test, when the optician looked at her, over his own glasses. 'She's extremely short-sighted,' he said, bluntly. He didn't add, but didn't need to, 'How could you not notice?'

Minette's parents acknowledged ruefully that there had been a few signs: the way Minette sat so close to the television, for instance, or her uncertain responses when things were pointed out to her – 'Look at that blue bird, Minnie!' – but she was a bright child who had compensated for her poor vision in other ways. When the optician put the heavy test glasses onto her face, and slipped in the correct lenses, Minette cried out, 'Oh, I can see lots of things!' and her mum burst into tears. Minette couldn't understand why. Hadn't she just been given the precious gift of sight?

She loved her glasses, though they were chunky blue National Health ones that got her teased throughout primary school. If Tilly needed glasses, thought Minette – hopefully she wouldn't – it would be such a different experience. When Minette went to the optician now, to get new contact lenses, she admired the children's glasses wistfully. Post-Harry Potter, glasses were cool, and even the free frames were attractive. She still had a pair of glasses, more flattering than the ones of her youth, for the brief periods without lenses first thing in the morning and last thing at night.

But one of her great pleasures, since she was six, was to remove all visual aids and allow herself to sink into Blur World. She could only do at it home, in a familiar setting, but oh, the comfort of it. Abe didn't understand it. He felt sorry for her poor mole-like state, said if he was half as short-sighted as her, he'd have laser surgery like a shot. But when Minette took out her lenses, and the room lost its edges, shifted to a colourful fog, she felt herself relax. It wasn't just, as Abe suggested in one of his amateur psych moments, that she'd regressed to childhood, to that time before anyone knew she couldn't see. It was more than that: it was also an abdication of responsibility. 'I can't see,' says the inhabitant of Blur World, 'don't ask me to do anything.'

Abe was at work, and Tilly was having a nap, worn out after a stressful trip to Toys R Us. She'd got upset in the soft toy aisle because Minette wouldn't let her keep hold of a cuddly tiger. Minette quickly pushed the buggy into the next section. But Tilly's wailing got louder, her arm stretching back towards the aisle where the tiger was, body twisting against the buggy straps. Minette felt that other parents were judging her. One woman pushing a toddler glanced at Tilly and then stroked her child's hair, as if thinking, glad I haven't got a spoiled brat like that.

'I'm going to take you out of here if you don't behave,' Minette snapped, and when the crying didn't stop she made good on her threat. But as she pushed the buggy hurriedly through the exit, Tilly's screams became even more desperate, and people in the street turned round to look. Minette started crying too. 'Will you shut up if I get you that stupid tiger?' she hissed, and stormed back to the shop. As they went back in Tilly's sobs slowed down, and by the time Minette had bought the bloody thing and shoved it into her hands, she was smiling broadly, the tears still wet on her cheeks.

Now that Minette had finally made the decision not to go back to work, there were going to be a lot more days like this. She sighed. But Cath was right – she wouldn't get this time again. She took out her lenses and lay on the bed, gazing at the ceiling, which in Blur World was a fuzzy white expanse, with a blue sparkly blob in the centre (the lampshade).

We'll all be dead in a hundred years.

No one had ever said anything like that to her before, and it was a revelation. Minette had always been a high achiever. Her glasses excluded her from the cool gang, so she naturally formed alliances with the geeks and nerds, the hardworking kids. She never really had a rebellious phase. Not when her parents split up; and not even in her teens. She went to university, got a good degree while working hard at a series of part-time jobs, and settled down into a career with a pension and a steady relationship with Abe. They had a very conventional life. He worked, she looked after the baby, they saved a little money each month, did the recycling and sponsored a child in Africa. Minette had never been too drunk to brush her teeth before bed, had never left her seatbelt off, never slept on a beach.

One of the few times she'd ever thrown caution to the wind was when she suggested to Abe that they stop using condoms. Even that wasn't much of a risk. Both agreed it would be nice to be parents while they were still young. She got pregnant the third or fourth time, and after a heart-stopping moment of uncertainty, staring at the little white stick, they'd quickly got used to the idea.

Minette relaxed her eyes until the circles of fuzzy light around the blue blob danced and split apart into little stars. Yes, life had been pretty smooth, until Tilly's arrival revealed the Miltons to be neighbours from hell. Minette told herself she'd been pushed into a weakened state by their persecution, because otherwise surely she would never have contemplated kissing Liam. Such recklessness was out of character.

And yet, all the time, there existed a parallel universe she hadn't known about, a world in which she could have been guided by the straightforward philosophy of 'we'll all be dead in a hundred years'. Minette was honest enough to admit to herself that she had seized on Cath's attitude to justify what she wanted to do anyway. But imagine if, instead of working hard at her homework, maintaining a steady Grade A, she'd gone out dancing and boozing like the majority of her class-mates. So many of them had dropped out of education completely, got work as shop assistants and hairdressers and gardeners. What if Minette hadn't gone to university after all, but had remained in her Saturday job in the chemists, asked to be made full-time? They'd wanted her to stay, had given her such a lovely send-off, presenting her with a bag full of the make-up she'd admired when she tidied it on the shelves each weekend. She still had some of it: an eye pencil in the most perfect grey, now little more than a nub, and a Chanel lipstick, which she only ever used on special occasions.

What if she'd lived in this parallel universe? What if she'd thought, it doesn't really matter what job I do? Shop assistant, tourism officer, brain surgeon: we'll all be dead in a hundred years, after all. If she hadn't gone to university she wouldn't have moved to Brighton, or met Abe, or had Tilly. But she would have done other things. Travelled round South America on a motorbike, perhaps. Or become a burlesque artiste. Met a crazy man, maybe met her animus, with fair hair and brown eyes, and fallen tumultuously in love. And not cared, because 'we'll all be dead in a hundred years'.

I'm lucky, thought Minette, snapping her eyes back to attention so that the orbs of lights stopped dancing around the blue blob. I have a lovely man, and a gorgeous daughter, and, and, and. She conjured up a Kodak moment of Abe, him holding Tilly as a tiny baby on Brighton beach last year, father and daughter squinting into the wintry sun and, in their woolly hats, looking very much alike.

Her mind drifted away from Abe, to the recent encounter with Liam. Snogging like teenagers on her sofa, as she'd said to Cath, while Tilly slept upstairs.

'I'm bored with making this macramé bikini,' he'd said as she opened the door to him.

'Is there even such a thing?' she laughed, resigned to the fact that, yet again, he looked as hot as all get out and she looked rank. Tilly had spat up milk on her sweatshirt, and her hair was in its home-day pineapple top-knot. It was this moment, in fact, that made her resolve to book a hair appointment for the next day and ask Cath to mind Tilly.

'In my head, there is. You can model it and I'll take a picture for the front cover of Macramé Masturbators Monthly.'

'What have you really been doing?'

'Listening to my mum on the phone, being upset about my gran.'

'Oh no, why, what's happened?' She stood aside to let him pass.

'My mum saw her yesterday and Gran said she wanted to go home, and when Mum said, "You are home," she cried.'

'Poor them.'

'And poor me for having to listen to it. I need a treat after that, so I thought of you.' He smiled. 'Where's Tilly?'

'Asleep.' She showed him into the living room.

'This is a posh sofa.'

'Heal's. Abe's parents bought it for us.' Shut *up*, Minette.

Liam sat down. 'How long till Tilly wakes up?'

Minette, flustered, glanced at her wrist, though she wasn't wearing her watch. 'Half an hour? Maybe a bit longer?'

'Perfect.' He patted the seat next to him.

'Shall I make tea?' Minette said, hesitating.

'No thanks. Sit down please, Minette.'

She sat abruptly, looking at her lap so she couldn't see his face, his eyes, the path of wrongness they would lead to.

'You look worried.'

'I look a mess.'

'Yeah, you're a right old scruff-bag.'

That made her laugh. He put his hand on her cheek and gently turned her face towards him, so she had to look at him. 'You're beautiful, you know,' he said.

'Oh, I'm not . . .'

He leaned in, in his movie-star way, and kissed her, first lightly, then more urgently, until he was pushing against her, pressing her against the sofa. She felt overwhelmed, and she liked that feeling. In moments they were somehow lying down, him more or less on top of her.

'Liam . . .'

'I've still got one foot on the floor, so we're legit according to the 1950s film censors.'

'I don't think . . .'

He silenced her with kisses, glorious kisses, and she found herself just submitting, sinking. When his hand moved to her breast, she let it stay, because he didn't make any further moves, just caressed her over the top of the dirty sweatshirt. She wondered if, through the layers of that, her T-shirt underneath, and her padded bra, he could feel her nipple, sticking out like the word 'yes' made flesh.

Clearly he could, for he honed in on it, circling it tighter with his fingers, and as he pressed against her, she felt his erection, and made disloyal comparisons in her head about its size compared to Abe's. Like a steel pipe, she would have said if she was ever going to describe it to anyone, which she wasn't. She moved her hand down, deliberately not thinking about what she was doing. It's just touching the outside of his clothes, she told herself. Just kissing-with-extras.

They never moved their lips apart, the kind of long-term, in-it-for-the-duration kissing Minette hadn't experienced since Jamie, her first proper boyfriend. Liam once tried to move his hand from on top of her clothes to under, but she replaced it where it had been, again reminding her of Jamie, him moving his hand repeatedly from over to under. Yes, and she lost her virginity to him so her prevention strategy clearly wasn't very effective, was it?

She submerged herself in the here and now, keeping her eyes closed so she couldn't see what she was doing. Her senses focused instead on Liam's lemony scent, the warmth of his hand, the sound of his ragged breathing. She had no idea how much time had passed when she thought she heard another sound: a faint cry from upstairs. It couldn't be Tilly because she'd hear her much more clearly on the monitor and . . . bollocks! Minette's eyes snapped open and she struggled to a sitting position.

Liam, a dreamy expression on his face, said, 'What's wrong?'

'I don't think I put the monitor on.' She craned to listen.

'Monitor?' Liam was still far away.

Yes – that was definitely Tilly crying. Minette pushed Liam away and bounded up the stairs in what felt like two steps. Tilly was sitting up in her cot, an accusing look on her red, tear-stained face.

'Oh, baby, I'm so sorry.' Minette grabbed her and held her close, pressed the hot wet face against hers. 'Silly mummy didn't turn on the monitor.'

She carried Tilly downstairs, talking gently to her all the while about what a bad mummy she had been. It felt good to castigate herself, though which aspect of her recent behaviour she most needed to be told off about, she wasn't sure. Her voice soothed Tilly who transitioned, in classic baby style, from outraged sobs to smiles by the time they reached the living room. It was Liam's fault that she hadn't turned on the monitor, really. He'd knocked on the door just minutes after she'd laid Tilly down for her nap, distracting her from her usual routine. But when she saw him, looking concerned, and so devastatingly beautiful, her kisses practically still damp on his mouth, she smiled at him.

'Is she OK?' he said.

'She is completely fine. Aren't you Tills?'

'Hey, sweetheart. Sorry we didn't hear you. We were, uh, busy, weren't we Minette?'

Minette wasn't sure about risqué banter in front of Tilly. 'I'd better give her some milk,' she said.

Liam said, 'Oh, I'd like to see that.'

'I'm not breastfeeding anymore,' she said, feeling an odd mixture of affronted and titillated.

'I know,' he said, eyes wide and innocent. 'I find all the baby routines fascinating. Even milk in a bottle is of interest, rather than in those charming receptacles it has been my immense good fortune to have just been fondling.'

She laughed. 'You can give her the milk, if you think it's so fascinating.'

'Bring. It. On.'

She left him holding Tilly while she made up a bottle of Aptamil. Her nerves were soothed by the comforting routine. Fill the little blue plastic scoop with the white fluffy powder, Baby's Own Cocaine, Abe called it. Mix it with the right amount of cold water and heat it gently in a pan, the instructions said, though she and presumably everyone just put it in the microwave. She tried to collect her thoughts. What was she doing? Abe might be home in an hour. She couldn't work out how she felt. She went back into the living room. Tilly was sitting happily on Liam's lap, playing with a pink plastic teething toy.

'You look like this Athena poster I had when I was a student,' she said.

'What, the black-and-white one, guy with the cute baby? Did you have Che Guevara too?'

'No. Athena man, *Withnail and I*, and Uma Thurman in *Kill Bill*.'

'You're a movie geek. I'm starting to pigeon-hole you now. So, were you the coolest girl on campus, Minette?'

'I was not.'

'I've been meaning to ask you about your name. It sounds foreign.'

'My mum is French.'

'So – French, into movies: you are Juliette Binoche and I claim my five pounds.'

Minette handed over the bottle. 'Have you done this before?'

'I could do with some guidance.'

'It's pretty straightforward. She likes to hold it with you. Tip her back very slightly. That's it.'

'Oh, look! I'm doing it. God, you can hear it going glug glug.'

'Yeah, she's a noisy eater, like Abe.' Oh god, why the hell had she mentioned Abe, again?

'Minette's a beautiful name,' Liam said. 'Makes me wonder why anyone would choose to call you by some ridiculous joke around your surname instead.'

There was a silence. She knew he was getting back at her for bringing Abe's name up. She searched around for something to say, to take the taste away. 'So, when are you going to see your gran?'

'At the weekend. Josie and I will take her out to lunch.' Josie. Touché. Were they even now? Liam gently wiped a drop of spilled milk from Tilly's cheek. The sight of his large hand steadying the bottle next to Tilly's tiny one made Minette feel like she might well up. She looked away. Whatever this thing was between them, it was more than just lust, surely?

'You don't really want to talk about my aging relatives, do you?'

Minette shrugged. 'It's a safe topic.'

'Are you sorry I came round today?'

'No! God, no. It was lovely. But. You know. We shouldn't. You're married, and so am I. Sort of.'

'I don't know how much longer I'll be married.'

'Oh, Liam, why?' She put her hand on his arm.

'Things are just really shitty at home.'

'I'm so sorry. But it still doesn't make it right. We shouldn't be doing anything.'

'We've barely done anything. Yet.'

'I think she's finished.' Minette took Tilly back onto her lap, and the decisiveness of this brought Liam to his feet.

'Minette, it was wonderful. You're wonderful. I'll drop by again soon. If you're not into it, just tell me.' He ruffled Tilly's hair, then lifted Minette's hand and kissed it, like a gallant knight. 'I know you French ladies like that,' he said, and left. He certainly was the master of the suave goodbye.

A week went past, during which, thanks to Cath, she not only got her hair cut, but also discovered the existence of the carefree parallel universe she might have been living in this whole time. In that week she didn't see Liam at all. She googled 'young Frank Sinatra' and could see what Cath meant. She only remembered Sinatra as an old, jowly guy singing 'My Way' in Vegas, but as a young man he was skinny and gorgeous. She liked one black-and-white photo in particular, Sinatra leaning against a wall, suited and wearing a trilby hat at a cocky angle, hands in his trouser pockets. There was something about the smile, the lines creasing on his face, that made her skin tingle in recognition. She downloaded it for her desktop picture.

One morning she thought she saw Liam walking past her house, and she grabbed Tilly and ran outside to see if she could casually catch him up. But when she was a few yards away, he turned round and it wasn't Liam, just some other tall man. His hair wasn't even the right colour. Though no one witnessed this, apart from Tilly, it made her feel oddly out of control.

She rang Ros that evening, when Abe was out seeing a friend. Ros was already a couple of glasses of wine down. 'I always got time for you, honey,' she said, 'but I got to try and put my eyelashes on at the same time.'

'Where are you going?' Minette said, making her voice light.

'Oh, some club with the gang. Someone knows someone who's done the décor, or something. I wasn't really listening, honey, to be honest, you know what Marcus is like when he explains stuff, I'm just going, uh-huh. Bristol's amazing, like Brighton used to be, new clubs springing up every week. When you going to come visit?'

'What would I do with Tilly?'

'Why can't she stay with Abe? She's not tied to your titties any more, is she? Oh shit it. Dropped one of the little fuckers. Hang on.'

Minette waited while Ros did whatever she was doing with her false eyelashes.

'I'm back! You should see me, I look like a manga cartoon, big crazy eyes. I'll take a photo for you later.'

'Ros, things are a bit shitty here.' She consciously borrowed Liam's phrase. 'With Abe, I mean.'

'Are they?'

'You don't sound very surprised.'

'Sorry, hon. But that's babies for you. Just about everyone I know who's had one has split up.'

'Thanks a lot!'

'Last time I stayed at yours, when was that, January? It wasn't exactly the Love Boat,' Ros said.

'Was it really that bad?'

'Oh my god, Abe was tiptoeing round the whole time because of your bastard neighbours, kept telling me to keep the noise down when I was just talking, you were strung out with the titty-feeding. God, I came home, I went to Marcus, you can ask him, I went, "We are *not* having a baby any time soon." Sorry hon.'

OK, so Ros was a bit pissed, but had she always been this tactless? It had felt a lot easier talking to Cath. 'You'll be going back to work soon, though, won't you?' Ros went on. 'Things'll improve then.'

'Oh.' Minette switched the phone round to her other ear. 'Didn't I tell you? I've decided not to go back.'

'No, you bloody didn't tell me. You crazy, girl?'

'The early years are so important, Ros. Essential. Tilly needs me. I rang Harry the other day and told him they'd need to appoint someone else.'

'Bet he was gutted, he always fancied you.'

'He did *not*.'

She didn't feel quite so much like telling Ros about Liam now, but she ploughed on. 'There's this man, in the street . . .'

Ros screamed. 'Ooh, you naughty! So *that's* why you want to stay home. Good on yer!'

'Nothing much has happened.'

'Yeah, sure hon. I believe you, thousands wouldn't. Oh,

god, that's Marcus. Gotta go, hon. You be careful now, yeah?'

Yeah.

Minette turned onto her side and squinted blindly at her big-numbers alarm clock. She could give Tilly another forty minutes. It felt naughty, indulgent, just lying here. Think of Cath, filling every minute of the day with activity. She did as much in a day as Minette did in a week. She ought to see if Cath wanted help with her fundraising. It would give her something to do, and anyway she was becoming fond of Davey. They'd had an interesting conversation about Aztec life at the hospital, while Cath talked to the doctor. Davey's homework was to copy a picture of an Aztec mask.

'That sounds like fun,' Minette said.

'Our computer isn't set up yet.'

'Well, you don't have to always look stuff up on the internet. You can copy it out of a book. We've got an encyclopaedia, and loads of history books. Shall I look for you?'

Davey regarded her with his unnerving stare. 'Yes, OK,' he said finally, making her wonder who was helping who. She had in the end just gone on the internet herself, and printed out three different Aztec mask pictures. When she took them next door Cath looked surprised, and said how kind, but if Davey asked again she should mention it to her first, because he was meant to be learning how to look things up in books. Minette, embarrassed that she'd effectively gone behind Cath's back, said she would, of course. Cath thanked her again, more warmly, and then said, 'Oh, I ought to tell you, in case he asks to use yours, that Davey isn't allowed to use a computer.'

'Good lord, why ever not?'

'It's bad for his muscular dystrophy. Typing even for short periods weakens his arm muscles, and makes his whole upper body hurt for days.'

'That's awful.'

'I know, and kids love those screens. I feel terrible, but I don't want to have to take him to extra physio just because he wants to play Angry Birds or whatever.'

'We've got an iPad he could borrow, you hardly have to move to use that, Abe lies on the sofa half-asleep playing it.'

'That's kind of you but we've tried one before, it has the same effect. He's completely wiped out after just a short time.'

'Must be because he has to concentrate so hard. The poor thing.' Minette marvelled again at how much Cath had to think about. She really was an incredible person.

There was a knock on the door, and Minette slipped on her glasses and a smear of her Chanel lipstick. She looked a mess, so there was no doubting who her visitor was.

'Hey, Liam.' She leaned against the door frame. 'Finished knotting my bikini?'

'I have. Want to try it on?'

'I think I'd better.'

'Nice haircut.'

'I'm not sure it goes with my glasses.' She pushed them onto the top of her head, and let herself slide into the irresponsibility of Blur World.

'I like that strict librarian look you got going on. So.' He studied her, slightly unsure of his welcome. 'I'm having a crappy day, how about you?'

'Tilly's asleep.' She smiled, and her meaning was unmistakable. 'Would you like to come inside?'

Chapter 11

Davey

Davey's mum let him stay off school. He told her he felt ill, and he did have a bit of a headache so it wasn't a fib. She gave him Calpol and tucked him into bed. While she took Lola to nursery, he started working on his five least favourite insults. It didn't always have to be best favourites, Adam pointed out. Least favourites were interesting too.

1. Spazzo. This was new. Those Year 5 boys called him it in the playground yesterday. One of them kicked the wheel

of Davey's chair.

2. Retard. Till spazzo this was Davey's worst. He was called it a lot when they lived in Harrogate. It was always older boys. People his own age never seemed to call him names.
3. Crip. Davey knew this was rude. He'd never been called it but had heard an older boy at the clinic in Harrogate call himself it.
4. Freak. Some girls said this once when he was in town with his grandma, and they laughed. But he wasn't 100 per cent sure they meant him.
5. Ironsides. A student doctor who worked with Dr Patel to help him learn how to use his new wheelchair had called him this. He said it loudly like he was trying to be funny, but Dr Patel told him off. Davey liked her a lot anyway. This was just another reason why she was one of his favourite doctors.

Davey heard his mum come back. She sat on the bed and stroked his hair. 'How you feeling, little one? Head any better?'

'A bit.'

'I'll bring you some fresh water, lovie.' She went into the bathroom and he heard her running the tap. He stretched out his legs and cuddled Waffles closer. Sometimes home was better than school, and sometimes school was better than home. When he was ill, home was best. His mum's voice went all soft. He sipped some water, and went back to sleep for a bit.

After lunch, his mum drove them to a village hall in a place called Portslade. 'I promised Julia we'd come along, lovie,' she said, 'so I'm glad you feel a bit better.'

Davey didn't know who Julia was, but he was used to support group meetings. In Harrogate they'd always been in church halls or village halls, big rooms with good echoes. They had to be somewhere big enough for all the wheelchairs.

This one was like the others: apple juice and biscuits for the children, never very good biscuits, and tea and coffee for the grown-ups. Five or six boys sat in wheelchairs in a circle, their mums next to them. A squashy woman wearing a red T-shirt welcomed them, all excited, 'Oh you're our newbies, lovely.' She was called Julia, and she told them who everyone was. The boys nodded at Davey. They all looked a lot worse than him. Some were a bit fallen over to one side in their chairs. One had a head going in a different direction to his body. Another one was trying to eat a biscuit and making a mess of it. He reminded Davey of Eric, back at the Harrogate support group. Eric was funny, he couldn't eat properly but he knew more knock-knock jokes than anyone. Davey and Eric always sat together at these groups and pretended they were somewhere else. Davey smiled at the Eric-alike boy but he didn't smile back.

Davey and his mum joined the group and all the grown-ups started talking about boring things. The boys all looked at Davey, except the one whose head went the wrong way. None of them said anything to him. His mum was all smiling and happy. She loved these groups. 'People who understand,' she said on the way in the car. 'They're all going through the same thing.' She'd got a notepad out now, and was writing down things they were telling her: places to get stuff, places to go, the friendliest doctors, best physios. She was doing her biggest smiley face. The red squashy woman, Julia, gave her a coffee and offered Davey the plate of biscuits. He took a custard cream. Medium sort of biscuit. The boy whose head went the wrong way took four digestives. Davey thought about listing his favourite biscuits but he basically couldn't be bothered.

Chapter 12

Cath

Carrying Davey down the stairs, Cath felt something twang in her back. She sat down abruptly, holding tightly onto him.

'What's the matter, Mum?'

Her back felt cold, just below the shoulder blades. 'I've hurt myself. Give me a minute.'

Davey's face loomed close to hers, his breath warm on her face. 'I can go down by myself.'

'It's all right, lovie, it's easing a bit. I'll get us down on my bottom.'

Cath bumped them both gently down the stairs to where the wheelchair was waiting. Lola came into the hall to watch. 'What you doing?'

'I'm realising we gotta sort Davey out a downstairs bedroom, Lolly. I'll make a start on it today.'

Cath deposited Davey into his wheelchair, then got carefully to her feet, her hand pressing into her back. 'Ahh!'

'I like my room,' Davey said.

'I'll recreate it down here, lovie. Look, we knew this was coming. You're getting bigger.'

'Daddy can carry him,' Lola said.

Cath and Davey both looked at her.

'Maybe you haven't noticed, Esmie,' Cath said, 'but Daddy isn't actually here right now.'

Both children gasped. 'Not Esmie!' Lola shouted.

'You told us we must never . . .'

'All right Davey, thank you very much, I know what I said. I made a mistake, OK? Lola, stop damn well winding me up. Get out of my sight for a minute, please.'

Lola retreated to the living room and Cath heard her crying.

'Mum, please,' Davey said. 'I want to be upstairs, with everyone else.'

'Look,' Cath said, opening the door to the dining room, 'I think it's bigger than your room.'

* * *

Cath dropped the kids off at school and nursery, then went back home and lay down on the bed. She was exhausted, no wonder she'd made such a stupid error. She thought of the children as Davey and Lola now, but clearly their original names could still come out under pressure. She was aware of some early warning signs – shortness of breath, a hollow sensation at the back of her head – that meant she was starting to get overwhelmed. If left unchecked, these could lead to 'the wiry feeling'. She couldn't describe it any more clearly than that. It was as if the nerves in her body, particularly in her arms, were made of thin metal wire, the sort you get inside pipe cleaners, and the wires were lifting up inside her, straining towards the surface of her skin, threatening to burst it open.

She'd explained it to Gina's mum, Fay, years ago – she'd just been a young kid then, fifteen or sixteen. 'Anxiety,' Fay called it, and suggested various coping strategies, including breathing exercises, focusing on a small task, visualisation and having a bath. But nothing soothed the wiriness down as successfully as Cath regaining control of a situation. Like that time when she was so worried about little Libby going home and not getting the treatment she needed. Cath stepped in when no one else was willing to, had taken charge, and the wiriness had tamped right back down. Or what about when Darren, no, don't think about Darren.

Another of Fay's suggestions, which sometimes helped, if

the wiriness wasn't too far advanced, was to sleep it off. Cath tried that now, falling asleep quickly and luckily not having any dreams. When she awoke forty minutes later she felt refreshed, the feeling little more than a fading tingle now. She updated her notebook with some more details about Josie next door, Liam's wife. She'd been chatting to her this morning. Josie was thirty-three – she mentioned this twice – and asked Cath how old she was when she'd had Davey. Cath locked her notebook away, then called round for Minette, inviting her to come for a swim. Exercise sometimes helped, too.

'You were so clever to find out about this,' Minette said, as they took Tilly into the crèche at the leisure centre. A smiling young woman in a brightly coloured jumper distracted Tilly with a Fisher Price activity centre, so that she didn't even notice Minette leaving. 'I can't believe it's so cheap. I'll be here all the time now.'

Despite having lived here for only six weeks, Cath knew considerably more about the local facilities than Minette. She'd told her about the baby-friendly café in the North Laine, and the weekly film screenings you could take under-ones into. She'd also introduced Minette to the exciting possibility of getting your hair done while someone looked after your kid. There was a lot to admire about Minette, but she was sometimes a bit wet. Ha, good one, Cathykins, cos she was currently soaking, doing that fancy front crawl with the proper breathing on each side. Cath moved up and down the pool with her slower, more splashy crawl, breathing randomly every three or four strokes.

Afterwards they sat with coffees in the leisure centre café. Cath put her stats into her phone. 'Twenty lengths, not too bad. Got to build up to thirty.'

'You're doing well.'

'It ain't fast but I get there in the end,' Cath said. 'But hey, you're a really good swimmer. You should do the triathlon with me.'

Minette shook her head. 'I'd love to help you with fund-raising. But I can't do the actual race. I don't like cycling.'

'I don't either. Go on, we could train together, it'd be a laugh.'

'I got a bit put off bikes when my friend Ros broke her wrist.'

'Oh yes, I remember you saying. She your best mate?'

'Yes. She and her husband moved to Bristol so I don't see much of her.' Minette looked a bit sorry for herself.

'Listen, speed doesn't matter at all. You can cycle slow and careful like me. Long as you finish, what's it matter?'

Minette said, 'I did run a bit before Tilly came along.'

'You'd help me raise so much more. And I'll tell you one massive advantage of training for something like that.'

'Lose my baby belly?'

'You haven't got one. You do get fit, sure, but more important, the training gets you out of the house. Legitimate excuse to have a break from the chores.'

'That's true. I could train when Abe gets home from work.'

'Lunchtimes too. Didn't you say he comes home for lunch?'

Minette nodded thoughtfully. 'And I could do mornings, it's not like he goes into work early.'

Cath knew when to leave an idea to percolate. 'How much longer we got?' she said.

'Fifteen minutes.' Minette leaned back in her chair. 'Oh, this is bliss. I might have another coffee.'

'It's not *that* nice.'

'I know. I don't even like coffee much. But it's a hot liquid I can drink in peace.'

'Yep, I remember that stage. I'll get them.' Cath fetched two more lattes, or the brown soap bubbles that passed for them. Then she asked Minette if she would help design a poster.

'Sure! What's it for?'

'I'm organising a quiz night at Davey's school, next Friday.'

'God, Cath, your schedule's exhausting. It takes me half the day to work up to going to the shops.'

'I was like that when Davey was little.' I was never like that, Cath thought.

They collected Tilly and went to Cath's house, where she showed Minette the start she'd made on the poster. 'Can you do something with this? You're the publicity professional, after all.'

'Oh, I'm not! I just did a bit of marketing for the Pavilion.'

While Minette worked on Cath's laptop, Tilly at her feet, Cath went up and downstairs, shifting Davey's things into his new room, formerly the dining room. She was standing on a stool putting up his green-and-blue racing car curtains when Minette came in with a print-out.

'Oh, that's perfect,' Cath said. 'I'm going to have you do all my publicity.'

Minette looked pleased. 'Anything else I can do?'

Still bored at home, lovie?

'Well, I've took out the drawers, could you help me bring down the chest?'

They went upstairs, and together began to squeeze the empty shell of the chest of drawers through the doorway.

'It's heavier than it looks,' Minette said. 'You prefer to be back or front?'

'Is that what you say to all the boys? I'll go backwards, it can land on me if you drop it.'

'How are you going to move the rest of Davey's furniture?'

'I don't know. I done my back in this morning.'

'God, you shouldn't be doing this, in that case.'

'It's all right. Swimming loosened it up. The only problem for tonight is his bed. It's well heavy, proper hospital bed that you can crank up and down. Took two big mover blokes to get it up there.'

'I could ask Abe to come round this evening?'

'Ah, that'd be fantastic. I'm sure I can get someone else to give him a hand. Talking of neighbours, I been meaning to ask,' Cath said, 'any recent sightings of ol' blue eyes next door?'

'Um. I can't remember.'

'Yes, he is so very unmemorable.'

Minette laughed. 'I think his eyes are brown, actually. Let's get this thing downstairs first, I'm out of puff.'

They manoeuvred the chest into the dining room, and pushed it against the wall. Tilly was still sitting where she'd been left, though she'd managed to tip over some books Cath had piled on the floor.

'Oh, Tilly, you monkey.' Minette started to put the books on the shelves, then she noticed a framed photo on the desk. 'Is that your husband?'

'Yes,' Cath said. 'That's Davey's favourite picture.'

The photo was taken a couple of years ago at a park, Andy on the swing with Davey on his knee. They were both laughing, Cath remembered, at some daft joke of Andy's.

Minette said, 'He looks nice.'

'Well, he used to be. It's a bit complicated.'

'Relationships are, aren't they?'

'He was nice yesterday, though. He was in Germany. It was cold there, he was wearing a massive jumper.'

'Do you talk regularly?'

'We Skype every week.'

'When's he back?'

'I don't know.' Cath felt it was time to open up a little. 'I think maybe we're having a bit of a break.'

'Oh Cath, I'm sorry to hear that.' Minette put the picture down.

'It's all right. Don't say anything to the kids. I haven't told them yet.' Cath finished hanging the second curtain and stepped off the stool. 'It was love at first sight when we met, if you can believe it.'

'Was it really?'

'For Andy, not for me.' Cath giggled. 'No, he wasn't looking his best. I was working nights in Birmingham.'

'As a nurse?'

'No, lovie, as a hooker. Yes, of course, as a nurse, at the old Queen Elizabeth hospital. They've built a new one on top of it now with the same name. I liked that old building though. Knew it like the back of my hand.' Cath began lining up soft toys on top of Davey's chest of drawers. 'I was on the children's ward but they was short-handed one night on medical. And there was Andy, in a right old state with a ruptured appendix.'

'Painful.' Minette picked up some books.

'Yes, he was feeling pretty sorry for himself. He fixed onto me, kept grabbing my hand, going, "Nurse, nurse, am I going to die?" I said, "Only if you keep grabbing me, lovie."'

'He fell for your smooth bedside manner.'

'You don't know the half of it.'

Minette looked up. 'Ooh, tell me!'

Cath smiled. 'You tell me something first.'

'About Abe?'

'I'd rather know about Liam.'

Minette cast her eyes down. 'Oh god. I feel awful about it.'

'Pretend I'm your Mother Confessor.'

'I wouldn't tell this to my own mother. In fact, she's the last person I'd tell. Jesus. OK. Well, we, uh, have, um, got to know each other a bit better. Shall I put these big books on the lower shelf?'

'Does that mean you've shagged?'

'Cath!'

'But does it?'

'Mmm.'

'Well, good on yer, lass.'

'We'll all be dead in a hundred years, after all,' Minette said.

'Ah, Grasshopper, you have learnt well.' Cath checked her watch. 'I got to collect Lola in a minute. She's only doing a half-day today. Want to walk with me, give me the gory details?' She knew Minette would jump at it.

'That'd be great!'

Once Tilly was settled in her buggy with a bottle of milk, the two women walked along the street.

'So, tell me,' Cath whispered.

Minette looked round to check they weren't overheard.

'It didn't end too well.'

'That's surprising. He looks like he'd be pretty good at, well, everything.'

'Oh I don't mean that. The actual, er, time we spent together was amazing. Cath, it was unbelievable. Right up until the minute Abe walked in, unexpectedly early.'

'Holy moly!' Cath put her hand over her mouth.

'It was all right, we were dressed and in the kitchen. But I practically had a heart attack,' Minette said. 'I'm not cut out for the cloak and dagger.'

'So, are you seeing him again?'

They crossed over, into another street. Minette said, 'I don't know. He texted today. I'd give anything to see him again. But I mustn't.'

'Tough call, I can see that. Will you have mind-blowing no-strings sex with your gorgeous neighbour, or won't you?'

Minette laughed. 'I know, but it's not no-strings, is it? I feel awful about his wife, and terrible about Abe. I was really feeling all, let's go for it, "we'll all be dead", etc., but when Abe walked in on us I realised I'm not the type to be unfaithful.'

'Is there a type?'

Minette shrugged. 'Trouble is, Liam's having a crazy effect on me. I keep drifting off, daydreaming. Yesterday I even forgot to put Tilly down for her morning nap, that's how addled I was. Couldn't understand why she kept grizzling. Then she fell asleep in her lunch.'

Liam must be incredible in the sack to be messing with Minette's army-style baby routines. 'Hasn't Abe noticed you've been a bit distracted?'

'No, he's not the most observant chap. Once, not long after we moved here, I went out for the day. He was at home, unpacking. When I got back in the evening he hadn't realised I'd been out.'

'Didn't he think you'd been a bit quiet?'

'We probably had some really interesting conversations while I wasn't there.'

Cath laughed. 'Anyway, don't you think Liam's daydreaming about you, too?'

'I doubt it,' Minette said, going red. 'So, what was that about your bedside manner with Andy, then?'

Minette had a lot to learn about deflecting awkward questions, but Cath decided to let her get away with that unsubtle shift. She knew enough about Liam for now, anyway. 'Oh glory, I'll be struck off if you tell anyone.'

'Lips are *so* sealed.'

'OK. One night, when there was only me and one other nurse on, I drew the curtains round Andy's bed and, shall we say, gave him some oral relief from his pain.'

'No! In your nurse's uniform? No wonder he married you.'

'Well, you know the old saying. A cook in the kitchen, a nurse in the bedroom . . .'

'I don't remember it going quite like that.'

'Here we are.' They'd arrived at Busy Tigers Preschool. 'Handy for you, soon, for Tilly.'

'That's a great idea! I'll ask about their waiting list.'

Cath introduced Minette to Sharon, the manager. While they were talking, Cath went over to Lola, who was sitting on the carpet listening to one of the gormless young nursery assistants read *Little Red Riding Hood.* She wasn't even really reading it, she was playing a tape of someone else reading, while she held up the book on the relevant page. She couldn't have looked more bored. But Lola was nonetheless enthralled, and pouted when she saw Cath.

'I want to hear the end.'

'I'll listen with you,' Cath said, sitting on the floor next to her. She became aware that the tingling in her arms had started up again. A couple more pages were lazily turned – the assistant was actually chewing gum – and Cath started to feel a rising panic. Her breathing was all wrong, her arms felt wiry. The story was up to 'What big eyes you have!' when Cath gave a yell that made every head turn in her direction.

'What the hell's this?' Cath screamed, holding up a sweet packet. She jumped to her feet. 'Oh my god, who gave this to Lola?'

Sharon ran over and turned the story-tape off. 'What's wrong, Mrs Brooke? What has someone given Lola?'

'Look at this, what Lola was holding.' She held up the packet. 'Peanut M&Ms!'

'Oh no,' Sharon said. 'Lola, did you eat any of these?'

Lola started crying.

'Lola, we need to know,' Cath said. 'Why was the packet in your hand?'

'I don't know!' Lola wailed. 'I didn't know it was.'

'Mrs Brooke,' Sharon said, 'we take Lola's allergies very seriously. We don't allow peanuts on the premises, we . . .'

'Yes, I can see that,' Cath snapped. 'I'm going to have to take her to casualty straight away.'

'No!' Lola sobbed.

'I'm sorry, lovie, if you've eaten peanuts . . .' Cath got the epi-pen out of her bag. 'Does your tongue feel swollen? Is your mouth itching?'

'I don't know! Maybe a bit itchy.'

'Oh god,' Minette said. 'Can I do anything, Cath?'

'Phone for a taxi, Minette, would you? I don't have time to get the car, and I know how long an ambulance will take.'

Minette moved away to make the call. Cath looked up and saw that a little circle of gaping toddlers and nursery staff was gathered round her. She knelt next to Lola. 'I'm sorry, lovie, better safe than sorry.' The wires were just below the surface of the skin, threatening to burst through.

Lola was shivering, her tears still pouring, but she was quiet now, waiting. Minette reported that the taxi was on its way, and she held Lola's hand while Cath banged the epi-pen into Lola's thigh. Lola yelled, as usual.

'All over now, Lolly.'

Sharon handed over Lola's bag and coat, looking worried. 'Shall one of us come with you, Mrs Brooke?'

'I'll go,' Minette said.

Cath went outside with Lola to wait for the taxi. She could hear Sharon giving Minette a load of explanations and justifications. Worried that Minette wouldn't apply there now, probably. She ought to be worrying about getting sued instead.

Minette came out as the taxi arrived. 'Oh,' Minette said, 'I hadn't thought about a car seat for Tills.'

'You can hold her on your lap,' the driver said.

'That's not very safe, though, is it?' Minette said, hesitating.

Cath rolled her eyes. 'Minette, we've got to go.'

This is not all about you.

'Oh god, sorry, yes.' Minette got in, and put the seatbelt right round her and Tilly, holding her tight, like that would really help if they crashed.

At A&E, a nurse gave Lola some chlorphenamine and hooked her up to an oxygen-saturation probe. Lola sat quietly as the staff whirled about her.

'We're all right now, Lola,' Cath soothed. 'Everything's going to be OK.' The wiry feeling had gone, and she relaxed for the first time in days. Hospitals were so homely and comforting. When she was little, and had to go to hospital to have her tonsils out, or her appendix, she'd never felt sad or scared to be away from home. Her mum was always so kind to her when she was ill. And she loved being looked after by the nurses. She smiled now at the pretty Chinese nurse looking at Lola's readings. And then, of course, working as a nurse had been a joy. Happiest days of her life, mostly.

'Isn't Lola good?' Minette marvelled.

'Sadly she's quite experienced at this,' Cath said. 'Oh, that stupid nursery. I thought everything was going too well.'

'The manager was saying she couldn't understand how the sweets got in there.'

'Well, clearly they don't check thoroughly enough.'

The nurse told Cath that Lola had no signs of any breathing problems. 'Her mouth looks fine. We think she might not have actually eaten any.'

'What a relief,' Cath said, 'thank you *so* much.'

'We'll just keep her here for twenty minutes to make sure.' The nurse gave Lola some comics to look at.

'I seem to be making a habit of coming to hospitals with you,' Minette said.

'I appreciate it.' Cath wiped her eyes, and Minette put her arm round her. 'Times like this, it's lousy being a single parent.'

'You poor thing. I really want to help you more. I've decided I'll definitely do the triathlon with you.'

'Oh, that's fantastic!' Cath gave Minette a hug. 'I'll get you signed up right away.'

When Lola was free to go, they got another taxi back to Sisley Street.

'Jeez Louise,' Cath said, 'look at the time. I'll have to get Davey in a minute.'

'Your life's so busy,' Minette said.

'Yours will be too, now you're going to do the triathlon. So,' she moved closer and whispered, 'we didn't finish the conversation about Liam. What you going to do?'

'Not see him again, I suppose,' Minette said, making a sad face.

'You don't want to beat yourself up, lovie.' Cath glanced at Tilly, cuddled in Minette's arms. 'You was just a bit bored, weren't you? When we're bored we do crazy things.'

'I hate being bored. I never was, before. It's not Tilly's fault.'

'Course it's not. Listen, after today I owe you a whole bunch of favours. So you can always use my house to meet a certain person, if you're worried about being walked in on.'

'Oh, Cath, you are very bad for me,' Minette laughed. 'Get thee behind me.'

'Offer's there. We'll all be dead in a hundred years.'

'Thanks, but I'm going to try and keep out of trouble from now on.'

Back in her house, Cath put the telly on for Lola, then went into Davey's new room, and admired the neatly-ordered bookshelves. It would be a real shame if Minette finished things with Liam so soon. They made such an attractive couple. She took the photo of Andy upstairs, and locked it back in her bureau. She didn't want Davey seeing it and getting all upset.

Chapter 13

Davey

Davey didn't like his downstairs bedroom. His curtains were up and his America map was on the wall but it didn't feel like his room. It had the same flat green carpet as upstairs. He really wanted to ask about the computer but he didn't want his mum to get that look. Then Adam Purcell reminded him about a good way to ask things. Davey went into the kitchen and said in his smallest voice, 'Mummy, I don't feel well.'

'Again, lovie? You poor thing. Another headache, is it?'

'Tummy ache.'

His mum stopped making packed lunches and gently touched his tummy. 'Here? Here?'

'Yes. Could I have a quick bath?'

His mum looked at the clock. 'Oh dear, we're going to have to go in twenty minutes. Do you think a bath would soothe it?'

He nodded. She always sat with him while he had a bath and he could talk to her there. She would be nice to him because of his tummy ache. She carried him slowly upstairs, making a face because of her back, and let him look out of the round window while she ran the bath. Davey heard voices below and craned to see. The lady next door with the swishy black hair and kind face, Minette, was standing in her front garden talking to her boyfriend. They sounded cross. The man had a louder voice than Minette. Davey heard him say, 'I've got to get to work.'

Minette was wearing stretchy clothes like his mum wore for running. She said something Davey couldn't hear, then said more loudly, 'Not going to be long, am I?' The man went inside with the baby, slamming the door. Minette stuck out her tongue at the closed door which made Davey smile. He had never seen a grown-up do that before. She started running slowly up the street. Davey wanted to watch until she was out of sight but his mum came and carried him into the bathroom. She let him take off his pyjamas himself but she still picked him up in the nude to put him in the bath. It was embarrassing. 'I can get in myself,' he said, but she took no notice. She told him to lie down and let the warm water work its magic. Even though they were in a hurry to go to school, she looked like she was in a good mood.

'Is that feeling better, little one?'

'A bit.'

'I knew it.'

'Mum, when can we set up the computer?'

'Oh lovie,' she said, but she didn't sound cross, just tired. 'Do you know how many times you've asked me that?'

He knew he had asked a lot, but she hadn't answered him properly on any of those times. He didn't say anything, and after a minute she said, 'All right Davey, listen up. That stupid computer doesn't work anymore. It musta got broke in the move.'

'I could fix it.'

'I don't think so. You feeling well enough to come out?' She picked him up and wrapped him in a warm blue towel. 'A computer guy came and said it was really very broken. But I'm going to get you one of your own soon.'

'Really?'

'Promise. One of your very own. Well, to share with Lola. I can't afford one each.'

'That's brilliant, Mum, thank you.'

'You're welcome, my little one.' She sat him on her lap.

'You look peaky. I think you should stay home today. I'll have to take Lola to nursery, you'll be all right till I get back, won't you?'

'Yes.' He began drying himself, and he was ready to say the next thing. 'I need new trainers.' This wasn't as important as the computer but it was becoming a problem.

'You want the moon on a stick, don't you?' His mum called downstairs, 'Lola! We are going to be LATE. Finish your breakfast NOW. What's wrong with the old ones?'

'They're from Asda.'

'Christ, peer pressure is it now? That's all I need. I suppose the kids here are a bit more into style than in Harrogate. All right lovie, I'll think about it.' She put him down on the floor. 'I don't have time to get you down, Lola will be super-late. You stay here, put your PJs back on, and when I get home you can snuggle in bed, all right, little one?'

She ran downstairs, and he heard her talking fast to Lola. 'I didn't finish the sandwiches, I'll just put the slices of bread and cheese in and you can make your own. Do-it-yourself. OK?'

That made Davey think of his dad's bad joke:

Q: What cheese should you use to hide a horse?

A: Mascarpone.

His mum and Lola called goodbye, and the front door slammed. Davey put on his pyjamas and sat on the landing. He pushed the door of his mum's room. He wanted to see if he could fix the computer. But the door wouldn't budge. He pushed and pushed. Then he saw that there was a silver padlock on a chain, attached to the door handle. It was stopping the door from opening.

While he waited for his mum to come back, he told Adam his five favourite trainers:

1. Air Max
2. Adidas
3. Converse
4. Gola
5. Asda

The new floorboards all had slightly different grains. Davey traced the pattern of one which looked like ripples in a pond. He only stopped when he heard a noise in the street, and made his way over to the round window. He was just in time to see Minette next door coming back. Her face was red. He waved to her, but she didn't look up.

Chapter 14

Minette

Minette usually enjoyed having Abe's parents over. She always made an extra-special effort with her cooking for them, revelling in their compliments, their genuine affection for her. They were appreciative of her role in Abe's life, she knew. And she in turn was grateful for their role in *her* life, for the whole-hearted welcome they had given her, their unstinting love for Tilly and, of course, their kindness in financially supporting them.

Minette remembered the incredulous expression on Mr

Milton's face the day she and Abe moved in next door. He clearly couldn't understand how 'people like them' – young, scruffy, not even married – could afford to buy a house in their street. He didn't know that behind Abe stood a pair of well-off, middle-class parents, who loved him dearly. Parents who'd given Abe a cheque for a deposit on a house the minute they heard Minette was pregnant.

There was something so solid and cosy about her in-laws, particularly compared to her own parents, who'd acrimoniously separated long ago. Her father, Richard, had remarried many years before, and her mother, Élise, had moved back to France when Minette went to university. Though they were both perfectly fine as parents, they'd never been as warm as Abe's. And since she'd had Tilly they'd been, in truth, a bit disappointing. Richard's second wife had four children, all with kids of their own. Minette thought he probably considered that he had enough grandchildren. He sent a huge teddy bear – too huge for a baby, and with a label that said it was unsuitable for children under eighteen months. And he hadn't managed to visit them until Tilly was already six weeks old.

Élise offered to come over and stay when Tilly was a newborn, and Minette had been delighted. She expected the first few weeks with a baby would be challenging, but imagined it would be homely and loving as well, with her mother's support. In fact, it had been the most horrible time. They were all rattled by the hostility from the Miltons, and Élise had become obsessed with Minette giving up breastfeeding. 'Formula was good enough for you,' she said, on several occasions, insisting that Tilly would cry less if she was properly fed.

But Abe and Minette had not sat through four sessions of Brighton's NCT classes without learning that formula was a synonym for neglect. Though Minette found breastfeeding difficult, and so painful that she cried at most feeds, she was determined to persevere. After a week, Abe told Élise that her intervention wasn't helpful, and she spent the rest of the stay in a sulky silence. It was a huge relief when she went home. Abe's mum Julie then stayed for a week and was brilliant.

Julie was delighted by Minette's French heritage, would exclaim over quite simple recipes that Minette had learned as a child. Today she made *salmon en croute* and a *tarte tatin*, knowing Julie would love them, but her usual pleasure in cooking seemed to have deserted her. She could hear Abe playing with Tilly in the living room. Abe was a good man, a great dad, so why was she mucking about? The joie de vivre of 'we'll all be dead in a hundred years' had left her. Now she just felt heavy. Guilty. She was *having an affair*. She was *cheating on her partner*. She was *the other woman*. The phrases, such awful clichés that they ought to have lost their meaning, felt slap-in-the-face shocking now they were applied to herself. She couldn't stand the thought of Abe finding out. It had been way too close a call that last time they made love. The only time, because the whole thing unnerved her so much that she had brusquely brushed Liam off since. He'd dropped round a couple of times when Abe was at work, but she'd not let him in. The second time he'd said plaintively, 'We're both at home during the day, after all. Can't we be friends?'

'I can't have such good-looking friends,' Minette said, looking nervously at the street behind him.

'Ah, you flatterer. Can't I just come in for five minutes? A tiny chat?'

It was lucky he didn't know just how much willpower it took to say no. But she said, 'I'm sorry, I can't,' using an image of Josie and Abe walking by to strengthen her resolve, and shut the door quickly.

Their last proper encounter – the *only* one, she kept telling herself, as if Abe was listening to her thoughts – was now nine days ago, not that she was keeping notes or anything. If it was all there was going to be – and it would be, OK, Abe? – then it was a pretty amazing one.

'I'm having a crappy day, how about you?' Liam had said.

'Tilly's asleep. Would you like to come inside?' she'd replied.

'Fuck, yeah,' he whispered, and followed her into the

house. He looked incredulous as she pushed him onto the Heal's sofa and stripped off her clothes. She couldn't quite believe it of herself, now. He was clearly wondering what the hell had happened to the demure girl of a few days earlier, who wouldn't let him put his hand under her top. But it was only later, as they lay in a deliciously sweaty naked embrace on the living room floor that he said, 'Wow, that was a slightly better reception than I was expecting.'

'Why's that, neighbour?' She felt him smile against her shoulder at their private joke.

'You seemed kind of unsure last time.'

'Yes, well, we'll all be dead in a hundred years.'

'What does that mean?' He propped himself up on an elbow to look at her properly, and she gazed back at him. God, he was impossibly lovely. His hair mussed, his broad naked shoulders, that steel pipe . . . thinking about it now, Minette had to put down the rolling pin for a moment and take a couple of calming breaths.

'It means,' Minette said, trying on the bravado she'd admired in Cath, 'I'm tired of always being sensible.'

'I seem to have lucked into a marvellous new change in attitude, then.'

Minette smiled, and ran her fingers along his thigh. 'Maybe we're both lucky.'

When the monitor crackled into life with a wail, they were in the middle of a second act. 'Don't stop,' Minette breathed, 'she'll be all right for five minutes.' It was even less than that before they were both calling out more loudly than before and clinging to each other.

'Jesus,' Liam said, as Minette rolled off him. 'You'd think that a crying baby would put me off my stroke.'

'It didn't seem to,' Minette purred, greatly enjoying her new persona.

'Fairly galvanised me, I'd say.'

Minette threw on some clothes and ran up to rescue Tilly. She brought her downstairs to the kitchen, calling out, 'Come through when you're dressed.'

Liam did so, quickly, and leaned against the fridge. She felt him watching her while she moved around, making up the bottle, Tilly on her hip.

'You are fucking gorgeous, you know that?' he said.

'*Pas devant l'enfant!*'

'She can't understand me yet.'

'She will soon, we'll have to start being careful.'

Liam sat at the table. 'Well until then, I'm going to say what I think. And what I think is, fucking hell, lady, you are one hot piece of ass.'

'You've gone all American,' Minette said.

'I've caught it off Cath next door, with her "neighbourhoods" and "jumping snakes". I just had to change nationality to express the incredibleness of that last shag.'

'God, I'm blushing.'

'I love it that someone who screws like you blushes so easily.'

'It was awesome,' Minette mumbled, sitting down to give Tilly her bottle.

There was a noise at the front door, followed by the unmistakeable sound of a key turning in the lock.

'Oh, fuck, fuck, fuck,' Minette whispered.

'Hi honey, I'm home!' Abe called from the hall.

Minette and Liam stared in horror at each other, and moments later, Abe, whistling, walked into the kitchen. 'Oh. Hello, Liam,' he said flatly. Abe hadn't been keen on him, not since Liam had been snitty about Cath's charity appeal. Minette's heart thumped so loudly she was sure Abe could hear it. The two men shook hands, watching each other warily. Minette wondered if Liam had washed his hands since . . . oh god. She didn't dare look at him.

'I just popped round for a cuppa,' Liam explained to Abe, his voice at a higher pitch than normal. 'I wanted to ask if your brother, is it? The teacher? Would mind having a chat some time? About what I can expect on my course?'

'Luckily, you're back early,' Minette said, wondering if she sounded as mad as Liam.

'Yeah, there was a gas leak in the street outside the Bureau,' Abe said. 'Us and the whole row of shops have had to close for the day.'

'What does it mean, a gas leak? Is it dangerous?'

'I dunno. They've got British Gas out. So, where's this tea then, Dougie?'

'Oh, I haven't even put the kettle on yet. I've been doing Tilly's bottle. Liam only just got here a few minutes before you, Abe.'

Gradually Minette's heartrate returned to less critical levels. Liam choked down his tea, thanked Abe for the email address, did a show of good-lord-is-that-the-time and left, managing one raised-eyebrow glance at Minette.

Yes, way too close for comfort. Remembering it now made her feel sick.

She put the *tarte* in the oven and started rolling out more pastry. As long as she was sensible, and didn't meet Liam at her house any more – or anywhere! she slapped herself down – there was no reason why Abe would find out. Minette was uneasy, though, and not just because of almost being caught. It had been a bit weird the other night, when Abe went to help Cath move Davey's bed downstairs. She was grateful to him for doing such a nice, normal, neighbourly thing like that. It seemed to somehow counterbalance her own less-wholesome neighbourly relationships. When he came back, she handed him a beer, and he raised it to her in toast.

'Cheers, Dougie.' He flopped onto the sofa.

'Was it very heavy?' Minette asked, sitting next to him.

'Weighed a ton, yeah, but that bloke Liam was there as well.'

'He was?' Shit, what was Cath playing at?

'Yeah. He asked after you.'

'Oh, really?'

'The way he said it. All concerned. Think he fancies you.'

'Don't be daft!' She took a big gulp of wine.

'Thought you'd be flattered, good-looking lad like that.'

'Mmm. Anyway, is Davey's room all finished?'

'Yeah, we shifted all the furniture. I'm stronger than that friend of yours, even if he's taller. He kept having to stop for a rest.'

Minette felt embarrassed for Abe, and hoped he hadn't made a show of himself in front of Liam. 'Well, thanks for doing it, hon. I was thinking of making *salmon en croute* for your parents, do you think they'll like it?'

'Course they will. Aren't we cute little stereotypes?' Abe said. 'You doing the cooking, me doing the macho lifting.'

Now, as she placed the pastry carefully over the salmon, Minette worried about just how much she'd revealed to Cath. What had possessed Cath to get Liam round at the same time as Abe? Was she trustworthy? She was friendly with Josie, after all. What if she . . . Slow down, Minette told herself. Probably Liam was simply the only other neighbour who was available at the time. Even if, worst case scenario,

Cath *did* tell, which Minette couldn't picture her doing, Minette could say truthfully that it was just the once. A stupid indiscretion, a one-time crazy moment that would never be repeated. Abe was not a black-and-white sort of person. Though he would be terribly hurt, and disappointed in her, he understood that people made mistakes. That's why he was so good at his job. A lot of the people he advised had made dreadful mistakes, but he never judged them.

The doorbell rang – Julie and Roy were always punctual – and Minette put on her hostess smile. She was quickly enveloped in Julie's warm embrace. Roy kissed her and then commandeered Tilly, carrying her into the kitchen and making her laugh by pretending to steal her nose. Soon they were having lunch, glasses of wine in front of them. Tilly sat up proudly at the table, with her own portion of flaked salmon, beaming at her grandparents, who beamed delightedly back. Minette looked round at all the beloved faces and thought, OK, I can do this. I can have this as my whole life and it will be fine. I don't need anything else. She pushed away an image of Liam kissing her, and drank down half her wine.

'This is sensational,' Julie said. 'You're better than Nigella.'

'And even more glamorous,' Roy said, raising his glass to her.

Minette smiled at them. 'It's a very simple recipe.'

'You're too modest. Isn't she Abe?' Julie said.

'She is, and that's why I love her,' Abe said.

Minette was astonished to feel a tear trickle down her face. 'Excuse me,' she said, and ran out, aware that everyone was looking at her with concern. She locked herself in the bathroom, took some deep breaths, and washed her face. There hasn't been a single day, she said to herself, not a single day in which she felt normal since Tilly was born. It wasn't Tilly's fault, not even a tiny bit, but since having her Minette's life had gone off-kilter.

She paused in the hall outside the kitchen, not exactly listening but sort of listening.

'Those awful bloody people, excuse my language, Tilly,' Roy said.

'They've been gone nearly two months, though,' Abe said.

'It takes a long time to get over something like that,' Roy said firmly. 'I think Minette has been traumatised by their behaviour.'

The Miltons.

'She does look rather drawn and anxious. Is everything all right, Abe?' Julie said. 'Between you?'

'Well . . .' Abe said. Oh Jesus. Minette was torn between barging in to prevent Abe from speaking, and wanting to know what he would say. Might he tell them he suspected her of having an affair? Or that they hadn't had sex for nearly a year? No, no one in the history of the world would ever tell their parents that.

Abe said, 'Far as I know, everything is completely fine.' Minette let out her breath. 'She's decided not to go back to work, which I support as she says it's the right thing for her and Tilly. And also,' Abe went on, 'she's started training for a triathlon.' Minette was astonished to hear the pride in his voice; so far his only comments had been sarky ones about Ladies Who Run in their Lovely Lycra. And earlier that week, when she'd gone for a morning run, he'd complained that she would make him late for work, and they'd argued in the front garden like people off *EastEnders*.

She crept back up the stairs and did an elaborate play of stomping down them loudly. When she went in, Abe was telling Roy, slightly stiltedly, about a viniculture evening course he was going to take.

'You all right, love?' Julie asked her quietly, as Minette slipped back into her seat.

'Yes thanks. I was just thinking about how lovely things are with the new neighbours, compared to the Miltons, and I felt a bit upset for a silly moment.' Minette was pleased with the way she'd managed to use this explanation.

'Yes, I thought it might be that,' Julie said, relieved.

Minette busied herself with her food, now cold.

'This triathlon sounds like a terrific thing to do,' Julie went on. 'Can we sponsor you?'

Julie and Roy each pledged £250, and Minette's eyes filled up again.

Roy, discreetly changing the subject away from Minette, said to Abe, 'I see you've displayed my picture.' He pointed to the noticeboard, to the lovely photo of Tilly he'd taken last time they visited.

'You're going to need a bigger board,' Julie said, 'Tilly's not a year yet and it's almost full.'

'We're putting some of Dad's best ones into frames, we just haven't got round to it yet,' Abe said.

Minette remembered she still hadn't cleaned the frames, which she'd stacked in the under-stairs cupboard. She avoided Abe's eye.

'Where's that photo of you two I've always loved, from when you went to France to see your mother, Minette?'

'The one where I'm wearing the green dress? It's still there somewhere, probably covered over.'

'It's important to have some markers of the time before you were parents!' Julie said, with a meaningful glance at Abe. She went over to the board and tried to find it. 'No, it's not here.'

'I didn't take it down. Abe, did you?'

'Maybe,' he said vaguely, trying to put one last spoonful of salmon into Tilly's mouth. 'I'll look later.'

In the afternoon Abe and his parents took Tilly to the park, while Minette went for a run. She had a good look at Liam's house as she jogged past but there was no sign of anyone. She remembered how much she used to like running.

There was nothing like it for clearing the head, and after five minutes she wasn't thinking about anything except her breathing, and her stride.

After a quick shower she joined Abe and his parents for tea and more food. Once they'd gone home, with many hugs, and Tilly was in her cot, Minette and Abe crashed out in front of the TV.

'Think your parents had a good time?'

Abe was flicking through the channels. 'Course. They love seeing us. Could do without any more of Dad's bloody photos though. He took another few million today. I must get those frames sorted.'

'I've nearly finished cleaning them, all right? No need to go on.' She knew she was being touchy but she couldn't stop herself.

'I wasn't, Dougie. Sorry. I didn't mean anything,' Abe said. He stopped at a war documentary. 'This?'

'Can we find something light?'

Abe continued surfing. 'Are you OK? It was a bit weird when you started crying.'

'Did *they* think it was weird?'

'No, they just assumed you were having post-traumatic stress.'

'Maybe I am.'

'Maybe so.' Abe looked at her thoughtfully. 'What about this? *Him and Her*.'

'I'm not in the mood to watch other people in their pants.' Minette took the remote from him and turned off the sound. 'Why don't we . . .' she snuggled into him with an unmistakeable invitation on her face.

'Bit knackered, sorry love,' he said, and moved a tiny distance away, unmeasurable by tape measure, yet actually an enormous gulf. He clicked the sound back on, and watched the telly couple snogging. Minette sat up, and stared at the screen. Do you find me ugly? Do I smell? Why don't you want to? There are other people who do, you know. She said, 'We haven't done anything for ages.'

'It's not been that long.'

'Yes it has, Abe. It's been . . .' she couldn't bring herself to say the actual amount of time, it seemed so shocking. 'It's been a long time.'

'Come here.' He kissed her forehead and pulled her close, but the gulf was still there. 'It's just been a bit of a weird time. New baby and everything. Things will settle down soon.'

They sat together, his arm round her shoulder, watching people on telly who were having more fun. For the first time, Minette thought about their sex life not in terms of its recent absence, but about what it had been like long ago, before Tilly. After an exciting couple of months when they started dating, it had gone a bit quiet. There were periods when nothing much happened for several weeks, and other times when – and Minette sat up straighter, realising – she had always been the one to make the first move.

'You uncomfy, Dougie?'

'Just check on Tills. Back in a sec.'

Tilly was fast asleep, breathing warmly in her cot. Minette went into her own room, grabbed the iPad, sat up in bed, and googled 'animus'. Quite a lot of the sites were confusing, full of psychobabble that her tired brain couldn't follow. But then she found a less formal site, written by a psychology student:

> Love at first sight was explained brilliantly by Carl Jung's animus and anima. We're talking basically a force of nature here, guys, so don't try and resist. You see your 'other half', your female or male self, you are so not going to be able to help yourself. You just fall, and worry about landing some other time.

Liam was much better looking than Paul. Well, he was much better looking than everyone. But there was something of Paul about him. They both had the same certainty and confidence, which came, she supposed, from knowing how irresistible people found them. They both had a similar way of seeming to see right through her. And when they touched her, it had the same electrifying effect. Minette hadn't looked Paul up for a long time, but now she searched for his Facebook profile. There were a lot of Paul Munroes, but only one with his face. He looked exactly the same. Cocky, tanned, and smiling that let's-fuck smile. How hard she had worked – unsuccessfully – to make sure that he only turned that smile on for her. 'Status: in a relationship with Lindsey Unwin.' *She* was new. Last time Minette had looked it had been some other name. She clicked on Lindsey, saw a tall slim woman in a tiny black dress, a model type, and turned off the iPad.

She'd only spoken to Paul once after they split. She and Abe had been going out for a couple of months, and she'd bumped into Paul in a pub. Abe was at the bar, and the girl Paul was with – not Bella, Minette's ex-friend – was in the loo. In the few moments that Minette and Paul were alone, he managed, once again, to totally disturb her equilibrium. 'Ah, so you're seeing Mr Interesting Moncrieff,' he said, glancing over at Abe. 'Punching a bit above his weight, isn't he?'

Paul's stunning new girlfriend appeared at his side and they disappeared in, it seemed to Minette looking back, a flash of sparkling light. Then Abe came over with the drinks, and normal reality resumed.

In the bathroom she took out her lenses, and stared at her blurry reflection: pink oval, halo of black, dark smudges for eyes and mouth. In her head, she listed the possible explanations for Abe's lack of interest:

1. He was gay.
2. He was asexual.
3. He was having sex with someone else.
4. She was physically repulsive.
5. He just wasn't as into it as her.

She quickly rejected the first four. Abe had never shown the slightest interest in men; he did like sex when they did it; he didn't really have much opportunity to be with anyone else; she knew she was quite attractive. Liam clearly thought so. The possibility that jangled her nerves, the one that contained an element of truth, was the last one. Minette had read enough problem pages to be familiar with the concept of sexual incompatibility. One of you wanted it all the time, one of you never wanted it. She and Abe clearly had a mild form, in which she wanted it sometimes, and he wanted it only occasionally. Her vision became blurred by more than just her poor eyesight. It was painful to realise how many times Abe had rejected her; how many times she'd made the first move and been so cleverly rebuffed so that only now did she realise that that's what it was.

I'm a reject, she thought, and there was Liam's handsome face in her head, as clearly as if he was in the room.

Not to me, you're not, he said, and she picked up her phone, and quickly typed, 'When you free this week?' pressing send before she could think too much about it.

Chapter 15

Cath

'How's the training going?'

'OK, Gee, apart from the damn cycling. Wish someone could do that bit for me.'

'Ah, would if I could. That's a lie, I wouldn't. You're bloody mad. You sound knackered. Sleeping still shit?'

'Not brilliant. But I'm done in cos I've just been for a run with that skinny minny next door. She's faster than me.'

'Everyone's faster than you, babe. Sponsor money pouring in?'

'Pretty good, three-and-a-half grand. Minette's already got a few hundred and she's hardly started. Then there's the school quiz tonight.'

'Good luck with that. Listen, Rubes, reason I rang, Ry and me are going away for a few days.'

'Finally pinned him down to a mini-break, didya?'

'Got five nights for the price of three, spa hotel in Yorkshire.'

'Yorkshire? Hope it's not in sodding Troubletown.'

'No, it's, uh, in Sheffield.'

'Sheffield? Oh, that's well romantic, that is. He gets to go to the football, tarts it up as a holiday . . .'

'The match is only a couple of hours,' Gina snapped. 'And there's brilliant shopping in Sheffield.'

'All right lovie, I'm only teasing,' Cath said.

'Anyway, I won't be here for a few days next week, from Thursday. I'll have the mobile though.'

'Heard anything from you-know-who lately?'

'No more emails. The cheques have come in fine, though. He still always puts in a note for you, do you still not want them?'

'Like I said. Bin them.'

'Seems a bit . . .'

'You're not hanging onto them, are you?'

'Course not.'

Hmm. 'OK. Better go, Gee, got some people coming round.

Have a dreamy time in Sheffield, won't you? Hotel next to the football ground, is it?'

'You're just jealous. See ya.'

Cath hung up, and grinned. Poor old Gina. Talk about being taken for a ride. She knew who'd be paying for the football trip, and it weren't going to be Toyboy Ryan. Cath went upstairs to Davey's old room, which was now the spare room, and made up the new guest bed with crisp white sheets. She put two neatly folded towels on top, checked everything else was in place, and went downstairs. The post was lying on the mat: bills, takeaway menus and charity envelopes with no address on, their shape revealing a give-away pen inside. Like a cheap biro would make people want to donate. Andy used to say she should work for a charity, she'd probably double their funding. Ah, there it was, at the bottom of the pile: an envelope franked with the local NHS trust's logo. At last! She ripped it open and scanned it hurriedly. Excellent – Davey's referral, and soon, too: only two weeks away. Good old Dr Ogueh.

'Please allow up to three hours for the appointment.' For Pete's sake! Bit over-thorough. 'You will be seen by members of the multidisciplinary team including a consultant in rehabilitation medicine, physiotherapist and occupational therapist.' Cath ticked them off on her fingers. OK, she could handle all that. She just needed to be prepared.

She filed the letter in her 'Davey hospital' folder, and just then the doorbell rang. She let Minette in, who was babbling in her stressy way as she stepped into the hall.

'Are you sure this is OK? It's so nice of you. I feel awful. But it is really kind of you. Oh god, are we sure about this?'

'Hey, Tills,' Cath said, taking the baby from her agitated mum. 'She looks tired. Hopefully she'll sleep all right here.'

'Yes, she hasn't had her nap yet. God, oh god. He not here yet? I don't know what's worse, him coming, or him not coming.'

Cath considered whether Minette was in the mood for a joke about hopefully them both coming, and decided not. Instead she said, 'Shall I show you where everything is? Then I can clear out before he gets here.'

'Oh no, please wait with me, Cath, I'd feel even weirder on my own. I've never done anything like this before.'

Yes you have, thought Cath. You just haven't been so, what's the word, premeditated. 'Well, it sounded like you couldn't carry on meeting in either of your houses.'

'Talk about unlucky! It must be some kind of bad karma.'

'I don't believe in karma.'

'I don't either, not really. But one time only at mine, and Abe walks in. Then one time at Liam's, and Tilly almost falls down the stairs.'

'Horrible.' Cath had heard all this already, how the mood had been ruined, how upset they'd both been, but nodded and tutted again and said her line: 'Well, they're all open plan in there, aren't they?'

'They'll have to sort that out if they're going to have children. I said to him, how are you going to put stair gates on open stairs with no bannister? How are you going to watch telly when the baby's sleeping? There's no doors between one room and the next.'

'What, not even on the loo?'

Minette laughed. 'I didn't check. But anyway,' and she lowered her voice, though there was no one else there, 'he said that babies weren't likely as they haven't had sex for months.'

Cath loved it when Minette's face went all confiding. Since they'd started training for the triathlon together they'd become close. There was no one else, really, that Minette could talk to about Liam. She'd hinted that she and her friend Ros were drifting apart, and she was generally pretty isolated.

Cath led Minette upstairs, and showed her the spare room. 'I just made up the bed. And you can use the shower, uh, after, if you like.'

Minette blushed. 'That's so kind.'

'You can stop saying that, it's a pleasure. And next door, in Lola's room, I've put a travel cot, look.'

'Oh yes. Isn't it a nice cot, Tilly?'

Not really, Minette – it was a large yellow and blue plastic eyesore. 'So even if she isn't asleep, she'll be safe in there. Godsend this was, when Lola was little; I stuck her in it while I sorted Davey out. Like them 1970s playpens.'

The bell rang again and Minette jumped. 'It's him!'

'I'll finish getting ready and clear out.' Cath handed Tilly back to Minette, and trotted downstairs to let Liam in. He looked absurdly handsome standing in the hall.

'Thanks for this, Cath. Really appreciate it.'

Minette came slowly downstairs and muttered a hello at Liam. He said, 'You OK?'

'I'm fine. Just hope no one saw us come here.'

'So what if they did? We're allowed to visit Cath. Even at the same time.'

'She's a worrier, this one,' Cath said. 'I'm just loading the car, then I'll be out of your hair. Why don't you go into the living room?'

They traipsed in, looking so much like teenagers on a first date that Cath had to stop herself laughing. She hovered outside the door.

'It just feels wrong, being here,' she heard Minette say. 'Settle down, Tilly.'

'Does she want to play with my phone? Here you go.' There was a pause, then it went quiet. Cath gave them a moment, then coughed before going into the living room. They were sitting very close and the top two buttons of Minette's shirt were undone. 'All right, you lovely people, I'm off. I'll be back about four.'

'You sure we're not forcing you out of your home, Cath?' Liam asked.

'I have to get ready for the quiz. Right, where's my bag? See you later.'

She smiled to herself as she shut the front door, and drove to the school. They had two hours to get a bit more relaxed. Young love, eh? Or young lust, anyway. Minette really needed something like Liam in her life. She'd enjoyed watching him square up to Abe, the night they'd moved Davey's furniture for her. 'This won't need two of us,' Abe told Cath, then practically burst a blood vessel trying to lift too much. 'Like two cocks facing off,' Cath said to Liam later, after Abe limped back home. 'One cock, and one *with* a cock, I think you'll find,' Liam replied.

'That's what I've heard,' Cath grinned. She gave Liam a glass of wine, and chatted about Minette, about how crazy she was about him. By the time Liam left, Cath knew he would keep on contacting Minette until she caved. It was good for her. She needed it.

The secretary was always the most useful person in any school, and Cath had made it a priority to get to know this one, Sophie Wallis.

'No one will be using the hall, now lunch is done. You've got it all to yourself, Mrs Brooke.'

'Thanks very much, Mrs Wallis. Hope you're able to come along tonight?'

'I can't, I'm afraid, but I'll definitely make a donation.'

'So kind of you.'

Cath set up her information boards around the walls. She'd got some nice pictures of kids like Davey, and two of her in running gear from a 10K she did a few years ago. Another board had some basic facts about Duchenne, and the last one explained how donations were used. Next, she put little decorations on all the tables, plus pens, paper and copies of her sponsor forms. When the quiz was underway she'd take a few photos for the local rag.

She remembered with amusement how uncertain and polite she'd been, the first time she approached a newspaper. She didn't suppose they'd be interested, but she was doing a sponsored parachute jump, might they be willing to mention it . . . She was astonished to find that they nearly bit her hand off. Talking to the young woman reporter who came out to interview her, Cath discovered that they were desperate for copy, and other papers were all the same. They were generally wildly understaffed, and a cute picture of a photogenic kid like Davey meant they could fill an easy half page. Mostly, the local rag in Troubletown just printed exactly what she'd written in the press release without changing a word. Hopefully the *Hove Gazette* would be the same. Though of course, there could be no more photos of her or Davey. Couldn't risk the wrong person seeing them, especially when papers posted everything on the internet now. It didn't matter. She had a lot of photos of a nice-looking Duchenne kid called Jerry. She'd taken them a couple of years ago at a fundraiser.

Papers didn't have the resources to check whether the person in the photo was the one mentioned in the press release.

The bell rang for the end of school shortly after Cath finished arranging the room. She found Davey in the playground, and bent down to give him a kiss but he ducked his head.

'Oh dear,' she laughed to another mother. 'He's already embarrassed about being kissed in public.'

The woman smiled. 'Mine are the same.'

'You coming to the quiz?' Cath said.

'I'd like to. I'll ask my husband.'

Cath smiled and turned to the next person. Ask my husband? Poor her. Cath didn't have to check in with *anyone*. She made all the decisions, did what she wanted.

She did sometimes find herself thinking about Andy, though it was pointless. There was no going back now. She'd been remembering this morning when Davey was born, and Andy just sat there staring at him with this crazy smile, like he'd got religion or won the lottery or something. 'Thank you,' he said to her, but it was the way he said it. She'd not forget that. Compared with the little boys round here – Ryan, Abe, Liam – Andy was a real man.

She knew she wouldn't be able to read the notes he sent to Gina. What would it be like, if he could still be in her life? But he couldn't, and that was that. She had to leave that all behind: Troubletown, the hospital and Andy. To snap out of it, Cath reminded herself of the feeling of his hand on her cheek, the sting and the shock of it.

Davey waited patiently while Cath prowled the playground, schmoozing the mums, reminding them about the quiz. 'For kids like Davey,' she gestured to him, 'and the school gets half the money so it's win-win.'

By the time they left to collect Lola, more than twenty women had promised they'd come, with or without husbands. Cath chatted enthusiastically to Davey as they made their way to the car, but he was monosyllabic. It wasn't like him to sulk.

'What's up, Davey? I've not gotten a word out of you.'

He didn't answer, and started to push himself across the road before she had time to check.

'Davey!' she pulled him back as a car whizzed past them. 'Crazy idiot!' She shook her fist at the driver. 'Not you, lovie, him. But you got to be careful, they can't see you so well down there.'

Once safely on the other side, Cath said, 'Listen, lovie, is it about your room? I know you didn't want to move, but I couldn't keep carrying you up and downstairs. Is there anything you want for it? I can't afford the computer yet, but we could get something nice, cushions or something.'

She was taken aback by the look Davey gave her. Sceptical, suspicious. She had never seen that expression on his face before, but it was familiar nonetheless.

'Gosh, you remind me of your father,' she said and ruffled his hair.

'Air Max trainers,' he said.

'Ah yes, your old ones are no good any more, I remember. Who's got them Air Maxes, then? Someone in your class?'

He shrugged. 'I don't want to look like a spazzo.'

'Pete's sake, Davey!' Cath put her hand on his chair to stop him. 'Who the hell called you that?'

'No one, I'm just saying.'

'I don't want to hear that word again, OK? That word is banned. We'll have a look for trainers this weekend. Come on, let's get Lolly.'

Once home, Cath instructed Davey to put on something smart, and told Lola to plait her hair. Minette and Liam were long gone, of course – it was nearly five – and Minette had stripped the bed and hung the towels up. Cath put on some make-up, and her favourite dress, a black shift with a low neck.

She called to Davey to get his coat on, and was juggling bags, boxes of cakes, and her coat, when he wheeled himself into the hall wearing a SpongeBob SquarePants T-shirt.

'Heaven's sake, Davey. I said something smart. Go on.'

She expected him to go back into his room, but he stood, or rather sat, his ground. Cath felt the rage building inside her. 'I'm not joking, OK? Put a proper shirt on. We're already late.' She started to push his chair back towards his room, but he put the brakes on, making her jolt her arm.

'You listen to me, mister,' she said. She pushed Lola out of the way and knelt in front of Davey, her hands on his chair. 'You know this event is important to me. To us. It will raise a lot of money. If you want me to even think about getting you trainers, get changed *right now*.' She hissed the last bit, and was mighty relieved when he wordlessly spun his chair round and went back into his room.

These rebellions were becoming increasingly frequent. He was already too big for her to manhandle against his will. She tried not to show him how she struggled to get him in and out of the bath; in six months she wouldn't be able to do even that. She felt a surge of exhaustion and wished she could stay home, crawl upstairs and get under the covers of her very own bed. Then her mummy would stop being angry, she was never angry when her baby was ill, she would come and smooth her forehead, kiss it gently, close the curtains, say 'get some sleep now, little one'.

Cath went into the bathroom and took a few ibuprofen, just double the recommended dose. She caught sight of herself in the mirror, and for a horrible, frightening moment, didn't quite recognise herself. Her eyes looked more widely spaced than she remembered, her skin paler and more papery. There were faint criss-crosses of lines under her eyes that she hadn't noticed before. She blinked hard, and the reflection turned back into her.

* * *

When she came downstairs Davey was in the hall, wearing a shirt and a filthy expression. So she'd won that one. She mightn't be so lucky next time.

Both kids were silent all the way to school, and Cath felt her tension start to build. The back of her skull felt hollow and loose, as if it was coming away from her head. No, please, not now. She forced herself to work through one of the strategies that Gina's mum had taught her: focus on a situation in which she had control. She turned her mind to the other week, Lola and the M&Ms, how she managed to sort that out. Her breathing started to calm down, though when they arrived at the school she saw how her arms trembled as she got Davey into his wheelchair. She stood for a moment in the carpark, gently rubbing her arms, soothing down the wires. Once inside the school, Cath relaxed when she saw how many people had turned up. The hall was buzzing. They were going to be sold out, in fact they had to squeeze in a few over the official fire safety limits.

Cath stepped up to the mic and welcomed everyone. She wasn't quite herself, but no one there knew who she was anyway. She was good at public speaking, and soon the crowd were laughing, and drinking, nibbling cakes, filling in her sponsorship forms, and arguing good-naturedly over the answers to the questions that she read out, slowly and clearly, in her warmest voice.

Chapter 16

Davey

Olivia's brother was called Empty. Anyway that's what it sounded like when Olivia said it. Olivia told Davey that Empty would let him use his phone. At home time Davey and Olivia went out of the gate together to meet him. Davey knew they had at least ten minutes, his mum was always late. Olivia didn't try to push Davey's chair anymore. She walked next to it, her hand on the arm. Davey liked it when she did that. Empty was tall, with straight brown hair like Olivia's. He was at big school. He nodded at Davey. 'All right?'

'Yes, thank you,' Davey said.

'Can he use your phone then?' Olivia asked.

Empty gave Davey his phone. It was small and old-fashioned, like Davey's dad's, before he got a new one. Davey knew straight away it didn't have the internet. On the back were two initials in Tipp-Ex. MT. Not Empty.

'Do you know the number?' MT asked, seeing Davey pause.

'Not exactly. I was thinking I could look it up.'

'You can't on that. I'm desperate for a smart phone but I'm not allowed till I stop losing things. But you can call directories and they give you the number you want.'

Davey looked hopefully at MT, and he said, 'Shall I do it for you?' He was kind, like Olivia. MT dialled a number and listened. Then he said to Davey, 'What's your dad's name?'

'Andy Purcell.'

MT repeated this into the phone, and then asked Davey for the address.

'Harrogate,' Davey said. It made him feel weird that Harrogate was a strange faraway place now, not the place he lived. Olivia had never even heard of it.

MT said, 'They need the whole address, you know, like the street.'

'We lived at number sixty-eight.'

'Do you know the street name, or the postcode?'

'Yes, the street was . . .' Davey stopped. He couldn't think. The only street he could remember was Sisley Street, but that was where they lived now. This was stupid. He knew this. He knew his old address. He must do.

Olivia said, 'What about your grandparents' number? You said they lived near your dad.'

'Yes, they live in Harrogate too.'

'Can you remember their address?'

Davey shook his head. His mind was blank. MT said into the phone that they only knew the number sixty-eight but they didn't know the street. He listened for a bit, then clicked the phone off. 'I'm sorry,' he said. 'If you find out the street I can get you the number.'

'OK,' Davey said. 'Thank you. What does MT stand for?'

'Milo Terrence, unfortunately,' MT said. 'That's why I'm called MT. I like your trainers.' He pointed at Davey's new Air Maxes.

'I want some,' Olivia said.

'Me too. Well, I could look something up for you on the computer at home,' MT said. He knew Davey didn't have the internet.

'Yes please, could you look my dad up?'

'Is he on Facebook? I don't really use that but I could do a search on it. What if there's more than one Andy Purcell though, how will I know which one he is?'

It hadn't occurred to Davey that there might be more than one. Andy Purcell was his dad, it seemed odd to think there might be others.

'I know,' MT went on, 'I'll print their pictures and you can tell me which one, OK?'

Davey thanked him.

'Well, we'd better go,' MT said, as though he and Davey were two parents chatting together, 'Olivia's got swimming.'

Davey's mum was the last to arrive again. She came running in all puffing. On the way to get Lola, Davey listed his five favourite boys' names.

1. Adam
2. Andy
3. Milo
4. Barry
5. Terrence

On the way home Davey asked his mum if he could go to Olivia's house. 'What, now?'

'She's at swimming now. Tomorrow?'

'No, I don't think so, Davey.'

'Monday, then.'

'We'll see. Hey, you two won't believe the fantastic surprise that's waiting at home!'

'What, what?' Lola said, all happy, but Davey didn't say anything. Lately, as Adam Purcell pointed out, the surprises had not been that great.

But it was: it was a computer. Davey's mum had set it up

in the living room. Davey and Lola raced over to it, wanting to be the first to turn it on. While they waited for it to load up, Davey tried not to notice how out-of-date it looked. It was probably older than MT's phone. It had an old-fashioned fat monitor and there was dirt in the keyboard. It wouldn't matter at all, as long as . . .

'Where's Google?' he asked. He and Lola turned to their mum.

'Oh,' she said, hanging up their coats, 'it doesn't have the internet. But the guy that sold it me gave me loads of games, look.' She handed them a shoebox full of CD games. Lola grabbed the box and tipped it onto the floor. She couldn't read yet but she recognised the pictures. 'Sonic the Hedgehog! Mario!'

'You can have first go,' Davey told Lola. Adam was right.

Chapter 17

Minette

Nap when your baby naps, says every child-rearing book on earth. Yeah, right. Minette, like most new mothers, she suspected, responded to this with a hollow laugh. First off, you never knew how long a baby would sleep for. You might get a solid half hour or longer, but you'd be equally likely to be woken two minutes after you'd sunk into a blissful, precious sleep. For another thing, even the tiredest person on earth would struggle to sleep on command. Quick, the baby's asleep, drop everything, leap into bed and . . . lie awake worrying about all the chores you should be doing.

All that said, Tilly was now sleeping reliably for ninety minutes in the afternoon, and so for almost the first time Minette lay down to 'nap when the baby naps'. She was certainly tired enough. She'd greeted Abe's lunchtime call of, 'Hi Honey I'm home,' with, 'Hi! Tilly's in her high chair, I'm going out for a quick bike ride.'

They faced off in the hall.

'Hang on! How long will you be?' he asked, his coat half off.

'Forty minutes, tops.'

'I thought we'd have lunch together,' he said, all wounded. She'd never before suggested he take over with Tilly at lunchtime, and she smiled as she put on her bike helmet. 'I'll have mine when I get back,' she said, shutting the door decisively.

Minette couldn't understand why she'd put up such resistance to cycling. The minute she got on the bike and started pedalling she felt incredible. She didn't think about Ros's broken wrist, she thought instead about the kilometres she was racking up, the wind on her face, the freedom of getting far away from home under her own steam. She was in Brighton before she knew it, and only turned back, reluctantly, when she saw the Palace Pier, lit up like a Christmas tree though it was the middle of the day.

Abe was fuming when she got home.

'I've got to go back to work now,' he said, holding Tilly to his chest like a rebuke.

'I'm bang on forty minutes, like I said.'

'If you're going to start going out at lunchtime, what's the point of me coming home?'

'That's a very interesting question.' Minette took off her bike helmet. She didn't know, till this moment, how angry she was. 'Because all these months I've been wondering myself what the fucking point *is* of you coming home for lunch. I suppose I thought it was so you could nag me about how I never do anything *educational* with Tilly.' She realised she was shouting but she couldn't seem to stop. 'Now for the first time, it *is* useful you being here: it gives me one tiny bit of fucking time to do what I want, by myself, in the whole of the long, draggy day.' It was so out of character for her to lose her temper that Abe took a step back.

'I'm sorry,' he said. 'You're right.'

Minette subsided immediately. 'No, I'm sorry.'

'You're training for this triathlon, and you don't have much time. I didn't think.'

'It's OK.'

'No, it's not. I've been rubbish. I'll take your form to work and get everyone to sponsor you. And I'll wait with Tilly now while you have a shower.'

'Abe, that's amazing.' She gave him a kiss. 'Sorry I yelled.'

No wonder she was tired after that unusual combination of physical activity and emotional outburst. Like a textbook mummy, she fell into a deep sleep almost instantly, and didn't hear her phone, which was in the hall, the first few times it rang. But gradually it seeped into her consciousness, pulling her out of an enjoyable dream about Liam, in which they were at a party. He was telling her that he'd slept with everyone in the room, and she was laughing. As she staggered blearily out of bed, she was slightly puzzled as to why she hadn't minded him telling her that.

She'd missed several calls from the same, unknown number. She rang it, and a woman said, 'Forest Lodge Primary?'

Minette explained about the missed calls, and the woman thanked her for phoning back. 'I'm Sophie Wallis, the school secretary. I'm sorry to bother you, Ms Fairbanks, but I'm afraid Mrs Brooke hasn't come to collect Davey.'

Ah, it was Davey's school. Minette squinted at the clock. Four fifteen. She'd been asleep for over an hour, no wonder she felt foggy and confused. 'Do you want Cath's number?'

'We've tried it several times but it goes straight to voicemail. Your details are listed in our records as Davey's emergency contact.'

'Really?' Minette was wide awake now.

'Well, you and a lady called Gina, but she's not answering her phone either. So I'm afraid as you've called back first, you've drawn the short straw. Are you able to collect Davey? I need to head off at five.'

'Oh! Yes, of course. I'll be there in about twenty minutes.'

'That's fine, thank you so much.'

Minette hung up, and put her lenses in. She'd only been to Davey's school once, when Cath drove her there, but she looked up the route; it was pretty straightforward. She roused Tilly, strapped her into the buggy, and went round to bang on Cath's door, but there was no answer. She set off, trying Cath's number every so often. It went straight to voicemail each time. Where was she?

The school was quiet, all the children having gone apart from poor Davey, who was sitting in the foyer reading a book. He looked up when she called his name, and regarded her with his habitual intense scrutiny.

'Hey, sweetie, you OK?' she asked, and he nodded.

The school secretary was wearing her coat, ready to go. She accompanied them out, and as they parted ways at the gates she said, 'Davey has a little sister, doesn't he?'

'That's right. Oh god, I guess I ought to collect her, too. But I'm not sure how to get to her nursery from here.' As with the school, Minette had only been there once, that somewhat traumatic visit with Cath when Lola had eaten the peanuts.

Davey said, 'I know the way.'

'You do? Can you show me?'

He nodded.

'And you can wheel yourself?'

'It's not very far.'

'He's amazing, isn't he?' the secretary said, looking relieved to be handing this problem over. 'Hopefully you'll hear from Mum soon.' She waved as she got into a red Mini Cooper. Minette, pushing Tilly, followed Davey across the road and into an unfamiliar back street. He was surprisingly fast, pushing the large wheels of his chair with practised ease. He must have incredibly strong arms. Minette had to trot along to keep up with him. They turned left into another street, went right at the end of that one, and then he stopped outside a building whose brightly coloured sign announced Busy Tigers Preschool.

'You are clever, Davey.' Fancy an eight-year-old being so savvy.

'I can't go in, there's no ramp,' he said flatly.

She asked him to wait, and took Tilly out of the buggy and up the steps. There were several children in the large playroom, the nursery presumably closing later than school. Lola was painting splashily at an easel. Minette spoke to the woman in charge, Sharon, who clearly remembered Minette from the M&M incident. Sharon looked worried.

'We can't release the child to anyone other than the people named in the file. You know Mrs Brooke is a real stickler for protocol.' She rummaged around in her cabinet till she found a folder with Lola's name and photo on the front.

'Here we are. Catherine Brooke, Gina Grainger and Minette Fairbanks.'

'Oh, that's me!' said Minette, surprised all over again that Cath seemed to have set her up to be in loco parentis, for this very eventuality, in fact, without mentioning it.

'Do you have ID?' Sharon said. 'I'm sorry to have to ask, but Mrs Brooke . . .'

Minette showed her bank card, and Sharon looked relieved. She explained gently to Lola that she was to go home with Minette. Lola accepted this matter-of-factly, and skipped off to get her things. Minette said, 'Has Cath given you information about Lola's allergies?'

'Yes of course,' Sharon said defensively, 'and we never found out who brought those peanuts in, everyone denied it, you know.'

'I'm so sorry, I didn't mean that, I'm not sure of all the allergies myself and wanted to check them before I take charge of Lola.'

Sharon gave Minette a look, as if to say, why are you taking charge of this child if you don't know her medical details? Minette started to feel aggrieved; she hadn't asked for this responsibility, after all. But then Lola came over and slipped her warm, slightly painty hand into Minette's, and her anger dissolved.

'She can't eat fish, or any kind of nuts, including peanuts, as you know.'

'Peanuts aren't really nuts,' chirped Lola.

'That's right, I believe.' Minette smiled at her.

'And she can't have milk either.'

'Poor old Lola,' Minette said. 'No hot chocolate?'

'Oh yes,' Lola said, 'I love hot chocolate.'

'The kind made with hot water,' Sharon said, firmly.

Minette let Davey lead the way home. This was still an unfamiliar part of town to her, and he clearly knew where he was going. Neither child seemed particularly upset about the absence of their mother. Minette had considered how to explain what might have happened, but she didn't need to – they didn't ask, or even mention Cath.

'We've got new taps at school,' Davey informed Lola.

'Why?'

'Because. They look like old taps. They say "Boss" on them.'

'Are they bossy?'

'It's the make.'

'What colour are they?'

'Silver. They stay on when you push.'

'I like taps like that.'

'You've never seen them.'

'I have!'

'Where then?'

'A place I went one time. You weren't there.'

How extraordinary to think that Tilly, enjoying herself immensely in the company of these two big kids, would be like them in just a few years' time. Able to walk, and hold a conversation, even bicker. To carry her own backpack, like Lola. To find her way home from a mile away, like Davey. With surprise, Minette found that they were at the top end of Sisley Street; she had barely noticed how they'd got there.

'You're a marvel, Davey, you know that? So, you guys better come to mine, and I'll give your mum another call.'

'I've got the key to our house,' Davey said. He pulled out a chain from around his neck that had a Yale key threaded onto it. Minette was taken aback. Surely this was independence taken a step too far? Minette had heard of the philosophy of free-range children, but wasn't he too young to be a latch-key kid?

'Are you,' she asked casually, 'often at home without your mum?'

'Sometimes,' said Lola, chirpily.

'Well, would you mind coming to mine for a bit? I have to do Tilly's supper and I can make something for you two, as well.'

Davey and Lola looked at each other, and then, as though they'd silently discussed it, they both said yes. Minette's hallway was wide, like Cath's, so Davey could get into the living room easily.

'Ooh, look at the big telly,' Lola cried.

'Do you mind watching CBeebies?' Minette asked. 'It's the only one that's suitable for Tilly.'

'We like CBeebies,' Lola said, all chatty. 'Can Tilly sit next to me?'

Minette gave them chocolate biscuits and left them happily watching, Tilly's attention torn between the telly and gazing adoringly at Lola. Minette dialled Cath's phone again, not expecting to get a reply, but it was answered. 'Cath? Oh, thank god. Are you OK?'

A woman with a Scottish accent said, 'Hello, I'm Sister McCarty. I'm a nurse at Brighton General.'

'Oh my god! I'm Cath's neighbour. Is she all right?'

'No need to worry, we think Mrs Brooke will be just fine.'

Minette breathed out. 'What's happened?'

'She was knocked off her bike earlier today. She's bruised and got a wee bang to her head. We've given her something to help her sleep it off. She had ID on her but her phone's locked, so we're glad you rang it. You don't know her next of kin, by any chance?'

'Her husband works away from home, and I've never met him. I'm looking after her children right now.'

'Ah, she'll be glad to know that, I'm sure. Are you able to look after them overnight?'

'Yes, of course, Nurse,' Minette said, sounding like her mother-in-law, who called taxi drivers 'Driver'. It would be nicer for the children to sleep in their own home. She could stay there, in the spare room. Don't think about the last time you were in the spare room, Minette. Focus.

'When Mrs Brooke wakes up I expect she'll want to speak to you, hear how the kiddies are doing.'

'How long will she be in for?'

'She should be able to come out in a couple of days, all being well.'

Minette suddenly wondered if Davey, being a clued-up boy, knew the passcode on his mum's phone. The nurse hung on while she asked him, briefly explaining to the children what had happened to Cath.

'It's 1531,' he answered, then added, 'She doesn't know I know it.'

'You star!' Minette passed this on, and waited while the nurse tapped it in.

'Great, I'm in. Do you know the husband's name?'

'Andy, I think. And she has a close friend called Gina. If you give me their numbers I'm happy to ring them, you're probably very busy.'

'Ah, that's kind of you. Hold on a minute while I look through the contacts. Here we are. I can't see an Andy. I'll look under "Husband". Oh yes, there's a number for "Hubby".' The nurse read out his number and Gina's, and Minette jotted them down.

She said goodbye to the nurse, and rang Gina first, but it

was another answerphone. She left a message, then wondered what to do about calling Andy. After all, Cath had said they were having a break. Clearly, their marriage wasn't exactly in a brilliant state. Minette could look after the children tonight, maybe a couple of nights, but they ought to have someone from their family with them. She was already worried about how she'd get them to school and nursery tomorrow, though she imagined that Davey had the routine down pat.

Minette rang Abe, and he said that of course she should call Andy, and added that he'd come home early to help out. Feeling like a shit because he was being so nice today, Minette texted Liam to say she'd be in Cath's house later that evening. In the last week or so they'd met there twice during the day. This would be another excellent opportunity, though more awkward, with the kids being there. Still, her skin prickled at the thought of Liam, his hands on her body, his mouth on her neck, her lips . . . And Abe would be safely out of the way, stuck in their own house with a sleeping Tilly . . . She pushed this unworthy thought away and dialled Andy's number.

He answered on the first ring. 'Hello?'

She'd barely begun to explain who she was, and why she was calling, when he interrupted. 'You've got the children? Are they OK? What's your address?'

Something wasn't right. His tone was too urgent. She said,

'I live next door to them.' She wasn't going to give him the address if he didn't know it.

'I swear to god, you're the voice of an angel. Please, just tell me where they live.'

'Don't you know?'

'You must know that I don't.'

'I don't know anything, honestly.'

There was silence. 'Hello?' Minette said.

'I'm still here.' He sounded as if he was crying. 'Listen, are they all right? How's Adam?'

'Who's Adam?'

'My son, my boy. Oh Christ, don't tell me she's changed their first names, too.'

Minette started to panic. 'I'm sorry, I think I've made a mistake. I thought you were their father.'

'I am their father! Adam's eight years old. He has beautiful dark grey eyes with thick lashes and he's smart as a tack. He's in a wheelchair. Esmie's four. She's got light brown hair and she usually wears it in two plaits. Her favourite teddy is Panda. I miss them so much my heart's broken.'

Minette's mind was reeling. 'I don't want to get in between something here.'

'I only want to see them. I'm terrified for them.'

'There's no need, they're happy and well.'

'They're not. You don't know the half of it. Ruby's not what you think.'

'I don't know a Ruby, I'm sorry. I'm going to have to hang up now.'

'I don't know what she's calling herself now. She used to be Ruby. Please don't hang up! Just tell me what names the children have now. Or the part of the country you're in. Or are you abroad? Please tell me something. Anything! Is Adam there? Could I speak to him? Just for thirty seconds?'

Trembling, Minette ended the call, and threw the phone down as though it was on fire. It immediately rang with Andy's number. She pressed 'decline', but it rang again straight away. She turned the phone off; she'd have to change her number if this carried on. She put her head round the living room door, thought about saying 'Esmie!' to see if Lola turned round, but knew she shouldn't get involved. There had clearly been all manner of domestic shit going down, and it would be wiser to stay out of it. Cath was a great parent. Minette had often marvelled over her patience, wished she could be as calm with Tilly as Cath was with her two.

Abe arrived, and was very reassuring. 'You did the right thing, Dougie. It was right to phone him, then when you realised it was a bit weird, you were right not to give too much away.'

'What the hell's going on there, though?' she whispered. 'Why has she changed their names?'

'Probably domestic violence. That's what it would be if it was a client at work.'

'Oh god, seriously? I hope I haven't put them at risk by ringing him.'

'Hang on, though, she had his number on her phone. Well, there's no point in speculating.' Abe had seen this sort of thing before. 'People's relationships are incredibly complicated. No one outside them can ever really know what's going on.'

He looked so concerned and caring. Minette wanted to warn him against herself. Oh, my love, sometimes people inside the relationship don't know what's going on, either.

It was enjoyably different, having a meal with older kids. Tilly ate everything without a fuss, following Davey and Lola's examples. Lola ate unconcernedly, barely paying attention to Minette's careful recital of the strictly non-allergenic ingredients she'd used. They were uncurious about their mother, beyond Davey wanting to check where they'd be sleeping that night. She wished she could tell Davey she'd spoken to his father. Hell, she wished she could ask Davey what was going on. She'd probably get more sense out of him than some of the grown-ups involved.

After they'd eaten, Davey asked very politely if he could use the computer. Abe said, 'Sure,' but Minette shook her head at him. 'Your mum told me you weren't allowed to, Davey; it's bad for your muscles.'

'Seriously?' Abe said. 'You'd think it would be good exercise.'

'I only meant a little go,' Davey said.

'Ah, let the kid, Dougie,' Abe said, which needled Minette. Why should Abe make her the bad guy, when it wasn't her rule? She wasn't going to run the risk of being in the wrong again with Cath, like she was over the Aztec mask thing.

'I'm sorry, Davey,' she said. 'Your mum was pretty clear about it. Is there something we can look up for you?'

There was a long pause before Davey said, 'No, it's all right, thank you.'

Abe suggested a game of cards, and both children were enthusiastic. He taught them to play rummy, and while they played Minette packed a small overnight bag. Then, heart thudding, she turned on her phone. There was a text from Liam – 'Brilliant. I'll be over later' – and four answerphone messages. Could have been worse – she'd been expecting dozens. Three were from Andy. The first said he was sorry he'd freaked her out, he just wanted to explain that he hadn't seen the kids since Ruby, or whatever she was called now, had left him in February, and just wanted to know they were OK. In the second message he said Ruby was an evil bitch who lied and cheated and he had the proof. Minette deleted that one before it had finished, and dreaded listening to the last one, but he was calmer again. He said he wouldn't keep phoning her, he understood she was Ruby's friend, he only wanted to be in his children's lives and he'd be really grateful if she could just ask Ruby to let him see them. 'I won't ask for anything more, I promise.'

The last message was from Gina, asking Minette to call her back. Minette did so, then instantly wished she hadn't. She'd barely started to explain the situation when Gina started yelling.

'Oh my fucking god please tell me you haven't called her ex.'

'Um, yes, well, I did ring him . . .'

'And you hid your caller ID, didn't you?'

'Er, no, I don't know how to do that.'

'You stupid twat!'

'Hey! Now, hang on a minute . . .'

'He's violent, did you know that?' Gina's voice rose into almost a screech. 'He whacked Cath, he whacked those kids.'

'I didn't know that Gina, how could I? Cath's not talked about it to me.'

'Could you not have used your brain for five minutes and thought, maybe I should check what the sitch is with her husband before ringing him up and blabbing?'

Minette's famously good temper was being tested to the limit today. She tried not to lose it again, like she'd lost it with Abe earlier, but she had never been called a stupid twat before. 'Don't you *dare* talk to me like that. I'm looking after Cath's children on my own, here. There was no one to ask. You weren't answering your phone . . .'

'I'm in fucking Sheffield!' Gina screeched, as she might have said 'Outer Mongolia'.

'. . . and Cath is unconscious in hospital. I didn't tell Andy anything.'

'Please tell me you at least rang him from a mobile, not your fucking landline.'

'I'm not going to speak to you at all, unless you stop swearing at me.' Minette pressed 'end' – what a horrible day – and waited for Gina to ring back. When she did, seconds later, Minette said, 'I mean it, Gina. I'll turn off my phone if you don't calm down.'

'Sorry. It's the last day of my holidays and we've been drinking all day. I'm just worried about Cath's safety, that's all. Sorry I came across a bit strong.'

'Hmm.'

'Please will you tell me what happened?'

'I rang him on my mobile.'

'That's great. OK. That makes it harder for him to find out where you are.'

'Well, surely he can't find out at all?'

'There are ways he can look up the phone number and find out who it's registered to,' Gina said.

'Oh god, really? Will it tell him my address?'

'Might do. It'll be on your contract.'

'But, hang on, if he can do that with my phone why can't he do it with Cath's? I know she speaks to him regularly, and Skypes with him.'

'She doesn't. I do all the liaison between them.'

Minette wondered how much of what Cath had told her was true. 'Actually, I don't have a phone contract, I'm on pay-as-you-go.'

'Seriously?' Gina laughed. 'Well, aren't you the sweet little student. We could be OK. Unless you just told him where you lived anyway?'

'No, of course I didn't. As soon as he called Cath and the kids by different names I knew something was up so don't worry, I didn't give anything away.'

'Don't suppose Cath's told you much about what happened in Harrogate.'

'I didn't even know she'd lived in Harrogate.'

'She takes a long time to trust people. Not surprising, after what she's been through.'

'Well, sure. But as I'm meant to be looking after the children, it would be useful to know some of this stuff.'

'Look, I'm back tomorrow morning. I'll come straight down and take over with the kids. I need to be there in case Andy does manage to work out where she is.'

Would Andy really turn up on Minette's doorstep? 'Should I be worried? Would he be, you know, violent?'

'I don't know. He might be. But he's working in Dubrovnik right now, if I remember his schedule rightly. He can't just drop everything and rush round to break down your door.'

Minette didn't feel greatly reassured. What a ridiculous

thing she had inadvertently got caught up in. You make one phone call, suddenly it's all violent men and crime scenes and Dubrovnik, a place name that always made her think of war even if it was peaceful now.

'Don't tell the kids anything, will you?'

'No, Gina, I'm not completely stupid. Despite what you called me.'

'Sorry. Hope you can forgive me. I'm famous for being rude when I'm plastered. I'll see you tomorrow and apologise in person.'

Minette hung up. It was gone six. She ought to get the children home and settled. She briefly outlined the conversation with Gina to Abe, who was amused rather than anxious, which made her feel better. 'We'll be OK, Dougie, I'll put a kitchen knife under my pillow.'

She kissed Tilly goodbye and took Cath's kids next door. Davey let them in with his key, and Minette went round turning on lights. It was chilly in the house, despite the warm weather, but Davey, in a rare lapse of knowledge, wasn't sure how to work the heating. 'We haven't turned it on yet,' he said. Minette was surprised to hear that, because when they first moved in, 11 April – the date engraved on her heart as the day the Miltons left – it had been cold.

'Mummy doesn't want to spend money on silly bills,' Lola said. 'We're saving up.'

'Do you have set bedtimes?' Minette wasn't sure what older children did.

'Lola goes to bed at seven, and I go at seven thirty and I read till eight.'

'And sometimes,' said Lola shyly, 'we have hot chocolate.'

'OK. Have you got the kind you're allowed, the type you mix with water?'

They went into the kitchen and Davey showed Minette where the hot chocolate was.

'Oh! But this is the kind you need milk for.'

Davey and Lola glanced at each other. Then Davey said, 'Lola isn't allergic to all milk.'

'Really?' said Minette, puzzled. She looked in the fridge. 'But this is just ordinary semi-skimmed.'

There was a piece of paper in Cath's handwriting, stuck to the fridge with a heart-shaped magnet, detailing Lola's allergies: symptoms, relative seriousness, other untried foods that might cause problems. It was quite terrifying.

'I know where the epi-pen is,' Lola said.

'God, Lola, I don't want to have to start using epi-pens and calling ambulances and god knows what.'

'I'll have hot chocolate,' Davey said, 'and Lola can have juice.'

'That's a great idea,' Minette said. 'I'll sort that, while you both get into your pyjamas. Then I can read you a story.'

They seemed excited by the idea of the story, and Lola

scampered upstairs to change. Maybe Cath didn't get time to read to them much. Abe had read to Tilly every night of her life, from when she was a few days old, prompting a raised eyebrow from Julie. But Tilly clearly loved being read to now. Minette wanted to ask Davey if he could get changed on his own, though god knows what she'd do if he said no. But he wheeled himself into his room and reappeared a couple of minutes later, wearing *Doctor Who* pyjamas. While they were choosing books she texted Liam, telling him not to come after all. Now she was here, it didn't seem right. She felt the urge to protect the children. God knows what horrible stuff they had experienced in their young lives.

She settled onto the sofa, Lola next to her, Davey in his chair on her other side. It was lovely reading to older children, who laughed in all the right places, and even read some of the words along with her. It would be amazing when Tilly was a bit older. In just three years she would be the same age as Lola, whose warm hand rested on Minette's shoulder as she craned to see the pictures. After a couple of stories, Lola asked for some more juice, and Minette took her cup into the kitchen for a refill. When she returned, Lola was full of suppressed giggles, and though Minette asked what was funny, Lola just shook her head. Minette supposed she wasn't usually allowed two glasses of juice.

At seven, Minette took Lola up and supervised her teeth-brushing. When Lola got into bed, she raised her face for a kiss. Feeling a bit awkward, Minette gave her a quick peck, but Lola's arms went round her neck and she was pulled in for a proper hug. She was warm, and smelled almost milky, like a baby. Minette said, 'If Mummy doesn't come home tomorrow, I'll take you both to see her, shall I?'

'I don't mind,' Lola said, letting Minette go and putting her arms round her toy panda.

Davey was waiting for Minette in the living room, a new book on his lap. He looked up at her with his familiar thoughtful expression. Minette felt sure there were some things he would like to tell her, and there was certainly a lot she'd like to ask him. But she reminded herself that, though he was old beyond his years, he was in fact only eight. She mustn't treat him like a little adult.

'I got this from school,' he said, as he handed her the book. It was called *Visiting My Daddy*. Minette looked at Davey questioningly and he looked blankly back. OK, then. She started to read. The story was illustrated with photos of a little girl called Moira, whose parents had divorced. It was one of those 'how to explain difficult issues to children' books that Minette remembered from her own childhood. She recalled a book, perhaps even in the same series, about having to go to the opticians, which her parents had read to her after her initial visit to get glasses. In Davey's book, Moira was sad because her daddy had moved away, and she and her brothers now lived only with their mother and a large number of pets. But by the end Moira had gone to stay with her dad – no new wife in the picture, Minette noted – and was all smiles.

Minette didn't know what to say. Things in Davey's life were clearly pretty complicated. 'Do you, uh, do you want to see your dad?'

'Yes.' The dark eyes held hers.

'I'm sure you will soon.'

'Mum doesn't want us to.'

'Oh. I'm sure she has good reasons.'

Davey didn't reply. Then Minette's phone rang, and she saw that it was Cath. Or Cath's number at least – maybe the nurse again? She sent Davey to the downstairs bathroom to do his teeth, and answered the call.

'Cath?'

'Yes. Just woke up about ten minutes ago.'

'How you feeling?'

'I'm all right, lass. How are the kids?'

'They're absolutely fine. I'm round your place with them. Lola's in bed and . . .'

'God, isn't Gina there? The nurse said you were going to phone her.'

'I did, but she's in Sheffield. She's coming back here tomorrow.'

'Oh god, oh god, I thought she was back. They won't let me out tonight.' Cath sounded quite panicked.

'Don't worry, I'll sleep here. I've already made up the spare bed.'

'You can't stay there, Minette.'

'Course I can. It's all sorted. Abe's with Tilly.'

'Davey and Lola will be perfectly all right on their own. Go home.'

'What are you talking about? I can't leave two small children in the house alone. I think it's illegal. Anyway, I don't want to! I'm really happy to be here. It's not putting me out at all.'

In a voice Minette barely recognised, Cath said, 'I'm not talking about putting you out, Minette. I'm telling you, I don't want you staying there.'

What the hell was going on today? Minette took the phone away from her ear and stared at it, as though it was a live snake.

'Hello? You still there?'

'Yes, Cath, just about.'

'Look. I'm going to ring Gina, see if she can get there tonight.'

'You're being bizarre. Even if she left Sheffield now and drove like the clappers, she wouldn't get here till about midnight.'

'That's fine. I'll get her to do that. Honestly, it's all right. Please leave, you can leave.'

Cath hung up, and Minette shook her head, breathless

with disbelief. She went to say good night to Davey. He was lying under the duvet reading the Moira book to himself. She had no idea how he'd got himself out of the chair, which was parked next to the bed, but presumably he was an expert at this.

'That was your mum. She, um, she seems to be feeling better.'

'OK.' Those dark eyes again! Minette searched for something neutral to say.

'I like that.' She pointed to a large US flag, which hung on the wall above Davey's bed. 'Have you been to America?'

'No. We've got relatives there. I thought we were going there when we left Gina's but we came here.'

'Oh, well, maybe you'll visit there some day. I've been to New York, I loved it.'

'Have you got photos?'

'Loads. I can show you them tomorrow if you like.'

'Yes, thank you.'

'Well, night then, love.'

As she got to the door, Davey said, 'You are staying here, aren't you?'

Minette wondered if he'd overheard her conversation with Cath.

'Of course! I'll be in your spare room. If you need me, can you get into the hall and shout up?'

'Yes. Night.'

She went upstairs to check on Lola, who was already asleep on her back, arms flung wide, the panda lying on her chest. Christ, Cath must have had a massive bump to the head to think that her children could be left alone at night! Minette heard her phone ringing in the kitchen and hurried down.

'Minette, I'm very worried. I spoke to Gina and she said you'd rung Andy.'

Christ. 'Yes, I'm sorry. I didn't know what to do at the time.'

'Gina doesn't think he can trace your address. She's really good at that stuff. So it looks like we're safe, for now.'

'Listen Cath, I'm sorry I rang him, but I had no idea that things were so bad between you.'

'I know. I promise I'll explain, when I get out of here. Anyway, Gina's too sloshed to drive, so she'll come tomorrow. But as I said before, there's no need for you to stay.' Cath's voice was light, as if her tone would detract from the oddness of what she was saying. Minette realised how easily she always accepted Cath's pronouncements, perhaps because of the confidence with which she delivered them. Even now, she had to fight all her natural instincts not to comply with an authoritative voice; she could almost hear herself saying, 'Of course, Cath, I'll leave them on their own if you say that's OK.'

Instead she answered, 'And as I said before, I will of course stay.'

There was a pause. 'I don't want you to, OK?'

'I hear you, but I don't think you're quite in your right mind. No offence.' Minette spoke calmly, as if to a child. 'So I will spend the night, and we can talk tomorrow.'

'Minette, please don't make me order you to leave my house.'

Minette laughed, it was so ridiculous. Who was this person? 'How you going to do that, Cath?' She added quickly, 'You're clearly concussed. Both kids are in bed and fine. Don't worry about anything, Cath, OK? Get some sleep. Bye.' Minette didn't wait for an answer, just turned her phone off. She felt as though she'd stepped into a bizarre through-the-looking-glass world, where nothing was quite as it seemed.

There was a knock on the front door. Fuck, what now? Suppose it was Andy? She peeped through the glass and saw it was Liam.

'Didn't you get my text?' she said, opening the door.

'Nice to see you, too. Can I come inside?' He smiled at their private joke, but Minette didn't smile back. She tapped on Davey's door, not wanting him to worry, and said, 'It's just Liam from next door, come to see how we're getting on.'

'OK,' Davey said.

She followed Liam into the kitchen. 'This is sexy, like having your boyfriend round while you're babysitting,' he said. 'So, what's happened to Cath, then?'

'A bike accident. They said it wasn't that bad, but I'm just off the phone to her and she was saying some pretty weird stuff.'

'I knew cycling was bad for the health. Least we won't have to pony up the sponsor money now.'

'Is that really your first thought?'

He held up his hands. 'Joke!'

'Hilarious. Anyway, I'm doing the triathlon too, remember.'

'I remember.' He put his arms round her and drew her in close. 'I expect you look super-hot in your Lycra.' He ran his hands round her waist, started trying to undo the button on her jeans. She pushed him away. 'I'm not feeling it, Liam. I'm worried about Cath's kids.'

'Aw, they're not going to say anything.'

'I don't mean that, I mean . . .'

'Come here.' Liam pulled her towards him, and kissed her on the mouth gently, then more forcefully. She wanted to pull away, then she didn't. God, whatever it was he did to her, it was bloody addictive. She thought of Cath saying 'he's your animus'. She whispered, 'Davey's in the room next door.'

'Well, let's go upstairs,' Liam said, smiling. 'He can't exactly come up and disturb us, can he?'

'I'm not enjoying your sense of humour this evening, Liam.'

'I can see that, Mrs Po-Face. But look, I'll be starting my course in a couple of months. Me and Josie are away half of July. We ought to carpe diem, oughtn't we?'

Minette knew he was right, but she couldn't completely shake her head of Davey and Lola. Liam undid a button on her shirt, and slipped his hand inside her bra. She shivered.

'What happened to "we'll all be dead in a hundred years"?' he said.

'Yes, fuck it, let's do it.' She let him lead her upstairs, push her onto the spare bed, and gently undress her. She lay passive while he moved down the bed and began kissing her inner thigh; soon his tongue flicked inside her and she felt herself grow warm, her whole body opening up to him. She closed her eyes, let the sensations wash over her.

When they crept downstairs, Minette looked in on Davey. To her relief, he was asleep; she could hear his steady breathing. Liam said he'd better split and she didn't argue. She closed the door quickly behind him, then locked it and turned her phone back on. There was a text from Abe sent at eight forty, which she quickly answered, so there wasn't a huge delay, and a long text from Cath saying that Minette should 'respect her wishes and leave the children be, they didn't need fussing'. Fussing? To have an adult in the house at night? Minette wondered just how well she really knew Cath.

Despite her afternoon nap, Minette felt shattered. Though it was still early she went upstairs intending to sleep. But then she saw that Cath's bedroom door was unlocked. On those occasions she'd stayed here with Liam she'd noticed that it had always been padlocked on the outside. The padlock was there, but hanging open on its chain. Presumably Cath had left it unlocked, thinking she'd be coming right back after her cycle ride. Before she could think too hard Minette opened the door and went in.

It was an ordinary room. Bed, wardrobe, bureau. A closed laptop was sitting on top of the chest of drawers. Minette tried to open the bureau but it was locked. Cath was into her security, clearly. Minette couldn't bring herself to open drawers, nor search through Cath's computer. What was she even looking for? Then she noticed what looked like a small fridge, sitting underneath the bureau. Weird, having a fridge in your bedroom. Maybe Cath liked that hotel touch. Minette pulled at the handle and opened the lid, releasing a great blast of freezing steam. Wow, it was cold in there – much colder than her freezer at home. She peered in, waving the steam away. All that was in it was a test-tube rack, the sort Minette remembered from science lessons. It was stacked with small glass vials. Cath pulled one out, but it was far too cold to hold, the sort of cold that can burn. She laid the vial down hastily on top of the bureau and carefully wiped the condensation off it with a tissue. It contained a dark red substance, blood, presumably. It must be something to do with one or other of the children's conditions. Weird thing to keep in your bedroom. Using the hem of her top to hold it Minette replaced the vial, shut the freezer and went out. After a moment's thought, she locked the padlock around the chain. Then she went into the spare room, slipped into the sex-scented sheets and fell asleep straight away, worn out by the strangeness of the day.

Four in the morning. A noise. Minette sat up in bed, straining to hear. Oh god, there it was again. Someone was moving about downstairs. There was a coldness in her throat. A burglar? Or maybe Andy had found them. Jesus. Come on Minette, get a grip. Most likely just Davey using the downstairs toilet. She turned on the torch app on her phone, and padded quietly downstairs. Yes, she could see the light on underneath the loo door.

Something made her look in Davey's room, and her heart thudded into her mouth; though it was dark, she could clearly see that his wheelchair was still by the bed. Fuck. It wasn't him in the toilet. She remembered that scene from *Pulp Fiction* when Bruce Willis goes back to his flat to get his father's watch, and realises that someone – John Travolta, it turns out – has broken in and is using his toilet. Bruce had a massive machine gun to deal with that situation, whereas all Minette could find in the hall was a long-handled umbrella. Clutching it, she sat on the stairs, where she could see the person who was going to come out of the loo before they saw her. If not Andy, perhaps it was Cath, absconded from hospital, come to throw Minette out. But the front door hadn't been opened, the bolt was still slid across. So someone might have come in the back door. Minette trembled, from a combination of cold and fear, realising she stupidly hadn't checked it was locked. The umbrella shook in her hand and she dropped it. Realistically, what was she going to do with it anyway? Even if it was Andy, who she had recast in her mind as a tall, bullet-headed neo-Nazi, she wouldn't be able to hit him or run him through with it. She had never hit anyone in her life.

The toilet flushed, and she stared at the door, every bit of her tense and alert. The door opened, and out stepped . . . Davey.

Minette had never been so astonished in her life.

Davey didn't see her at first. He was walking, unsteadily yes, but walking nonetheless, making his way back to his room. Then he saw her and stopped dead, rooted to the spot.

There was a moment's silence. They stared at each other.

He said, 'Don't tell Mum.'

'Don't tell Mum?' Minette repeated. She stood, spreading her arms towards him. 'But of course we must tell her! She'll be so excited! How long have you been able to . . .' Her voice died away, because she was starting to understand what he meant. Those steady, dark, sad eyes.

'She knows,' he said.

She knows.

Minette stepped forward and took him in her arms. He felt small and vulnerable as he leaned into her, his arms loose at his sides. She wished she could think of a different interpretation for his words. Quietly, gently, she said, 'Davey, do you mean, don't tell Mum I saw you walk?'

He nodded, a tiny movement of his head against her chest, barely there. She thought he might be crying. They stood together in silence for a couple of minutes. Minette's mind was racing, slamming into brick walls at every turn. At last she said, 'You'd better go back to bed. You're cold.'

'OK.' He stepped back, not looking at her. He *had* been crying. 'Night.' He went into his room and shut the door.

Minette sat on her bed, unable to think straight. She tried to work it out, went over every possibility. This, then, was why Cath had been so dementedly against her staying the night; she was terrified that Minette might find this out. Did that mean that Gina knew? Or would Davey have been more careful to hide the truth from Gina? Minette knew she would have to confront Cath. But how could she, without giving Davey away?

It was starting to get light. She got back into bed and lay on her back, thinking. But by the time Lola awoke, at six thirty, Minette had still got no further in deciding what she should do.

Chapter 18

Cath

The bruise on her right leg still ached, her shoulders were stiff, and she'd had another lousy night. Up to check on the children four times, finally falling into a horrible sleep, full of escalators that went down when she wanted to go up. But the triathlon was only just over a week off, and it was looking more important than ever that she do it, and do it well. She knew, from her 10Ks and other events, that a surprisingly large number of donations came in afterwards, when people saw the publicity.

Cath's running shoes felt as though they were full of cement, and it was one of the hottest days of the year so far, with a heavy blue sky and squinting bright sunlight. But she managed the full 5K without stopping, along the seafront and back. It was slow, but it was there. Sweat pouring off her, she walked straight into one of the touristy Brighton rock shops, and rewarded herself with a can of Coke.

So, she was ready. Good work, Cathykins. She could run five kilometres, swim thirty lengths, and she could even cycle 20K, though she was glad she didn't have to go near the bike till the actual day. Still, every cloud and all that: her tweets and blog about the bike accident had done wonders for sponsor pledges. She was up to more than £8,000 now. The most recent press release she'd written – 'Plucky mum vows to compete despite crash' – was coming out in the local paper today and should generate another wave of pledges.

Julia at Duchenne Together had rung to see how Cath was doing. She said, laughing, admiring almost, 'Every triathlete needs a gimmick,' then hastened to add that she obviously didn't advocate being knocked off your bike. Bit literal, was Julia. But bless her, she'd linked Cath's blog to the Duchenne Together Facebook page, which had thousands of friends who'd all shared it with their thousands of friends, plenty of whom had clicked to pledge.

When she walked down Sisley Street, Cath glanced at

Minette's house, expecting to see her and Tilly out on the bench in the sunshine, but there was no one there. Cath showered and made a sandwich. She was almost looking forward to hearing what Minette had to say; however bad, it would be a relief after the last three frustrating days. Gina hadn't been able to find out anything about the night Minette stayed over. Davey had completely clammed up, the little whatsit, and Lola, as usual, knew sweet Fanny Adams. Cath didn't trust Davey not to have done something daft. He was so keen to see his dad, he might forget their golden rule. Suppose Minette had let him talk to Andy on the phone? Cath's head ached at the thought of it. She just had to find out if anything had happened, and try and win Minette back round. Or, failing that, decide what to do.

Cath hoped she hadn't pushed Minette too far when she'd spoken to her from hospital. Hopefully she would understand that she'd been concussed, and not in her right mind. She remembered her saying as much at the time.

She'd tried again to ask Davey about it this morning. He wheeled himself into the kitchen, wearing his school uniform, a book in his hand. He went over to the cupboard where the cereal was kept, but Cath stood in front of it.

'Before you get settled, I need to talk to you.'

He pushed himself over to the table, and opened his book.

'Davey, can you put that away?'

He moved the book slightly out of reach, but she could

see that he was still trying to read it. She snatched it up and put it in the bin.

'Hey! That's a school book,' he said.

'Tough.'

He treated her to his sceptical Andy face. She'd retrieve the book later but there was no need to tell him that. 'Focus on me, please, Davey. The other night, did you remember our golden rule? What is it?'

'Don't tell anyone more than they need to know,' he intoned.

'That's right. So, what did you tell Minette? Anything she didn't need to know?'

He didn't say anything.

'Just tell me what happened, from the moment Minette collected you from school.'

'Don't remember.'

Stubborn little swine. 'Davey, you *will* remember if,' she searched round for something that was important to him, 'if you want to have breakfast.' She hated threatening, but honestly, it was blood out of a stone.

Davey glanced at the cupboard. He was always starving in the mornings. He took a deep breath. 'Mrs Wallis stayed with me when you didn't come. Then Minette came and I showed her the way to Busy Tigers. At Tilly's house, me and Lola and Tilly had pasta and watched CBeebies and played rummy with Abe.'

'Very good.' Cath opened the cupboard so Davey could see the cereal. She moved the Shreddies, his favourite, to the front. 'Then when did you go to our house?'

'After tea. We had stories, then went to bed.'

'Absolutely nothing else to tell me, Davey?'

'Oh. The man next door came round.'

'Abe?'

'No, the other one.'

Oh, did he now? 'Did you talk to him?'

'I was already in bed.'

Cath could work out the rest of that herself. She took down the Shreddies. 'OK. And then the next morning?'

'I woke up at six thirty-three. Minette gave us breakfast,' he said, looking meaningfully at the cereal, 'then we took Lola to Busy Tigers, then Minette took me to school. Gina collected me. Then you came home.'

Cath saw she wouldn't get any more. She had to hope that Davey was telling the truth. She kissed him and poured out a large bowl of cereal, which he started eating before she'd even put the milk in.

Now the kids were at school and Minette was fifteen minutes late. She said she'd be here at ten thirty. Every minute that passed made Cath feel more agitated. She unloaded the dishwasher, put the kettle on, and was just wondering if she ought to text again when there was a knock at the door. Minette was alone, looking flustered. 'Sorry I'm late.'

'Hey, don't worry! Lovely to see you.' Cath kissed Minette's cheek. Minette let her but didn't move towards her, or reciprocate. 'Where's my Tilly?'

'Home with Abe.'

'Well, I'm honoured you're using precious child-free time to come see me.'

'Mmm.'

This was going to take a bit of work. 'Cup of tea?'

'No, thanks.'

'Or water? I need some. Rehydrating after my run.'

'You're still doing the triathlon?'

'Of course! I've raised loads of money, local businesses are sponsoring me. I'm all over the Duchenne Together website. It's not that bad anyway, I'm just a bit bruised.'

'What happened?'

They sat at the kitchen table, opposite each other in their usual seats.

'Someone in a parked car opened their door on me and I just came straight off the bike.'

Minette winced.

'It might have been so much worse. I could have been run over but the car coming along stopped in time.'

'Were you unconscious?'

'Must have been. I remember turning into the London

Road, then I don't remember anything till I woke up in hospital.' Cath wasn't going to tell Minette – or anyone – how much more she could remember. She launched into her prepared speech. 'I was so grateful to you for looking after the kids on Monday.'

'Yeah?' Minette laughed, shakily. 'You could have fooled me.'

'You're angry with me. I'm so sorry.'

'Are you surprised, Cath? You were so weird about the whole thing, and rude, actually.'

Oh, was I, actually?

'The thing is, I was concussed,' Cath said. 'The nurse was cross with me for talking to you. I wasn't supposed to ring anyone.'

'Well, I wish you hadn't. You really upset me. And Gina was just as bad.'

'She's a bull in a china shop sometimes.'

'You both are.'

Minette wasn't being quite as politely restrained as Cath had expected. Well, good for her. 'I'm really sorry, Minette.'

Minette took a deep breath, before starting what Cath recognised as her own prepared speech. 'You know, Cath, I thought I was doing you a favour by picking up the kids. And you clearly expected that I would, because you'd put my name down as a contact.'

'I had to give two names, and we'd only just moved here and I didn't know many people.'

'Don't you think you ought to have mentioned it? It came as a complete surprise.'

Cath leaned across the table and put her hand on Minette's arm. 'You're right, I should have. It just slipped my mind. I know I keep saying I'm sorry, but I am. And another thing I'm sorry about is not giving you more background about me and Andy, before you got an ear-bashing from Gina. Can I tell you now? Being honest with you is the least I can do to make it up to you.'

Minette sat back in her chair and folded her arms. 'Go on.'

Cath marshalled her thoughts, working out the best way to start. Well, the beginning, of course. 'Gina and me go way back, you know. We were at school together in Eastbourne. I lived with her and her parents for a few years, after my mum died. Gina got married young, she didn't pick well. This was years ago, I was in Birmingham and I didn't see her that often. Then one time I dropped in unexpectedly and couldn't believe the state of her. Bruises everywhere. Broken arm. Gave me all that walked-into-a-door crap, and I got her out of there, it weren't pretty, but she got out. That man she married, well he's dead now and he's definitely not in the upstairs department, if you know what I mean.'

'I'm sorry for Gina. But you were telling me about Andy?'

'Sure I can't do you a drink? I'm going to have one.'

'No, thanks.'

Cath put the kettle on. 'Gee and me, we made a pact that we would never stay with a man who laid a finger on us. And we've stuck to it. Well, she's never been with another bastard, 'scuse my language. Not saying I like her boyfriends cos I don't, usually. Ryan for instance, he . . .'

She thought she heard Minette sigh, and she moved on quickly. 'Anyway, Andy and me had a good marriage, I thought. I'm skipping a lot here. I never thought he was the violent type, not at all. Then one night, back in, where we lived then, Troubletown . . .'

'Harrogate?'

'Yes. We had a massive row and he walloped me.' Cath's face darkened, thinking of it. 'Have you ever been hit?'

'No.' Minette looked concerned, for the first time.

'You can't imagine what it's like. The shock. No way as I saw it coming. One minute this man is your other half, you're a team. The next you're on the floor, your face hurts like buggery and he's standing there, you don't even recognise him.'

The kettle clicked and she stood up, poured water into a mug.

'Actually, please could I have a cup, Cath?'

'Of course.' Thank god for that.

'Gina told me he hit the children.' Minette said it fast, like she wanted it out of her mouth.

Cath hesitated, weighing up how much to tell Minette. She'd spoken to Andy, after all, and who knew what he had said. She put the mugs down on the table. 'He did love those kids very much.'

'I sense a but.'

'But Davey heard us fighting, came in, tried to stop us, got in the middle, and he got hit too.' It was the truth, after all. Cath had hardly ever spoken about this, apart from to Gina, and briefly in an email to Verna. It was good to say it, hear the words out loud.

Minette looked like she might cry. 'That's just terrible. Poor, poor Davey.'

'Next morning Andy had to go away for work, and while he was gone I took the kids, we came down south and stayed with Gee for a while. Some friends got out the furniture I needed, like Davey's bed and that. Finally Andy sent through some money and we put the deposit down on this place.'

'So you aren't in contact with him anymore? Skyping him every week, that's not true?'

'No.' Cath stared at her hands. 'I shouldn't have told you that. I was embarrassed. I haven't spoken to him since we left. He pays the mortgage but he sends the money to Gina.'

'And you've all changed your names?'

'Andy told you a lot, didn't he? What else did he say?'

'I don't know what to think, Cath. Half of what I thought

I knew about you turns out not to be true, including your name. Your real name's Ruby, isn't it?'

'Please don't take it personally.' Cath felt on the verge of tears. 'I just don't tell anyone what's gone on with Andy. I've been so ashamed about it.'

'You shouldn't be ashamed if he was violent.'

'I am, though, lovie. Everyone thought we were great together, that we had a perfect family. Even though we all know that there's no such thing. All families have their secrets.' She didn't look at Minette when she said this. 'Davey's too young to understand any of this. I know that if I left him for five minutes with the internet he'd track Andy down, and he'd come after us. I have to lock the computer in my room.'

Minette remembered seeing the laptop when she'd gone into the room. She wanted to ask about the freezer, but didn't want Cath to know she'd been in there. She asked instead, 'So is that why he can't use computers? It's not anything to do with his muscular dystrophy?'

Cath shook her head, no.

Minette exhaled. 'Heavens, Cath, this is a tangled web. You really ought to explain some of this to Davey.'

'But you can't tell a kid not to love his dad, can you? Even if that dad is bad for him.'

Minette sipped her tea. 'Cath, there's one more thing I need to talk to you about.'

'Sounds ominous.' Cath smiled, her heart pounding. Here it came.

'When I was looking after the children, I saw Davey walking.'

'Oh yes, well of course, he can walk a tiny bit. You know that, right? If he has to get out of his wheelchair and into a chair that's not right next to it, he can do a few steps.' Cath wasn't entirely unprepared for this. From the moment Minette had insisted on staying over, Cath knew there was the possibility of her seeing things she wouldn't understand. She felt the familiar groundswell of anxiety begin, making her breathless, and she told it to lie down. *Not now*. But she knew you couldn't make anxiety go away just by wishing it. Gina's mum understood that. She suffered a little from anxiety herself.

'This didn't seem like a few steps. It looked like proper walking.'

Slow down the breaths, Fay used to say. Make sure you exhale all the air. That's it. That's what I do to get my breathing back. Then I tell myself, I'll deal with this in just a minute. Hold it in till I'm on my own, in a safe place, then I let the feelings come out. That way, I don't say or do anything I might regret.

Cath forced herself to slow down her out-breath. 'Well, Minette, it wasn't proper walking. He has muscular dystrophy. He was wobbly on his feet, wasn't he?'

'Yes, but . . .'

'In a year or so he won't even be able to do those couple of steps.'

'Cath, he said . . .'

'What did he say?' Cath took another slow, calming breath, and said more gently, 'He's a little boy, Minette. He doesn't have any idea what's going on.'

'If I tell you, I want your solemn oath that you won't be angry with him.'

'Is that what you think of me?'

'I don't honestly know what I think, right now.'

'Scout's honour.' Cath did the salute, trying to keep her tone light.

'He said you know he can walk.'

Minette sat back with the expression of someone who's done their bit. Oh, the confidence of her middle-class certainty. It's not me who's screwing around, lovie, Cath thought, so you can take that self-satisfied look right off your face. She swallowed this down in less than a second, and said, 'Let me tell you about Davey. He was four when he started limping. I knew straight away what it was, I'd just been nursing a kid with Duchenne and his mother told me it began with a limp. And in a fortnight Davey went from being able to walk upstairs to being full-time in a wheelchair. With the diagnosis comes a shortened life expectancy, did you know that? He'll have to have his back straightened when he's older, to prevent his spine from crushing his lungs. But even so, he probably won't make it past thirty.'

'Cath, you're shouting.'

Minette was staring at her, and Cath quickly pulled it together. 'Sorry for going on,' she said, in a normal volume. 'Bit upset. You've just misunderstood, lovie. He can walk a tiny bit, that's it. That's what he means, when he says that I know.'

Minette looked at her watch, and stood up. 'I'll have to take over from Abe, he's got to go to work.'

'I'd hate that you were thinking badly of me,' Cath said, trying not to sound desperate. She followed Minette to the front door. 'Are we all right?'

'Yes. I just need to have a think.'

'Of course.' Cath knew she needed to let Minette go, much as she wanted to force her to stay, to talk until she convinced her. 'It's been very weird for us, having to start a whole new life. I wish I'd told you more before. I don't always know who I can trust.'

'I don't either. I'm really sorry you've had such a horrible time.'

Cath felt sure Minette wouldn't want hostility between them. 'Thank you. I knew you'd understand what it's like to face aggression, after your experience with the Miltons.'

Minette said coolly, 'Well, I wouldn't say it was quite the

same thing.' She opened the door, said, 'See you,' and went out without a kiss.

Cath went back into the kitchen and sank into a chair. *Let the feelings come out.* A net was closing round her. Andy was a loose cannon. God knows what he had told Minette. For the dozenth time she cursed herself for leaving his number on her phone, or at least for not hiding it more subtly than 'Hubby'. She assumed it would be protected by the passcode but somehow the hospital had managed to get past that. She was so exhausted, she could barely lift her hand to push a loose strand of hair behind her ear.

How blissful it had been to wake up in hospital. For those first few minutes, before she knew they would insist on keeping her in, going so far as sedating her 'for your own safety', she was the happiest she had been for months. Maybe years.

She'd seen the car door opening ahead of her in slow motion. She had time to stop. It was a split-second decision not to. She didn't know she was going to let fate sweep her along until she did it. She was just so damn tired of keeping everything going. She knew that if she didn't brake there would be a short period of not being in control. That desire, to hand over responsibility, overwhelmed her, stopped her thinking about the pain. She loved being in control. But she sometimes hated it too. The door opened, making the decision for her, and knocked her off the bike, a whooshing sound as she arced into the air, patch of blue sky, feathery clouds, mackerel clouds her mother used to call them, she thought she heard her mother saying, 'Oh my little one, let me kiss it better,' and then she woke in the clean white sheets of a hospital bed, a familiar smell and bustle around her. Nurses. Busy, careful hands keeping her safe. Home.

She'd only made two slight miscalculations. Firstly, she'd not took into account how terrified of lawsuits hospitals were now. Five years ago she'd have been allowed out, soon as she said she felt fine. Now they couldn't risk the tiny chance that she might black out on the way home and sue the backside off them. Secondly, she'd got wrong by one day Gina's holiday dates. So hard to remember everything. So hard, when you're tired.

Come on, little one. Feel better for mummy. Right. Onwards. There was a lot to do. She was just going to have to move faster, that was all. She'd reckoned to being here between six months and a year. So what if it was three months? Verna had made it clear that she was completely flexible.

Cath logged onto her site to blog her latest training stats, and checked the current total amount: £9,245. The newspaper must have come out, that was another big jump. Put that together with all the other money: the quiz, sponsorship, Minette's pledges, and the nursery, and it would be pushing eighteen grand. She'd been really pleased about the nursery, that had turned out better than she expected. And then there was Liam. She hadn't even spoken to him yet. She needed to find the right moment.

She got everything ready that she needed for Davey's appointment, then drove to school to collect him. On the way she stopped at a garage to buy the *Hove Gazette*. Her article was on page five, accompanied by two large photos she'd sent them: one of cute Jerry in the wheelchair, the other of a mangled bike. Not her bike, sure, and not her child, but no one would check. She smiled when she saw that they'd printed the complete url of the 'Doing it for Davey' page. They really were desperate to fill the space.

Chapter 19

Davey

Davey's mum collected him from school in the middle of a spelling test, so he wasn't sorry to leave. He knew he'd got 'disappointed' wrong. His mum was quiet all the way to Haywards Heath. All she said was, 'We've got to get this right, Davey, OK?'

'OK,' he said.

The clinic was very white and there were comics and his mum let him buy a KitKat from the machine. The doctor, a lady, took them into a room and asked his mum lots of questions. Davey got bored, so he told Adam his five favourite doctors.

1. The one in Harrogate who gave him six stickers when he was only meant to have one. Plus he let Davey have a go at listening to Lola's chest with the stethoscope.
2. Dr Barry in Accident and Emergency, that wasn't for him, it was when Lola had eaten tuna. He had funny eyebrows he could wiggle and he told them lots of knock-knock jokes. The best one was Knock Knock! Who's there? Interrupting cow. Interrupt . . . Then you had to say moo! You had to say it quickly before they finished saying interrupting cow. He told it to his dad later and his dad laughed, and said, 'That's a good one!'
3. Dr Patel who fitted him with his wheelchair and said Davey got the hang of it very quickly.
4. The one at Eastbourne when they were at Gina's, and they'd run out of steroids. That doctor kept saying, 'I don't think this boy should be on steroids, they are not necessary.' His mum said all huffy, 'No offence doctor, but his specialist at our last hospital would disagree with you.' And the doctor said, 'We are all only human and doing our best, madam.'
5. The doctor in Liverpool, he couldn't remember much about her because they moved away when he was little, but she had long swishy hair and a smiley face.

When Davey started concentrating on the doctor again, he realised his mum was getting a bit upset. 'I have explained all this a hundred times already,' she said.

'I understand, Ms Brooke,' the lady said. She wore a red shirt and black trousers. She had three patterned gold rings on one hand, and her name badge said Dr Chowdry. 'I know it is annoying to have to repeat yourself. But please bear with me, as I want to go through it for my own satisfaction. So Davey has not yet had his muscle biopsy?'

'Yes, in our last town, but we don't have any record of it! When will you people do any kind of joined-up working? I already told Dr Persaud and Dr Ogueh in Brighton about our situation, and they agreed we could postpone the repeat biopsy.'

'That is fine.' The doctor made a note on her paper. 'I'm scheduling it for six months' time. Now, without the biopsy we are going to have to do the diagnostic blood test.'

'Just to let you know, doctor, that his last creatine kinase test showed clearly the very high levels in his blood.'

The doctor looked at Davey's mum with a serious expression, like a teacher. Davey felt excited. Was she going to tell his mum off?

'Ms Brooke, in the absence of Davey's records, we obviously have to do the test again.'

His mum sighed and said, 'Well, I suppose you can't just take my word for it.'

'Not really, no.'

'Typical NHS bureaucracy.' Davey realised his mum was now in a good mood. 'Worse than when I was nursing, and it was bad enough then.'

The doctor laughed. 'Ah yes, where would we be without our paperwork, eh?' She didn't, Davey noticed, ask his mum about being a nurse, like most other doctors did.

She turned to Davey. 'How are you getting on at school, Davey?'

'All right.'

'He's at mainstream school, yes?'

Davey's mum nodded.

'OK Davey, so you are going to see a few different doctors today, I'm sorry about that. One will take a blood test, the physiotherapist will look at your legs and give you some exercises to try, then we will check whether you are on the appropriate medication. The dose of prednisolone, the steroid you are on,' she looked at her paper, 'is quite strong but on the other hand you do seem to have good muscle strength so maybe they are helping with that. We will take some X-rays of your back to check the steroids are not causing bone problems.'

'Jumping snakes, Davey, we'll be here all day.'

'I hope not.' The doctor smiled. 'Please take a seat back outside.'

Davey added the doctor to his list of top five, replacing

the swishy-haired doctor. He liked the way she spoke to his mum, as if she wasn't afraid of her.

Back in the waiting room, his mum said, 'Come in the loo, I need a pee.' They went into the disabled loo together, and his mum locked the door. She unzipped her bag and took out some cotton wool and white tape. 'Give me your arm, lovie.' Davey held out his arm and his mum rolled up his sleeve. 'There's not enough room in here to swing a cat, is there?' Just above his elbow she put a piece of cotton wool and stuck it in place with the tape. 'It's totally unnecessary to repeat the test, we've done it before.' She rolled his sleeve back down. Then she went back into her bag and took out a little glass tube.

'Here's one I prepared earlier.' She grinned and put it in her pocket. 'Now I just need to see what initials they put on these, and which colour lid, and then we're done.'

'Shall we tell them?'

'No, lovie, we won't. I won't, and you won't either, OK? We don't want to have a blood test if we don't need to, do we? A horrid scratchy needle?' His mum held his chin in her hand, and turned his face to look at her. 'Can I just remind you again of our golden rule, Davey? Do you understand?'

'Yes.'

'Sometimes I'm not sure you do. What was going on in

your mind, for instance, when Minette stayed that night?' Her face was very close to his. He could see the pattern of lines underneath her eyes, like a noughts-and-crosses grid, and big holes on her skin. Pores, they were called. 'You must have been pretty noisy for her to wake up.'

'I needed the loo.'

'Funny how you never normally need it in the night.' He couldn't move his face to look away, so he turned his eyes up to the ceiling.

'Hmm,' she said. She let go his chin. 'Remember, lovie.' She pretended she was zipping up her mouth. 'Zip! That's what I do.'

They went back outside, and Davey's mum went over to the desk to look at the blood bottles. She took a yellow lid when no one was looking, and went into the loo again to write on the label. When she came out, Davey watched as she carefully put the sample in the box on the desk.

A different doctor examined Davey's legs. 'The calf muscles are in very good shape,' he said. 'If anything, they are smaller than we would expect. Many children with muscular dystrophy have enlarged calf muscles.'

'I know,' Davey's mum said. 'I'm a paediatric nurse.'

'Oh, are you?' the doctor said, all smiley.

'Well, I'm not working at the moment of course, got enough on my plate right now.'

The doctor patted Davey's head. 'Well young man, you're clearly in very good hands here.' He showed Davey some ankle exercises. Davey copied the doctor, and was told how very good he was at them. 'Please encourage him to do these, Ms Brooke,' he said. 'Try and make them fun and part of the daily routine.'

'Of course, doctor,' Davey's mum said.

Davey wanted to tell the doctor that he didn't need the exercises, that every morning and every night he practised walking round and round his bedroom. He didn't want to forget how to do it. But he thought the golden rule would probably say not to. Instead, he said that he liked the doctor's watch. It was silver, with three little clocks on its face. Davey liked those extra clocks.

'You're an observant boy,' the doctor said. 'It's a Breitling, a gift from a grateful patient.' He looked at Davey's mum and laughed. 'A grateful and wealthy patient!'

They went back to the waiting room, and after a while a nurse said she would take a blood sample.

'Oh!' Davey's mum said, all smiling and surprised, 'We've already had one.'

'Really?' The nurse's badge said Helen McLaine. 'That's odd.'

'Show the nice nurse, Davey,' his mum said, and Davey rolled up his sleeve so she could see the place where his mum had put the cotton wool and tape. 'It was another nurse,' his mum went on. 'I don't know her name. She had the initials SR?'

'That'd be Stella. She was here first thing but she's gone off to do another clinic.'

'Yes, that's what she told us. We were one of her last ones.'

'I thought she'd already left when I came in.' The nurse looked from her clipboard to Davey's arm. 'Hang on a minute.' She went over to the desk.

'Sit tight, Davey,' his mum said. She looked at a magazine on her lap. It was open at a page which said, 'Get ready for bikini season!' Her leg was jiggling up and down underneath it, and she rubbed her arm as though she was cold. The nurse came back and said, 'Sorry about that. Typical communication breakdown! The sample is there, so we can tick that one off.'

'Great,' Davey's mum said. 'I'm a nurse, though not working at the moment, so I know how hectic the handover gets sometimes.'

'So true. Where were you last nursing? Do you miss it?'

'I miss it like anything. I love it so much. Love everything about it.'

'Ha, you've forgotten some of the bad bits. I still don't really like phlebotomy, I wouldn't mind dropping that . . .'

They started talking, and Davey repeated 'phlebotomy' to himself. It had the word 'bottom' in it, and he wanted to remember it so he could make Lola laugh.

There were more doctors, and his mum had to fill in questionnaires, and he had another KitKat, and then they left. His mum sang along to the radio on the way home. In between songs she kept saying 'Finally! We can get a diagnosis again, Davey, stop all the mucking about.'

They collected Lola from nursery. When they were getting out of the car at home, they saw Minette and Abe coming down the street with Tilly. Davey's mum was all chatty to them but Davey could see that Minette wanted to go. She gave him a big smile. Davey thought about Abe playing rummy with him and Lola, about Minette reading him a story. He wondered what it would be like to be Tilly and live in that house with them.

Lola was excited to go on the computer. Davey sat with her while she played Super Mario. It had been a long time since he'd heard anyone say the name 'Adam' out loud. Lola used to slip up and call him by it all the time. Then for a while she called him 'he'. But now she called him Davey without thinking. He whispered, 'Lola, do you remember my name?'

Her eyes staring straight ahead at the screen, she said, 'Davey.'

'No, I mean the name I had before.'

'I don't know.'

It was all going to be down to him.

Chapter 20

Minette

Minette fell asleep almost immediately. There was so much going round in her head, she just shut down like an overtaxed computer. But now the early morning June sun poured into the room, waking her and flooding her with the worries of the previous day. They came at her one after the other: Davey walking out of the bathroom, that fraught encounter with Cath, four days' silence from Liam. Minette rolled onto her back, stared at the blue blur of lampshade, and let out an involuntary groan.

Abe whispered, 'What's wrong, Dougie?'

'Oh! I didn't know you were awake.'

'You've been restless all night.'

'God, have I? Sorry. I didn't mean to disturb you.'

'I know that. Come here.'

Minette turned on her side to face him and he put his arms round her. He was warm, the feel of his body familiar and comforting.

'You've been in a funny mood lately. Why don't you talk to me? Maybe I can help.'

Minette felt a lump in her throat. She knew she'd let herself become distant from him. She had sort of fallen in love with someone else, and now it seemed that the someone else was backing away. Where did that leave her and Abe?

'It's a long story.'

'I'm in no hurry.'

So she told him about seeing Davey walking, and the strange thing he said, and Cath's defensiveness about it.

'Jesus, Dougie, this is massive. Was it just a few steps that you saw?'

'I don't honestly know. Sort of. He made it from his bed to the bathroom and back. I supposed it depends on your definition of a few. He was unsteady, that's certain.'

'Anyone would be unsteady if they spent all day sitting down.'

'I know. But also, I feel awful for Cath, because you were right, they've changed their names because the husband was violent.'

'Those poor kids. Being in a violent relationship can make people do weird things. But why would she pretend Davey can't walk? I'm struggling to come up with an explanation.'

'And you've seen a lot of strange people.'

'Well, look. We have to do something.'

Minette liked that 'we'. She pressed herself closer to Abe, and found that he had a hard-on. She stroked him, gently, expecting him to push her hand away, as he had so often during the last year. But instead he pulled her closer towards him and kissed her, properly, on the mouth, and because it had been so long it felt unfamiliar and exciting, almost a stranger's kiss. In a few minutes they were making love, and though she couldn't say in truth that it was as good as with Liam, nowhere near, it was still good. And afterwards was better, because there was no guilt, no racing heart, no fear of discovery. For a few minutes, as they lay in each other's arms, the world seemed the right way up again.

'That was nice to come back to, after a bit of a gap,' Abe said, and Minette knew that was the most she would get out of him about the drought.

'I guess we felt awkward with those horrible people next

door listening to our every move,' she offered, and he eagerly agreed.

They lay cuddled together until Tilly began her morning yodelling. Minette usually had a lie-in on Saturdays, but this morning she wanted to get moving. She made tea for herself and Abe, put on her dressing gown and took her cup outside, to the bench. She looked up at Cath's house, wondering what the hell was going on in there, and a movement caught her eye. There was someone at the round window, the one that overlooked them. Minette shaded her eyes because the sun was making her squint, and also to show the person at the window that she was watching them. Was it Cath? She couldn't tell. Then the dark figure put their hand flat on the glass, as if saying hello, and she saw it was Davey.

All this time, it had been Davey, watching her from that window. And all this time, he had been trying to tell her something. She knew how high the window was; she'd looked out of it herself when she'd been in Cath's house. It was too high for him to see out of, if he was sitting down.

Minette, look. I can stand.

Minette waved, and the hand against the glass moved, a tiny bit. You could just about call it a wave. Then he disappeared. She watched for a while longer but he didn't return.

Abe came out and set Tilly gently down on the little patch of grass. He sat close to Minette, and they watched Tilly examine and dissect a series of daisies as though they held the secrets of the universe.

'Here's what I think we should do,' Abe said. 'Phone Cath's ex again.'

'Really?'

'Yes. We're not going to get an unbiased account from anyone. Cath's too embedded in whatever this thing is, the children are too little. We might as well find out the husband's story.'

'What would I say to him?'

'Be honest. Tell him straight, say you've heard that he hit Cath, and you want to get his take on it.'

'What if he is a wife-beater, though?'

'Well, what can he do to you over the phone?'

Minette hadn't told Abe about Gina and Cath's paranoia about being traced. She decided to keep that to herself, for fear of worrying him.

'Plus, even wife-beaters are also people. Bad people, maybe, but they are sometimes worth listening to.'

'Get you, Mr Citizens Advice.'

'Should have gone into social work, shouldn't I?'

'You'd have been brilliant.'

He slid an arm round her and pulled her in for a kiss. She closed her eyes, the sunlight flickering under her eyelashes. Having sex had made her feel tender towards him, for the first time in forever. Maybe he felt the same.

They broke apart when Tilly called out, 'Dud-ud,' her new word, which Abe was thrilled by every time. He admired the dismembered daisy in Tilly's palm. 'Well done, darling,' he said. 'Can you do the bindweed now?'

Minette said, 'I saw Davey at that window a few minutes ago.'

Abe turned to look. 'Interesting . . . you sure it was him? OK, so, playing devil's advocate, Cath could have carried him upstairs, and he could have been leaning against something. Maybe his condition's not so bad yet, perhaps he can stand if there's something to support him?'

'Oh god, it's all so complicated.'

'Go phone the wife-beater. Don't stay on too long.'

'Why?'

'I know it sounds a bit *In the Line of Fire*, but I think the longer you're on the phone, the easier it might be for him to trace you.'

'Jesus, Abe.'

'Not that he'll be trying to, of course. Don't worry. We need to hear from him.' He stretched his legs out in front of him. 'Good idea of mine, to put the bench here.' It was his way of finally apologising about the stupid row they'd had over it.

Minette sat on her bed and turned off 'show caller ID' on her phone, which she now knew how to do, though it was pointless as Andy already had her number.

He picked up on the first ring, with, did she imagine it, a slightly desperate 'Hello?'

Minette's mouth was dry. 'Um, hi Andy, it's Minette, we spoke the other day.'

'Thank you, thank you so much for phoning back. I'm so sorry about my idiotic answerphone messages.'

'That's OK. I've been thinking a lot since we spoke, and there are some things I want to ask you, is that all right?'

'Yes, absolutely.'

Minette relaxed a little. If he was a wife-beater, he was a very polite one.

'So, uh.' She couldn't leap straight in. Thank god for small talk. 'Are you still in Dubrovnik?'

'I'm about 2,000 kilometres further east. You heard of Vileyka?'

It sounded nice and far away. 'No, but I'm terrible at geography.'

'It's, well I suppose it's a town, I haven't seen much of it. It's in Belarus.'

'God, that sounds pretty remote.'

'It is. Terrific mobile signal though. Talking of which, isn't this call going to cost you a fortune?'

'I've got this bolt-on deal thing for international calls. My mother lives in France.' Too much information, Minette! 'How much longer are you away?'

'Another week or so. I take longer jobs now there's no one

to come home to.' He coughed. 'Zig-zagging about as far as Georgia, eight drop-off points on the way back.'

'So, you really are a lorry driver, then?'

'Yes, why?'

'Well.' Minette took a breath. 'Things seem to be rather unclear here, and I'm trying to work out what's true and what's not. I'm going to jump right in, so forgive me if this seems a bit personal. Understatement, sorry. Ruby said,' Minette congratulated herself for remembering to say the right name, 'that you had, er, hit her and that's why she left.'

There was a silence. She could hear him breathing. Oh god, suppose it wasn't true. Jesus! 'Hello? Andy?'

'I'm still here. That's very hard for me to answer.'

'Well, I don't want to sound like a lawyer, but either you did, or you didn't.'

He let out a long breath. 'Yes. I did hit her. Once.'

'Once is enough, I guess.' So it was true. Minette felt terrible she'd doubted Cath.

'The right question here, I think, is why did I hit her?'

'Excuse me, but that's not the right question.' Minette was clear on this point. He'd hit his wife, he was not to be trusted, there was nothing to be gained from continuing the conversation. She was about to start wrapping up the call when he said, 'I think there is, maybe, one excuse.'

Minette had always prided herself on being a feminist. So, she might be a stay-at-home mother now, cooking pastry from scratch and freezing homemade purees. But that was her choice. And as a feminist, there were unwritten rules she held to be self-evident. No means no; women can wear whatever they like; a woman doing the same job as a man should get the same pay; and there's never a justification for hitting a woman.

'There's never, ever, any excuse.'

She was already starting to take the phone away from her ear when he said, 'Not even to protect my child?'

'I'm sorry?' Minette sat up straight.

'I admit it, I lost my temper, there were a dozen other ways I could have handled it, but I just got that red mist. My tiny girl, my Ezzie.'

Abe put his head round the door. Minette gestured him in, and discreetly slid the phone onto speaker.

'What happened to Esmie?' Minette said.

'She has a lot of allergies,' Andy said. 'For instance, she can't drink milk.'

'I know.'

'What a palaver that was, when she was tiny, god bless her. Soya milk, rice milk, all disgusting, poor little kid. Anyway, a few months ago I'm in some crummy hotel near Leipzig, and I Skype with Ruby after her night shift, and she's in that weird a mood I feel worried. She says something's happened at work, something to do with a kid she was fond of, Darren. He had leukaemia, I think. She keeps saying, I told them it was serious, no one believed me. She's not herself, she's all worked up, can't sit still, keeps walking away, forgetting that we're on Skype. The kids were with my parents, thank god. I'd only seen her like this once before, years ago back in Birmingham, when a kid called Libby died and she was in a total state.'

Minette said, 'I thought you were telling me about Esmie.'

'Yes, sorry. I'm a rambler, Ruby always says I come at a story from three miles away. I'm trying to explain. So Ruby's not expecting me back for a couple of days but I feel that worried about her I drive fourteen hours straight, I just want to get home. So it's late, ten, I think, I'm knackered, and when I come in there's Esmie, sitting in the kitchen with a hot drink. All pleased to see me. "I couldn't sleep, she says, so Mummy made me hot chocolate. Try it, it's yummy." "It's all right sweetheart," I say, "I don't like soya milk, you know that." "Oh, she says, there wasn't any soya so Mummy made it with proper milk." So I try it, and it does taste like proper milk, and I go to the fridge, show her the milk carton, she says, "Yes, that's the one." So I'm trying not to panic, don't want to upset her, I calmly get the epi-pen. Then Ruby comes in wearing a towel, she's been having a bath, shocked to see me home, says, "What do you need the epi-pen for?" I say, "Has that hot chocolate got proper milk in?" She starts denying it, but there's no soya milk in the house and no empty carton in the bin, so she can't explain what happened.'

Minette was bewildered. 'Oh my god, how could she, did she forget about the allergy or something?'

'I haven't told you the best bit yet.' Now he'd started talking, Andy couldn't seem to stop. 'I tell Ruby, "Never mind that for now, I'll give her the epi-pen then we'll get her to A&E," but before I can do anything Ruby kind of crumples. Instead of helping me she sits at the table, she says, "Look, we're all tired, she'll be OK." I yell, "She won't be OK!" I'm properly stressed now, I get the lid off the epi-pen, then Ezzie goes, "But Daddy, I've had this kind of milk before."'

He stopped, out of breath. Minette knew she ought to hang up, she'd been on for ages. If he was tracing her call he could have easily done it by now. But she had to know what happened. 'Go on.'

'She'd drunk most of it, the worst symptoms would have showed by now, breathing problems, vomiting. I'd read a lot about allergies, as you can imagine.'

'So . . . what on earth?' Minette stared at Abe, sitting next to her on the bed.

'Ruby's got nothing to say, so I take Esmie up and tuck her in, tell her to call me if she feels ill. Then I go down, say, "Well what the hell, Ruby, what's going on?" She's the one who got Esmie's allergies diagnosed at the hospital, she's the one who's always been so on top of it. There's a note on our fridge about it. It's still there, I didn't want to take it down in case they . . . well, anyway. First she says, "Look, she wanted hot chocolate, and you know how she whinges, and I'm knackered, and you're away all the time." So now it's my fault. I say, "But just because a child whinges . . ." then she says, "Well, actually it's fine because Esmie's grown out of her milk allergy." "What, I say, why didn't you tell me?" "It only just happened," she says. But something's not right, and I ask her lots of questions and finally she bursts into tears, I'd hardly ever seen her cry like that before, proper sobbing, and she says Esmie isn't allergic to milk. Isn't allergic now, never has been.'

'Jesus, Andy.' Minette remembered Davey and Lola the other night, Davey's awkward explanation that some milk was fine. Lola had been very giggly, and smelled milky when Minette had hugged her at bedtime. She must have sneaked some of Davey's hot chocolate, presumably with his agreement.

'I shout at Ruby, so is Ezzie allergic to any of the other things: nuts, or fish, all the rest of it? And she won't answer. I never do get an answer to that.'

'But look,' Minette said urgently. 'I was with Ruby only a few weeks ago, when we thought Esmie had eaten peanuts. She was really upset, we rushed to the hospital, it was awful.'

'And what happened at the hospital?' His voice was quiet.

'They did tests, they checked her breathing.'

'But they didn't find anything wrong, did they?'

'Well, no. They said she probably hadn't eaten the nuts after all.'

'That's what they always say. No hospital has ever found anything wrong, all the times we've dashed there.'

Minette's head was spinning. 'Why then did Ruby . . .?'

'Six million dollar question. She wouldn't tell me. I asked her over and over that night. I've been trying to work it out ever since, you can imagine, and I'm none the wiser, Minette. There are mental patients, loonies, I've read up on them, who pretend their kids are ill, no one really knows why. For attention, or to get one over on doctors, or something. It's an illness itself. But why would Ruby be like that? She's smart, clever, confident, she's even a nurse.'

'What happened in the end?'

'We argued. Well, I did, Ruby kind of sat there, curled up, wouldn't look at me, wouldn't give me no explanations. I knew something at work had really got to her. But I started to get angry. I got angry about all the times we stabbed poor Esmie with an epi-pen and maybe didn't need to, all the crazy dashes to hospital. Even all the times I've told Esmie "no" about food she coulda had. I say, "That poor child, I'm going to look after her myself from now on," meaning I'm going to try and be around more, get a local job. I didn't mean I was going to take her off Ruby. But Ruby goes berserk, runs at me, starts hitting my head. Screaming, "These are my children, mine, you'll never get them off me!" We're both yelling, I'm not proud of it, I called her a monster and other bad things, and she hits me again and again, and finally I hit her back. Just once, round the face, a slap not a punch, to stop her hitting me, but if I could take back one thing in my life I would take that back, that's not who I am but it's all you know of me.'

Minette looked at Abe, her eyes wide. He nodded encouragingly. 'Andy, the other thing Ruby said was, this is hard to ask, she said D—, uh, your boy, I can't remember his real name, came in during this row and you hit him too.'

Andy let out a blast of air. 'No.'

'That's what she says.'

'No, no, no. *She* hit him. Oh, she didn't mean to. Adam came in all right, he'd heard us fighting. He wheeled himself between us, he was crying, "Stop, stop." I was trying to get him out of the way, and Ruby was screaming at him, "Your father hit me." It was such a mess, then she ran at me again and Adam pushed himself in front of her and he got a smack in the head off her that was meant for me. It was an accident and he wasn't badly hurt. It stopped the row, that's for sure, which might have been his intention.'

Minette felt like she too had been smacked in the head. 'This is just so awful. I don't know what to think.'

'It's her word against mine, isn't it? I can see why you'd believe her. I hit my wife so I'm capable of anything.' He was crying properly now. 'I had to go back to work next day. Five day job. When I got home, they were gone.'

'I'm so, so, sorry. Bringing it all up again.'

'You haven't, it's always there, all the time.' He moved away from the phone and she heard him blow his nose. 'Thought I'd done all my crying. I mostly keep it together, for my parents' sake.'

So there were grandparents on that side. 'They must really miss the children?'

He laughed. 'You could say that. They got old overnight. My mum keeps reading up on those cases, you know, where a parent kidnaps a child. No one can believe it happened to me. I didn't go to the police because Ruby left me a note saying she'd tell them I hit her if I called them. I was in that much of a state, and I didn't want my mum to find out I'd hit her, that's not how she brought me up. Private detectives are shit, excuse my language, it's not like on the telly, and anyway when they caught up with Gina she said she would cut off contact all together with me if I ever tried that again. I've had a lot of false leads, and you're my best hope, but I'm not going to pressure you. I know what Ruby's like, she's very convincing, you'll have to reach your own conclusions.'

'Are Ruby's parents in the picture?'

'Her mum died years ago, before I met her. And she didn't know her dad. He was some friend of the family, older bloke, who got her mum pregnant when she was only seventeen. Ruby reckoned it was rape but nothing was ever done about it.' He exhaled. 'Least, that's what Ruby told me! Who knows? They're probably living in a retirement home in Marbella.'

Minette knew she should ask whether he had any suspicions about Davey's condition, but she really wanted to get off the phone. She felt she couldn't handle any more right now.

'You've given me a lot to think about, Andy, and I promise I will, really carefully.'

'Thank you. Can I just ask? Are my children all right?'

'They're fine. I saw them very recently. I'm going to have to stop now, I have to see to my own daughter.'

'How old?'

'Eleven months on Monday.'

'Wonderful. A lovely age.'

'I'll call you again.'

'Please do. Hope I haven't upset you.'

Minette clicked off her phone, and she and Abe gazed at each other. 'Oh my fucking god,' Abe said, 'it's like a thriller.'

'It's not, Abe, it's horrible.' Minette started to cry. 'If it's true, there are two children living next door with a psychotic, potentially dangerous mother.'

Abe put his arms round her. 'The Miltons don't seem so bad now, do they?'

Minette managed to laugh through her tears. 'I didn't really manage to keep it brief, did I?'

'Well, he didn't let you get a word in edgeways.'

'What was that illness he mentioned?'

'I was looking it up while you were talking.' Abe read from

his phone, 'Munchausen syndrome by proxy. I saw a documentary about it, years ago. It's where the parent pretends the child has an illness.'

'She could have that! She clearly pretended about Lola, and she might be pretending about Davey too. Oh my god, it's all pointing to Cath being the weirdo, but I so don't want to believe it. We're friends! Well, I think we're friends.'

'Look, we shouldn't jump to conclusions. We only have Andy's word for the Lola thing, don't we?'

'But he did sound genuine, don't you think?'

'I don't know.' Abe looked thoughtful. 'His story was pretty pat, wasn't it?'

'Do you think?' Minette wiped her eyes.

'All that, yes, I hit her but there's only one good reason, that's to protect my child. It all sounded a bit, well, rehearsed. It was all told in the right order.'

'Maybe you're right.' Now Minette no longer had Andy's voice in her ear, but Cath's, and it was saying, 'I never thought he was the violent type. Then one night, he walloped me.' What was the truth? 'Oh, god, I'm going to have to talk to Cath again.'

'Yep.'

'Maybe I should go this evening, with a bottle of wine? Keep it friendly.'

'And not so much like the Spanish inquisition? Yes, good plan.' He kissed the top of her head. 'You know what you need? A day out. Let's take Tilly to the pier. You can have a sea swim to practise for the triathlon and we can try and put all this out of our heads for a bit.'

'I do love you, Abe.' Minette leaned against him. For the first time in months she felt properly supported and cherished. Nothing to bring you together better, she mocked herself, than by sharing the horrors of someone else's parenting.

'I love you too, and I'm glad you're not a psycho mom.'

'I'm glad you're not a psycho lorry driver.'

'I could be, if I wanted. I have an HGV licence.'

'You do not. You don't even like Yorkies.'

'Yorkies aren't obligatory, you can have Wagon Wheels.'

The relief of surfacing after the intensity of the phone call made Minette giggly. 'What about having to read the *Sun*?'

'I could hide the *Guardian* inside it. Right, I'd better check on Tills. She might be watching something unsuitable, like *Peppa Pig*.'

It was Tilly's first trip to the pier, and she adored the noise and colours. They held her up to a penny falls machine in the arcade, and when a coin they pushed in for her made some other coins come out, her mouth went into a perfectly round circle of surprise. Later, Abe sat on the pebbles and fed Tilly a pot of homemade mush, while Minette ploughed up and down in the sea. Every few minutes she stopped to wave, and Tilly, who had only just learned how to do it, waved enthusiastically back.

'How was it?' Abe asked, as Minette came ungracefully up the beach in her wetsuit, hobbling on the stones.

'I think I'm getting the hang of it. It's very different from swimming in the pool. I'm having to look up all the time to see where I'm going, and make my stroke longer.' She peeled off her wetsuit, and sat on the warm stones in her swimming costume, watching Tilly crawling about. 'You'd think she'd hurt her knees.'

'She's made of tough Moncrieff stock.' Abe passed her half a bag of chips he'd been eating. They weren't hot, but were nice and salty. 'Think, soon she'll be walking.'

'And talking, and slamming doors and asking for her ears to be pierced. Actually, I can't wait.'

'Hey, isn't that whatsisname?' Abe pointed down the beach. 'That annoying pretty bloke?'

'Who?' Minette turned to see, and her heart skittered. It was Liam. He was walking hand in hand across the pebbles with Josie. Dimly, she registered what a handsome couple they were; Josie in a short mint-green summer dress, long auburn hair loose, Liam in one of his casually cool outfits, a tight-fitting blue T-shirt and grey chinos.

'They look like they're doing a photoshoot for Next,' Abe said.

Minette hastily pulled on a T-shirt over her baggy old

swimsuit, then turned her head away and stared at the sea, in the childlike hope that if she couldn't see them, they couldn't see her. But seconds later she heard Abe say, 'Hi!'

She scrambled to her feet, and tried to look welcoming. She pulled a towel around her waist, but there was no getting away from the fact that she was wearing a naff old Oasis T-shirt and no make-up, her hair wet and scraggly. She looked at Josie, not Liam. 'Hello! Isn't it lovely and warm?'

'Not warm enough for me to go in,' Josie replied. 'You *are* good.'

'You know Abe and, er, Minette, don't you?' Liam said to Josie. 'Two doors down?'

'Liam has to tell me who everyone is, I'm hopeless.' Josie had a beautiful smile. 'I miss all the social occasions.'

'I suppose you work long hours for Hilton, don't you?' Abe said, all puppyish enthusiasm. 'Must be awesome working there.'

'It is . . . awesome,' she agreed. 'They're a good company. With great benefits.' Unexpectedly she giggled, and for the first time Minette glanced at Liam. He was looking worriedly at Josie.

'Good perks, huh?' Abe said. 'You're lucky. The only benefit I have is working up the road so I can have lunch at home.'

'That's pretty nice, though,' Josie said. 'I'd like to give up commuting. It would be lovely to be at home in the day, like Liam.'

'And Minette,' Abe said.

'Where's Tilly?' Liam asked, almost cutting across Abe.

'Right behind you,' Abe said, 'doing very important beach work, piling stones into a cup, then emptying it out again.'

'Oh, she's gorgeous,' Josie said.

Minette was conscious that Liam looked super-awkward, that he had failed to reply to eight texts, and that she hadn't said anything since 'Isn't it lovely and warm'. She took a step back, and said, 'We'd better be going, Abe. Tilly's nap.'

'Really?' Abe looked at his watch. 'She's fine for a bit longer.' God, he was so fucking dense sometimes.

'We've got to go, anyway,' Liam said. He seemed stunned by their unexpected meeting. 'I need some new clothes for my teaching course.'

'Jackets with leather patches on the elbows?' Abe said.

'Yeah, that kind of thing. Well, see you.'

Josie leaned towards Minette and said, 'Hope I'll see a bit more of you soon.'

'That'd be great,' Minette said in a robotic voice.

As they walked away, Josie stumbled on the pebbles in her silly platform sandals, almost turning her ankle, and Liam took her arm, saying, 'Careful, baby.'

When they were out of earshot, Minette began berating Abe for not taking seriously her comment about Tilly's nap. 'I don't say these things lightly, Abe. I could see she was getting tired.'

'Sorry, Dougie. Let's get going now.' He started putting their stuff away.

'Do you think actually that you could stop calling me Dougie?' She hadn't known she was going to say that, so she was as surprised as Abe. They stared at each other for a moment.

'Oh! Sure. You should have said you didn't like it.'

'It's just. Well. Other people call their partners by more loving names.'

'Honey-bunch? Sugar-plum? That kind of thing?'

'Forget it.' She rammed Tilly's toys into the rucksack and stood up.

'Angel face? Darling-pie? Cuddle-chops?'

'Fuck off, Abe.'

They worked together for a few moments in silence, packing everything away. Then they climbed onto the promenade and began walking towards home. 'That bloke's a bit odd, isn't he?' Abe said. He was trying to move on from their row. 'Went to all that trouble to get Johnny's email address, to ask about teaching, but Johnny said he never heard from him.'

'Yes, that's a bit strange,' Minette agreed.

She spent the rest of the day in a state of disconnect. What with Andy, and Cath, and Liam and Josie, the world seemed very bewildering. Who was truthful, who was lying, who knew what?

As evening approached, Minette felt like a condemned prisoner. She was dreading talking to Cath. 'Do I have to go?' she wailed to Abe.

'No, of course not,' he said, ever reasonable. 'But it would be good to put what Andy said to her, see if we can work out what the hell's going on.'

He was right. There was no other way forward than to ask some awkward questions.

'If you're not back by nine I'm coming round.'

'Jeez, Abe, what do you think she might do?'

'Nothing, Min.' He looked serious. 'It'll be fine. But she might be unpredictable. Don't drink too much. Have you set up the recording?'

Abe had downloaded an app onto Minette's phone which would record the whole conversation.

'I feel like I'm wearing a wire,' Minette said. 'I'm Big Pussy in *The Sopranos.*' She clicked 'start' on the app and slipped the phone into her pocket.

'Good luck, Pussy,' Abe said. 'Try not to get whacked.'

Minette went next door, her heart thudding, and when Cath answered her ring Minette immediately held up her peace-offering, a bottle of wine and some homemade biscuits. To her relief, Cath smiled welcomingly. 'Ooh, I love Chardonnay. You know, I considered Chardonnay when I changed my name,' she said as they went into the kitchen.

'Seriously?'

'Not really, but I did think of a lot of fancy names before I settled on Cath.'

It was encouraging that Cath was being so honest about her circumstances. 'How did you choose it?'

Cath got out two glasses and unscrewed the bottle. 'It was just a name without baggage. I didn't know anyone called Cath, couldn't think of any famous Caths.'

Minette picked up her glass. 'Cheers.'

'Cheers. Thanks for coming round. I didn't like the way as how we left it yesterday.'

'Me neither. Are the kids in bed? I brought some biscuits for Lola.'

'Aw, that's nice of you. She's already asleep. Davey's just watching telly.' Cath put some crisps in a bowl and set it in front of Minette. 'He had his referral yesterday, at the neurology place.'

'Oh yes, did it go well?'

'Really good. Once I get the diagnosis letter from them, I can use it to get benefits, educational equipment, loads of things.'

'That sounds extremely useful.'

'Oh, you've no idea. I've been waiting for it for ages. So, how are things with you?'

'Fine, thanks. How's your training going?' Minette said. Answer a question with a question. Cath had taught her this.

'I've stopped now. Haven't you? Only a week to go, so we need to rest.'

'One more run, then I'm all about the carb loading.' Minette took a gulp of wine. Come on, girl. Don't be a pussy. Be Big Pussy. 'So. Can I ask you . . .' She stopped, unsure how to start.

'Some fairy-tale from Andy, is it?'

'What makes you say that?'

'I know you spoke to him the other day. I know what he's like, he'd say anything. You can't believe a word.'

'He did say rather a lot.' Minette sipped some more wine, then remembered Abe's warning and put down her glass.

'Well, go on, then,' Cath smiled. 'Tell me what he said and I'll tell you which bits are true. If any.'

She was making this easier than Minette had expected. 'Thanks, Cath.'

'Hey! We're friends, aren't we? You were the first person to welcome us when we moved in.'

'OK. I'll just say what he said, then you can tell me your version.'

'The facts, you mean?' Cath was still smiling.

'Andy admitted he hit you, but only because . . .'

'Ha! Here it comes, the excuse.'

'He says he hit you because he thought you were harming Lola.'

'And how was I harming her?' Cath's eyes glittered, and Minette wondered if she could go through with this.

'He – uh – he said she doesn't really have allergies.'

'Bullshit. You know she does. Next.'

'But . . .' Minette drank some wine for courage, 'how do I know she does?'

'Oh my god, Minette, what the hell? You were there that day at nursery! You called the taxi. I was so grateful you were with me. You think that wasn't real? That I would make something like that up?'

That authoritative, convincing voice again. Minette put her hands palm down on the table, bracing herself. 'I don't know, Cath. Andy seemed so certain.'

'Oh yeah, I bet he did. He'd do anything to get back at me. Anything. You don't know jack shit about abusers, Minette, excuse my language. Jack shit.' Cath poured herself another glass. 'So, go on.'

'It doesn't matter, Cath. Let's leave it.' Minette felt she'd had enough.

Cath shook her head, as if to clear her thoughts. 'Look, I'm sorry. I'm trying not to overreact. But I do feel slightly shocked that you might believe *him*, who you've never met, over me, your friend.'

'I would never have even thought of believing him, Cath, if it hadn't been that thing with Davey.'

'You're on Andy's side,' Cath said.

'I'm not! I'm not on anyone's side . . .'

'You're certainly not on mine.' Cath stood up and started

opening cupboards, then closing them again. 'No one ever believes me.'

'I am, I do, it's just . . .'

'You can't be on both sides, Minette.' Slam went the cupboard door. 'You can't sit on the fence.' Slam. 'If you support me, you can't be questioning me, suspecting me, not trusting me. That's not what friends do, is it?' Slam.

Minette couldn't stand it. 'Sit down,' she said quietly, taking Cath's arm. 'I didn't mean to get you all upset.'

Cath's breathing was very fast. She shook Minette off, and rubbed her arm where she had touched her. 'Don't patronise me. Just be honest. Are you for me, or against me?'

'It's not really that black and white . . .'

'It is, to me.' Cath's expression made Minette alarmed. Perhaps the same alarm that caused Andy to drive through the night. There was something out of control on Cath's usually calm face.

'I just want to know the facts,' Minette said.

'Against me then,' Cath said. 'That's how it is.' She wiped her eyes with her sleeve – Minette hadn't realised she was crying – and said, 'Well, at least I know where I stand.'

'Cath, it isn't like that!' Minette cried. How had the conversation slipped so far out of her grasp? 'I only want to know about Davey . . .'

'Talking of Davey, it's getting late, isn't it?' Cath went to the door and called him. Minette heard the television go off, then he wheeled himself into the kitchen. She said, 'Hello.' Unusually, he didn't look at her, but stared at the ground instead.

'Oh, Davey, just one thing,' Cath said. 'Minette here thinks she saw you walking the other night.'

'Hey, Cath, that's not . . .'

'Not just your few steps that we know you can still do, lovie, but proper walking. What do you say to that?'

Davey's face was blank. 'I can't walk more than a few steps.'

Minette was horror-struck. 'Please Cath, stop this.'

'There you go, Minette, straight from the horse's mouth.' Cath stroked Davey's hair. 'Bed now, lovie. Say goodnight.'

Davey muttered 'good night' and went out, without looking at either of them.

'That was hardly fair,' Minette said. She picked up her glass, found she was trembling, and put it down again.

'How so? You accused me of something, and I've just given you evidence that you're wrong. Shall I bring you a copy of the letter when I get it? It'll say "Duchenne muscular dystrophy" in black and white.'

'I don't mean not fair to me, I mean to Davey. He'll say whatever you tell him to.'

Cath smiled. 'You need to be careful, Minette. Say what you like about me, but don't you dare suggest that my son is lying.'

Minette stood up. She was surprised to find that she felt

more angry than frightened. 'You know that's not what I mean, Cath. I'm going home now.'

Cath said, quietly, 'It's so horrid, isn't it, when a family breaks up? Nasty. I know as how you went through it yourself, as a child.'

'When my parents split things weren't great,' Minette said. 'But no one had to change their names.'

'No. You were lucky. And you've been lucky to meet a nice, kind man like Abe. Though,' Cath paused, then said in a rush, 'it's not all roses round the door, with you and him, is it?'

'We're fine.' Minette went into the hall and picked up her jacket. Cath followed her.

'If you was all fine, you wouldn't need to invite certain handsome blond animuses round when you're in my house, looking after my kids. Not exactly appropriate, is it?'

Minette looked at Cath. Were the gloves finally off, then? She wasn't sure if she was more tired or sad. She looked at her watch: eight fifteen. 'I'd better go.'

Cath said, 'Sure. But before you do, there's something I really ought to show you. And I've got something to tell you as well, some good gossip I found out today.'

'It's all right, I don't want to know.' She moved towards the front door.

'You'll like this, it's about Liam.'

Whenever Minette looked back on this scene, this was the

point at which she metaphorically slapped herself around the head. Why didn't she just walk out the door? But some part of her felt she owed Cath the courtesy of listening. Even if this Cath didn't seem like the person she knew, the old Cath had been amazing about her fling with Liam, had encouraged her to do the triathlon, had looked after Tilly, and helped her navigate the world of life with a small baby.

Plus, Minette's curiosity was roused. 'Go on, then.'

'Josie's pregnant.'

'She's not.' Minette reacted instinctively.

'You've gone white as a sheet, lovie. Come back, come and sit down.' Cath's voice was gentle.

Minette's legs felt weak, as if she hadn't had enough to eat. She allowed Cath to lead her back into the kitchen and sat, still wearing her jacket. Cath put a topped-up glass of wine in front of her and Minette mechanically took a sip.

'Yes,' said Cath conversationally, looking into her own glass. 'Josie was *mucho* in evidence in the street today. Got chatting and she said as how she wasn't supposed to tell anyone but she couldn't keep it in any longer. She's only a few weeks but she's never missed a period before, apparently they've been at it like rabbits. She didn't say it in quite those words, but she did a lot of cute blushing and saying things like "second honeymoon". Isn't it sweet? You must have given him his mojo back.'

'I don't believe you.'

'Uh-huh. Because you think I'm a liar now. OK. Well, you can easily verify this, you only have to ask Liam.' She looked at Minette. 'Or ask Josie. She's just busting to tell.'

Josie on the beach earlier, stumbling in her sandals. Giggling. Wanting to give up work. Her hand on Liam's arm. Minette knew instinctively that it was true.

He said they weren't sleeping together.

'What's the thing you wanted to show me?' Minette said, keeping her voice steady.

'Oh yes! It's upstairs. Hang on a tick.' Cath went out. Minette's mind couldn't process what she'd just heard. Liam had lied. He'd been sleeping with her and Josie at the same time. Jesus. It was disgusting. And it was breaking another feminist rule she'd just remembered: don't fuck another woman's husband. She drank the rest of her wine in one go and poured herself another glass. Then she thought abruptly of the phone app in her pocket, recording her conversation. For god's sake, it had all that stuff about Liam in it. She couldn't play that to Abe! She looked at her phone. It wasn't immediately clear how to erase the recording, so she just deleted the whole app. Cath came in as she was doing this, carrying a cardboard folder, and said, 'Texting your boyfriend are you?'

'Which one?' Minette shot back, trying to regain some ground.

'Oh, ha ha, very good. This one,' Cath said. She took a

large black-and-white photo from the folder and put it on the table in front of Minette.

For a moment Minette couldn't understand what she was seeing. It was a porno picture, a couple having sex, why was Cath showing her this? She'd said 'this one'. That was a clue. Yes, the man, though his face was half-hidden between the woman's thighs, was clearly Liam. Christ! Was Cath showing her a photo of Liam with Josie? Just to prove that Josie could be pregnant? What the hell . . . But slowly, Minette saw that it wasn't Josie in the picture. Wine-flavoured bile rose in her throat and she thought she was going to be sick. She covered her mouth.

'You all right, lovie?' Cath's voice came from far away.

'Yes,' Minette said vaguely. Then, 'How did you get this?'

'You're a smart cookie,' Cath said, filling Minette's glass again – Minette didn't remember finishing it. 'You've got a degree, and everything! You can figure it out.'

'I can't.' Minette knew she should be able to work it out but she couldn't. She felt utterly exposed. Cath had seen this photo, this private moment: her head flung back in ecstasy, legs spread wide apart, her cunt on display. Minette's eyes filled with tears. She knew that younger people, the generation below hers, sent each other photos of their genitals, their tits and arses, like it was nothing. Maybe if she was more like that this wouldn't be such a horrible shock. She had never even seen herself like this, so to think that someone else had . . . 'Please tell me how you got this.'

'Let's work it out together,' Cath said, her voice quiet and calm. 'Do you recognise the room?'

Wildly, Minette scanned the photo for clues. There was a bedside table she didn't recognise; the sheets could have been any sheets. She looked up, a thought occurring to her. 'Have you photo-shopped our faces onto other bodies?'

Cath laughed. 'You are so sweet. You maybe don't know Liam's gorgeous body too well, looks like you had your eyes shut, but I would have thought you would recognise your own. Whose little birthmark is this, just here?'

Minette watched as Cath's finger alighted on a small mark on the woman's hipbone. 'Yes,' she said. It was her body. Her breasts, her arms, her legs. The bedside table stopped being unfamiliar.

'How did you take it? Were you here all the time?'

'Gracious, Minette, I have a life! I'm doing a triathlon next weekend. I've got two sick kids. I don't have time to hang around taking pictures of my neighbours.'

'A camera on an automatic timer?'

'See? I said you was clever. Davey helped set it up, he's great with technology, that one. Reckon he might be a computer programmer or something like that when he's older.'

Minette knew it was probably futile, but she ripped the picture into shreds, let them fall to the floor.

'Didn't like that one, huh? Fair enough, you looked a bit fat in it. What about some of these?' Cath opened the folder and held it up in the air. Photos cascaded down onto the table. Some colour, others black and white. Photos of Minette sucking Liam. Him holding her breasts. Her straddling him, him straddling her, him fucking her from behind. Hundreds of them, all different, some clearly taken only seconds apart.

'Just pointed the camera at the bed, and off it went. You two should make one of them sex-tapes.'

Minette was too stunned to feel anything, other than sheer disbelief. She felt so full of disbelief, it crowded out every other emotion. 'Why?'

'Why a sex-tape? Well, you both look good, especially Liam. I think it would be popular.'

'Why did you take them?'

'Oh, I have my reasons. Didn't think I'd ever show them to *you*, to be honest. Didn't imagine I'd be using them so soon.'

'How will you use them?'

Cath began to put the photos into a neat pile. 'That one's nice, isn't it? So many people prefer digital photos these days, but I think there's nothing better than an actual physical picture that you can hold in your hands. I don't want to have to show them to Abe or Josie. I should think they'll be a bit upset. Her specially, what with the pregnancy and all.'

Minette was beginning to understand. The fog was clearing.

If she kept quiet about Cath's secrets, about Davey and Lola, Cath would keep quiet about the pictures. It seemed, now, as if all the craziness and excitement of the affair with Liam had just been leading up to this point. This horrible, tawdry point.

'It's a shame not to show them around, really, because they're such nice pictures. You could put some of them in those frames Abe nicked from a skip.'

'And what if I say that Liam and I are going to run off together, and I don't care?' Minette made an attempt to brazen it out.

'Well, then, you've nothing to worry about. Though will he, if his wife is pregnant? I think he's pretty keen to have a baby, bless him. He's just about to start his course, too. I'd be amazed if he wanted to rock the boat now.'

Josie, so long just a shadow, someone she deliberately didn't think about, now appeared in Minette's mind in sharp focus. Josie was Liam's *wife*. They were going to have a baby. Seeing these photos would ruin her life. Minette couldn't quite believe that she had been so careless, so cruel, about another person's feelings. She had never behaved like that in her life before.

Cath spoke into the silence. 'And if you and Abe split, will he be reasonable about custody of Tilly and that sort of thing, if he sees these? I just don't know for sure. I guess he's had his suspicions about Liam for a while, hasn't he?

From the moment you put that bench outside so you had an excuse to hang out with any bored out-of-work Tom, Harry, or should I say *Dick*, passing by.'

Minette was too stunned to respond. Cath went on, 'We reckoned as how Liam was your animus, didn't we?' She held up another photo and said, 'He does look particularly good in this one. I forgot to tell you the rest of what Jung said about that. Let's see if I can remember. Ooh, it was a long time ago I did psychology. Yes, he said, "You have an image of a man, of *the* man. Then you see that man, and you fall in love." Sound familiar? And afterwards, says Jung, "you may discover that it was a hell of a mistake." Wise words, don't you think?'

Minette looked at her watch. Christ, it was eight fifty-five; Abe would be coming round any minute to check she was all right. He'd see the photos, strewn over the table . . . She stumbled to her feet. 'I'm going.'

'Sure. Thanks for the wine. See you soon. Oh, and if you don't want to do the triathlon no worries, totally understand. I'll just add the money you've raised to my overall total. Joint effort.'

Somehow Minette was outside. She was sweating, and cold at the same time. She couldn't get her key in the lock because she was drunk, and because her hand was trembling. She let out a whispered prayer – 'please god come on just let me please let me get inside please I'll do anything' – till at last the door opened. She stepped inside quietly, and stood in the hall.

Abe called from the kitchen, 'That you, Dougie? I mean, Minette, sorry. You've been ages. You OK?'

She had to get herself together, put on one hell of an act for him. She couldn't think straight, yet she knew one thing for certain: she would die if Abe saw those photos. Who would she be, in his eyes, if he saw them? No longer Minette, his best friend, love of his life, mother of his child. But Minette, a whore. She hadn't felt like a whore till she saw the pictures. And that's what Abe would see. It would change the way he felt about her; there would be no coming back from it. She had to avoid that happening at all costs. Think, Minette, for fuck's sake, think. She would tell him Cath had convinced her all was fine. Just for now, to buy some time, while she worked out what to do. She'd tell Abe that something had gone wrong with the app. That Andy was unreliable. A wife-beater after all. She'd ring Andy tomorrow and say she couldn't help him any further.

She took out her lenses, and cupped them in her palm. It would be easier to lie if she couldn't see Abe properly. Then she pushed open the kitchen door.

Chapter 21

Cath

'What's she doing?' Cath asked Davey. He was looking out of the round window while she painted the tiles in the bathroom across the hall. The Miltons had chosen hideous salmon pink tiles, with a grey fleck that looked like dirt. Cath was painting them white. They looked miles better.

'Nothing. Still sitting on the bench. She's showing Tilly a book.'

'God, some people have nothing better to do on a Sunday but lounge about.'

'Oh, she looked.' Davey ducked down from the window.

'Did she see you?'

'I don't know.'

'You oughta stop now, anyway. You'll get tired, you're not supposed to stand for long, remember.'

Davey sat on the floor outside the bathroom. 'Stinks.'

'Yeah, it's smelly paint. I'm done now. You can help me collect the last bits of sponsor money. There's about eight houses where they're never home in the week.'

Cath cleared up and checked in on Lola. She was watching TV, a half-empty packet of Bakewell tarts in front of her.

'How many of those have you had, Lolly?'

'Dunno,' Lola said, another one on its way to her mouth.

'Make that the last one, lovie, OK? Listen, Davey and me are going out for ten minutes. Do you want to come?'

She shook her head. 'Want to see the end of this.'

'OK. We won't be long. I'll lock the front door, all right?'

'All right,' Lola said, her eyes never moving from the screen. She probably hadn't heard a word.

'I'm really tired, Mum,' Davey said.

'You can't be! You haven't done anything today,' Cath said, laughing.

'I think it was standing up at the window.'

'Come on, fresh air will do you good.' Cath gathered up her file. 'I need you with me when I'm collecting sponsors.'

She ushered Davey out, locking the mortice so that Lola was safe inside.

Kirsten was first on her list. 'Hey!' she said when she opened her door to Cath and Davey. 'How are you guys? Must be nearly triathlon day.'

'Yep, one week today.'

'I've got a 10K in a few weeks and I don't feel ready at all.'

'Me neither,' Cath laughed. 'It'll be all right on the night, though.' She took out her list. 'We're just collecting the money now, if that's OK. It's always such a bore doing it afterwards, you know . . .'

'Oh! Sure.' Kirsten grabbed her purse. 'What did I put down?'

'You were really kind, you put £100.'

'Wow, I *was* feeling generous. Listen, I only have £50 in cash, I'll do the rest in a cheque, shall I?'

'Can you make it out to me?' Cath said. 'I'm going to collect all the money and give one big cheque to Duchenne, they prefer that.'

'Course. Here you go.'

'Wonderful. While I'm here, can I sponsor you for your 10K?'

'Thanks!' Kirsten handed Cath the form. 'Where's your sister, Davey?'

'She's at home.'

'What, on her own?'

'Yes,' Davey said.

Cath laughed. 'He's such a messer. No, she's with the sitter. She was too tired to come out but Davey doesn't mind giving me a hand, do you lovie?' Cath ruffled Davey's hair.

They said goodbye and Cath consulted her list. 'OK, let's try Martin now. Davey, for god's sake, what was all that? What happened to the golden rule?'

'I don't feel very well,' Davey said.

'Ah, c'mon, lovie, we've only just started.'

'I really am tired, please can we go home.'

'We'll just do a few more.' Cath pushed him past the scruffy student house to number 41. She hoped Martin would answer, but unfortunately it was Sarah, his unfriendly wife, who looked suspiciously at Cath. She leaned on her old-fashioned flowery stick, an unattractive accessory for a young-ish woman. There were far cooler sticks you could get now. The Duchenne kids who didn't yet need wheelchairs had some great ones: fluorescent ones, ones with skull handles, or ones covered in rhinestones.

'Lovely to see you,' Cath said, and explained about the sponsor money.

'What, in advance? You haven't even done the race yet, have you?'

'No, but the charity likes it . . .'

'Bit dodgy if you ask me.'

'It speeds up their admin, anyway, how is everything with you guys? How's Callum, haven't seen him out on his skateboard lately.'

Sarah was not easy to deflect. 'Well, I don't even know how much Martin sponsored you, so you'll have to come back later.'

Cath looked at her form and said, 'He pledged £80.'

'He what? That's ridiculous. He must have been drunk. We'll give you a tenner. *After* you've done the race.' She started to close the door, then looked down at Davey and said, 'Oughtn't you get that kid home? He's wrecked.'

Cath saw to her amazement that Davey was fast asleep in the wheelchair, out cold. 'Oh!'

Sarah shook her head, and shut the door.

Poor Davey. Cath was furious with herself. He was genuinely unwell and she had forced him to come out. You are a terrible mother, a monster, she told herself as she pushed him quickly back home.

She told Lola, still gazing at the telly, cakes all gone, to turn down the volume. She had to wake Davey gently to get him into his bed.

'How do you feel, lovie?'

'Head hurts. Tired.'

Cath drew the curtains. 'You do look very pale. Nothing worse than a sick headache. Do you want a cuddle?'

'OK.'

Cath lay on top of the covers and put her arm round Davey. His small soft hand curled loosely round her wrist. His other hand clutched onto his toy bear. Cath closed her eyes. 'I can't tell whether I'm touching your arm or the teddy. They're both so soft.'

'Waffles.'

'My mummy had a long fur coat when I was a little girl. Fake fur, she called it, all soft, like your Waffles.'

'He's brown.'

'Yes, her coat was brown too. Pretend mink. I didn't have my own teddy, but I loved pressing my face against her coat when it was hanging in the cupboard. Mummy didn't like me touching it, though, she thought I would make it sticky. She was a very busy lady, you know, very important. She worked in a big department store in Eastbourne. She was always rushing, rushing.'

'Like you.'

'Me? I'm not like her at all, lovie. I don't even have a job now. My job is to look after you and Lola.'

'OK.'

'So anyway, she'd always be running out in her fur coat. But sometimes, if I wasn't well, she would stay home. She would put me to bed, like you are now, and close the curtains, and bring me little trays of food.'

'What food?' Davey sounded like he was drifting back to

sleep. Well, no wonder he was tired. He'd got to bed pretty late last night, disturbed by her row with Minette. She was tired too, after that.

'Soft boiled egg and soldiers, maybe . . .'

'Yuck.'

'No, you don't like that, do you. Or toast and marmite, you'd prefer that. And a special little glass of juice. And her voice would be different from her busy voice. It was like an angel's voice, really. I wish you'd known her. She died a long time ago, long before you were born.'

Davey was asleep. Cath stayed still, so as not to disturb him. She knew that sometimes he said he felt ill when he didn't. All kids did that, for the attention. She certainly had. But he never normally slept in the day. She wondered how much of the row he'd heard. He came out of his room some time after Minette had gone home, maybe nine thirty, saying he couldn't sleep. Real shame about Minette. Cath had thought for a while that they were going to be proper friends. It wasn't to be, sadly. You couldn't be friends when there was no trust. The things that Minette had implied! Cath counted herself lucky she'd had the sense to put things in place to protect herself.

She wished she could stay where she was, drift off to sleep with Davey. But there was too much to do. She carefully extricated herself from Davey's clasp, and stood looking down at him. So beautiful. Like a sudden blow, Cath felt the absence of Andy by her side. When the children were tiny and she checked on them when they were asleep, she would often call Andy quietly. 'Oh, come look, they are so cute.' Standing silently by the children's beds, Andy would put his arm round her, and they'd admire the rounded curved cheeks that they together had made, smiling at the little snuffles and moans, their funny sleeping positions.

God, snap out of it, Cathykins. She shook her head violently. Remember Troubletown, remember having to leave work, remember what would have happened if she'd stayed. Remember Andy's face. There was no going back. Andy wasn't any kind of solution. He was the problem, really. He would make her deal with a load of stuff she didn't want to. Moving forward, that's what was needed. She didn't really miss any of that crap, anyway.

She went into her own room and updated her notebook. She put a big tick through the page for Kirsten. Only £100! When you thought about the size of the renovations Kirsten had been doing. Still, it wasn't too bad, considering Cath hadn't made much progress with getting to know Kirsten. She saw she'd written a note on Kirsten's page to book Lola in for a cranial appointment with her; that was another ball she'd dropped. Ah well, can't win 'em all. She turned to Martin and Sarah's page, and noted that she would need to wait till Wednesday evening, when Sarah went out to some evening class and Martin was in on his own.

She put the book away and fired up the laptop. She hadn't had a chance to look at her email for a few days, and there were three from Verna. She replied:

> Dearest V
>
> I was just thinking about Mum today so it's funny you mentioned her. It will be twenty-eight years next month. Looking forward to hearing more of your memories.
>
> Sorry that I'm changing like the wind here. You're right, it might be sooner after all, rather than later. Still not sure of eta, things a bit up in the air, can I keep you posted? Thanks for looking into the stuff for me. Thought Duchenne might get better benefits there, bit of a shame. Still, turns out the easiest way to transfer UK benefits is to get Gina to collect and send them on.
>
> R xx

Typing Gina's name reminded her that they hadn't spoken for a few days. She dialled her number.

'Hey,' Gina said, 'I was just about to ring you.'

Cath leaned back in her chair and smiled. 'That's nice. Great minds. I miss you. Don't suppose there's any chance of you popping down this evening, is there?'

'Oh . . . I'd like to but I can't, I got this thing with Ryan . . .'

'Sure.'

'I'll pop down tomorrow. And I'm coming next weekend anyway, aren't I, for your crazy triathlon? So listen, bit of a weird one from Andy this time.'

'I don't need to know about it.'

'He's enclosed a letter from the hospital. Where you used to work?'

How funny that she'd just been thinking about it, and now here it was.

'It mentions that boy who died. Darren? It says something about a disciplinary.'

'Tear it up, Gee, there's a love.'

'Sure?'

Cath straightened her shoulders. Moving forward. 'Yep. That's all in the past now.'

After they'd hung up, she looked up the *Harrogate Advertiser* online. It was there, on the homepage: 'Police investigating child hospital death'. There was a school photo of Darren. A lousy picture but there was no hiding that cheeky grin. She smiled back at the picture. Absolutely lovely kid, one of the best she'd ever nursed. She realised that she must have had Darren in her head when she came up with Davey, another D name. She scanned the details of the report, but it didn't mention her or any of the other staff. It just mentioned those mysterious 'irregularities'. Yeah, pretty irregular, not recognising when a child was properly ill, not listening to his nurse, not giving him the treatment he needed.

Still, no one believed her then, and there was no way that they would believe her now.

She turned off the laptop, went downstairs, and checked on the kids. Davey was asleep, Lola still staring at the telly. Then she popped out to collect the rest of the money, giving Martin and Sarah's house a miss. By the time she got home she was carrying almost 500 quid. Not bad for half an hour's work. She put the money carefully in her 'Duchenne' cash box, and locked her bedroom door.

Chapter 22

Minette

Minette finally gave up on texting, and as soon as Abe had left for work she rang Liam.

'I'm sorry,' she said, when he picked up, 'I don't want to stalk you. But we didn't seem to be getting anywhere with texts.'

'No, well, I've been pretty busy.'

She knew from his voice that it was over between them. Then she told herself to get a grip. It was already over, the moment she saw those photos. No, it was over the moment Cath told her Josie was pregnant. Then she homed in on it.

It was over the moment she saw Liam with Josie on the beach. His face, the way he looked at her. *Careful, baby*.

'I promise it won't take long,' she said. 'Can I pop over now?'

'No, I've got some stuff to do this morning. Uh, with Josie.'

'I'm doing my last training run at lunch time. How about joining me?'

'I haven't been for a run for weeks.'

'I go pretty slowly.'

They arranged to meet at the end of the street. Minette hung up and turned round, to find that Tilly was no longer sitting on the floor where she'd left her, but was holding onto a chair and standing up. 'Oh, Tilly, you clever girl!' Minette said, and had a little cry. Whether it was about Tilly, or over Liam, she wasn't sure. When she'd composed herself, she made a phone call she'd been working up to for a few days.

'Hi, Harry?'

'Minette! I was just thinking about you, and cursing you, in fact.'

'Oh dear, why's that?'

'I got lumbered with pulling together this damn job description.'

'Does that mean you haven't appointed anyone yet?'

'I think you've forgotten how slowly the wheels turn here, my sweet. We haven't even sent out the damn advert yet.'

'In that case would this be a good moment to ask for my job back?'

'Really? Are you kidding? Tell me again.'

'I want to come back. Part-time, if that's OK.'

'Yay! Did you hear that? That was the sound of me ripping up the job advert. When can you start? I'll sort everything out with personnel, don't worry. Just get your lovely self back here pronto.'

Minette was in her running clothes when Abe got home. She told him about deciding to go back to work. 'That's great news,' he said, and kissed her. 'I'm not sure being a stay-at-home mum really suits you.'

'Well, you say that, but if I hadn't been here I'd have missed Tilly standing up . . .'

'Oh my god,' he said, running into the kitchen. 'Show me, Tills!'

As Minette jogged to the corner, she thought how sad it would be, to be a single parent. No one else in the world was as fascinated by Tilly as her, except Abe. People like Cath had no one to share that stuff with. And how close Minette had come to throwing that away. Well, she wasn't going to allow Cath to try and ruin things for her. But then . . . she slowed down. What about helping Davey and Lola? Jesus, there were no easy answers. Someone was going to get hurt, however it played out.

Liam was waiting outside the shop, looking hot as all get

out in running gear. He gave her an odd little nod, and set off at a ridiculous pace. She jogged after him, not trying to keep up, and after a moment he turned round and said, 'You're not going for speed at this triathlon, I take it?'

'If we're to talk, you'll have to slow way down.'

He settled into a more manageable pace alongside her. 'Where are we headed?'

'I usually go down as far as the pier.'

'Bring it on.' He was already slightly out of breath. 'So, what is this vitally important thing you have to tell me that requires eight texts on a weekend?'

'I'm sorry. You don't know me well enough to know how out of character that is.'

'I'll take your word for it. Go on, then.' They turned the corner and ran down towards the seafront.

'I saw Cath at the weekend . . .' She paused while they crossed the road. 'Liam, she's taken dozens of photos. Of us.'

'What do you mean? Us at her party?'

Minette stared straight ahead at the path. The Palace Pier glittered, off in the distance. It looked impossibly far. 'Photos of us, er, in bed.'

'She's got sex photos of us?' Minette could feel Liam looking at her. 'How?'

'I think she set up a camera in the spare room.'

'Can we please wait a minute?'

They stopped running, and Liam bent down to get his breath, hands on his knees. Minette thought that he was really upset, but when he straightened up, he was grinning. 'Are they good?'

'Pardon?'

'Do we look hot in them? Have you got one? I'd love to see them.'

'Aren't you shocked?'

'Well, it explains a lot about Cath. Everyone's got a kink, Minette.'

'She didn't take them for some sexual purpose. Christ, Liam, she's threatening me with them.'

'Oh, come on, Minette, I know you love the movies, but this isn't *Dial M for Murder*. This is Cath we're talking about, middle-aged mum next door who, we now know, gets off on perving over nudie pictures of her neighbours.'

'You're not listening.' Minette started running again, fast, as if that would get her away from the situation. 'And there's no one else I can talk to.'

Liam chased after her. 'So you can go faster if you want. Look, Minette, it doesn't make any sense. Why would she want to blackmail you?'

'Because I know something. Something bad.'

'What is it? Christ, slow down a minute.'

'I can't say.' Minette changed her pace back to a talking speed. 'But let me ask you this. Do you think her kids are OK?'

'They seem fine to me.'

'Great teacher you're going to make. Razor-sharp instincts.' Minette was out of breath now.

'Well, what am I supposed to have noticed?'

'You don't think she's like, a little bit odd with them? That night I looked after them, when you came round, she told me to leave them in the house on their own.'

'She was concussed, you said.'

'And Davey has his own front-door key.'

'Isn't that quite impressive, though? Yes, she's hands-off. But you know, there's a balance, isn't there, between laid-back parenting, and over-protectiveness.'

'Meaning I'm over-protective, I suppose.'

'You know what, Minette? I think we should keep out of it.' Liam was breathing hard. 'How much further are we going?'

'You want another rest?'

He shook his head. His face was beetroot, his hair plastered flat onto his forehead, and there were sweat patches down the sides of his vest. If she'd been trying to cure herself of lust, she couldn't have found a better way.

'Look,' he said, 'Cath's a bit odd, sure. But those kids are not our responsibility. I think we should back off a bit. You certainly shouldn't confide in her any more.'

'Believe me, I'm not planning to. She made it clear that if I told anyone what I knew, she would show Abe the photos.'

'Well, that makes it very simple. Don't tell anyone. I don't even know why you're telling me about it.'

'Because she said she would show Josie as well.'

Liam stopped dead, panting, and grabbed hold of her arm. 'Fuck's sake, how did Josie get dragged into this? Why did you even tell Cath you knew this mysterious secret? What's wrong with letting sleeping dogs lie?'

'Never had you down as a head-in-the-sand type, Liam.' Minette pulled away from him. 'I'm worried about those kids. I *had* to tell her.'

'No, you didn't. You wanted to.' Liam's voice got louder. 'You were like a bored child putting a stick into a hornet's nest. You're just another under-stimulated mummy, in search of a hobby. Poking your nose into someone's else's life is a bit more interesting than feeding the baby, isn't it? You need a fucking job, you know that?'

Minette stared at him, her hands on her hips. 'I see. That's what you think of me. Good to know. Oh, one more thing, on the topic of babies. Cath told me that Josie's pregnant.'

'What? How the hell does she know?'

'So it is true.' Minette started running again. 'Congratulations.'

'Minette, please wait.' He raced after her. 'I'm sorry. I was going to tell you.'

'When, exactly? Next time we had sex? The time after that? "By the way, Minette, you know I said I wasn't sleeping with my wife? Oops." And of course, I would reply . . .'

'Don't, Minette.'

'I would reply, "Oh that's OK, Liam, I don't mind being lied to and made a fool of."'

'My god, the drama. Look, Josie and I *weren't* sleeping together when you and I first met, I didn't lie.'

'And when you later reunited, you forgot to mention it?'

'Not being funny, Minette, but I was hardly going to cock-block myself, was I? The sex was amazing, you got to admit.'

'So is your conscience finally blocking your cock now she's pregnant?'

'You're hot when you're angry.'

'Do fuck off, Liam. I'm not finding any of this remotely amusing.'

'I'm not either. Christ, can't we walk for a bit? I'm done in.'

'You're a big man, but you're out of shape.'

'How *did* Cath know? Josie's barely seven weeks gone. We just had the first doctor's appointment this morning.'

Seven weeks. Minette did some rapid calculations. 24 June today. Cath's party was at the end of April. So yes, technically, when they met at the party, he could have been telling the truth. But he must have got Josie pregnant at almost exactly the same time as he was starting the affair with her. It was Paul all over again. Paul trying to juggle her and Bella, everyone knowing but her. Liam was a player. A total fucking player. What an idiot she was, what a first-class fool, to risk her proper relationship with Abe on a pretty-faced bastard. Abe was worth twice what Liam was.

'How did Cath know? Well, Liam, I'd say voodoo, except that as you pointed out, she's just a middle-aged mum next door. So I guess logic dictates that Josie must have told her.'

'I very much doubt it. We said we wouldn't tell anyone till twelve weeks.'

'Not even me?' She laughed into his silence. 'It's all right, Liam. I know we're through. Now, I've got a triathlon to train for. See you.' She broke into a proper run, a sprint, knowing she could keep it going until she reached the pier.

Chapter 23

Davey

Davey woke up feeling more like Adam Purcell than he had done for ages. The light coming in through the curtains looked the same as in his old room in Harrogate, and made him think he was back there, with the stripy carpet, red, blue, orange, blue, his dad whistling and frying bacon downstairs. Just like that he remembered his old address: 68 Parkside Avenue, Starbeck, Harrogate. He got up quickly and wrote it down.

* * *

At school he waited at the gate for Olivia. He was lucky because MT was dropping her off today. MT gave him the printout of faces he'd promised. 'There are millions of Andy Purcells,' he said. 'These are just the first ten. Is he any of these?' Davey looked through them quickly – too old, too young, wrong colour, too fat, too bald – and shook his head.

'It would be easier,' MT said, 'if you come over to play with Olivia and we go through them together.'

'OK,' Davey said. He knew his mum wouldn't let him go there, or if she did, she'd tell Olivia's parents not to let him use the computer. But anyway, it didn't matter. He triumphantly produced the piece of paper with his address on. MT put it in his pocket, and saluted. 'Well done, I'll call directory enquiries at lunchtime.'

Davey went into school feeling brilliant. It was a lucky day because their teacher was away, and they had a supply teacher, a nice man with floppy hair. When he said it was time for ICT Davey went over to choose a DVD as usual, but the new teacher didn't seem to know that Davey wasn't allowed ICT because he said, 'Come on, there's a lift isn't there?'

At last, the internet! Davey could hardly believe it. He stared at the screen. There was so much he wanted to do. He had really missed Wikipedia, and Olivia had told him about a cute animal called a tarsier with enormous eyes that he wanted to look up. But first he typed in 'Facebook Andy

Purcell' and some links came up. He clicked on the first one and there was a long list of Andy Purcells, MT was right. He couldn't see his dad, all these ones were from America. At the bottom of the page it said 'You must sign up for Facebook to see the full results.'

The school secretary came in, and said something to their teacher. The teacher said, 'Davey Brooke?'

Davey looked up. He knew what was coming.

'Can you go with Mrs Wallis, please?'

Feeling everyone's eyes on him, Davey wheeled himself out of the room. He heard someone say, 'Spazzos aren't allowed to use computers.' No one in his class had called him 'spazzo' before. They were copying those Year 5 boys.

Davey followed the secretary along the corridor. 'Well, that was lucky timing,' she said. 'I went to the classroom to get you and what do I find? You're only up in the blooming ICT suite. I think,' and she winked at him, 'we won't tell your mum, maybe?'

They got in the lift and she let Davey press the button.

'Where are we going?' he said.

'Oh, you've got this meeting with the ed psych.'

'The who?'

'Educational psychologist. Your mum's already there.'

The lift beeped, and they were at the ground floor. Mrs Wallis walked alongside Davey to the library, and opened the door for him. 'Here he is!' she said.

Davey's mum was sitting at a table with a woman with red curly hair. 'Hello, Davey,' the woman said. 'Please join us.'

'All right, lovie?' Davey's mum said. 'Was it ICT? What film were you watching?'

'*Toy Story 3*.'

'Again?' Davey's mum laughed. 'You must know it word for word by now.'

'I'm Ilena,' the woman said. 'The school has asked me to have a chat with you about how you're getting on.'

'He's doing really well,' Davey's mum said.

The woman didn't say anything to that. 'I'm just going to run through some questions, Davey, OK?' He nodded. 'So, how are you finding the access in the school? Can your wheelchair go everywhere you need it to?'

There were lots more questions like this, about moving about, whether his hands got tired writing, how much help the teachers gave him. Davey answered them with short answers. He felt his mum staring at him and he didn't want to get things wrong, or mess up the golden rule. Then the woman said, 'You have had a lot of time off since you arrived at school. Why is that, do you think?'

'Hospital appointments,' his mum said.

'Yes, but there are also quite a few where he was off sick, according to the register.'

'No more than other children.'

'Yes,' the psychologist said, 'more than most.'

'Well, you know, he gets so tired with the Duchenne. He has headaches, and tummy aches. I used to, as a child, too.'

Davey noticed the woman's eyes flicker. Not a normal blink, a kind of double blink. She made a note on her paper. Then she asked Davey's mum more questions, about when she was little, whether she missed a lot of school, what sort of headaches did she have? Davey's mum started answering but then she got cross. 'Why are you interrogating *me*? I thought we were here for Davey.'

'We are.' The woman smiled calmly. 'Thank you very much for your time, Ms Brooke. I'll have a few words with Davey on his own.'

'I'll stay.'

'It's completely standard to speak to the child alone. After our chat, I'll also speak to his teachers and then we'll all of us meet with you to discuss suggestions for extra support that Davey might need.'

'It's just about support, then.'

'That's right.' The woman stood up and held out her hand. 'Lovely to meet you, Ms Brooke. I'll make sure Davey gets back to his classroom when we're done.'

Davey's mum left the room slowly. She didn't want to go. She turned back to look at him and shook her head a little bit. When the door shut, the woman didn't say anything, she just sat smiling at him. Finally Davey said, 'I'm not allowed to use the internet.'

'And if you could use it, what would you do?'

'I'd look up my dad,' Davey said, 'but I need a bit of help with Facebook.'

'That's the trouble, Davey,' she said. 'Your mum doesn't want you to look up your dad.'

'Why?' Davey said.

'She hasn't given us the full details, but reading between the lines, it will be because he wasn't very nice to you all.'

'He *was* nice.'

'Sometimes grown-ups have to make difficult decisions, Davey. Why don't you try asking your mum tonight? She might tell you a bit more than she has done already.'

'My mum doesn't always say the truth,' Davey said. He stared at his hands, waiting for the woman to say something. But she didn't understand him properly. Not like Minette would have.

The woman said, 'Parents can't always give their children the whole facts, not when they're young, anyway.'

Davey shook his head.

She said, 'Did you mean something different?'

He looked at her hopefully, and nodded. She made some notes. 'I think it would be a good idea if I had another chat with your mum soon.'

Davey couldn't see how another chat would help. Still, it didn't matter. MT would have got his dad's number. But when the bell rang for the end of school, and Davey and Olivia went outside, MT was on the phone, and he shook his head at them.

Olivia went over to ask him what had happened. She told Davey, 'He says it's extra-terrestrial.'

'What's that?'

MT came over. He was off the phone now. 'I'm sorry Davey, that number is ex-directory.'

'What does it mean?'

'It means it's not listed in their phonebooks, I think. I was just trying another directory service but they said the same. I don't know why some numbers are like that.'

'Oh.'

'Your mum must have your dad's number on her phone.'

'Yes, but she doesn't let me use it.'

'Just borrow it, quickly, when she's not looking. Get the number and then you can use my phone to ring him.'

'Thanks, MT.'

Davey was last to be collected again. 'Sorry, sorry,' his mum said, not looking sorry. 'Feel like I only just left here from seeing that psychology woman. I don't know why school finishes so early, it was four o'clock when I was a kid.'

All the way home his mum asked what the woman with red curly hair had asked him, and he told her some of his answers. He and Lola watched telly when they got in, eating Mr Kipling's jam tarts. Their mum always got them a packet of Mr Kipling's on the way home. She said she loved them when she was little. Davey's five favourite Mr Kipling's cakes were:

1. Viennese whirl
2. Almond slice
3. Cherry Bakewell
4. Jam tart
5. Apple pie

He waited till he heard his mum go upstairs. He knew she had got their computer in her room. It wasn't really broken. He'd heard her in there tapping on the keys. He went in the kitchen to see if her phone was charging. Yes! It was there. He typed in the passcode he'd seen his mum put in before, but it didn't work. He tried it again, but it still said 'Wrong passcode try again'. She must have changed it. Then he heard her coming down the stairs.

Davey burst into tears. He hated crying, he didn't want to cry, but he had tried so hard and nothing worked.

'What's wrong?' his mum said, coming into the kitchen.

'I want to see Daddy. Why can't I see him? Why?'

'Come here, lovie.' Cath sat down, and Davey wheeled himself over to her. She put her arms round him and he leaned his head on her shoulder, making it wet with his tears.

'I knew this would happen, that stupid woman today asking questions, raking up stuff. Do you know, she left a message saying she wanted to speak to me again? Like I've got nothing better to do than keep running up to the school. OK, I'm going to be honest with you, like I should have been all along. I didn't want to tell you. You're only a little boy. You shouldn't have to have this great big burden on your shoulders.'

'Tell me what.'

'I know you love your dad. But he isn't a good man.'

'He *is*.'

'He isn't. He does love you, I know that. But he hit me. He tried to hit you. And there's worse things.'

'What?'

'Don't hate him, if I tell you this?'

'OK.'

'He said it would be better if you were dead.'

'He didn't.'

'I'm sorry, lovie, he did. When we found out about your Duchenne, and the short life expectancy, the medical problems, I said, well we are going to get the best care, the best support, this child is not going to have a short miserable life if I have my way. And your father said, maybe it would have been better if he had died at birth.'

'It's starting, Davey!' Lola called from the living room.

'It's my programme,' Davey said to his mum.

'Well, now you know the truth. That's why I don't want you to try and contact him. He's a bad man, a bad dad, and

I am frightened that he will hurt you and Lola. Do you believe me?'

Davey really wanted to watch his programme. 'Yes,' he said.

No.

Chapter 24

Cath

'Breakfast of champions, this is,' Cath told Davey, noting the disgusted expression on his face. She spread another thick layer of peanut butter onto her bagel.

'Looks like poo,' Davey said. They didn't usually have peanut butter in the house, because of Lola.

'It's high in protein, which I need. So, you looking forward to watching me? It's going to be a beautiful day. Gina's meeting us there.'

He didn't say anything, just carried on shovelling cereal into his mouth. Cath shrugged and looked through the race notes as she ate. It said to get there an hour before the start but she knew that was unnecessary. She was anxious about cycling, and there was no sense hanging around with the other competitors getting more nervous. Particularly if certain other competitors did actually turn up.

'If I could walk, would we go back home?' Davey said suddenly. His mouth was full, so Cath wasn't sure she had heard him right.

'What did you say?'

'Nothing.'

'Yes, you did.'

He looked up from his book. 'I just thought. Why can't we go home?'

Cath wanted to cry. Of all the days! 'You think you can walk now, do you, because of something that silly woman next door said?'

'Dunno.' He put his head back down.

'Davey. Look at me. We aren't going back there. I can't. We can't even stay here much longer. We'll have to move on.'

'You're shouting, Mum.'

'I'll shout if I bloody well want to.'

Davey put his hands over his ears, and something in Cath snapped. The wiry feeling seemed to come on more often than it used to. She rubbed her arms to soothe the nerves back down, but it didn't help.

'You want a wallop, do you?' She yanked his hands away from his ears and put her face right up close to his. 'You are trying the last limits of my patience, Adam.'

'Davey,' he whispered.

'I'll call you what the fuck I like. Adam. Davey. Spazzo.'

Davey pushed his chair away from the table and started racing out of the room. Cath was horrified at herself. 'Christ, I'm sorry, I'm sorry.' She ran in front of him, stopping him, and put her arms round him. 'Forgive me?'

'Yes.'

'You'll be so pleased with me when you find out where we're going.'

'I don't want to move.'

'I know. But you'll love it.'

'America?'

'I'm not saying, lovie.' She leaned in closer and stroked his hair. 'It's a big move, all right, and we're going to have to leave a lot of things behind. But you, me and Lola will be together, and that's the main thing. There's some not-nice people out there, and we have to get away from them.' She stepped back from him, so she could see his face, then wished she hadn't. There was that sceptical expression she'd seen before. She'd seen it the afternoon of the quiz, when he wouldn't change his shirt. She'd seen it when she prevented him from having to suffer through a blood test at the clinic. She'd seen it on his father's face.

'Let's not talk any more now. Remember, don't tell anyone more than they need to know.'

Cath went upstairs to get into her gear, and to chivvy Lola along, who was attempting a new world record in slow dressing. Cath worried about Davey, and what she'd said to him. She didn't know the right way to handle him anymore. Sooner they got away, the better. It was sad to be leaving Gina, but it was the right thing to do. As when she had left Andy, Cath felt frightened and energetic in equal measures. It was scary to leave safety nets behind, but also very freeing. It was too easy to get constrained by safety nets, tangled up in them.

Cath had collected all her sponsor pledges, and Minette's too, or at least, all the ones before they fell out. She was going to have to let the last ones go, but it wasn't going to make much difference, what, fifty or sixty quid? Duchenne Together didn't ask people to collect money before the event, but they were out of date. Most of Cath's pledges had come in advance via her 'Doing it for Davey' donations page, so what difference did it make asking cash pledgers to pay up front also? It meant the charity got the money much quicker.

Things were starting to come together. The report from the clinic arrived yesterday. Cath wanted to kiss the envelope when she saw it. 'Davey Brooke has been provisionally diagnosed with Duchenne muscular dystrophy.' At last. The proof that she needed. No one ever believed her. Doctors, nurses, doubters like Minette. Libby and Darren had both been seriously ill, but no one would listen to her. No one believed her, till they died. She hadn't wanted them to die, she had wanted someone to take her seriously when she said how ill they were. And some people didn't believe her about Davey, but they would have to, now. All that work getting people to see that there was something wrong with him had finally paid off.

Lola still wasn't down, so Cath went now to re-read the letter. But as she took it out of the 'Davey hospital' folder she felt completely and unexpectedly deflated. Her earlier energy quite slipped away; she slumped down on a chair and stared at the letter without seeing it. She felt the same as she'd felt the night when Andy had come home and caused that massive row, and she hadn't been able to keep up a brave face any more. Like then, everything all at once seemed utterly pointless.

The front at Seaford was teeming with cars, but Cath drove along till she found the row of disabled spaces. She pushed Davey through a mass of people, who were all walking around in that aimless way spectators do before a race has begun. Gina was waiting for them near the registration desk, and Cath, not normally a hugger, held her tightly.

'You OK, Rubes?'

'Bit nervous.'

'You'll be fine. This is exciting.'

'You said it was stupid.'

'It is, but it's exciting too. Your leg going to be OK, after coming off the bike?'

'My back's hurting more than my leg.'

'You're a right old crock. We're going to have to push you round the course in Davey's chair.'

'Gee, you know I love you, don't you?'

Gina stepped back and looked at Cath.

'Oh my god, you soft old cow, you're not planning to drown yourself, are you?'

'Only if it looks like I'll come in last. No, look, I just thought, well, I haven't told you how much I appreciate everything you've done for me. For us.'

'God, you *are* nervous, aren't you? You're shaking.'

'Just cold. Right. Better sign in.' Cath joined the queue of competitors, and was given her coloured swimming cap and race number, eighty-seven, which she wrote on her arm and cap with a waterproof pen. She put her wetsuit on over her tri-suit, and Gina zipped her up at the back.

'You won't be able to get Davey's chair onto the pebbles,' Cath said, 'so you might as well watch from the esplanade. It's higher up anyway.'

'Are the kids OK? They're very quiet,' Gina said, looking over at them. Lola was perched on the arm of Davey's chair, her arm round his shoulders, and they were gazing out to sea.

'You weren't in the car on the way here. Lola never shut up for one second. She's all talked out.'

'Speaking of which, there's that neighbour of yours, the one with the blabby mouth.'

Cath turned to see Minette and Abe walking towards them, Minette in a wetsuit. So she was going through with it, after all. Cath's stomach felt heavy, but she forced on a smile, and said hello to Tilly, who was in Abe's arms. She didn't look at Minette. 'Are you here to cheer us along, Tilly? That's so nice.'

'We thought you might like Abe to watch the children while we're racing,' Minette said.

'Oh, there's no need, Gina's here.' Minette's tone infuriated Cath. *Actually*, she imagined Minette saying in that smug little voice of hers, we thought we'd better as you're the sort of mother who thinks it's fine to leave your kids on their own.

'I haven't seen you since, ooh, last weekend, wasn't it?' She needed to remind Minette of their last encounter.

'That's right. But everything's OK,' Minette said pointedly. 'I'm just here to do my bit for the charity.'

Dozens of racers were gathering on the pebbles, and hundreds of onlookers standing around, chatting and laughing. It was a beautiful day, clear blue skies and warm sunshine. The swimmers started to make their way to the water's edge.

Cath pulled on her cap. 'Looks like we're getting ready to go in.'

'Good luck,' Abe said. He kissed Minette.

Gina gave Cath a hug. 'You're mad, you know.'

Cath laughed. She bent down to kiss Davey and Lola. She could see, as she could increasingly now, his father on Davey's face. With a last look at him, she followed the other swimmers across the stones, keeping her distance from Minette. The crowd were in party mood. Several people she didn't know slapped her on the back, and called out, 'Good luck, eighty-seven.' Snatches of conversation followed her as she passed:

'. . . all look the same in the wetsuits . . .'

'. . . which one's dad? . . .'

'. . . didn't remember the sun cream . . .'

'. . . lovely day they've got for it . . .'

'. . . we can get sausage and chips . . .'

'. . . going to run away again.'

The last one was a child's voice and she stopped, whirled round, but she couldn't see who'd said it. She was too far from the esplanade for it to have been Davey, anyway. Come on, Cathykins, focus. At the edge of the sea she joined the mass of seal-like people in black wetsuits, the odd crazy person wearing just a swimsuit or trunks. Now she really had lost Minette. They were herded into a penned-in area to acclimatise to the water, while the race organisers told them a load of health and safety stuff that no one listened to. The gun cracked for them to start and Cath was in the water, churning it up, in the first wave of swimmers. Reach, arm plunge in, face in the water, breathe, other arm comes over, face, breathe, keep moving, breathe, try to avoid getting hit by the arms and legs flailing around her. After a few minutes the course began to thin out, and she sensed that she was roughly in the middle, which was fine. She wasn't aiming for any particular time. Her stroke settled into a decent rhythm and she was able to turn her mind to Minette. Cath had not expected her to turn up today; she had assumed that Minette would keep well away. She'd gambled that Minette wouldn't want to jeopardise her relationship with Abe, nor risk ruining Liam's marriage, but that's all it was – a gamble. A calculated risk, based on what she knew about Minette.

If only Cath hadn't come off her bike. Because of that, Minette had stayed over, seen Davey, jumped to conclusions, and Cath's carefully planned moves had all been forced too early. And in a short while she was going to have to get back on that damn bike. She mistimed a stroke, choked on a mouthful of sea and trod water while she coughed. One of the rescue boats immediately made its way over to her, and a bearded man in the boat called out to ask if she needed help. He looked outdoorsy, at ease with the water, his skin tanned and weather-beaten. As he came closer, Cath could see the creases at the edge of his eyes, the silver flecks in his hair. She managed to gasp that she was fine, and he waved and rowed away. Oddly, she felt disappointed, and had to fight an urge to call him back. There was something about his face that made her want to open up, talk it all out, tell him all her fears.

She looked ahead to the furthest swimmers, who seemed a long way off. The ones at the front had already turned and were making their way back towards the beach. Cath started swimming again, slowly, aware that she felt exhausted, worn out with the effort of keeping everything going. Keeping the show on the road. She remembered Minette saying sea swimming was very different from swimming in the pool, and Cath had put it down to Little Miss Cautious doing everything by the rulebook, but right now it didn't seem so stupid. Her stroke, so reliable in the pool, didn't seem to be moving her forward in the way she would expect. Two or three older swimmers passed her easily, and she went even slower, her arms leaden, her legs thrashing out of sync. It was the same give-it-up-can't-go-on tiredness she'd felt earlier today, the same as when Andy came home unexpectedly and asked why Esmie was drinking hot chocolate.

Darren had died the night before the row with Andy, died like little Libby, sweet stubborn Libby with her Pippi Longstocking plaits. Cath was immediately suspended because of Darren, would almost certainly be struck off if she had stayed around for the disciplinary. There might even be criminal proceedings. Negligent at best, the consultant had said. He didn't say what it would be at its worst. She hadn't told Andy, though he'd know by now of course, if he didn't before, with letters arriving at the house. Being a nurse was such a big part of what Andy liked about her.

That night, he'd asked her over and over what the hell, why, why why, and she had no answer for him. She had no answer for any of it, really. Not Esmie, not Adam, not Libby, not Darren. She went to bed after their fight thinking she would just talk to Andy calmly in the morning, explain everything, ask him to accept and forgive her, and start again. She could try and explain to him about the wiry feeling, the way it sometimes seemed that she would explode from the inside, her blood vessels shattering like ice, if she didn't get rid of that feeling somehow. The weight she had carried round for so long, since her early days of nursing, since Libby's death, seemed to partially lift. That night she didn't wake up once, and her dreams were pleasantly unmemorable. She woke feeling refreshed, her energy back. She woke knowing that she couldn't talk to Andy, wouldn't be able to explain, couldn't bear to stay after being suspended from work, that Andy was all tied up with the mess and that, in fact, life with the children would be considerably easier on her own.

If only she could just call back that bearded man on the

boat, look into his kind face, and say, I've had enough, I want to stop now. Can I come aboard?

Cath reached the buoy marking the halfway point and, with a tremendous effort of will, set her sights on getting back to the beach. She was near the back, but her stroke was smoother now, a little faster. A swimmer was a short distance ahead of her and she determined that she would overtake them. Come on, Cathykins, you can do it.

It was Gina she felt bad about. It would be amazing if Gee would come with them. Maybe she would, in the future, when things went tits-up with Ryan, as they would eventually. But Gina hadn't moved around like Cath. She'd always lived in the same town, got her life there, her family, her drippy toyboy, her friends, her beauty business. Till a few years ago she'd had her lovely mum too.

Cath knew Gina could manage without her. But Cath didn't know if she could manage without Gina. Still, she was going to have to, at least until Gina decided she was ready to be a bit more adventurous. Cath didn't know if the salt water on her lips was tears or the sea.

There were only a few metres to go now, and Cath pulled ahead of the swimmer in front just as they reached the marker for the finish. The people noting down times called out congratulations to them both. The swimmer pulled off her cap, and Cath saw that she was a grey-haired woman in her sixties. Ah well. You take your victories where you find them.

The woman said, 'Well done, you made a big last effort there,' and Cath smiled, too tired to speak. She stepped stiffly onto the beach, retrieved her beach shoes, and made her way up to where Gina and the children were waiting.

'You did brilliantly,' Gina cried. 'Was it hard?' She handed over a bottle of water, and Cath drank half of it down in one go.

'Well done, Mummy!' said Lola, clinging onto Cath's leg.

Cath started to struggle out of her wetsuit. Davey said, 'Lots of people came out before you.'

'Minette already come by, has she?' Cath asked Gina.

'Yeah, a while ago. She said to say good luck when we saw you. Her boyfriend's taken the baby for a walk or something.'

'Did she talk to you?'

'No, she was only here a minute. She chatted to Davey.'

'I was thinking about your mum while I was swimming, Gee.'

'Was you?' Gina helped pull the wetsuit off one of Cath's legs.

'I really miss her.'

'So do I. Cancer's a fucking bastard.'

'Least you had the chance to say goodbye to her.'

'Mum made sure of that,' Gina said. 'Why we discussing this now, Rubes? You gotta keep moving. Give me the wetsuit and let's go.'

* * *

The bike start and finish area was a short walk behind the esplanade. Looking back at the sea, Cath could see a couple of people still in the water, but most had already started on the cycle route. She put on her shoes and helmet, and pushed her bike over to the mount line. As she sat on the saddle and Gina clipped her shoes onto the pedals, she felt a chill of fear, a trace memory of the accident, and held tight onto Gina's shoulder. The official counted her down and she set off, wobbling slightly as she waved to the kids. Which was a waste of time as they weren't even looking her way.

She followed the circuit down Cliff Gardens and back onto the esplanade. At last, her anxiety started to recede. The warm breeze ruffled her damp hair, and from here the sea looked beautiful, covered by sparkles of golden light, much more benign than when she'd been in it. Her legs felt strong as she sailed smoothly past the spectators lining the route, all cheering her on, because she was the only cyclist at this point. She rounded the corner and headed towards the Martello Tower, where the course was narrower and there was no room for people to stand and watch. She'd loved the funny museum inside the tower when she'd visited as a child. Davey would like it too, if she only had the time to take him. Mind you, there was probably no disabled access. She remembered steep steps going down into it, like a mineshaft. Oh, Davey. She shook her head to try and rid it of the terrible name she'd called him this morning. Pointless to beat herself up. Try and be better, that was the thing. Make it up to him. He would know she didn't mean it, that she was just stressed. Worrying about the race.

Cath felt herself freeing up, getting faster. After the route merged onto lovely flat Marine Parade she rocketed along. She saw Minette on the opposite side of the route, already coming back, way ahead of her. Minette's strong point was the swimming, but she was also a reasonably fast cyclist, so she would be in quite a while before Cath. Well, she had a good ten years, more, to her advantage. You don't do so badly, Cathykins, she told herself. She waved – Minette was doing this for Davey after all – but Minette didn't see her.

Cath managed to pass a few older cyclists, some of whom looked quite fit, though there were also a couple of fat ones who were alarmingly red-faced. She turned at the halfway point, gave a thumbs up to the official, and made her way back along, cheered on by more spectators. All the training had been worthwhile. She felt as light as air. Silly to worry about losing Gina. Verna was lovely, she would be the new Gina. It would all be fine.

In what felt like minutes she was back at the Martello Tower, cruising along on autopilot, the finish point only five minutes away. Then a man stepped out in front of her holding up his hand. She screamed, swerved to avoid him, and went clattering into the seawall. She just about managed to stay upright and on the bike, by clutching at the edge of the wall. The man came over. It was Liam.

'What the fuck you playing at?' Cath yelled. 'I'm in the middle of a fucking charity race!'

He put his hands on her handlebars. 'You're a hard woman to track down.'

Her legs started shaking. 'I need you to unclip my shoes.' He looked at her, uncertainly, and she shouted, 'Liam, I'm going to fall, please help me.'

Liam quickly unclipped her shoes and she dismounted ungracefully, scraping her shin. She sat on the ground, her back against the wall, breathing hard, and tried to stop trembling. Liam propped the bike onto its stand and sat next to her. Three cyclists zipped past, a blur of legs and wheels. Then another came past and slowed down, called out, 'Are you all right?' It was the grey-haired woman Cath had overtaken at the swim.

'I'm fine,' Cath called back, waving. 'Just fell off. I'll get on again in a minute.'

'OK.' The woman pedalled away.

Cath looked at Liam. 'Weird time to insist on a chat,' she said, trying to smile.

'I'm sorry, I don't mean to hold you up for long. But it's not like I haven't tried to contact you. Phone messages, notes through the door, personal visits, the works.'

'I've been busy.'

'Last time I knocked, a builder answered, and when I asked if he knew when you'd be back, he said, "Sorry, mate. I'm only measuring up the kitchen, I ain't got her diary."'

'I like your comedy Cockney accent. So Liam, what's so urgent?'

'Minette says you've got pictures of us.'

'Does she, now?'

'Dirty pictures. Of me and her in your spare bed.'

Cath laughed. 'Really? I wonder why she would say that.'

'I don't think she's lying.' Liam looked at her, and Cath saw the uncertainty on his face.

'Maybe she got confused. When I saw her the other night, she was pretty upset about Josie's pregnancy.'

'Yeah, thanks for telling her.'

'Sorry, lovie, it just slipped out. So can I go now? I am sort of busy.'

'I just need to say this one thing.' Liam looked straight ahead rather than at Cath, his jaw set. She wanted to laugh at how much he looked like a model from some naff clothing brand, his eyes gazing out at the horizon.

'Go on, then.'

'If you ever show one of those photos to Josie – if you even so much as hint that you have these photos – I will track you down, and I will do you some serious harm.'

He turned to look at her. She felt a little afraid, but her instincts told her that this was, in all probability, a hollow warning. 'These imaginary photos must be pretty hot stuff, if you're making threats like that.'

'I mean it, Cath.'

She decided she might as well do this now, rather than later as she'd planned. 'OK Liam, let's get serious. What are they worth?'

'The photos?'

'I don't want Josie to see them, either. But I think you should put down a deposit, to remind me that I don't want to.'

'So it is blackmail. Minette was right.'

'Not at all. I have something you want, and you're paying me for it. It's a basic transaction.'

'How do I know that you'll keep your word?'

'You don't, I suppose. But I will.'

'How much?'

'You tell me. What's it worth to you?'

'This is a one-time-only payment, all right? I'm not going to have you shaking me down every month.'

'I'm not planning to be around here for much longer. It's a one-off. To go towards "Doing it for Davey". It's a good cause.'

Liam sighed. 'Five hundred?'

Cath laughed. 'Come on, Liam, you were a banker. Still are, if we change one letter.'

'I was a city trader.'

'You'll have stashed enough away. I'm not greedy. Call it five grand and we'll leave it there.'

'Jesus, no way!'

'You ought to see this particularly nice picture of you with your dick in Minette's mouth . . .'

'All right, you fucking cow, five grand.'

'Can you make sure you've paid it into my website by the time I get home today? I don't want to have to chase you for it.'

Liam nodded. 'I'll do it now, if you promise that's it.' He took out his phone and started searching for her site. 'That's it, Scout's honour,' Cath said. She stood up, and her legs trembled and nearly gave way. She realised she wasn't going to be able to get back on the bike. Not now. Maybe not ever. She waited till he'd paid in the money, then said, 'Are you feeling strong, Liam? Strong enough to do "some serious harm"?'

'Why?'

'I need you to break my bike.'

'Seriously?'

'Just do it, please.'

'Why should I help you?'

'It would make sense for you to do me a favour, maybe.'

Liam shrugged, picked up the bike, held it as high over his head as he could, and hurled it to the ground. The mirrors shattered and a couple of bolts came off, god knows where from, and rolled away. The wheel rims chipped but looked intact.

'Harder.'

'What's my aim here?'

'I need to not be able to ride it.'

'Oh, in that case . . .' Liam brought his foot down hard against the chain with all his weight, then again, and the chain snapped. 'I remember from my cycling days as a lad. There's no coming back from a broken chain.'

'Thanks. I'll push it the rest of the way and say I crashed it into the wall.'

'Won't they disqualify you?'

'Not if I finish the course.' Cath stood up. Knowing she didn't have to cycle any more made her feel skittish. 'I must say, you look particularly handsome today, Liam.' She braced her hands on the handlebars. 'Something I've always wanted to ask you, how come you never tried to make it as a telly presenter or something?'

'I did try, years ago, but nothing came of it.' He gave her his Man At Armani smile. 'Whatever I've got doesn't come across in front of the camera.'

Cath began walking away from him, pushing the bike, which was all over the place, like a wayward supermarket trolley. 'Yes. I can see that.' Luckily there wasn't far to go. 'Weak chin,' she called over her shoulder, and then she turned the corner.

She wasn't the only one walking to the end of the route. A couple of other competitors ahead of her were also pushing their bikes, and one youngish man was limping along with bloodstains down his legs. It was good to know that she wouldn't be quite last. She reached the finish and explained to an official about her chain. Gina came running over.

'Oh my god, I was getting worried. What happened?'

'Tell you later. But I'm never getting on a bike again.' Cath drank some water and looked over at the kids. Lola was playing with Gina's phone.

'She was getting a bit bored,' Gina said.

'Bring them over to watch me run.' Cath changed into her trainers and went to the start line. Gina and the children came across to wave her off.

As Cath began to run, she realised something wasn't feeling right. She tried to shake it off, but it nagged away at her. She did a mental checklist of her body: legs, aching and a little trembly still, the scratch on her shin stinging. But basically OK. Feet, fine. Arms, tired but OK. Back, neck, shoulders, all OK. What was it, then, Cathykins? The runners ahead of her were a long way in the distance; the runners behind a long way back. It was just her and the tarmac, her panting breaths, the echo of her feet thudding in her ears.

She thought of Gina's anxious face as she saw Cath pushing the bike. She'd been the cause of a lot of Gina's anxious faces lately. The days when she'd been the one to rescue Gina were a long time past.

That first night after leaving Andy, four months ago. The kids were asleep in Gina's spare room, and she and Gina were in the living room, making up an airbed for Cath to sleep on. Cath smoothed down the cream duvet cover and said, 'This is nice. Egyptian cotton.'

'John Lewis,' Gina said. 'Nothing but the best for you, Rubes.'

'Cath, now.'

Gina sat down on the sofa and began putting a matching case on the pillow. 'Rubes, I'll do everything you ask. I will always be there for you and the kids. I'll do my best to remember whatever new damn names you've given them. I'll liaise with Andy and I swear on my mother's grave that I will never tell him where you are. But the one thing you can't get me to do is call you Cath. Oh, of course,' she said quickly, anticipating Cath's objection, 'I'll call you Cath in public. But in private, when no one can hear, you're still Ruby. You were Ruby when you were the only one to talk to me in Mrs Blaker's class. You were Ruby when you held my hair that time I puked on Hastings seafront. You were Ruby when you lived with us after your mum died. You were Ruby when I was your bridesmaid, and Ruby when you got me away from that shitty bastard.'

'Gee, are you crying?'

'Fuck off, I'm not.'

Cath emerged from her thoughts in time to see Minette pass her going the other way. This time Minette did wave, and called out 'Good luck!' Cath waved too, but didn't wish her luck, she didn't need it. In ten minutes, maybe less, Minette would be at the finish. She was going like the clappers too, almost sprinting. Cath, on the other hand, was beyond tired now, her running little more than a fast walk. She couldn't shake the irritating voice in her head telling her something was wrong. Cath always thought of her unconscious the way she'd seen it depicted in a psychology textbook during her nurse training. It was a drawing of a man's head in profile, with the brain inside, a tiny bit of the top of the brain marked 'Conscious' and coloured in red, the much larger part, nine-tenths, in blue, labelled 'Unconscious'. The literal-minded tutor had been at pains to tell them it wasn't really like that inside their heads, but the image had stuck for Cath. She imagined sifting through that large blue area, flicking through the possibilities. The wiry feeling was more or less in check. She was feeling bad about Gina, sure. But that wasn't it. Was it something to do with Liam? No, she'd handled that encounter well, considering how startled she'd been. Minette? That was still a gamble, of course. But there was no way Minette would tell Abe. Still, it was a bit weird that she'd come to race today after the way their last encounter had ended. Why had she? She'd not tried to confront Cath, and it seemed she hadn't even talked to Gina . . .

The thing that was wrong suddenly hit Cath between the eyes, like a physical slap, and she stopped dead in her tracks. The phone in Lola's hand . . . Oh god, oh god, what an idiot she was. She turned instantly and ran back towards the start, almost colliding with a runner who was running in the same direction.

'Hey!' the woman yelled. It was her old friend, the one with grey hair. 'You didn't get to the turn point.'

'I'm not cheating, it's an emergency. I have to get back to the start.'

'Yeah? You don't look ill,' the woman panted. 'I'm going to have to report you to the race officials.'

'Report away, grandma,' Cath said, and picked up speed. She thought she would never get to the end, the slap of her feet against the ground pounding in her head, all thoughts blotted out except that she had to get back there right now. At last she reached the finish point. She didn't stop to get her number noted down, and the official called after her. She ignored him, scanned frantically round for Gina. Oh god, where were they?

'Miss, I'll have to disqualify you if you don't come back now,' the official said, coming over and taking hold of her arm. She shook him off, feeling she might sob, and the official must have seen the despair on her face because he let her alone.

Every part of her was exhausted and aching, and now

there was this. She knew what was coming and she was powerless to stop it: the only option was to leave tonight and she didn't have the energy, but Christ she was going to have to find it. She ran here and there like a crazed person, and at last she saw Gina, sitting with the kids next to a cold drink stall.

'Oh!' Gina gasped as Cath appeared. 'What happened? We were going to come to the line to watch you come in. You can't have finished yet.'

'Where's your phone, give me your phone.'

'It's here, hang on.' Gina got it out of her bag and Cath snatched it from her hand.

'What's the matter, Rubes?' Gina said.

Cath didn't answer, just pressed buttons frantically. Her fingers were sweaty and it took for ever. There was nothing there, just endless calls to Ryan. Texts, then. She scrolled through the list. There were texts to Ryan again, to her, to various members of Gina's family. There was nothing there. But she knew. That blue area of her brain knew, had known all along.

She swung round to face Davey. 'You've deleted it, haven't you?'

Davey looked at her with his Andy-expression, and didn't answer.

'Davey, you little shit, don't give me that innocent look, I know you have, I can see it on your face. It was Minette, wasn't it? She told you.'

'What's Minette told him?' Gina said.

'Gee, I'm going to need your help tonight like I've never needed it before.'

'Oh my god,' Gina said, getting to her feet, 'will you please tell me what's going on?'

'Are you in, or out?'

'In, of course. What is it, Rubes?'

Cath sank down onto the ground, and started to cry.

Chapter 25

Minette

Nap when the baby naps. Minette was too exhausted even for her usual cynical laugh. Last night she was kept awake by her thoughts, whirling round and round. She prayed that she'd done the right thing, imagined terrible scenarios that were all her fault. She finally dropped off about two, only to be woken barely an hour later by noises from next door. She was too tired to get up and see what was going on, and went back to sleep, the noise weaving in and out of her dreams. Then Tilly woke for the day at five thirty. After Abe went to work, Minette spent the morning in a zombie-like state, trailing wearily round the house after a manically toddling child. When Tilly showed the first signs of readiness for her pre-lunch nap, Minette was beyond relieved. She whisked Tilly into her cot, yanked out her lenses, and crawled gratefully into bed. She was asleep in moments.

She briefly surfaced sometime later, disturbed by a vehicle in the street. Its engine shook the floor beneath her bed, then it cut out and there was silence again. Her brain groggily flickered, trying to remember if she was expecting any deliveries, decided she wasn't, and drifted back to sleep. A couple of minutes later she was woken properly by someone ringing the doorbell. She lay inert, her limbs reluctant to uncoil. She was so warm and comfortable. Let the guy leave a card. Or if it was a parcel for a neighbour, he could sod off. She closed her eyes again. Then someone started hammering at the door. For god's sake! They'd wake Tilly, the idiot. She put on her glasses and tore downstairs. If it was Liam, come to try and make things up, she would give him such a bollocking. But it would also be fantastic to see him. She flung open the front door, but the man standing there wasn't Liam. He was stocky, medium height, scruffily dressed, messy sandy-coloured hair. Two sharp vertical lines on his forehead made him look worried. An enormous lorry was parked in the street behind him.

'Are you Minette?'

It seemed a bit forward to use her first name, but maybe his company had the misguided notion that it was friendlier.

'Er, yes.' He didn't have a parcel in his hand. 'What's it regarding?' She sounded like her mother-in-law.

'I'm Andy. We spoke a few times on the phone.'

Minette's tired brain took a few seconds to catch up. Then she understood. Oh, clever Davey!

'Oh god, hello, sorry. Do you want to come in?'

'No, I want to know where they are.' He pointed at Cath's house. 'There's no one there.'

'Well, the children will be at school and nursery. Cath's probably at the shops, or something.'

'There's no one there,' he said again, his voice rising into a wail. 'They've gone.'

Minette stepped outside and closed the door behind her. Tilly would be OK for a bit longer. She and Andy walked up to Cath's door, and Minette rang the bell. There was no answer. Andy beckoned her to look through the ground floor window, Davey's room. The hospital bed was neatly made up. His books, the ones she herself had put on the shelves, were still there, and the American flag was on the wall. But all the drawers were hanging out of the chest, emptied of clothes, and something about the atmosphere of the room told her Andy was right. They had gone. She turned to Andy and saw her shock reflected in his eyes. 'But, but, I saw them yesterday,' she said.

'Adam sent me a message yesterday, on Gina's phone.'

'I know.'

'He sent me his address.'

'I told him to,' Minette said. 'I gave him your number. I told him to delete the message after he'd sent it. I don't understand what's happened. Where have they gone?'

'Thank you.' He clasped her hand, and tears poured down his face. 'Thank you for trying.'

'Eastbourne's not exactly a tiny place,' Minette said. 'We can't just go there and knock on doors.'

Abe was home, having taken a half-day's leave in response to Minette's phone call, and was drawing a blank on the electoral roll. Gina Grainger had almost no internet presence. The two links that mentioned her name didn't give her address. One link just had a photo of her and a younger man looking rather drunk outside a football ground. They'd given up phoning her – she simply wasn't answering.

Andy was slumped on the sofa, berating himself for not having arrived sooner. From the moment he got Davey's message, he'd driven through the night. 'But if I'd gone faster, I might have been in time.'

'I don't think so,' Minette said, remembering the noises that had woken her. 'I think they left in the early hours.'

'Something I don't understand,' Abe said, turning away from the computer, 'is that the other week, when you came back from Cath's, you said you'd got it all wrong, that she'd been telling the truth.'

Minette opened her mouth to explain, then realised she couldn't. That night she'd stumbled back from Cath's, reeling from seeing the photos, she'd excused her addled state to Abe by explaining that she and Cath had made up and got pissed together. 'Andy's clearly not to be trusted,' Minette had said, looking straight at Abe. She couldn't see him properly, which made things easier. 'Cath's got an official diagnosis of Davey's condition, and Davey showed me the few steps he can do. I also saw the hospital letter about Lola's allergies. It's all legit.'

To her shame, the lies came easily. It's to save us, she reminded herself, and to save Liam and Josie. It's the right thing to do. Abe asked her twice if she was quite sure. 'Absolutely! Like you said, Andy had his excuses down pat. It's all good with Cath.'

She said she was exhausted and went to bed, pretending to be asleep when he came up. She knew she had just added another layer of deception to her relationship with Abe, but she didn't know what else to do.

'Ruby's very convincing,' Andy said now, saving Minette from having to answer.

'But what made you change your mind back again?' Abe said, staring at Minette. 'And why didn't you text the address to Andy yourself, once you'd decided to tell him, rather than give the number to Davey?'

'Because I *didn't* decide to tell him,' Minette said, hoping Abe wouldn't notice that she was only answering the second of his questions. 'I knew it had to be up to Davey. All I did was give him the means to call his father, if he wanted to. How you getting on with Gina's address there?'

Answer the question with a question. How could she explain to Abe that it wasn't about changing her mind, so much as having the balls to make the right choice: protect her relationship and Liam's marriage, or protect Cath's children? She had spent the last week in a state of torment, trying in vain to find a solution which allowed her to do both. In despair, she rang Ros, not expecting great things, just wanting to hear a different voice to the one in her head. To her surprise, she found she was talking to the old thoughtful Ros. It was Ros who came up with the halfway house answer, to give Davey the means of contacting his dad if he decided to, allowing Minette to distance herself from whatever came afterwards. 'If he's as savvy as you reckon,' Ros said, 'he won't say who gave him the number.'

Minette would one day tell Ros the exchange she'd had with Davey at the triathlon, while Cath was still in the sea. But she'd decided not to tell Andy, because she didn't want to upset him any more than he was already. And she wasn't going to say anything to Abe either, because it would raise yet more questions that she couldn't answer. He was looking at her rather oddly now, and to escape from his scrutiny she went to make more tea.

'Davey,' she'd said in a low voice, crouching uncomfortably in her wetsuit next to his wheelchair, 'do you sometimes watch me out of your upstairs window?'

'Yes.'

Minette kept a careful eye on Gina, who was walking round the esplanade shouting into her phone at her boyfriend, and said, 'Have you been thinking that maybe I could help you?'

Davey's eyes grew big as he gazed at her. He nodded.

'For god's sake, Ryan!' Gina yelled. 'It needs to be delicates. Right, you can just buy me a new one. No, today. Before I get home.'

Minette and Davey grinned at each other, and Gina saw. 'Got people gawking here,' she said, and moved further away.

Minette said, 'I'm going to ask you one more thing. Think carefully before you answer, but whatever you say, I won't tell on you, I promise. Davey, are you ever frightened by your mum?'

'Yes.' Not a second's hesitation.

'I don't mean when she shouts, I mean . . .'

'I know what you mean,' he said.

'And your dad? Did he ever frighten you?'

'No.' Emphatic. 'No.'

'OK. I don't know the truth about what's gone on in your family, Davey. Your mum would tell me not to interfere. But you're a bright boy. I think you'll be able to decide what to do about this.'

She handed him a tiny slip of paper, which she'd been keeping in her kit bag. On it was written Andy's number, and her own. She asked Davey if he thought he could memorise them, in case he lost it. As she spoke, she prayed that she was right about Cath, that she wasn't doing the worst thing in the world: putting a woman and her children in danger.

'I'm good at remembering numbers,' Davey said, staring at the paper. His lips mouthed them out silently.

Gina came over, and he slipped the paper into his pocket.

'You won't believe what that eejit I live with has done,' Gina said to Minette. 'Only took it into his head to put my brand new Elle Macpherson silk teddy in with his red Sheffield jersey. On a hot wash too, thank you very much.'

'Mummy washed my teddy,' Lola said, 'and his fur went funny.'

'Yeah, well it sounds like the fur on my teddy's gone bloody funny,' Gina said.

Davey said, 'Gina, can I show Lola your phone?'

'You're not allowed to use the internet, Davey, and anyway there's no 3G here,' she said.

'We don't want the internet, I just want to show her the calculator,' Davey said.

'Why can't you kids just sit nice and quietly?'

'Pleee-eeese,' Davey moaned. Minette thought she saw him nudge Lola, and the little girl immediately starting whining. 'WANNA LOOK AT THE PHONE! PHONE! PHONE!'

'Oh, god, OK,' Gina said, and handed it over.

Minette didn't know how Davey was going to make a call discreetly, but she had to leave it with him. She could see that he was going to act quickly and she wanted to get out of there, remove herself from suspicion. She ran over to Abe, got out of her wetsuit and onto her bike, and suggested Abe take Tilly for a stroll along the promenade.

'He sent me a text,' Andy said, which explained why Gina hadn't seen Davey make a call.

'How did he know how to do that?' Abe asked. Both Andy and Minette started answering at the same time – 'he's incredibly bright' and 'he's very resourceful' – and smiled at each other.

'Couldn't believe it when I saw it. I didn't know the number, because Gina's never given it to me. Thought it was a hoax at first. Then I just turned the lorry round and drove.'

'Where were you?' Abe asked.

'Spain.'

'My god, that's a hell of a way. Min, what about the school? Would Cath – Ruby, I mean – have given them a forwarding address?'

'I doubt it,' Andy answered. 'She'll have just not turned up, no explanation, that's what she did in Harrogate. But anyway, schools and nurseries never give out information like that. Believe me, I've come up against this enough times. Data protection.'

'That's it!' Minette cried. 'I know how we can get Gina's address.'

Andy kept apologising about the mess in the cab, the food wrappers underfoot, the dust on the dashboard. The lorry smelled stale, and so did he. He had five o'clock shadow, and then some; his clothes were crumpled and grubby. Minette wondered how long it had been since he'd had any sleep. She wound her window down a little – an old-fashioned manual handle – to let in some air, and gazed out at the streets as they passed. She had never been in a lorry before. Being so high up, the people down on the pavement looked very small and defenceless. How vulnerable we all were, really. It was incredible that anyone made it past infancy. All the things that could go wrong. All the random accidents. She thought of the people she'd known who'd died. Cancer, car crash, heart attack, brain tumour, septicaemia, stroke. And yet. Here she was, having made it through almost thirty years. Here was Andy. Here were all these other people, walking around.

Davey and Lola would probably make it too.

'Turn here,' she said, and Andy artfully manoeuvred the huge lorry into the side-street. He shut off the engine and she opened the door, climbed down onto the step above the wheel and jumped the last couple of feet. She ran into Busy Tigers, and saw with relief that Sharon, the manager, was at the front desk.

'Oh, hello, Mrs . . .'

'Fairbanks. Hello, Sharon.'

'You're a family friend of Lola Brooke's, aren't you? Didn't you collect her recently?'

'That's right!'

'Is she OK? She's normally in on Mondays, but her mum didn't answer her phone.'

'Oh, she's fine. Cath said something about her having a cold. So, er, I was wanting to get an application form, please.'

Sharon visibly warmed up. 'Great! For your little girl?'

'Tilly. Yes. In three weeks' time she'll be a year old. I think she'd really enjoy mixing with other children. And I'm going back to work.' How glad she was, to be able to say that.

Sharon opened the filing cabinet drawer and handed Minette a form. 'You can pop it in next time you're passing.'

'Thanks.' Minette put the form in her bag and started to walk away, then turned back as though only just remembering. 'Oh, there was one other thing. Cath told me I needed to update my details with you, on the named person form. I don't think you have my new mobile number.'

'Sure. Let me just find Lola's form . . .' Sharon rifled through the cabinet drawer while Minette held her breath. 'I must say, when Lola didn't come in I thought perhaps Mrs Brooke had decided not to send her here anymore. Now we've settled.'

'Settled?'

'You know Mrs Brooke sued us over the M&M business?'

'Good god, I had no idea.'

'Oh. Well. It was my first experience of the legal system. And the last, I hope. We settled out of court. My managers wanted it over quickly, to avoid the publicity.'

'How much was it?'

'Five thousand. Luckily our insurance covered it. I suppose our premiums will shoot up next year. Ah, here we are.'

She put the form in front of Minette, who quickly scanned Gina's details before saying, 'Oh, you do have the right number, I was more efficient than I thought.'

Sharon smiled. 'Well, do tell Mrs Brooke once again how sorry we were about the incident. And wish Lola better for us, if you see her.'

'I will,' Minette said. 'I'm hoping to see her very shortly.'

Minette expected that Andy would drop her back home before heading to Eastbourne, but he took it for granted that she would come along with him. She debated with herself whether to insist, then reasoned that she would just stay in the lorry when they got to Gina's. It would be stupid to be seen to be so involved; Gina would tell Cath, and then Minette would be in for it.

Andy was silent while he steered the lorry out of the narrow Brighton streets and onto the A27. Then he said, 'What made you decide to give Adam my number?'

'There wasn't just one thing.' Minette couldn't tell him about Liam, or the photos, or any of it, really. There was a solid honesty, an ordinary blokiness to Andy, that meant she wanted him to think well of her. She didn't want his disapproval. 'The key thing was the feeling that Davey – Adam – wanted me to help him.'

'Thank you.'

'You don't have to keep thanking me. It's my fault, really, if you think about it, that Cath's run off. By giving Adam your number, I scared her away.'

'You can't think of it like that,' Andy said. 'You did the right thing.'

'I wish I'd acted sooner, now. I wish I'd . . .'

'What?'

'Nothing, really.' Minette had been going to say, I wish I'd taken them away. Run as fast as I could and kept them safe. It wasn't the sort of thing that really happened. Anyway, the kids probably wouldn't have wanted to go with her. They hardly knew her. Instead she said, 'I was wondering why you didn't have Gina's address. I thought you sent her money for the children.'

'Yes, but that's to a PO box, not to her home. I just have that, and an email address. She and Ruby are both very careful. I always put a little note in with the cheques, telling Gina my side of it, and asking if she can get the kids to give me a call. She has my number though I don't – I didn't, till you gave it to me – have hers. All I knew was that she lived in Eastbourne, where she and Ruby grew up. After Ruby left in February, I went straight to Eastbourne, spent several days just driving around, looking for them. But I didn't find them.'

Minette wondered what it was like, to be Andy. To spend all your time alone, driving thousands of miles, with nothing but the radio and your thoughts for company. No one to come back to anymore, either. She knew she had to ask him about Davey, but wished she didn't.

'So, uh, this might seem an odd question, Andy. Or perhaps not. But Davey – Adam – he definitely has muscular dystrophy, is that right?'

'Oh, yes.' Andy slowed down for a roundabout and glanced across at her. 'Ruby took him for the blood tests, they all came up positive.'

The lorry trundled along the road, past Lewes and on towards Beddingham. Another roundabout. Minette waited.

'Shit,' Andy said. 'Shit, shit, shit. How could I be such a shitting idiot?' He whacked the steering wheel, hard, and gave such a cry of despair that Minette's eyes filled with tears.

'Ruby took him for tests at the hospital where she worked.

She could have lied, or doctored the results, or anything. Oh my god, I am such a fucking idiot.'

'I don't know if this is relevant,' Minette said, hesitantly, 'but when I was at the house once, I saw a freezer in Cath's room. It had blood samples in it.'

'I know, she borrowed it from work, years ago. Never gave it back when we left Birmingham. Little Panasonic portable, it is, lab freezer. She kept samples from kids she worked with once they'd been tested.'

'What for?'

'You're going to think I'm stupid, but I never really asked her. I thought she just kept them out of interest, or to do her own tests on. She was a nurse, not a lab technician, but she was always very interested in that side of things.'

There was a silence while they both thought about what Cath might have used the samples for.

'Such a fucking idiot,' Andy said, under his breath.

'Will the hospital in Harrogate let you have Davey's results, do you think?'

'I don't know. I could try. But if she substituted someone else's blood for his, what difference would it make? Anyway I can't even remember if she got him tested at Harrogate. We moved around quite a bit, and she worked in a lot of different hospitals. I can work anywhere but she often got fed up with jobs, wanted to go somewhere else.'

'Did she get sacked?'

'Well, she would have been sacked from her last job, from the nursing bank. Worse than sacked, I think. Letters came after she left, saying she had to go to a disciplinary hearing. There were question marks about the little boy who died, Darren. It looks like he was doing well, then Ruby took over his care and he quickly got worse and, well, he passed away.'

They were silent for a moment. Minette wanted to ask if he thought Cath had deliberately done something to harm the little boy, then checked herself. His own children were with her, and maybe he was frightened that they too were in danger. It didn't bear thinking about. But Minette couldn't imagine Cath harming Davey or Lola. Behaving oddly, yes. Pretending they were ill, certainly. But physically harming them? It didn't square with anything she'd seen of Cath. She wondered what had happened with the little boy who died. Whether it was just some of Cath's odd behaviours taken too far, or whether she had just slipped up, given him the wrong treatment or not enough of the right one, or something? Well, she probably wouldn't ever know.

Andy continued, 'I had to ring the hospital and explain that Ruby had left me. I think they'll have to drop it. Before that, no, I don't think she got sacked. When I met her she was working at the Queen Elizabeth in Birmingham, and I think I told you before how she was very upset about a little girl who died there, Libby. Ruby wanted to leave straight after that. We moved to Edinburgh, then Liverpool a few years after.'

'Andy, I really think Ruby's unwell. I looked up that thing you mentioned before, that illness with the weird name.'

'Munchausen syndrome by proxy.'

'Yes. Could it be that?'

'I don't know. Possibly.' Andy wiped his eyes with the back of his hand. 'To be honest, I don't really care. Having a name doesn't help. It doesn't explain anything, it just describes it. Minette. Tell me one thing. You saw the children yesterday. Are they really OK?'

'They really are.'

'Well, you know.' Andy laughed bitterly. 'Apart from all the lying and the mental health issues, Ruby is a pretty good mother.'

They passed the sign for Eastbourne – 'The Sunshine Coast Welcomes You' – and Andy followed the satnav's instructions to Gina's street. The lorry juddered to a halt, and Andy opened his door. Minette said, 'Good luck,' and he turned to look at her, surprised.

'Aren't you coming with me?'

'Well, no. I, er, wouldn't it be better if it was just you? Less overwhelming for Gina? In fact, I was going to say, it would make sense if she didn't know that Abe and I have been helping. Don't want her feeling like there's a whole load of us ganging up. Don't you think?'

Minette's plan – to sit tight in the lorry, slide down so she couldn't be seen – had taken everything into account, except the expression on Andy's face. He looked utterly bereft. 'Shit. I'm a bit anxious about going in there on my own.'

Minette's heart went out to him. Really, she wanted to go with him. But you can't, she told herself. You mustn't be any more involved than you already are. The photos, Minette, think of the photos. 'We don't want to be mob-handed, Andy. And suppose Cath's still there, she won't want to see me, will she?'

'She won't want to see me, either.' He had tears in his eyes, and she had to look away to stop her own eyes from watering in sympathy. 'No matter how this turns out, I just want you to know that I appreciate it,' he said. 'You're the first person who's really tried to help.' He climbed out of the lorry.

I don't know you, Minette thought. We've only just met. I need to protect myself. Even as she was thinking this, she was opening her door. She couldn't bear to let him go alone. 'I'll come,' she said.

She knew it would end badly. But she couldn't do otherwise. She knew that in the same situation, Cath would sit firm, would protect herself, would not think twice. But Minette wasn't like Cath; there was clear blue sea between them. Holding on to that thought, and letting all the other thoughts go, Minette jumped down from the cab and walked up to the house by Andy's side.

When Gina saw them she tried to shut the door in their

faces, but Andy put his foot in the jamb and pushed into the hall. Minette felt a flutter of fear as she saw how easily he did this. Christ, was his story complete bullshit? Had Cath been telling the truth after all? Gina looked like she thought so, as she backed away from them. 'Get out of my house or I'm calling the police.'

'Gina, are they here?' Andy said. 'I just want to know if they're here.'

'Took them to the airport this morning, so you can both just fuck off out of my house.'

Andy burst into tears.

'Christ, I need this like a fucking hole in the head,' Gina said.

'What's the problem, babe?' A skinny young man with a pronounced Adam's apple came down the stairs. Minette recognised him from the internet photo.

'Nothing, Ryan, they're just leaving.'

'Gina, please can we talk to you?' Minette said.

'You're on his side,' she said, flipping a thumb in Andy's direction. 'I don't trust you. Ruby thinks you gave Adam his number.'

There were so many confusing new names. Minette translated them in her head to the ones she was familiar with. She hoped Davey hadn't got into too much trouble. She herself was, she realised, already in trouble, even before she'd stood side by side with Andy. She was prime suspect number one for having given out the number, so it didn't matter so much about being here. Even if she hadn't come in, Cath still had justification to drop the hand grenade of those dirty photos into her house. Don't think about it, Minette told herself. Now she was here, she might just as well go all the way.

'Andy,' she said. 'Maybe you should wait outside.'

'Yes,' he said, stumbling to the door.

'Careful mate,' Ryan said. He turned to Gina. 'Shall I sit with him? Poor bloke looks a bit fucked.'

Gina nodded. Then she said to Minette, 'OK, come in here.'

'Want a cuppa, mate?' Minette heard Ryan say as she followed Gina into the living room. Gina shut the door and they sat opposite each other on two plump white sofas.

'You're like a sodding detective, you are,' Gina said, and Minette thought there was a note of admiration mixed in with the scorn. 'How'd you get Andy's number out of Ruby's phone? We never could work out how you got past the passcode. And how'd you find my address?'

'Let me ask *you* something,' Minette said. 'Andy told me that he's sent you loads of notes, telling you what happened.'

'What happened, according to *him*.'

'Yes, according to him. So you know both sides of the story. How come you have never believed his version?'

Gina shook her head. 'I met Ruby in reception class. We

was four. She held my hand when I cried after peeing my pants. We grew up together. She lived with Mum and me for six years, from when she was fourteen. I know her inside out, and she me. She looked after me. She rescued me.'

'That doesn't mean she's telling the truth, though.'

'You're missing the point. I'm with her all the way, through thick and thin.'

'Gina, Cath didn't leave Andy because he hit her.'

'He did hit her, though.'

'Yes, but he thinks he has cause, he . . .'

'It ain't never justified. You look to me like a lady who's never got herself into a bad situation with a bloke. So you don't tell me that "he has cause". There isn't never a cause.'

'OK. Look. She didn't leave because he hit her, bad as that was. She left because she was in serious trouble at work. And because Andy discovered that she was lying about the children.'

'La la, I'm not listening,' Gina said.

'So even if Lola doesn't really have allergies? Even if Davey doesn't need to be in a wheelchair?'

'Minette, I love those kids. But I'm loyal to Ruby, first and last.'

'Bloody hell.' Minette didn't know whether to be appalled, or envious of the women's friendship. 'Are you in love with her?'

'Why? Can't I just love her like a mate, she can't just be my soul sister, it has to be about sex?'

'Is she in love with you, then?'

'Rubes was right, you are a pervert.'

'Pardon?'

'I've seen the photos, sweetie. I seen you.' She stuck her tongue through her fingers suggestively.

Minette's face felt hot, but she ploughed on. 'Don't you think that's weird, then, Gina? That she took photos of me and Liam?'

'It was Liam's idea to set up the camera. He's a kinky bastard, isn't he? Looks like you was well into it, though.'

Minette no longer knew what was true and what wasn't. She didn't want to think about the photos for one moment longer. She turned her focus onto Andy. That was the one bit she felt she properly understood. 'Listen, Gina, there's a man out there, a father. He drove through the night the minute he heard from his child. You're the only one standing in his way. Can you really live with that?'

For the first time, Gina didn't answer immediately. Minette pressed on. 'His children want him, Gina. Davey told me so.' As she spoke, something occurred to her. 'And I think you feel the same as I do. After all, you're the one who gave Davey access to a phone.'

'I beg your fucking pardon?' Gina stood up, towering over her. Minette edged into the corner of the white sofa, remembering how hot-tempered Gina had been on the phone, that day Cath came off her bike.

'Sit down, please, Gina. I don't mean anything, really. I just wondered why, after all Cath's efforts to keep Davey from contacting his father, you were the one who . . .'

'Didn't fucking know what he was going to do, did I?' Gina sat down. Her cheeks were red. 'He just wanted to play a game on it.'

What was the point in pushing it? It wouldn't help the children. And she didn't want Gina to clam up on her completely. Or wallop her. Minette took a breath, and said, 'No, you're right, I'm sorry. But Andy's desperate to see the kids, just to know they're all right. Even seeing them once would be enough.'

Gina shook her head. 'There's no point asking me. Ruby won't. And anyway, he's an abuser.'

'Do you really think so?'

'He hit her. That's a solid fact.'

'She hit him too, though,' Minette said.

Gina laughed. 'Think it's the same thing? How much damage you reckon she could do him, skinny bird like her?' She looked more confident now. 'He hit Adam an' all. And you saw how he pushed in here. He ain't that tall but he's big enough. Shoves his weight in, thinks afterwards. Ruby don't want the kids exposed to that.'

She sat back in her chair. There was something about her

expression that told Minette she would never get any further appealing to Gina's sense of compassion. She tried a different tack. 'You'll miss Cath, won't you? Ruby, I mean? Now she's abroad?'

'I'll go out there, soon enough. Me and Ryan, we fancy a nice holiday.'

'Where is it?'

'Oh, ha ha, Minette, maybe you're not such a Sherlock as you been thinking.' Gina stood up. 'I think we're done here.'

Minette allowed herself to be led into the hall. She stepped round an obstacle then registered it as the laboratory freezer from Cath's bedroom. It was plugged in. 'See you've got Cath's freezer,' she said, casually.

'Keeping it safe for her,' Gina said, opening the front door. 'Expensive piece of kit, that.'

Andy and Ryan were sitting on the front wall, drinking mugs of tea in companionable silence. Andy looked up hopefully, but Minette shook her head, and he nodded, as though he had expected nothing more.

'We saw that Cath left a lot of furniture behind,' Minette said. 'Including Davey's hospital bed.'

'He was getting a bit big for it, anyway.'

'Will you be putting her stuff into storage, or getting house clearers in?' Minette asked.

'Couldn't say.'

'So, do you think she might come back one day?'

'Well luv, if she does, you'll be the last to know about it.'

'Bye, Gina,' Andy said.

'Bye Andy. Now you know my address, you might as well send the maintenance cheques here. Save me paying out for that PO box. But don't bother turning up again. Neither of you. It'll be a police matter if you do.'

'Now Gee, that's a bit much,' Ryan said.

'You keep out of it, Ryan.'

'All right, babes. Nice motor,' he said to Andy. 'Bit of a hassle to park though?' He laughed.

'You know,' Gina said quietly, as Minette was about to walk round to the passenger side of the lorry, 'I do love Rubes, but I'll be glad to have a little break from the drama. Know what I mean?'

Minette nodded. She felt like she had been stuck on a rollercoaster ride against her will. Maybe that was how Gina had felt for years.

Andy climbed up into the cab of his lorry. He looked so defeated, she wondered how Gina could stand seeing him, knowing that she had the power to help him. But Gina had already gone back into the house.

Minette said, 'I'm sorry.'

'It's all right. You did your best.' Andy pulled out of the street and onto the main road.

'I did too little, too late.'

'It was me, I didn't do everything I could. They were within my reach, and I let them slip away again. Now I've got to think about how to live my life without them. I was a father, but I don't know what I am now.'

'Why don't you stop Ruby's payments?' Minette said. 'Surely that would spur her into getting in touch with you?'

Andy turned and stared at her, making her worry because his eyes were off the road. 'You serious?' he said. 'Sever the only link I've got to my kids? Give Ruby the chance to tell them all over again how I don't care about them?'

'Sorry,' Minette said quickly, and Andy shook his head, and turned his attention back to driving. Minette tried to think of something to make him feel better. 'I'm sure Adam will remember your number. I told him to memorise it. When he's a bit older he'll be able to get hold of a phone, or borrow a friend's.'

'I doubt it,' Andy shrugged, his eyes on the road. 'After all, far as he's concerned, he called me this time and I didn't come.'

Minette suggested Andy stay the night at hers and Abe's. He looked like he could fall asleep at the wheel any moment. He agreed gratefully, said in fact maybe he could have a lie down when they got back. But when they reached Sisley Street, Abe flung open the door in a state of high energy. 'Any joy?'

Minette briefly explained what had happened, and Abe

nodded grimly. 'I thought it might not come to much. So I've already made a start.' They followed him into the living room, where the laptop was sitting on the table, surrounded by piles of paper.

'What's all this?' Minette said. Abe had his crusading face on. He looked the same way after taking on a client at work whose case he believed in.

'We just need to go about this systematically,' Abe said, taking some papers off a chair so that Andy could sit down. 'I've been making notes.' He picked up a pad. 'So, where might they have gone? Minette wondered if they've headed to the States.'

'Davey said there were relatives there,' Minette explained to Andy, 'and Gina did say she'd taken them to the airport.'

'It's possible. Ruby's cousin, Verna, is American. But I don't know her surname, or where she lives. It'd be a needle in a haystack.'

'God, if only I'd asked Davey a couple more questions,' Minette said.

'OK, so, first, we contact the American Duchenne groups,' Abe said. 'There's some national organisations such as Parent Project and MD Junction. They might be able to tell us if there's a new family in a particular area.' He indicated the papers on which he had printed out details of these groups.

'What if Cath drops the whole Duchenne thing?' Minette asked. 'She left the hospital bed behind, after all.'

'Got to start somewhere,' Abe said. 'And we can do the same with allergy organisations. Then you have Gina's email address, don't you, Andy? So we might be able to get some kind of trace on that, and if she uses it to communicate with Cath we can get her IP address. That's the location of the computer,' he said, misinterpreting Andy's befuddled face.

'Abe,' Minette said, 'if someone is determined to stay lost, it can be pretty hard to track them down.'

'If it was just Cath, I'd say sure. Leave it. Let her do what she wants. But there are two children, Minette, who haven't chosen to be lost.' He consulted his notes. 'Another strand is the house sale. Priya's sister should be able to find out whether Cath's dealing with the estate agent herself or if they're selling it through Gina. Either way, the estate agent will have some useful knowledge. So, that's as far as I got, but that's just for starters. There's loads we can do.'

Abe hadn't shaved today; something about the combination of stubble and his determined expression struck Minette between the eyes. Abe looked hot. She hadn't seen him this way for years, though right now she couldn't understand why not. He looked like a grown-up, not some skinny Sinatra boy. She smiled at him, but he seemed oblivious to her admiring gaze.

'You don't have to do all this,' Andy said. He looked completely confused. 'Why would you?'

'Couldn't live with myself if I didn't at least try,' Abe said. 'I'd want someone to help me, if Tilly disappeared.'

Surely we've already done enough to help, Minette wanted to say. After all, none of this was really any of their business. But she knew she was conflicted. Sure, it would be better for her if Cath was never found. But it wouldn't be better for Davey and Lola.

'What I mean,' Abe said, putting his arm round Minette, 'is that *we* couldn't live with ourselves. I know Minette feels the same.'

Torn as she was, Minette was overwhelmed with love for Abe. He was so good, so straightforward. And newly hot, which didn't hurt.

'Yes,' she said to Andy, and it didn't matter that she didn't quite feel it, 'we couldn't live with ourselves if we didn't try.'

The men spent the next few hours in front of the computer, while Minette made coffee, tended to Tilly, and supplied snacks at regular intervals. In the evening Abe went round to Priya's, and was grinning broadly on his return. 'She's totally on board,' he said. 'She'll speak to her sister tomorrow. And you'll never guess what else. Liam's wife, Whatsername, was round there and she's expecting a baby.'

'Oh, how lovely,' Minette said, doing a fair impression of someone who was hearing a) wonderful news for b) the first time.

'That's going to be one cute kid. Anyway,' Abe said, turning to Andy, who was lying on the sofa, trying to stay awake, 'the good news is Priya's sister will be able to get us the inside info about the house sale.'

'Don't you have to get back to work soon, Andy?' Minette asked.

'Yes, I do, really. I'll have to finish this lot,' Andy said, pointing at the window, meaning the lorry load outside, 'before my manager gets arsey. I ought to shift tomorrow.'

'That's OK,' Abe said. 'I'll keep going with all this.'

Andy said, 'I've been thinking. I'll give it a few days, then take some leave and go out to the States. Do a bit of searching of my own.'

'God!' Minette burst out. 'Where the hell would you start? It's a massive country!'

Behind Andy's back, Abe shook his head at Minette, meaning, don't piss on his parade. He was right: Andy needed something to hold on to, was clearly much more optimistic now Abe had got started on all this. So Minette smiled, and backtracked, said going to America was a great idea. 'So good to just get out there and feel like you're covering some ground.' She didn't point out that Andy hadn't been able to find them in Eastbourne, population under 100,000. America was on a slightly different scale.

'I don't know how to thank you for all this.' Andy stood up and shook Abe's hand, then turned to Minette. 'Both of you.'

'You couldn't be more welcome,' Minette smiled, her jaw aching.

In the morning Abe set off for work, but came back straight away to report that there was a lot of activity going on at Cath's place. They all went to have a look. There were so many people traipsing in and out – men moving out furniture, a building company fitting a new kitchen – that no one questioned them when they went in. Andy was glad to get the chance to see where the kids had been so recently. In Davey's room Andy picked up a jumper that had been left behind, Minette guessed because it was too small, and held it to his face. Minette saw that the book she'd read to Davey – *Visiting My Daddy* – was by the bed, and told Andy how much Davey had liked it. He read the title and added that to his mementoes. She also told him about the framed photo she'd seen in here, of himself and Davey on a swing; Davey must have taken it with him.

Upstairs, the posters were still on the walls in Lola's room, but everything else had already been taken out, and the furniture movers were now emptying the spare room. Minette asked one of them if the items were going into storage, but he shrugged. 'We just shifts it, love. Don't know where it goes.'

Minette watched as they heaved the guest bed down the stairs. She thought about the times she had been in that bed.

Her eyes fell on the travel cot that Tilly had slept in, on the occasions that Minette had met Liam here.

'Do you remember that cot?' she asked Andy. 'It was Lola's old one.'

'We never had a travel cot,' he said. 'She always slept in our wooden one. And when we stayed at my mum's Esmie used my old cot. This looks brand new to me.'

Minette looked at it properly for the first time. He was right – it clearly was new. Cath must have bought it specially for Tilly, to facilitate Minette and Liam's trysts. Jesus, was there no end to the ways in which she'd been played?

'The thing I don't get,' Minette said, back at their place, and trying to focus on one thing she didn't get at a time, 'is that new kitchen going in. Cath said she didn't have the money for one.'

'Thought you'd have worked that out,' Andy said.

Minette stared at him, puzzled. It was Abe who said, 'The sponsorship?'

Andy nodded. 'When she left Harrogate I got chased by the Duchenne group up there for some money she'd raised for them. It weren't much, couple of thousand, enough for her to get down here I guess.'

Abe looked up Cath's pledge page, "Doing it for Davey". The final total was £18,570.

'Plus the money you raised,' Abe said to Minette. 'You got nearly two grand, didn't you?' He turned to Andy. 'Cath insisted Minette collect the sponsorship money in advance.'

'Oh!' Minette remembered what Sharon at Busy Tigers had told her. It had got lost in all the other drama. 'And she got five thousand from the nursery in damages.'

Andy nodded, unsurprised. 'So something like twenty-five grand. Plenty enough to put in a kitchen and bathroom, sell the house at a nice profit and start a new life abroad.'

'Bloody hell,' Abe said.

Andy sighed. 'Next time I get married, I'm going to pick someone less interesting.'

Chapter 26

Milo

'Last time, I promise,' Davey's mum said.

'You sure you need to do this again, Ruby?' Aunty Verna said. 'Nobody knows you're here, after all.'

'It's just a precaution,' Davey's mum said. 'A fresh start, too. I already thought of mine. Sandra Walker. Sandy for short. Film-star's name, Sandy Walker, don't you think?'

'Doesn't it make things awful complicated? Having to get new documents for everyone?'

'It was a lot easier than I thought, back in the UK. You

just apply to change your name by deed poll. Did the same for the kids. Didn't even need to get a court order.'

'Well, I don't know how it's done here. But Wade will know. He's very well connected.'

When they first walked out of the airport yesterday, it looked how Davey imagined America, with big shiny buildings, but then they drove a long way to Aunty Verna's house and it looked like anywhere. Aunty Verna's house was tall and had two lots of stairs and air conditioning. Davey didn't know you could get that in a house, he thought only cars had it. He and Lola kept running outside with the thermometer, so they could watch the mercury rush up fast, then back inside again to watch it fall down.

'Sweating's good for you, gets all the toxins out,' Davey's mum said. She liked the heat.

Outside the house was a wooden platform called a porch. There was a flowery swinging chair that he and Lola could both fit into. His mum and Aunty Verna sat on the steps in front of the chair.

Davey had been thinking about names on the plane. 'I want to be Milo,' he said.

'That's a great choice,' his mum said. 'Milo Walker. It even sounds American.' She put on an American accent. 'Here we have Milo Walker on bass.'

Lola couldn't think of one. 'Tilly?' she said.

Their mum told her that they couldn't use the names of

people they knew. She didn't realise that Davey had chosen Milo because of MT. He grinned to himself.

'How about Tammy?' his mum said. 'That's like Tilly.'

Lola shook her head.

'Tessa?'

'No.'

'This was a lot easier last time, Lola, when I just told you what it was going to be,' Davey's mum said.

'Well, I tell you what, I always wanted a cute little girl,' Aunty Verna said. 'If I'da had one, I'da called her Breeze.'

'Breeze?!' Davey's mum said.

'Is that even a real name?' Davey said.

'I brought up three strapping boys, and I always wanted a little Breezey of my own.'

Lola said, 'I like it.'

'It's pretty, ain't it?' Aunty Verna said, pulling Lola onto her lap. 'Well, I guess we have a winner. How you doing, Miss Breeze Walker?'

'You Yanks sure do like a silly name,' Davey's mum said.

'Least we stick to the ones we get given,' Aunty Verna said, and his mum laughed.

Milo told Adam his top five things about Escondido.

1. Being able to walk.
2. Playing with Nathan in Grape Day Park.

3. The fireworks.
4. Aunty Verna and the books.
5. Sour cream.

Grape Day Park was such a funny name. Nathan was used to it but it made Milo laugh every time. He made up his own bad joke about it. Q: What do you say when you go to the park? A: I'm having such a Grape Day!

Nathan lived on Aunty Verna's street, six doors along. Milo met him at their Fourth of July street party. In America they had fireworks then, instead of on Bonfire Night. It was only two days after they arrived so his mum said, 'Isn't it nice of them to give us such a wonderful welcome party!' Every day since then Milo had been to the park with Nathan and some other boys who lived near. He loved playing football – soccer they called it – even though he wasn't very good yet. He didn't tell his friends he used not to be able to walk.

They came to America from Terminal 5 at Heathrow. They got priority boarding and went through to the next bit, then his mum did a big sigh. She said, 'Did I tell you I had a call from the doctor, Davey? He says you can walk now. It's quite rare but they have cured you. It was those steroids, they think.'

'OK. That's good.'

'It's more than good, it's fantastic! Stand up then. We don't need this hunk of junk anymore.' She pushed the wheelchair into a corner near the toilet, and a bit later they got on the plane without it. He knew that what she'd said didn't sound right, but he was so pleased to be allowed to walk that he didn't ask any questions. His legs were weird and shaky for a while, but they soon felt better. He and Lola each had their own little TV screen on the plane and they could choose any fizzy drink they liked.

Milo knew Breeze would take ages to remember all the new names. But his mum seemed more relaxed than when they were in England. She didn't shout if Breeze said 'Davey' instead of Milo. She didn't even make a fuss when Aunty Verna accidentally gave Breeze milk before bedtime. But she was worried all the time about Breeze's headaches. Breeze said the day they arrived that her head hurt, but that was after they'd been in an aeroplane for ages, and Breeze had drunk four different kinds of Fanta: orange, red fruits, icy lemon, and mango and passion fruit. Now whenever Breeze looked tired or was upset about something, their mum said, 'Oh dear, have you got a headache, little one?' and gave her Tylenol which was American Calpol. 'I'm going to take you to the doctors soon, we need to get to the bottom of these bad heads.' Breeze never said she didn't have a headache because she liked getting cuddled and she liked medicine. She said Tylenol was even nicer than Calpol.

They'd left a lot of things behind again. It didn't matter about the American flag, because you could get them everywhere here. And he'd got his clothes, and Waffles. But he missed his books. Aunty Verna said if he made a list of his favourites, she would replace them. He wrote down twenty-three books and she laughed and said she was not made of dollar bills but if he narrowed it down to his top ten she would take him to Barnes & Noble at the Gateway Shopping Center. It was tough to get the list down to ten because so many were series and you needed all the books. He was still working on the list.

The food here was different. The bread was amazing, really sweet. You hardly needed any butter on it, it tasted nice enough without. Milo's new favourite food was sour cream. The day they arrived, Aunty Verna made them jacket potatoes with sour cream. She called them 'baked potatoes'. Breeze didn't like them but Milo thought he had never had anything so delicious. 'If I'd known, I could have given you sour cream back in England,' his mum said. Milo couldn't believe that he had spent all these years without it.

Chapter 27

Sandy

Sandy felt light here, like being on holiday. There was much less to do, less responsibility. Verna was so good to them. She'd made up their rooms beautifully – Sandy and Breeze in one large room together, Milo in his own cute room. Verna told Sandy not to even think about apartment-hunting for a while, that they should stay cosy with her. Fact was, as Verna herself said, this was a good time to land at her door. She'd only just seen off the last of her boys – his work had taken him to San Francisco – and was itching for someone to look after. Sandy was thrilled to be that someone. It was wonderful to get a bit of mothering.

Sandy and Verna had kept in touch via Christmas cards, and more recently by email. But they hadn't actually seen each other for thirty-five years, since Sandy was a child of about eight. Verna would have been in her early twenties then. Sandy had a clear memory of her older, glamorous cousin visiting them in Eastbourne.

'Your house was not in a good state of repair,' Verna said, when Sandy asked what she remembered of that trip. It was early evening, a week after their arrival, and the two women were sitting outside the house on the front step, which was what everyone did in this street. Every so often Verna called out 'hi' to someone. The kids were playing catch with some neighbourhood kids along the road, just about in sight.

Sandy didn't like thinking about her old house. She said instead, 'Are we sure about Breeze for Lola? It sounds like it should be the name of some fragile little thing, and you know I love her, but . . .'

'She ain't exactly delicate, is she?'

Both women laughed.

'It's just a bit of puppy fat,' Verna went on. 'Cute name like that might inspire her, anyhow.'

This was a terrific town. The climate was gorgeous, for a start. During the day it was far hotter than it ever was back in England, but in the evenings, like now, it was perfect shirtsleeve weather. From the moment they arrived Sandy felt herself start to uncurl, like some kind of reptile. The people here were friendly, the streets safe for kids. She was sure that even if Andy remembered she had an American cousin, she'd never mentioned her whereabouts. For the first time in she didn't know when, she felt safe. The last two nights she'd even slept right through, hadn't needed to do her usual panicked check to see that the kids were OK.

Verna handed her a can of Coke, and she raised it in a toast. Enjoy the moment, Sandykins, she told herself. This was a good place to stop.

She leaned back against the step and when she was ready, said, 'Go on then, what were you saying about our house, that time you visited?'

'It was dirty,' Verna said straight away. She'd been waiting to be asked. 'You put something down on the counter, it came back sticky. The door handles, I didn't like to touch. The dust made me sneeze. And everything was broken, you didn't have a single chair in that kitchen that was safe to sit on. Your mother was a funny one.'

Verna's mother and Sandy's mother were sisters, though they'd never been close. 'Whenever Bernadette's name came up, that's what my ma would say: "She's a funny one." You can believe that she said it when *you know what* happened. To do that to your child. What were you, just fourteen? To do *that*, and let your daughter find you, like *that*. Well! A funny one don't seem to cover it, in my opinion. Even when you were a bitty thing, your ma left you on your own all the time, you know. She did it that time when I was staying, so I assumed I was meant to look after you. But Bernadette said, "Oh, no need, she can look after herself!" You were just a little kid!'

'She had to go to work,' Sandy said. She shaded her eyes against the evening sun and squinted down the street, trying to see Milo. There he was, in the middle of a group, playing some kind of tag. It was fantastic to see him running around like other kids.

'That's right, she was always high-tailing it off to that department store. I often thought about you when I came back home. Wondered how you were doing in that filthy, cold house.'

'Was it really that bad?'

'Honey, she never cleaned! After she did *you know what*, you went to stay with your friend, and I think it turned out to be the best thing for you. Your ma wasn't the most caring lady.'

'She could be, sometimes.'

'If you say so.'

When Gina dropped them at the airport, it was immediately clear to Cath that the wheelchair was now more trouble than it was worth. As they hurried through Heathrow, she couldn't suppress the feeling that everything she'd worked so hard for was now utterly futile. Davey would never consent to a biopsy and, anyway, what would be the point of one? It was time to move on.

Sandy wasn't worried about money – her savings were in good shape. And thanks to the provisional diagnosis they'd get UK disability benefits, sent to her via Gina, for six months, until the next assessment was due. There was nothing like those sorts of benefits in the States, but the diagnosis had got them a few perks, such as a new computer, and a free access pass for attractions and national parks.

Soon as they were properly settled, she would return the triathlon money, every penny. She'd only borrowed it to tide her over, pending the house sale. She reassured herself that she would even send back the money she'd borrowed from her last race in Harrogate.

The savings wouldn't last for ever, of course. But the children were getting older, Verna would help look after them, and Sandy could get a job. She could probably find work at a private hospital. Verna's son Wade knew someone who could help with getting ID and other important papers for them all. Maybe even a nursing certificate. It would be so fantastic to be nursing again. She felt liberated at the thought.

Away from the Heathrow crowds, Cath helped Davey out of the wheelchair and pushed it into a quiet corner near a toilet.

She held his hand and together with Lola they ran to the boarding gate. He couldn't stop smiling.

She still couldn't bear to think that she herself had called him that terrible insult. Yes, he was provoking, and yes, she needed to work on her self-control. But getting rid of the chair would remove any temptation to repeat her mistake.

And Davey was clearly getting much better at walking. Verna was right; she'd said it was a kind of miracle, and it was, when you thought about it. 'Can't believe it,' Verna had said, when she picked them up from the airport. Though she'd never met Davey before, she'd seen plenty of photos of him in his wheelchair. She led them to her car, asking about it all the way, how did it happen? What on earth it meant?

'You know,' Cath said, 'in all my years of nursing, I've learned maybe one important thing, and that is that doctors don't really know anything.'

Verna laughed. 'That's true, honey.'

'Sometimes you have to really prove to them that someone's ill, otherwise they won't listen till it's too late. Other times, they make stuff up, because they hate saying that they don't know.'

'It's kind of a miracle,' Verna said, reaching into the back-seat to ruffle Davey's hair.

'It is. So, tell me about Wade. Is that girlfriend of his still messing him about?'

'Oh glory, she is. Let me tell you what she did last week . . .'

Breeze broke away from the gaggle of children she'd been playing with, and trotted down the street towards them. 'Ah, here's my honey,' Verna said, and Breeze snuggled into her arms. 'What's new, Breezey?'

'Nothing,' Breeze said, and began to suck her thumb, a new habit. Sandy knew she should try and do something about it, but god knows, it didn't seem all that important in the great scheme of things. She was more worried about Breeze's recurring headaches. She started to ask Verna how they'd go about signing up with the local paediatrician, but she'd barely said a few words when Breeze unplugged her thumb and said, 'I don't want to go home.'

'England, do you mean? No, of course you don't, lovie.' Sandy reached across and stroked Breeze's hair. 'This is our home now.'

Breeze looked at Sandy with wide eyes. 'Davey said.'

'Milo, you mean? What did he tell you?'

'Nothing. He said it to Nathan. He wants to use Nathan's mum's phone.'

The two women exchanged glances. Verna shook her head slightly, meaning don't panic, don't get upset. 'I wonder who he wants to call,' Sandy said, making a heroic effort to keep calm, though her breath was running short. 'Did he say?'

Breeze didn't answer. Sandy sat up straighter. 'Why don't you whisper it to me, lovie?' she asked. Breeze leaned towards Sandy and said, 'Nathan is going to let Milo send a text to Minette.'

Sandy shivered. The evening heat seemed to have cooled right down.

'Now don't you worry your breezy little brain about that,' Verna said. 'You run along and play now, let us do the worrying, OK?'

Breeze nodded, and ran back to the other children, thumb in mouth.

'Five fucking minutes. That's all I get.' Sandy could feel the tears starting. To have come this far, and to fail at this final stage. 'Five fucking minutes of peace. Christ, Verna, what am I going to do?'

'Well you can watch your mouth to start with, darlin'. Ain't nothing ever been solved by cursing.' Verna put her hand over Sandy's. 'Is Minette that neighbour of yours?'

Sandy nodded. 'I don't know what to do! I don't know how to stop Milo from contacting people, using the internet, it was hard enough before but he's getting older, harder to control. How the hell can I stop him?'

'You don't try, honey.'

Sandy looked at Verna, puzzled. 'What do you mean? I have to try!'

'This Minette, how is she a risk? If she knows what you're running away from, why would she be a worry?'

'She believes Andy's version of events,' Sandy said quietly.

'That ain't too sisterly of her. I'd like to have a word with that little person. Well honey, you can't control Milo, OK? So you give up trying now. I speak as someone with three boys and I tell you, I weren't in charge of what they did since the longest time.'

'If I can't control him, Verna, I am never going to get any peace. Maybe I should talk to Nathan's parents? Which one is Nathan anyway?' Sandy squinted down the street but the children were now too distant to see properly.

'If not Nathan, it'll be someone else. Milo's only going to get more strong-willed. You give that up now, you hear? You're going about this wrong.'

There weren't many people Sandy would let tell her how to manage her life, but Verna was one. 'Let me guess. You're going to say there's more than one way to skin a cat.'

'I am.' Verna took a swig from her can of Coke. 'Look, you can't stop Milo from talking to whomsoever he wants. In fact, I am surprised you don't know that by now. Kids don't want to do what you tell 'em.'

'Except my Breeze.'

'Yep. She's a mommy's gal all right. She reminds me of another little girl who always did what her mommy told her . . .' Verna grinned, showing large teeth. 'You need to go at this from the other end. You need to make sure this Minette person don't do anything if Milo does manage to contact her. Does he even have her number?'

'I don't know, he could have, or he might be able to find it.'

'Can you warn her off? Encourage her to keep her big nose out?'

Sandy sat up straight. 'There is something that might work. What would be the absolute fastest way I could mail a photo to the UK?'

'Email, of course.'

'No, I want to send a physical photo. It will have a lot more impact.'

'Well, USPS or FedEx, they could do it in twenty-four hours, but it wouldn't be cheap.'

Sandy sat back. 'It doesn't matter. I'll pay whatever.'

'Also you would be giving those people kind of a big heads-up as to where you are located.'

'True.' Sandy thought for a moment. 'But, you know what? They'll only know I'm in the States. It's a big place. That's one of the things I like about it.'

'OK, honey, you know these people.'

'I hope I do. I really hope Minette takes the hint. Cos I don't have a Plan B.'

Chapter 28

Minette

Abe always went into work late on Fridays – one of his protests against the nine-to-five – and he was ambling about in his dressing gown when there was a knock at the front door. Minette was occupied with making French toast, so Abe went to answer it. Minette couldn't hear who he was talking to over the noise of the radio that she still gloried in playing loudly, but she heard the door shut. Then he called out, 'Blimey, never had a delivery from UPS before.'

'What's UPS?' Minette called back, but he didn't answer.

After a moment, he came back into the kitchen and said, 'What's this photo?'

Minette stood at the stove, her back to him, stock still, cold ice filling her mouth. Cath had sent one of the dirty photos. It was all over. But why now? With the small part of her mind that wasn't panicking, Minette rapidly searched for possible things she had done to trigger Cath's revenge. For instance, Cath probably knew by now that she and Andy had been to Gina's house. That was certainly enough to have triggered this. The bread started burning in the frying pan and she said, 'Shit,' and tried to prise it out but it was too stuck. She dropped the pan and bread into the sink and poured cold water onto the whole thing, splashing herself thoroughly as she did so. Then she turned round and waited helplessly for the guillotine to drop.

'This is weird,' Abe said. He was holding a brown envelope. 'What do you make of this?' Minette looked reluctantly at the picture in his hand. But it wasn't what she was dreading to see.

It was a photo of her and Abe, taken years ago in France. She still had very long hair, and was wearing a green dress she no longer owned. They stood with their arms around each other in front of a large cream-coloured building, Chateau Chambord, Minette remembered in some distant part of her brain. The photograph was creased where it had been folded into quarters.

'Didn't this used to be on our noticeboard?' Abe went over to the board, puzzled, and started looking underneath things to see if he could find it.

Minette's heart started to beat again. She dried her hands and took the envelope from Abe, but it held no clues, other than being from an American delivery service. She shook the envelope and put her hand inside, but there was nothing else. The typed label was addressed to Abe.

'How weird!' she echoed. 'It must be from Cath. So we were right that they're in America.'

'How do you know it's from Cath?'

Minette realised she had rushed into assuming it was from Cath because she associated Cath with having photos. She thought quickly. 'Well, you're right. It might not be. But we suspected they were in America, and that's where this is from. And I can't think of anyone else who might have taken the picture, she was an odd fish, for sure. It's exactly the sort of thing she might have done, taken it and forgotten to give it back. Let's put it back up, shall we?' She took it from Abe and pinned it on the board. Then she got out a clean pan, and started all over again with a fresh piece of bread.

She wondered when, and why, Cath had stolen the photo. And more pressingly, why she had returned it now. Was this just an opening salvo, a warning shot? Or could it be – and her heart lifted – the exact opposite, a kind of apology? This could just be Cath tying up loose ends, drawing a line under everything that had happened, returning stolen property.

Abe sat down and started tapping on his phone. 'Just telling Andy that we might have some evidence that they're in the States.'

Minette successfully turned the French toast over and said stiffly, 'Yes, good idea.'

Abe had never been so slow to get to work. He behaved as if it was a Sunday morning, and Minette was just about ready to scream by the time he finally left. She couldn't think straight with him there. She practically shoved him out of the front door, saying that she and Tilly were going to wave him off from the garden. Once he'd disappeared, she sat on the bench, Tilly on her lap, and looked up at Cath's house.

What she would give to see Davey's outline against the side window.

Tilly yawned, and Minette realised that she too was wrung out. She took Tilly up and then took off her glasses – she hadn't got as far as lenses this morning – and quickly fell asleep. She no longer mocked the 'nap when the baby naps' brigade.

She woke from a dream about Davey handing her a pomegranate – confusingly, it was shaped like a banana. Feeling refreshed, though no wiser about the photo, she checked her phone. On the home screen were the first few words of a text from an unknown number, and those words made her sit up so fast she felt dizzy.

Hi Minette this is Milo (Davey) now we are

'You are where?' she cried out loud. Had her dream summoned him? She swiped at the message so vigorously that nothing happened. She took a breath, wiped her hand on the pillow, and tried again.

Hi Minette this is Milo (Davey) now we are in America it is quite nice. My address is 1320 East Maple Street Escondido that is in California in America see you soon.

Minette dropped the phone as if it was a spider. She put on her glasses and sat against the headboard. She knew where Davey was! She could rescue him. But then, almost simultaneously, she knew that this was why Cath sent the picture. It wasn't an apology. It was a warning. Had it been an apology – you idiot, Minette cursed herself – of course Cath would have sent the photo to her, not Abe.

With a sick feeling, Minette realised that Cath was saying, don't look for me. Stop trying to find me. Ignore any other messages you may receive. Or some more photos will come your way.

After lunch, Minette put Tilly in the buggy and pushed her down towards the seafront. She was too restless to stay in the house. She thought about how she had run along these pavements during triathlon training, and of that run with Liam. Everything had seemed complicated then, but it was nothing compared to now. Every time she started towards her phone, to ring Abe, call Andy, tell them she knew exactly where the children were, she thought about the shock of the photos. Every time she considered doing nothing, just deleting the message and pretending it had never come, she knew she couldn't. Then she tried to imagine Abe's face when she told him about Liam, and what he would say, and she did an involuntary little gasp of horror. She couldn't do that either. Shit, shit, shit.

After half an hour Minette turned back, but was not ready to go home. She walked right past her front door, to the little park at the end of the street. She pushed Tilly on the swing, settling into the rhythmic back and forth, rocking slightly on her feet each time so she didn't actually have to move. Push: Don't tell. Push: Do tell. Push: Don't tell.

Push: He loves me.

Her marriage and family, or Davey and Lola's lives?

Push: He loves me not.

It would be better for Tilly if she did nothing.

Push: He loves me.

Could she live with herself, knowing she could have helped those children, but hadn't?

Push: He loves me not.

But what about Abe?

'Dud-ud, dud-ud,' Tilly called, and Minette came to with a start. Tilly was going far too high in the swing. Minette stepped forward to grab the chain and slow the swing, then realised that Tilly was laughing, delighted.

'More?' Minette called. 'You daredevil,' and Tilly laughed still harder – 'Dud-ud!' – as she was pushed higher into the sky.

'Hey Andy, seen this?' Abe said.

Andy looked over Abe's shoulder. 'Yes, it's only thirty miles from San Diego airport.'

'No, listen, it says here that in Spanish, Escondido means "hidden".'

'Ah! Ruby would just love that.'

Abe and Andy high-fived each other. They were so fired up, they didn't notice how quiet Minette was. She kept herself busy with cooking. Though both men told her not to bother, she was putting together a cassoulet and a vanilla soufflé. These were recipes which were usually guaranteed to take over her mind, but she was still constantly second-guessing whether she had done the right thing. I couldn't have done otherwise, she told herself. You could have, and you should have, she replied. She wiped her hand across her forehead; it was boiling in there with the oven going full pelt.

'Can I get that number Adam rang you on?' Andy asked Minette. She handed her phone over, then thought, why does he need that?

'You're not going to call that number, are you, Andy?'

'Not yet, not till I'm there,' he said, tapping away. 'So he knows I'm on my way.'

'But we don't know whose phone it is.' Minette put her hands on the back of Abe's chair to steady herself. I've done my bit, she wanted to say. I've already put myself at risk, over and over. As it stood, Cath wouldn't know how Andy found out where they were. She might guess but, knowing Davey's ability to keep quiet, it would only be a guess, nothing more. But if Andy contacted him with the number he'd called her on, it would be only too easy to work it out.

'Well, no, but it's clearly a phone he's got access to,' Andy said.

'Not necessarily,' Minette said, her voice rising in pitch. 'Suppose it's Cath's! Or someone she knows?'

Abe put his hand on her shoulder. 'Minette's right. You don't want to alert Cath that something's up.'

'But I didn't reply last time Adam got in touch, and it didn't make no difference,' Andy said. 'I wasn't planning to text anyway, till I was in the cab from the airport.'

'Turning up unannounced is far better,' Minette said. 'The element of surprise . . .'

'OK, maybe you're right,' Andy said. 'I won't.'

Minette looked at him, but he wouldn't meet her eyes. Oh great, another fucking thing to worry about.

Abe had been looking up flights and now he said, 'Here's

the best one. Leaves Heathrow tomorrow at 13.40, eleven hours later you pop up in San Diego, 16.55 their time.'

'Abe, I'm sure Andy can book his own flight,' Minette said, irritably. 'He does travel the world for his job, you know.'

'I don't go by air, though,' Andy said. 'Last time I booked a flight was before I met Ruby, lads' weekend in Spain, and I went into a travel agent to do it. That dates me.'

'I suppose all that driving round for work, you just want to be at home when you can,' Abe said, shooting a keep-it-together look at Minette.

'Not lately,' Andy said. He handed Abe his bank card to pay for the flight. 'But this is going to be the most exciting journey of my life.'

Chapter 29

Milo

Nathan had a best friend, a boy called Chip. A chip here meant a crisp. Nathan said he could have two best friends. But it wasn't the same as having a best friend all to yourself.

Milo told Adam his best friends from all the different places he had lived. He didn't tell Davey. He didn't miss Davey like he missed Adam. Davey was just a short time thing.

1. Kiera, from his nursery in Liverpool. He didn't remember her very well, apart from her pink strawberry hairclip, but

he remembered a painting she did of Father Christmas.

2. Sammy was at his nursery in Harrogate, then they both went to the same school. He'd have said Sammy was his best friend when he left Harrogate, but Sammy hadn't always been nice to him. He once laughed when an older boy said 'retard'.
3. Eric was the nicest boy at the Duchenne support group in Harrogate.
4. His granddad and grandma weren't exactly friends, because they were old, but Milo really missed them. He stayed with them a lot when his mum was busy.
5. Olivia was the nicest person at Forest Lodge school. And a special bonus entry from MT. Milo knew MT was too grown-up to really be his friend, but he liked him anyway.

Milo had been out at Grape Day Park, playing with Nathan and Chip. He'd not been back in the house long when there was a knock at the door. He answered it to a lady he didn't know. Her hair was in a long brown ponytail and she was very smiley. 'Hey, you must be Milo,' she said. Milo's mum came to the door, and the lady shook her hand and told them that she was Ashley, Nathan's mom. She held up her phone. Milo was frightened for a minute that she was cross that he had used it, but she was still smiling.

'I got a text today, I didn't see it till just now, and I think it must be for Milo!' She laughed when she said this.

Milo's heart started beating hard. Had Minette replied?

His mum turned to look at him. 'Why in the world would you be using Ashley's phone?' she said. She smiled too, not a real one. She said to Ashley. 'I am so sorry,' she said.

'Not to worry at all,' Ashley said. 'I let Nathan use it all the time. It's more his than mine.' She laughed again. Milo could see that she really didn't mind, but his mum looked very angry.

'So, er, what was the message?' Milo's mum asked. Her hand was holding very tightly onto the edge of the door. 'Who is it from?'

Ashley consulted her phone. 'It just says, "Hey Adam-Milo, I'll be there in an hour. Love you. D."'

Dad. It was from Dad. Milo couldn't believe it. He was coming. He was nearly here.

'Could I just have a look at that, Ashley?' Milo's mum said. Her face was white, clean white like Gina's sofa. Nathan's mum handed her the phone.

'My god, it was sent forty minutes ago,' Milo's mum shouted. Aunty Verna came running into the hall. Milo knew he was in massive trouble but he didn't care.

'I'm really sorry, is it a problem, can I help in any way?' asked Ashley. She'd stopped smiling and looked worried.

'It's a huge fucking problem,' Milo's mum said, and Ashley put her hand over her mouth.

'Excuse us please, won't you?' Aunty Verna said, and gave

back the phone. 'Thank you so much for coming round, it was really kind of you.' She shut the door in Ashley's face and turned to Milo. 'What on earth were you thinking of, honey?' she said, but she didn't seem surprised.

Milo's mum was walking up and down the hall, backwards and forwards. 'Think, think, I got to think.'

'Look, honey, why don't we just sit down and talk to Andy? I'm sure it will be OK, we just got to be rational about this . . .'

'It's not going to be fucking well OK, Verna.'

'Please, Ruby, not in front of the child.'

'Right.' Milo's mum stopped walking. 'I reckon we've got ten minutes. Can I borrow Wade's car?'

'Sure, honey, it's just sitting there on the drive. You absolutely sure you don't want to see Andy, put an end to all this?'

'It won't put an end, it will never end, it will just keep going on and getting worse. Do me a favour Verna, I'm going to grab some clothes and my laptop, can you throw a bag together for the kids? Change of clothes, toothbrushes, teddies, that's it, I can buy everything else and you can send me the rest of our stuff when we're settled.'

Milo's mum ran upstairs and Aunty Verna followed her. He went into the rumpus room where Breeze was sucking her thumb and watching TV.

'Daddy's coming,' he said.

'Who is?'

'Daddy, you remember?'

She looked unsure. 'He was naughty.'

'No, he was nice.'

'Mummy's nice,' Breeze said, and stuck her thumb in her mouth again. Milo sat down to watch with her. It was an old-fashioned cartoon, Milo couldn't think of the name, it was a duck with a funny voice. Milo had a long-ago memory of watching it with his grandparents back in Harrogate. He would see them again soon. He pinched the top of his nose so he wouldn't cry.

Their mum came into the room and turned off the telly. 'OK kids, we got to go. Get in the car, I'll explain on the way, Breeze. We got your brother to thank for this one. Don't think I won't be having a few words with you about this, Milo. Say bye-bye to Aunty Verna, hopefully we'll be back soon, we're just going on a little holiday.'

'I thought we were already on holiday,' Breeze said.

'Another one,' Milo's mum said. 'Car, now.'

Breeze ran out. Milo stayed where he was. 'Come ON,' his mum said.

'I'm not coming,' he said.

'You most certainly are. I'm not messing about. Get in the car. It'll be OK. We can write to Daddy, tell him we're OK. You can even talk to him on the phone, if you want. But we really have to go RIGHT NOW.' Milo's mum was crying. Her face was red now, not white. Milo felt sorry for her. But he knew he wouldn't go, not even if a policeman told him to.

'I'm not coming.'

His mum grabbed his arm, tried to pull him to the door. He held onto the table, so she tried tickling him so he'd let go, but as soon as his hand slipped off one part of the table he grabbed another part. She pulled harder at his arm and he couldn't hold on any more, so he dropped to the floor and grabbed the table leg with his free hand. The table started to move with him as his mum dragged him along the floor. The pink carpet was clean and bristly, and felt nice under his back.

Aunty Verna called from outside the room, 'Just popping a snack in the kids' bag. Listen, sugar, if you're going you oughta go.' Then she came in and said, 'What in the name of Beelzebub are you two doing? You planning to take my good table with you?'

Milo's mum said, 'Can you help me, please, Verna?'

'Help do what? Physically remove the child from this room? I don't think so.'

'He's just being silly. You grab one leg, I'll grab the other.'

'You listen to what you're asking, Ruby.'

Milo's mum let him go and sat down with a thump on the sofa. Aunty Verna smiled at Milo. 'Come on, honey, your place is with your momma.'

Milo shook his head, still holding on tight to the table leg.

Milo's mum said, in a quiet voice, 'What'll I do? He won't come.' She rubbed her arms, first one, then the other.

'Have you hurt your arms?' Milo said.

She shook her head.

'Well, Ruby, this is what I meant before,' Aunty Verna said. 'They gets to a certain age, ain't possible to make them do what they don't want.'

Milo sat up, and he and his mum stared at each other across the room. Milo's mum pushed her hand into her hair. It looked funny, stuck up at the front like a hedgehog. She said, 'Aren't you happy here?'

'Yes.'

'Then for Christ's sake, why did you send that message?'

'I want Daddy.'

'You can't have me *and* Daddy.'

'I want to.'

'You can't, Milo, it's one or the other. Do you understand?'

He didn't answer. She yelled: 'DO YOU UNDERSTAND?'

Milo thought about Minette saying, 'Are you ever frightened by your mum?' He nodded. 'I understand.'

'Boy wants both his parents, Ruby. It's only natural. Now, let me ask you one more time. Why don't we just talk to Andy? He probably feels so remorseful. He ain't going to be the first fellow who acted crazy then regretted it. He'll be a lamb, I promise you. You all can stay here while you decide what to do . . .'

'I can't.' Milo's mum stood up.

'So what are you saying?' Aunty Verna asked.

Milo's mum said, 'I'm going to have to go without him.'

'You crazy?' Aunty Verna shouted. It was the first time since they arrived that Milo had even seen her cross. 'You can't abandon your child! Think about what you are saying.'

'I'm not abandoning him,' Milo's mum said. She was properly crying now. 'He's abandoning me. He's made a choice.'

'But you could stay! I'll look after you all. I'll send Andy packing, don't you worry.'

There was a sound of a car outside and Milo's mum ran to the window. 'Christ almighty.' Then she turned back. 'Not him. OK. Verna, did you do the kids' bag? Thanks.' She took it from Aunty Verna, pulled Milo into a hug and kissed him hard on the cheek.

'Bye, Adam,' she said. 'I love you.'

'I know,' Milo said.

He felt her fingers press harder on his back. She stayed there for a long time, so long he wondered if she really was going to go. It was very quiet. Then she stood back, and looked at him.

'I wish . . .' she said, and looked from him to Aunty Verna.

'Yes, sugar?' Aunty Verna said.

Then Milo's mum shook her head, walked outside and put Breeze into the car. Milo stood in the doorway watching them.

'This is just crazy stuff,' Aunty Verna said to him. 'I am so angry at your mother.'

Milo could hear Breeze wailing, calling his name. He waved, and the car reversed suddenly, in a big jump, then bunny-hopped into the road. His mother got it going properly and the car roared away. Aunty Verna put her hand on his shoulder and they stood there for a few minutes, staring into the street, not saying anything. Then she said, 'Oh my gosh, I think she's gone off with your toy.'

'What one?'

'She told me to pack teddies for both of you. Your soft brown bear?'

A taxi pulled up, and before it stopped properly, his dad jumped out and ran to him.

'Adam! You're standing!' his dad said, and he flung his arms round him.

'Daddy,' Milo said, and tears went all over his dad's shirt, 'Daddy, Mummy has taken Waffles.'

Chapter 30

Minette

'Go and have a coffee,' Sharon urged. 'She'll be fine. Hey, Tilly, shall we play with the sand?'

She took Tilly's hand and led her to the sandpit. Tilly whooped in excitement when she saw it, practically dragged Sharon the last few steps. Sharon smiled, and made a shooing motion at Minette with her hands. 'Bye, sweetie,' Minette called, but Tilly didn't look round.

Outside, Minette raised her face to the sky and took a couple of slow breaths, looked at the clouds, wiped under her eyes with the side of her hand. There was a whole world out here, and she was on her own in it. She walked to the nearest café and ordered an espresso. Her mother Élise, unlike most of her French compatriots, didn't generally drink coffee, preferring tea after all her years living in England. However, when Minette was a child, Élise always celebrated any small achievement in their lives with *un café*. So it came to seem to Minette as though it was a treat, like champagne, though she too didn't much like it. She stirred in two lumps of sugar, and sipped it. Still too bitter.

Tilly's try-out at Busy Tigers was a success, and she started going there three days a week. Shortly after, Minette returned to work. Her old colleagues were delighted to see her, and she was plunged straight back into the rotas and new systems and gossip as though she'd never been gone. She found that she enjoyed it even more than she'd done B.T. – Before Tilly – because work was now a contrast to the rest of her life. While there, she could finish a conversation, have a coherent thought from beginning to end, eat a quiet lunch at her desk, go for a pee whenever she liked. Home became easier too, because Tilly was more tired now she was at nursery, and she began to sleep reliably through the night to seven o'clock. When they were students this would have been a brutal time to wake; now Abe called it a 'luxury lie-in'. Minette slowly began to feel like her old self again.

All four grandparents came to Tilly's first birthday party.

Minette's parents were civil to each other, which was made possible by Richard leaving his difficult second wife at home. They even paid jointly for a family photo of all of them, though they made sure to sit on opposite sides of the picture. Julie and Roy gave Tilly a huge soft lion, big enough for her to sit on, which she adored. Everyone loved the meal Minette made, the champagne sparkled, and Julie made a speech in which she described Minette and Abe as 'the best parents I have ever seen', to which Élise called out, '*Bien dit!*' It was one of the happiest times Minette could remember for a long time. She silently gave thanks to the God of Good Things that her life, as she knew it, remained intact. Despite everything, she'd managed not to screw things up.

The days went by, and Tilly started to produce more recognisable words, including 'Mama'. The way she said it made Minette's heart melt, every time.

At the end of July, a 'For Sale' sign went up outside Cath's house, and Minette went to look round, posing as a buyer. She knew Cath had painted the walls, and restored the wooden floors. Now she could see how much of an improvement the new kitchen and redecorated bathroom made. The house sold quickly, for £55,000 more than Cath had paid for it. Minette was glad. The more money, the better for Lola.

Minette and Abe were in close contact with Andy. He'd taken Adam, as they were learning to call him, straight home to Harrogate from Heathrow. But he Skyped them the following evening, when Adam was in bed, and gave them all the details of his dramatic rescue. How Verna had reluctantly driven him and Adam round for several hours looking for Cath, though Andy knew that Verna genuinely had no idea where they'd gone. How they'd eventually gone back to Verna's, where she'd cooked for them, and, after Adam was asleep, had mixed some strong cocktails, and told Andy a few things he didn't know about Cath. That her mother, who'd been 'a lousy mother, and I'm using mother here as short for a swearword, if you get me,' had hung herself when Cath was fourteen. 'Right in the kitchen, hanging from the beam above the flue.'

Cath was the person who found her. 'Well of course she was,' Verna said, 'she was the only person in and out of that god-awful house. Bernadette made no attempt to protect her.' Verna mixed another mojito. 'I always said that Ruby deserved a pretty big pass after that. She was allowed to be a little cranky.'

Her own mother, Bernadette's sister, travelled to England for the funeral and had wanted to bring Ruby back to live with them, but Cath chose to stay at school and was taken in by Gina's parents.

Andy hadn't known that Cath's mother had killed herself, and this shocked Verna almost as much as Cath abandoning Adam. But not quite. 'I still say she earned the right to a free pass, but I tell you, I am not feeling best pleased with her for leaving that boy. I know she never had a role model, but even she knows that is not what a good mother would do.'

Andy looked at Verna, and they smiled at each other.

'I guess,' Verna said, 'she is not necessarily a good mother.'

'Only perhaps in the sense that you used the word about Bernadette,' Andy said, and Verna said, 'Now that's going a bit far, Andrew. You do not have an unblemished record, yourself.'

Andy had tried to tell Verna his side of the story, but Verna said it would be better if she didn't know it, that whatever the rights and wrongs, she was still, and would always be, there for Ruby.

'Wow,' Minette marvelled, 'like Gina.' She was so impressed by, and yes, rather envious of, the unconditional loyalty that Cath inspired in others. But maybe that was part of Cath's illness – it was powerful enough that she was able to convince a lot of people to accept her version of the world.

Andy said he planned to get Adam settled, and back into school, then he'd leave the grandparents in charge while he returned to the States to find Lola. He spoke confidently of teaming up with Verna, and didn't seem to consider the impossibility of the task that faced him, so Minette didn't say anything. But a week or so later, Andy contacted them again, with the news that Verna had heard from Ruby. Though he was obviously relieved that there had been contact, he seemed unexpectedly flat. Minette felt terrified that something bad had happened to Lola, but Andy reassured her.

'Verna says Esmie is fine. She's even spoken to her. But it's like the arrangement with Gina all over again; Ruby will only stay in touch with Verna if she swears not to tell anyone, especially me, where they are.'

'Are they still in the States?'

'I'm guessing so, but Verna won't say. She has Ruby's new number and email, but of course she has to keep all this to herself. Verna just wants them to stay in touch, so she isn't going to do anything Ruby doesn't want.'

'Will you still go out there and look for her?' Abe asked.

Andy shook his head. 'I really want to, but Verna's insistent that I don't rock the boat. She says me going there will jeopardise things, tip the balance she's got now. Verna thinks that if we give her enough time, Ruby will come round. Maybe even move back in with her.'

Minette didn't think that sounded likely, but she nodded enthusiastically, along with Abe.

'And Verna's promised me that she'll check in with them regularly, three times a week. She'll speak to Esmie every time, to reassure herself, and if she's worried about her safety, then the deal with Ruby's off, and she'll tell me where they are.' He rubbed his forehead, smoothed down the two sharp vertical lines. 'It's about as good as I can hope for right now, I think.'

Andy admitted then that he was still kicking himself for alerting Cath that he was on his way. 'I wish I'd taken your advice and not texted,' he said. Yeah, Minette thought, I wish you had too. Gina had been right about Andy, when she said he acted first, then thought afterwards. Minette tried not to make him feel worse than he did already. He'd paid a hefty price these last few months for his poor impulse control.

'Lola will be fine,' Minette tried to reassure Andy, and he responded with his own desperate belief: 'When she's older, like Adam, she'll find a way to get in touch with me.'

Minette suspected that Lola wouldn't realise she needed to get away from her mother for a long time. She was a different character to her brother. She wondered if Cath had known she needed to get away from her own mother, before the decision was taken for her.

Adam came onto Skype afterwards to say 'hello', and was all smiles, clearly very happy to be home. His grandparents had bought him a new Waffles teddy, and he was back at his original school, only now he could walk and play football. He told Minette that she must try sour cream on her jacket potato, and she promised she would. Life for him was good. Apart from missing his sister.

Minette took Tilly to Kirsten's house for her last cranial osteopathy session. She suspected that Tilly's improved sleeping had happened naturally, without any outside help other than the tiring activity of nursery, but she didn't want to hurt Kirsten's feelings. Minette watched as Kirsten gently touched Tilly's head, and realised that she was seeing it through a new, cynical lens. It looked silly, like the laying on of hands. She didn't say anything, of course, because Kirsten was a good person who meant well. Minette handed over the £20 fee with the oddest feeling, as if she was paying off her former self: the naïve young girl who was fair game to every charlatan and charmer who passed by.

Kirsten walked Minette to the front door, and said, 'I see Cath's house is up for sale. Any idea where she's gone?'

Minette and Abe had agreed not to talk about what happened to any more neighbours, so Minette just said, 'No, none at all. She left in rather a hurry.'

'All a bit bloody weird, wasn't it? Blew in, made friends with everyone, then disappeared again.' Kirsten frowned. 'She sponsored me for my 10K, you know, and never paid up. £60, it's not like it was a small amount.'

'Oh dear, that's a shame,' Minette said. 'I guess she forgot, what with moving and everything.'

'Wouldn't mind,' Kirsten said, opening the door, 'but I gave her a hundred quid for hers.'

The weather was gorgeous that summer. On her home days, Minette's favourite thing was to sit on the bench with Tilly and read to her. The book Tilly most often chose was *Five Minutes' Peace*, in which Mrs Large, an elephant, tries to have a quiet moment away from her noisy children. Minette read it over and over, finding an odd kind of five minutes' peace herself in the repetition.

The days went by, and in early August the local Duchenne Together group rang Minette to ask when they'd be getting the money she and Cath had raised. They explained that Cath had given her name as the point of contact. Minette laughed. She had to admire Cath's style. Unlike poor Andy, Minette did not feel in the least responsible for the debt. She'd given all the money she raised to Cath in good faith. She pointed out that the group should not have allowed Cath to set up her own unregulated donations page. With Abe feeding her lines from his Citizens Advice legal knowledge, she asked if they realised they could put their charitable status at risk by such poor management, and Duchenne Together lost interest in the conversation.

A couple of weeks later a new family moved into Cath's house, a couple in their forties with a teenage daughter. The mother chatted to Minette across the wall, and mentioned how much her daughter loved babies, wanted to be a nanny in fact, and was a great babysitter. Minette had learned to be wary of gift horses. She thanked the woman, and said she'd bear it in mind.

August turned into September, and Davey's school rang to ask her if she, as the named contact, knew why Cath Brooke hadn't handed over the money she'd raised at the school quiz. Minette was a dab hand at these calls now, and the conversation only lasted five minutes.

It was the middle of September and Minette was pushing Tilly on the swing in the little park when she saw Josie walking towards them. Josie's pregnancy was just about visible, and she cradled her small bump protectively. Minette smiled at her, remembering how she'd done that. How enormous she'd felt, even at three months. Josie admired Tilly's purple dress, a gift from Minette's mother, who was coming into her own now that she could buy stylish French baby clothes.

Minette said, 'It must be about time for your twelve weeks scan?'

'Yes, we just had it,' Josie said eagerly. 'They said everything was fine, thank god.'

'That's brilliant.' Minette realised she hadn't seen Liam around for weeks, and indeed, had barely thought of him.

'I know I'm supposed to be feeling all joyful and maternal,' Josie said, touching her stomach again. 'But I'm filled with random worries instead.'

'I was the same,' Minette said. It felt now as if those anxieties had been experienced by someone quite other. Someone who had no idea how big and bad the real world could be.

'Oh, thank god you understand! My sister's got three kids, she says wait till it arrives, then you'll really start worrying. But that's all I'm doing now. I can't stop. The baby's health, what I should eat, the labour, my blood pressure, did I screw the little fella up by drinking too much before I knew I was preggers . . .'

Now Minette was able to see Josie as a real person, rather than just an inconvenient obstacle, she found something very appealing about her. In particular she liked the way Josie blurted out her feelings, emotions scudding across her open face for all to see. She seemed to be a person who didn't lock any part of herself away. Minette knew she wouldn't ever be ready for cosy couples' dinners, sitting across from Liam, her hormones jumping about despite herself. But she thought she might like to get to know Josie. Do I feel guilty for sleeping with your husband? Minette asked herself. *Yes*. Do I feel overwhelmed by it, such that I couldn't be friends with you now? *No*. Maybe there was something to Cath's breezy compartmentalising, after all.

We'll all be dead in a hundred years.

'After Tilly's had enough of the swings, would you like to come back to mine for a cuppa and a chat?' Minette said.

'I'd love to,' Josie said immediately. 'Liam's not much help, he's totally focused on his teaching course. No one in the history of the universe has ever wanted to be a teacher as much as him, of course. I don't think he'll register this baby until it's on the outside.'

'How's Liam managing to see his gran, now he's much busier?'

'Which gran?'

'The one in Cardiff, he said she'd been moved into a home?'

'Well, yes, years ago. He hasn't been there for ages, I'm always nagging him.'

By now, Minette was so used to the feeling of having been bullshitted that this barely left a mark. After a while, Josie said shyly, 'Maybe I could practise holding Tilly, even change a nappy?'

'It would be a bit different from a newborn, but yes, of course.'

The women smiled at each other, and Josie said, 'May I push her on the swing for a bit?'

'Oh god, be my guest, I'm dying to sit down.'

One morning at the Pavilion, Minette went into the foyer to meet the next school group she was to take round, and there was Liam, standing tall among a crowd of eleven-year-olds.

'Have you seen this one?' Paula on the desk whispered to Minette, all fluttery. 'Total babe.'

'He's my neighbour,' Minette said.

'You are *kidding*!'

Liam saw her, did a double-take, and flashed her his Sinatra smile. Minette felt the old rush of attraction, and there were Cath's words in her head: 'Always a hell of a mistake, to fall for your animus.'

'Phwooar,' Paula said, 'I'll be strolling up and down your street later, for sure.'

Minette went to greet him and the other teacher, an older woman.

'I'd forgotten you worked here,' Liam said to Minette.

She determined not to let it show that this hurt a little, and said, 'I thought you were specialising in macramé, not history.'

The other teacher looked slightly puzzled at the mention of macramé. 'Regardless of subject, we like the student teachers to experience all our activities.'

Minette led the group into the Banqueting Room and started the tour. She was aware that Liam was watching her as she talked. She was aware, too, that she felt differently about him. He was still beautiful to look at, no question, but the hairs on the back of her neck stayed resolutely flat.

When the children scattered around the building to fill in worksheets, Liam caught up with her.

'That was brilliant, really interesting,' he said. 'You're a very good guide.'

'Thank you.' She accepted the compliment calmly. 'How's teaching?'

'I'm really enjoying it. Hard work, though. And a lot of paperwork.'

'It's good to be back at work, though, isn't it?' Minette

said. 'I love it. I certainly didn't want to be one of those bored mummies, you know, in search of a hobby.'

There was a moment's silence, and then Liam said quietly, 'Minette, I'm sorry if I was a bit of a shit.'

Having given him a little dig, she decided to let him off the hook. It wasn't all his fault, anyway. She'd been just as much a driving force. 'Don't think twice about it. We had a good time. We're both better off as we are.'

You have been inside me, she thought. I revealed more about myself to you than to any other man. There are pictures somewhere out there that prove it. Now I don't know anything about you. I don't have a clue what you're thinking. And you probably don't know what I'm thinking, either.

'That's really good of you to say that,' Liam said, clearly relieved. 'It's weird, because I was convinced back then that Josie and I had run out of steam. But now, I'd be gutted if anything happened to us.'

'I feel the same way about Abe,' Minette said. 'I'd never say anything to Josie.'

'Oh, I know! I'm very glad you're friends with her. So . . . I hear that Cath and the girl are still AWOL.'

Minette nodded. 'I think Cath has really disappeared now.'

Liam lowered his voice. 'She was a piece of work, that Cath, wasn't she? She stung me for a right old wedge of cash.'

A boy came over to ask Liam if he'd answered one of the

quiz questions correctly. 'Ask this lady here,' Liam said. 'She knows much more than me.'

Minette told the boy he had the right answer, and he went off happily.

'Do you think Lola will be OK?' Liam asked.

'I don't know. I can't get her out of my head. But if I'm not to go mad, I have to tell myself that she will be fine.'

He nodded. 'I hope you're right.'

'I know much more than you, remember? You just said so.'

He smiled down at her. 'That's true. I think you do.'

That evening, Minette was about to write Ros an email when she realised she still had the Frank Sinatra picture as her desktop background. She'd stopped noticing it. She changed it for a photo Abe's dad had just sent, taken at Tilly's birthday party. In it, Minette was kissing a smiling Tilly on one cheek, and Abe was kissing her on the other. Roy had called the file 'Happiness'.

The days went by, and Minette noticed that they were passing more quickly. For the first time she could see what parents of older children meant when they complained about how fast time went. When Tilly was a baby, particularly when the Miltons lived next door, every hour seemed to last a day; there were days that went on for weeks. But everything seemed easier now. Tilly was fun to be around and to do things with, especially as Minette didn't have to spend every waking minute with her. Abe started to talk about having another baby, and Minette said that she would like to wait for a year or so.

One evening, when they were watching telly, Abe told Minette that, now she was earning again, he would like to drop a half-day at work and study viniculture at Plumpton College. This had long been his ambition: he dreamed of owning a small vineyard in France near where Élise lived. Minette said it was a terrific idea. Abe turned the TV off before the end of the programme and they made love on the sofa.

One afternoon when Tilly was asleep, Minette remembered the photo frames. She dug them out from the under-stairs cupboard, even more dirty than before. She sat on the bench and washed them, and no handsome neighbours came past to disturb her and she was mostly glad.

The days went by, and on every one Minette thought of Lola. One evening in October, when it was starting to get properly cold, Andy got in touch. The flurry of regular contact with him had tailed off; it had been about three weeks since they last spoke. As soon as Minette and Abe saw his face on the screen, they knew he had news.

'Verna rang me to say that Ruby's asked her to send on her things.'

'That's a good sign, yes?' Abe said. 'It means she's settled down.'

'Yes. Apparently Esmie's started school now, a good school in a nice area, and is doing really well. She can write her name.'

Which name, Minette wondered. Adam had told them that she was called Breeze now, though maybe even that had changed. Minette admired the stubborn way Andy still referred to her as Esmie.

Andy went on, 'Ruby asked Verna to send various things to me, as well, so I'm waiting on those.'

'Did Ruby ask after Adam?' Abe asked.

Andy turned, to make sure that Adam hadn't wandered into the room. 'Yes. She just said that she missed him every minute, and hoped he was happy.'

They were all silent for a moment.

'She really did love him, I think,' Minette said, finally.

'I know,' Andy said.

Ros came to stay, and she and Minette went out for a drink that turned into a meal that turned into more drinks. They visited their favourite student bars, all greatly changed, and moaned about how old they were compared to the current students. Ros listed all the things she didn't like about Bristol, and the things she missed about Brighton, and they plotted how she and Marcus could get their jobs to transfer them back.

Even just talking about it made Minette feel happy, and full of possibilities.

A few drinks down, Minette told Ros about seeing Liam at work.

'Did you still fancy him?'

'Oh, yes. I don't think that will ever go completely. He's my animus, you see.'

'Your what?'

'Never mind. But I still feel awful about betraying Abe.'

'What he don't know won't hurt him. And to be fair to you, Abe wasn't sleeping with you, was he? Not for ages?'

Minette shook her head. She felt rather drunk.

'There you go,' Ros slurred. 'Sexy gal like you, gotta get it somewhere.' She put her hand on Minette's arm. 'I don't want you to feel guilty about it, OK? You are a good person. You did a naughty little thing. Now it's finished. Don't beat yourself up about it, OK? That's an order.'

'Love you, Ros.'

'Love you too, you old pisshead.'

A couple of weeks after Andy Skyped them about Ruby, he texted Minette asking if he could talk to her in private, without Abe. As it happened, Abe was out at the supermarket with Tilly. While Minette waited for Skype to connect she wondered what the hell this was. Was Andy going to declare his love for her? She giggled at the thought. Or – and the giggling stopped instantly – was there something up with Adam that Andy wanted a female perspective on?

When Andy's face appeared on the screen, Minette asked him how Adam was doing.

'Good days and bad,' Andy said. 'He misses Esmie a real lot, you know.'

'Course he does. So do you. Well, we all do,' Minette said.

'He talks to her all the time, you know, pretending she's with us. Tells her about his day, makes lists of his favourite things for her. Do you think that's normal?'

'Yes,' Minette said, firmly. 'It's really good that he isn't forgetting about her.'

'Verna's still hopeful that Ruby will turn up on her doorstep any day now,' Andy said.

'I'm sure she's right,' Minette said, thinking the exact opposite. 'So, was Adam what you wanted to talk about?'

'Ah. No, it was, er, something else.' Andy coughed. 'Maybe I should have done this by email.'

Minette was still in the dark. 'What is it, Andy?'

'Verna sent me some things Ruby asked her to forward. Adam's clothes, though he's grown out of most of them. Esmie's jacket, I'm not sure why. A few toys. We've got two Waffles now. And this.'

He held up a large brown envelope, and Minette went cold. 'Oh god,' she said.

'I'm sure Verna didn't open it,' he said.

'But you did,' Minette said faintly.

'I closed it again straight away when I saw what it was, Minette,' Andy said.

I bet you did, Minette thought to herself. Straight away, just a couple of sweaty hours later. You're a man, after all. 'Can you destroy them, please?'

'Of course. I was planning to. I'll do it soon as we finish talking. There's also a memory stick in the envelope.'

'With the photos on, I suppose?'

'Um, yes. They're all there.'

Well of course, he had to check, have another look at his favourites. Minette shook her head. Come on, Minette, it's not his fault. Anyone who was sent a pile of dirty pictures would look at them, it was human nature. She was probably the only person in the world who would put them straight back in the envelope and put the whole thing through a shredder.

'So, erm, do you mind if I ask?' Andy said.

Yes, of course I bloody do! 'No, go on.'

'I don't think that was Abe in the pictures, was it?'

Minette let out a flat laugh. 'No, Andy, it wasn't.'

'OK, say no more, say no more,' he gabbled, like the dodgy bloke out of Monty Python.

'Why do you think she sent them to you?' Minette asked. She moved out of webcam range for a moment and took out her lenses so that she couldn't see the envelope, nor Andy's embarrassed-but-titillated expression. That was better. The screen was just a page of light, Andy a splash of colour, her own face a smaller splash in the corner.

'I don't know. I can't pretend I'll ever understand anything Ruby does. I suppose she thought it would be safer than sending them to you, in case Abe might see them?'

Nice idea, Minette thought. But it went to show how little he really did know his wife. 'Will you destroy the memory stick as well?' she asked.

There was just the slightest hesitation before Andy said, 'Well, sure. Consider it done.'

Minette said goodbye and logged out, with some difficulty, as she couldn't see what she was doing. Then she lay on the bed and tried to work through it logically. If there was a memory stick, there was a digital version of the photos. That meant there was a computer somewhere with the photos on, and possibly another memory stick. Or lots of memory sticks.

'I hate you, Cath,' Minette said aloud. As soon as the words were out of her mouth, she told herself that was wrong. Cath had a mental illness, she wasn't well, she didn't have control over her actions . . . it didn't feel like that, though. It felt actually as though she had perfect, extraordinary control. But no, that type of control-freakery was part of her illness. Probably. Wasn't it? Did that excuse it? Of course it did. Minette shut her thoughts up, they really weren't helping.

She needed to be practical, think clearly. What were the most likely scenarios for Cath sending Andy the pictures?

Possibility one: Cath wanted to get rid of the baggage from her previous life and make a fresh start. But in that case, why not just ask Verna to destroy them? OK, why, because Cath knew Andy would tell Minette, then get rid of them, decent chap that he was, and Minette would know that they'd been destroyed and have that burden lifted. Bit embarrassing for him, very embarrassing for Minette, but all over. No more photos. Likelihood: zero out of 10.

Possibility two: Cath wanted to send Minette a message. The message was: I could ruin you, like you tried to ruin me, but I am bigger than that. So I am letting you know that I could have done something harmful with the photos, but I haven't. All copies of the photos have been destroyed. Likelihood: 3 out of 10.

Possibility three: Cath wanted to send Minette a message. The message was: You shouldn't have intervened. It wasn't like I didn't warn you. I still have the photos. So get ready. Andy first. Then Abe. Likelihood: 9 out of 10.

Minette hadn't spent all this time trying to get into Cath's head without some understanding of the way her mind worked. She didn't know for certain, though, and she knew that Cath wanted it that way. Minette rolled onto her back and gazed at the blurry lampshade above her, letting the warm tears scroll down her face. The front door banged, and

Abe called out, 'Hey, we're back! Tilly's bought you some flowers.'

So now Minette had to decide. Tell Abe about her affair now, or wait until her hand was forced. *If* her hand was forced. If she didn't tell now, could she bear to live her life in a state of constant anxiety? To always have to intercept the post? But then, Cath could just as easily use Abe's work address. Or the photos could turn up in an email, or on Facebook. Or on some public-access website.

The morning after she'd spoken to Andy, everything seemed in suspended animation. She watched Abe as though from a long way away, watched as he poured himself coffee, opened the dishwasher to put the teaspoon inside, kissed Tilly, and sat at the table, spread the newspaper out in front of him and let out a contented sigh. He was so very dear to her. She didn't want to lose him.

If she told him, she might ruin everything they had. Perhaps needlessly, as the photos might never turn up. But if she didn't tell him, and then they arrived, would that be worse? How would he react if, one morning, another envelope arrived from America containing a different kind of photograph? If she told him about them, pre-empted it, at least she knew the photos turning up couldn't hurt things any worse than they were. But what would he do when she told him? Leave? Take Tilly? Stay, but hate her? Stay and never trust her again?

There was a knock on the door, and she froze.

'I'll go,' Abe said, getting up.

'No! You've just sat down. I'll get it.'

'But I'm expecting a parcel . . .'

Minette was already in the hall. She flung open the front door and stared at the parcel courier. 'Delivery for Mr Moncrieff?' the man said.

'That's me,' Abe said, behind Minette, and reached for the package. Minette got to it first and held it behind her back.

'Minette! What's the matter? It's for me,' Abe said. He thanked the courier, and closed the door. 'Come on now, it's a surprise for you,' he said. 'I don't want it spoiled.'

'I need to look at it first, please,' Minette said, trying to keep her voice steady.

'What the hell is going on? Sweetie, why are you crying? It's just that book you wanted, the one about George IV's wife.'

Minette slowly brought the parcel round in front of her. It said 'Amazon' on the front.

'I know we're not supposed to be using Amazon but it was half the price,' Abe said.

Minette laughed through her tears, and handed the package to him. He gave it back to her. 'It's for you,' he said.

So, if she didn't tell him, that was her future. Her heart jumping every time the doorbell rang, or the post landed on the mat. Every time he turned on the computer. Every time he came home from work. Every time, for who knew how long.

'Abe,' she said, and stopped.

'Yes?' he said. His eyes were full of concern. 'What is it, sweetheart?'

Sweetheart. She sat down on the stairs, the parcel on her lap. She loved him so much. 'Abe,' she said, 'there's something I need to tell you.'

'Is it about Liam?' he said.

She stared at him, feeling her mouth drop open into a round 'O', like Tilly's when the penny falls machine on the pier paid out. 'Pardon?'

'Budge up a bit,' Abe said, and sat next to her.

She looked down at the parcel. 'I didn't know you knew.'

'Well, I'm not a complete idiot,' Abe said.

'How . . .'

'That time I walked in and you and he were in the kitchen.'

Of course. It was, after all, bloody obvious.

'You weren't bad, but his acting was appalling. I thought something might be going on. Then I knew for sure that day we met them on the beach and you acted so weird.'

'Abe, I'm so, so, so, sorry.'

'I did give you a few chances to tell me, but you didn't want to take the hint.'

'If I could only turn back the clock . . .'

'Shh now, shh,' he said, putting his arms round her. 'It's all over now, isn't it?'

'Oh yes,' she said, emphatically. 'It's been over for a long time. Do you believe me?'

'Yes.'

'Do you . . . hate me?'

'What?' He sat back a little way from her, and lifted her chin, made her look at him. 'How can you think that? I love you, you know that.'

'But I've done this awful thing.'

'What is it he says, at the end of *Brief Encounter*?'

Minette started crying again. 'Oh Abe, don't.'

'Go on, tell me. I'm pretty sure you know it by heart.'

'He says, "Thank you for coming back to me."'

'Yep. That's me. The boring husband. That's how I feel.'

'Are you serious? You're not angry with me? You don't want to split up?'

Abe laughed. 'No, do you?'

'Jesus, no!'

'So, what is it that we're expecting in the post?'

Minette explained quickly about the photos. She toned it down a bit so it sounded like there were just a few. She faltered slightly when she got to the bit where Andy had seen them, and Abe winced. 'Still,' he said, recovering quickly, 'it's not like his wife is a model of domestic stability.'

'They could turn up. I don't know if she's got them still, or what.'

'Right. Well, just so you know, I'll be really happy not to see the photos, OK? I've managed not to create many visual images of this thing in my head, so far. I'd like to keep it that way. So if an unexpected email or package comes for me, I think I'll get you to open it first.'

Minette had never felt so relieved in her life. She put her arms round him and hid her face against his shoulder.

'So is that everything?' he said. 'No other unexploded bombs secreted away? No pregnancies where we'll need a DNA test to find out which of us is the father?'

'I've got my period,' Minette said. 'And we, er, took precautions.'

'La la la!' Abe said, reminding her of Gina doing the same, when she refused to hear anything unpleasant about Cath. He covered his ears. 'Trying to avoid any visual images, remember?'

'Yes, sorry.' She sat up. 'Christ, I can't believe that you're not angry.'

'I have been angry, of course I have. And really upset. But all this business with Cath and Andy and her kids, it's made me think a lot about what's important, and what isn't.'

'Abe, I don't deserve you.'

'That's true. No, don't be silly. You're amazing, and clever, and kind, and interesting, and much too pretty for me.'

'What about when I'm old and plain?'

'We'll renegotiate the contract at that point. Listen.' For the first time his face went completely serious. 'We've been through a turbulent time this last year; it's not surprising that something had to give. You've always been so sensible, so steady. Maybe too steady. You know that my parents think you're perfect, and that's not an accolade they've ever given anyone: you're up there ahead of Mother Teresa, Nelson Mandela and Nigella.'

'Oh god, your parents.' The thought of losing their good opinion set Minette off crying again.

Abe smoothed the tears from her cheeks. 'It's rather exciting to find out that you're more reckless than I thought. More reckless than you thought as well, perhaps.'

'How can you be so bloody understanding?'

'I'm practising the rakish, libertarian attitude that goes with being a vineyard owner. Also, let's face it, Liam's a force of nature, isn't he? If he'd have been up for it, I'd probably have slept with him.'

Minette threw her arms round Abe again. She recognised that as a line he had prepared, and she loved him for it. 'You are an amazing man.'

He kissed her hair, and said quietly, 'Yeah, well, one time only, OK? I won't be so understanding a second time.'

'Promise. Cross my heart.'

They sat still for a moment, holding each other close, and

into the silence they heard Tilly in the kitchen, trying out all her words. 'Mama! Dud-ud! Today! Pretty!'

They smiled at each other.

'See? That's us she's talking about,' Abe said. 'We're her Mama and Dud-ud. She needs us both. Let's try not to fuck it up.'

Let's try not to fuck it up. As a mantra to live by, Minette preferred it to 'we'll all be dead in a hundred years'. They got up, and went to see if Tilly had finished her breakfast.

Acknowledgements

This has been a funny year, and I have relied on the comfort of friends. Thanks are particularly due to Alison Hutchins, Anne Lavender-Jones, Gerry Warner, Jo Bloom, Rachel Wojtulewski, Rosy Muers-Raby and Trish Joscelyne, for being there.

For bigging-up of my first book beyond the call of duty, thanks to Lucy Wilkes, Robyn Adams, Sam Knowles, and my fellow writer (and mother-in-law), Heather Castillo.

For their helpful comments on various drafts of this book, and for many other kindnesses, thank you to Saskia Gent and Juliette Mitchell. For doing his debugging thang on the first draft, thanks to Tim Ward. For suggesting I remove a character who was getting in the way, thanks to my agent, Judith Murdoch (she was right, of course). For ongoing writing encouragement, support, and extra commas, thank you, as always, to my writing buddies – Liz Bahs, Clare Best, and Alice Owens. For gentle and helpful edits – oh, and for publishing the book – thanks to Gillian Green and Emily Yau at Ebury.

For telling me everything I needed to know about the storage of blood and creatine kinase, thanks to Dr Catherine Wykes. And on the subject of research: of the accounts I read by people who had a parent with Munchausen syndrome by proxy, the most useful was *Sickened*, by Julie Gregory.

For giving me more time to write, thanks to the owners of *Viva Lewes*. For helping me seek new directions, thanks to Claire Kirtland and Mark Bridge.

For being so proud of me, thanks to my children. I will never forget the looks on your faces when the first copy of *When We Were Sisters* arrived in the post.

Finally, for all the loving support, the staggering levels of belief, the confidence-boosting, the sheer delight in my achievements, thank you to John. And thanks to the God of Good Things, for sending me John.

Reading Group Questions

1. Both Minette and Cath have different parenting styles in this book. In what ways are they good mothers? And can bad behaviour be excused if it's in the best interest of the child?

2. Both Minette and Cath's characters in *The Good Neighbour* have their flaws. Do you think you have to like the protagonists for a story to work well? Do you think there are 'good' and 'bad' characters in this book, or is that too simple a classification?

3. Was Minette naive to trust Cath so much? Was it a positive or a negative that Minette had learned to be less trusting by the end of the book?

4. How much do you think Davey understood about what was going on? Do you think his decision to reach out to Minette was one of bravery or fear? Or both?

5. For Cath, her identity and that of her children are closely linked with their names. That plus the diagnosis – and in Cath's case, lack of diagnosis – of their illnesses. Do you think names/labels are important? Do you think the book would have played out differently without them?

6. Do you feel sympathy towards Cath? Did your opinion of her change after finding out about her diagnosis? Does this excuse the way she behaved with her children?

7. Cath's quick-fire decision to take Lola and run, leaving Milo behind, was one of desperation and panic. Do you think, had she not been taken by surprise, she would have taken a different course of action?

8. This is a story that could continue long after its ending. What do you think happens to the characters in the next

few years? Will Andy be reunited with Lola? Or will Cath be successful in forging a new life for herself and her daughter?

9. One could say that the meaning and significance of the word 'neighbour' has changed drastically over the last few decades. What do you think this book has to say about community and privacy? Can you truly have both?

10. What do you think of the phlosophy, 'We'll all be dead in a hundred years'? Is it a positive or negative outlook to have on life?

Author questionnaire with Beth Miller

1. What inspired you to write this novel?

I was reading an article in the local paper about a woman who'd run lots of marathons. Her child was very ill, and she was raising money for the relevant charity. I think most people reading such an article would probably feel sorry for the mother and child, but my first thought was, hey, what if she was pretending, and her child wasn't sick after all? Then I felt ashamed of myself and channelled the bad thought into a fictional story.

2. Were you previously familiar with Duchenne muscular dystrophy and/or Munchausen by proxy? What did your research entail?

I've been interested in Munchausen syndrome by proxy since I first heard about it as a psychology student. That someone – often a mother or a nurse – would deliberately harm a child by pretending that they were ill was fascinating to me. It goes against all expectations of the caring female. I read several accounts from people who'd been brought up by someone with the syndrome. These were awful. Unimaginable – that the person who should protect you was the one who caused you to suffer. I couldn't find any accounts written by people *with* the syndrome. I imagine it's not something you acknowledge to yourself, or anyone else. It is a hidden thing. I wanted to try and get inside the head of someone like that. To write Cath, I had to think very hard about why she behaved as she did. As I'm a wishy-washy liberal type, my key question was what had happened to her that might have caused her to be like that? I realised that the behaviour must serve some kind of function for her; that it must soothe her stress and anxiety, and therefore must be very compelling to her.

Duchenne I didn't know anything about initially. I was thinking about what Davey was like, when I heard a mother being interviewed about her son's Duchenne on *Woman's*

Hour. She said that within a fortnight, her son had gone from being able to walk down the garden, to being in a wheelchair. The awful speed of the deterioration. Cath would know about Duchenne from her nursing and would know how to forge the blood markers that test for it. A doctor friend answered all my questions about the marker (creatine kinase), and the storage of blood.

3. What do you want people to take away from *The Good Neighbour*?

I hope they all start to suspect their neighbours of dodgy doings. OK, not that. Maybe something profound about the mystery and complexity of human behaviour? Or perhaps, that diagnosis is a starting point, not an end in itself? I feel very in tune with Andy when he says to Minette that even if it's true that Cath has Munchausen by proxy, it doesn't actually explain anything. It's just a description – all the same questions are still there even if you have a label.

Really, I just hope people enjoy it as a story about families and secrets.

4. Your last novel *When We Were Sisters* deals with a range of subjects, from those explored in *The Good Neighbour* such as dysfunctional families and adultery, to others such as religion and the clash of cultures. Did you find inspiration from your previous writing or do you start each new book with a blank slate?

You're right, I do seem slightly obsessed with adultery. Hmm.

As befits a first novel, *When We Were Sisters* had a lot of autobiographical elements (though not the adultery). But *The Good Neighbour* is entirely fictional. As far as I know, I've never met anyone with Munchausen by proxy. The odd thing is that characters in both books spend quite a lot of time in hospitals. I don't understand why, because I know nothing about hospitals and have scarcely ever been in one, except to have my children. Maybe there's a frustrated doctor in me, trying to get out. Or an evil nurse [maniacal laugh].

5. Many writers say that their characters are often based on aspects of themselves. Would you agree? Would you compare yourself to either Cath or Minette? (Or indeed, any other character from *The Good Neighbour*?)

Like Minette, I am very short-sighted. And of course I am young and beautiful. Also like her, when I had children, I found the baby stage a bit exhausting and unexciting. But that might be a fairly universal feeling. The few people I met who seemed to breeze through that stage, like Cath, were people I greatly envied. I think I'm probably most like Abe. Dorky but essentially sound.

6. How do you plan your writing? Were there any surprises in terms of plot, or had you had it mapped out from the beginning?

I wrote *When We Were Sisters* into a void, having no idea what would happen. That might be why it took twelve years to write. In a reaction to that, I planned *The Good Neighbour* before I started it. Though it changed a lot, it was nice to have a road-map. The ending is very different to my original plan. When I read it through with the first ending in place, I was furious with the rotten author who'd written such a dystopic conclusion. I rewrote it straight away. I like happy-ish endings where people forgive other people.

7. Do you have a favourite time of day to write? A favourite place?

My preferred time of day – between 2 and 9pm – is incompatible with family life. I just start to feel inspired when I have to down tools to collect children from school, make tea, etc. I've learned to force myself to write during school hours and snatch other time when I can. For instance, I am writing these answers while sitting in my children's martial arts class. My favourite place to write is at my desk in the attic. But I also love writing on trains.

8. Have you always wanted to write? What other jobs have you had? And if you weren't a novelist, what would your dream career be?

I've had a lot of jobs. I've been a psychology lecturer, a journalist, a sexual health trainer, a creative learning manager (still not sure what that is), an alcohol counsellor, a volunteer coordinator and an audio-typist. I've worked in a bread shop, a chemist's, and a stationery shop. My worst job was temping in a stockbrokers, where my sole task was to put thousands of old newspapers into date order. My best job was working on a computer magazine, the long-defunct *MicroDecision*, because it was the old-school days of journalism when everyone smoked in the office and went out for three-hour lunches. This makes me sound contemporaneous with Evelyn Waugh, which is odd as I am only twenty-three.

I told a teacher when I was seven that I wanted to be a poet when I grew up, and she kindly said, 'I'm sure you will be, dear.' She was wrong; I am a terrible poet. I loved writing at school, but then got out of the habit and didn't start again till I was in my thirties. In all my many jobs, though, I always made sure that writing was involved. If I wasn't writing handouts and booklets, it was newsletters. I love a good newsletter.

I now mix writing books with teaching writing and book coaching. My dream career is exactly what I do, except much better paid.

9. Who are your favourite authors? What are you reading at the moment?

I've waited so long for someone to ask about my favourite authors that when it finally happened, I went temporarily blank. Like Rob in Nick Hornby's *High Fidelity*, when he was asked his top five records. OK. In alphabetical order, they are Douglas Adams, Jane Austen, Judy Blume, Laurie Colwin, Monica Dickens, Nora Ephron, Margaret Forster, William Goldman, Howard Jacobson, David Lodge, John O'Farrell, Anne Tyler, Molly Weir and PG Wodehouse.

I'm a member of a slightly niche group called 'Debut Novelists aged over forty' and I'm currently trying to read all their books. There's more than thirty of us in the group, so it's taking a little while. Some cracking reads in amongst that lot, though.

10. Which book do you wish you could have written? Which classic have you always meant to read and never got round to?

The book I wish I'd written is *Heartburn*, by Nora Ephron.

There are so many classics I have never got round to. *Ulysses*, of course, but also *Crime & Punishment*, *Catch-22*, *Don Quixote*. . . I suppose I haven't read them because they didn't much appeal. The one I would like to read is *War & Peace*, because I love *Anna Karenina*, and I imagine it's quite similar, right?

Enjoyed *The Good Neighbour*?
Read on for a taster of Beth Miller's
WHEN WE WERE SISTERS

'I never think of Laura as my step-sister,
but that's what she is.'

Once they were the best of friends, inseparable as only teenage girls can be.

That is until Miffy's Jewish father runs off with Laura's Catholic mother and both of their families imploded – as well as Laura's intense relationship with Miffy's brother. . .

Twenty years on, they're all about to meet again. . .

Also available from Ebury Press

Melissa

24 February 2003

I turn on the stairs when I hear that name.

Miffy.

Not my real name. A nickname. No one has used it for more than twenty years.

Laura stands framed in the doorway of her room. I'd know her anywhere. I try to focus on her face, on her dark eyes with their thick lashes, but against my will my own eyes keep sliding down to her stomach.

She raises her hand as if she's going to wave, then the hand changes direction and smoothes her hair, the lovely sleek black hair I used to envy. Cut shorter now. She's still beautiful, though not the way she was at fourteen.

Last night I deliberately avoided her. Said hello but nothing more. It didn't look too obvious. After a death, normal rules don't apply.

She says, 'Do you want to come in for a minute, Miffy?'

I knew being here would mean facing Laura. She was once such a significant figure in my life; a symbol of everything that went wrong. Now I know she's just a person who did some stupid things.

And haven't we all, as Dad would say if he were here.

Laura

14 February 2003

You know those women who say, 'Oh, I only take five minutes to get ready'? I always want to say, 'Yes, darling, I can see that, but what did you do for the other four minutes?'

I take my time. Always have. Hair, make-up, clothes. It's so important to do it properly. You can tell when it's been rushed.

Huw says I'm high maintenance. Used to mean it as a compliment. Now it's: *Laura, what have you been doing for the last hour?* Now it's: *Laura, you look no different from when you went upstairs.* Thanks, honey bun; love you too.

Don't tell him, but tonight's session *has* been a bit of

a marathon – nearly two hours. Partly because of my sodding chin and its plucking hair (ha!); and partly because it's been hard to get the exact blend of foundation to disguise the bruise.

The crowd is roaring on the TV downstairs. You know what? Huw should be pleased. He didn't want to miss the football, and now he's had time for the game *and* the inevitable post-match recriminations. Dopey Paige is down there too, doubtless staring at the telly with her mouth open, drool trickling from her lower lip. The only nineteen-year-old in Wales with no plans for Valentine's, bless her hefty backside. I know it's a waste, paying her to babysit while we're still here. But my chin hairs have started to instantly replace themselves, like a sustainable forest.

'What's happening, *cariad*? Was wondering if you'd died up here.'

Huw's face looms behind mine in the mirror. Eleven years my senior, but looks fresher than me. His silvery blond hair flops onto his forehead, giving him a boyish air. Slim, clean-shaven, eyes the same bright fall-in-love-with-me blue I fell in love with.

I know I look older than thirty-seven. My hair's cut in what passes for a sharp bob in North Wales: basically a straggly bob. I used to think my Spanish heritage was a gift: thick black hair and olive skin, like my mother and

Frida Kahlo. But these days I'm more of a flabby old peasant-type, whose key resemblance to Frida is the facial hair.

'Can you see the bruise?' I ask.

Huw peers at my forehead. 'No, it's hidden under a trowel-load of cement.'

Did I mention this bruise? It's all right, it's not hurting that much any more. I put on some more smouldering purple eye-shadow. My big brown eyes, once my best feature, have so many lines round them I've been considering Botox, even though it's just *not done* here in the back arse of beyond. Not done because if you bother with your appearance beyond wearing matching socks, everyone thinks you're trivial. And literally not done, either, because there aren't any proper clinics. You'd have to go somewhere metropolitan, like Liverpool. I once mentioned my interest in Botox to Ceri, and she reacted as if I'd told her I was considering having my boobs grafted to my head. Which I will do, if they slide any lower. That's the bit I don't like about being pregnant: the way your tits just kind of sit on your stomach, reminding you that the gravity-defying part of your life is over.

'Come on, *cariad*, let's go, if we're going. You look fine.' His Welshy sing-song accent used to charm me, but he surely knows by now that I find it irritating.

'I do not look fine! I look like a fucking dog's dinner!'

'Dog's bollocks, more like. Well, you could maybe try

a different colour on your eyes. What with the bruise, people'll think I took a swing at you.'

'*Daaa*-ddy!' The Ruler of the House is calling, demanding an immediate audience with her most favoured subject. Huw trots off to attend to Evie, and I squeeze into what used to be my reliable going-out dress, before my tummy began to resemble a bowling ball.

Did I mention I'm pregnant? Memory like a sieve. Well, I am. Keep your congratulations low-key. No one but me is particularly happy about it.

I pause outside Evie's door. 'I don't want you to go out, Daddy.'

'Well, darling,' Huw says in his talking-to-children voice, 'it's important for mums and dads to go out together, isn't it? To talk, and enjoy each other's company.'

Doesn't sound like any evening Huw and I have had for a while. But now I'm ready, I want to go. I'm starving, and Jenny-and-Paul are good cooks. Which almost makes up for them holding hands and droning on about how fucking happy they are.

I look into the living room, where Dopey Paige is staring – yes, mouth open – at the telly. I pull on my coat, and hover at the bottom of the stairs. Huw takes his time, being extra patient with Evie to get at me.

It's a fifteen-minute drive to the dinner party – time enough to fit in a good row.

Me: 'Just don't embarrass me tonight, that's all I ask.'

Him: 'Why should I embarrass you?'

'Let's see. Hmm. How about snogging some *girl* in front of everyone. Yes, I think that qualifies as embarrassing, don't you?'

'One fucking kiss!'

'So there was fucking as well, was there?'

'Hilarious! You should be a stand-up. One fucking kiss in fifteen years!'

'What do you want, a long-service medal?'

'I want you to stop going on about it.'

'I'll stop going on about it when you tell me why you did it.'

'Why does anyone do anything? I was pissed, I suppose.'

'Yeah, right. Just a coincidence.'

'Just a coincidence, what?'

'That it happened when it did.'

'What, on New Year's Eve?'

'Fuck New Year's Eve! It was two days after I told you I was pregnant.'

'It was New Year's Eve! The traditional time for getting pissed and snogging people! It's practically obligatory!'

'Just a coincidence, then.'

'Will you stop saying that?'

'I'll stop saying that when you stop snogging other women!'

And so on.

We don't always argue like this. You're not seeing us at our best. We've had our ups and downs: marrying too young (me); a broken marriage (him); then step-children (me); then Evie, our very own home-grown dictator (both of us). Then the miscarriages (me again). Not to mention both having come from complicated family lives. Though who doesn't?

Till recently, we had a strong marriage.

Not lately, though. As I'm sure Huw would put it to the girl from New Year's Eve, or any other totty he has hidden away, we are 'going through a rough patch'.

We're so late, Jenny-and-Paul have assumed we aren't coming and have removed our chairs to make more room. They squeeze us back in, but they're very much not thrilled.

'We should have called,' I say.

'Never mind, you're here now,' Jenny says tightly. 'There's some lamb left.'

She's only gone and decorated the room with red hearts. Spent this morning cutting out crêpe paper, bless her girlish little soul. I wouldn't exactly say she is a friend, in case you're wondering. I met her through Ceri, my boss. For a couple of years, Huw and I, Jenny-and-Paul, and Ceri-and-Whoever-She's-With-This-Time have taken it in turns to host a monthly dinner. I used to fantasise that it would be a sophisticated salon-type thing, but forgot where I was and the sort of people I was dealing with.

Ceri's all cosied up next to Rees. Since her divorce she's been through most of the single men in Gwynedd, so I felt obliged to set her up with Rees, the last man standing. I've known him since my student days. Despite not being bad-looking, he's never been married. Soon as he opens his mouth, you know why. 'Well, hellooo, curvy lady,' he says, leering at me.

Ceri shoves his arm; Huw pretends not to hear; I say, 'Yes, Rees, a baby-belly is this season's must-have accessory.'

Jenny plonks a sparse helping of dried-up lamb and potatoes in front of me and Huw, and we respond with stratospheric cries of gratitude. Jenny sits back down and pushes her dessert bowl aside. She hasn't noticed the stain on her blouse. 'We were worried about you,' she says. 'Wondering if something had happened' – stage whisper – 'with the baby,' indicating my stomach with her eyes.

'Oh, no, everything's fine.' I improvise: 'The sitter was late.'

'Thought you'd decided to have a romantic Valentine's night in,' says Paul.

Rees gives me a creepy wink.

'Can't stand Valentine's,' says Huw. 'Commercial shite.'

'Rees agrees with you,' Ceri says. 'Thinks giving flowers is playing into the hands of The Man.'

'Rip-off, yeah?' Rees does his Woody Woodpecker laugh. 'They double the prices on February fourteenth.'

'I'd be happy getting flowers on the fifteenth,' says Ceri.

'White, red or fizzy, Laura?' Paul says. Thank God, I thought he'd never ask. I'm not drinking but I really need something to get through this.

'Paul!' Jenny cries, miming an enormous stomach. 'She's pregnant!'

'I can have half a glass.'

Jenny shakes her head at Paul, and he pours me some water.

'Better safe than sorry, right?' Jenny's one of those fascist Americans, the sort that tells complete strangers to stop smoking or eating brie if they happen to be pregnant. Ceri makes a sympathetic face at me. I make one back; she needs it more than I do. She's the one dating Rees.

'Nice decorations, Jenny,' I say.

Ceri gives me a tiny smirk.

'Are you all right?' Jenny mouths across the table at me, touching her head. This time it's about my forehead. I suppose the mark's started to show through the foundation, damn it.

'Fine.' Nothing a glass of wine wouldn't help. Cow. 'Slipped.'

'Oh, walked into a door, yeah?' Rees laughs, moronically.

'No,' I say, just as Huw blurts, 'She was literally banging

her head against the wardrobe.' He's already drunk a few while watching the football. 'So pissed off about nothing fitting. Said to her, "Well, *cariad,* if you will insist on getting up the duff..."'

People laugh nervously.

'Huw! Just ignore him.' I smile. *I'll kill you later, you bastard.* 'I slipped and banged it on the edge of the sink. Centre of gravity's shot to shit, you know.'

All right, so I did hit my head against the wardrobe. You're thinking I'm a psycho, but I'm not. It wasn't about nothing fitting. Huw knows that. It was about everything. Valentine's Day. He never even buys a card. Him snogging that girl. Him not wanting the baby. And, yes, about feeling fat as well. I really want this baby – you've no idea how much – but it doesn't mean I'm totally cool about my weight. I'm not one of those wanky hippy chicks who don't care what they look like. Anyway. That's a pretty long list of upsetting things. Some venting is normal, isn't it?

Jenny, sitting next to me, turns and breathes Rioja into my face. 'Changing the subject slightly, we were trying to work out the gap between Evie and the new baby.'

'Well, Evie's eleven.'

'Twelve by the time the baby comes,' says Ceri, grinning at Jenny. The look they give each other makes me realise our arrival has interrupted a delightfully bitchy conversation about us.

'You *are* brave,' says Jenny, holding out her glass for Paul to refill. 'It's like having two only children, really.'

'It'll be fine,' I say, watching the lovely red wine glug into the glass. 'I can concentrate on the new baby, and Evie will help.'

'But such a big gap will be very challenging. They're in two completely different places,' says Evil Jenny.

'Ours are the opposite extreme,' says Paul. 'Only eighteen months apart.'

'They play together so well, don't they, Paulie? We were lucky, though. Not everyone can have babies when they want to, can they? Paulie only has to look at me, and bam!'

Rees says, 'Good on yer, mate!'

Ceri discreetly makes a puking face that only I see.

Jenny now completely oversteps the mark, not that she hasn't already. Leaning her head to one side to indicate deep understanding, she drops into a counsellor-type voice. 'I know you've had some fertility problems, haven't you?'

'Who'd like coffee?' says Paul.

I catch Huw's eye, willing him to rescue me, and the bastard just looks right through me before draining his glass. I hate Huw, but I hate Evil Jenny more.

I picture Jenny in a documentary called *Women Who Live A Lie*. She's being interviewed by a thin, blonde, faux-sympathetic journalist. Jenny is wearing her horrible stained flowery blouse.

Faux-sympathetic Interviewer: Why did you pretend you were happy?

Jenny *(weeping)*: I wanted everyone to envy me. I'm so ashamed. Everyone thought Paul was such a stud. No one knew he was gay and went out every night as a male escort. *(Sobs louder.)*

F-s Int: And the children…

Jenny *(wiping her eyes, suddenly looking evil)*: Mail order from Thailand. Little brats. Wish I could send them back like I'd send back this hideous M&S blouse, if only I hadn't spilled tiramisu down it.

Ceri says, 'Just because you have them close together doesn't mean they'll be friends. Look at my step-kids. Two years apart, fight all the time.'

'So do Huw's boys,' I say gratefully. Now, finally, he looks at me, and raises his glass in a sardonic toast. I toast him back with Jenny's wine glass and take a long, deep, lovely drink before she says, 'Erm, I think that's mine.'

'Yes, we've had a minor fertility problem,' I say. 'Couple of miscarriages, nothing unusual.'

'Did anyone say they wanted coffee?' says Paul, louder than before.

'Well, darling,' says Huw, and I think, no, don't say it, don't tell them there were five miscarriages, don't tell them we'd agreed not to try again, don't tell them I changed my mind without consulting you. If you say any of that in front of these horrible people, I will walk out of here and I will walk out on you and never come back.

'Well, darling,' he says, 'at the very least, it was a happy accident, wasn't it?'

He smiles, and Paul relaxes, and Ceri asks if they have decaf, and I unclench my arse because now I don't have to cause a scene. The rest of the evening passes off boringly with a long anecdote from Rees about the personnel department at Welsh Water, during which he twice flicks out his tongue at me in a manner which some fool – not Ceri, I hope – has told him is sexy.

I drive us home. We're both under-fed, and Huw's over-wined.

'Well,' he says, 'that was a predictably shitty evening.'

'Yes, it was.' I'm glad we can agree on something.

'I hate those people. Let's never do this again.'

'We're sort of committed to this monthly dinner thing. And Ceri likes us there for moral support. Jenny-and-Paul's loved-up scene intimidates her.'

'Well, now she's got the fascinating Rees.'

'She won't be able to stand him for long.'

'No, boyo, then it'll be a sad day down the Llandudno Junction branch of Welsh Water, yeah?' Huw takes off Rees's voice perfectly.

The house is quiet. Evie's asleep and Paige is still in front of the telly. She looks as if she hasn't moved at all, but the chocolate digestives have disappeared from the plate in the kitchen. I pay her and she gets up slowly.

'Come on, Paige,' says Huw, 'I'll drop you off.'

'I'll take her; you're way over the limit.'

'Worried I'll embarrass her outside the Halls of Residence?'

'Huw, you're only embarrassing yourself. Why don't you get some coffee? I'm terribly sorry, Paige, he's had too much to drink.'

Paige, wakened briefly by this outburst, clambers into the car and gazes at me with spaced-out eyes. 'Dr Ellis isn't normally like that in lectures.'

'Yes, well I should hope not. He doesn't drink at work. I don't think.'

'Do you know if you're having a boy or girl?'

'Not yet. Evie wants me to have a girl.'

Big lie. Evie doesn't want me to have anything. I lapse into silence, thinking how separate Huw, Evie and I are right now. We were such a strong unit when Evie was little.

As she levers herself out of the car, Dopey Paige says, 'Oh, there was a phone call for you. Your mother, I think. She said can you call back no matter how late?' She wanders off in her vague studenty way. I go through my bag for the mobile phone before remembering I ran out of credit yesterday.

Back home, Huw's sprawled on the sofa watching telly, a glass in his hand.

'Oh, good idea, more alcohol.'

'Piss off.'

I ring Mama, but when she picks up the phone I can't hear her. I say, 'Hello, hello?' like an old-fashioned telephonist until finally I realise she's crying.

'Can't hear you properly, Mama. Shit! I'll come down straight away. Tomorrow. Try to get some sleep. No, well some rest, then.'

I hang up, and Huw looks at me questioningly.

'Michael's been rushed to hospital. Heart attack.'

'God, I'm sorry, *cariad*.'

My make-up has been gently melting all evening, and in the living-room mirror I look like a worried clown. Huw puts his arms round me. I move my head so I can't smell the alcohol on his breath. I used to find this smell a turn-on but now it just makes me nauseous. The pregnancy-enhanced sense of smell, I suppose.

'Poor Olivia, how is she? She must be in a right state.'

'I could barely make out a word. Poor Michael, too. He's not all that old. Sixty-five. God, though. Mama will completely fall apart if he, you know.'

'I'm sure it won't come to that.' He strokes my back and says, 'Would you mind terribly if I didn't come with you tomorrow?'

I walk to the mirror, start rubbing at the mascara under my eyes. 'Luckily, half-term starts on Monday, so I can get Evie out of your hair, too.'

'Oh, Laura, that isn't what I meant.' He tries to touch me, but I sidestep away. 'Of course, I'll come if you really want, like a shot, just say the word. But I'll be in the way. Your mum needs you. You can focus on her and your stepdad.'

It's just another little let-down from Huw. I'm getting used to them. My mind races through lists of what I need to organise. It helps to make lists. It's better than thinking about Michael, frail in hospital, Mama distraught at his side.

'I'm just saying it would be handy if I didn't have to cancel that devolution group meeting thing on Tuesday.'

'Can't have you missing a meeting. Must get our priorities right.'

'It's not a meeting, it's *the* meeting, the one I've been working towards for months.'

Is he still talking?

'I already said, you don't have to come.' I'm working out what clothes Evie will need, and whether we can share a holdall, when I think of something else, something bigger, and sit down abruptly on the floor with an 'Oh!'

Huw kneels next to me. 'What is it, *cariad*?'

I go dizzy for a moment; the room tilts and bleaches out. I bend my head forward. Huw puts his arm roun me, saying, 'Hey, hey, hey,' in a soft voice. It takes me a minute to recover, then I sit up slowly and look into his worried face.

'I was just thinking,' I say, 'that if Michael's really bad, they'll send for . . .'

I haven't said their names for a very long time, and can't seem to bring myself to say them now.